Andy Malice

Crypto Fools

A Novel

Published By Karnival Kingdom Entertainment Inc. By arrangement with the Author.

Crypto Fools
Copyright © 2012 Andy Malice

ISBN: 978-0987937131

KARNIVAL KINGDOM
ENTERTAINMENT

****

To the pursuit of rational thought

CHAPTER 1

I pretended like it wasn't happening. It wasn't real. I ignored the repulsive fact that somehow, something had gone horribly wrong with my day. The source of my denial lay mostly in the realization that I was in a car travelling at speeds nearing terminal velocity, upside down, and screaming something along the lines of, "Holy shit! I'm gonna die!"

The vehicle hit the ground and smashed into a parked car, sending countless shards of tempered glass flailing through the air. When it finally came to rest, I pulled my knife from the glove compartment and quickly jumped out, filled with the rage of a cornered beast. I ran like a cheetah toward the other car where my nemesis sat, silently watching in amazement. Partly amazed with the fantastic scene he had just helped create, but mostly with the fact that I seemed completely unscathed and was now running very quickly toward him with a shiny blade in my hand and lunacy dancing in my eyes.

How this little "situation" developed was–about 3 hours ago, while sitting quietly at my desk, dozing off to the steady drone of the anthem of our lives, a voice snapped me out of my zombie-like stupor. I was, as always, suffering from an insatiable, mind numbing boredom, and found myself surfing the internet for a weird assortment of pornography, fascinated with what some people were willing to shove into their available orifices as long as there was a camera around. I had, of course, been warned about this type of behavior at work in the past, but the bumbling pack of nerves I called a boss simply couldn't handle being challenged by crazy eyes and jabbered screams of defense. As luck would have it, it was his voice that suddenly grabbed my attention.

"Excuse me, Mickey?" I hurriedly shoved my monitor in the other direction, away from authoritative eyes "Ah... MmMickey. We ah, we have an issue I need to speak to you about."

"What it is now, Grant?" I asked. "I stopped electrocuting Barbara a long time ago."

"Ye... Yes, Mickey. Now, listen. The IT guys have informed me that you have been, you know, looking at inappropriate things on the internet again. Now, I don't need to remind you that the computers at work are for work. You can't do that here. Do it at home where you are free to do anything you like. Now, there's nothing I can really do for you. I have to send a report to head office. I'm sorry, but that's company policy. I have no other choice."

"Well," I sighed. "When you have no choice in the matter, you have no choice, right?"

"Ye... Yes, Mickey. I'm sorry."
I was filtering through the situation when a sudden flash of genius erupted in my mind. It was a long shot, but what the hell, I was fucked anyway. When there's nothing left to lose, go for the impossible.

He was just turning away from me, still mumbling nonsense, when I stopped him in his tracks. "Hey, Grant," I said, and he returned to my cubicle, nervous as ever.

"Ye... Yes, Mickey. What is it?" he was seemingly annoyed with me now. I leaned in closer with devious eyes and whispered into his flushed face.

"I saw you."
His demeanor suddenly changed, as if I had struck a nerve and sent his ever present paranoia to an excruciating climax.

"Saw... Saw what?" he asked cautiously.
I grabbed the side of my monitor and slowly turned it toward his face, exposing the random thumbnails of wet orifices and erect organs. His eyes grew wide while I pointed toward the screen accusingly.

"I saw *you!*" I repeated.
His body tensed sharply as though he was about to snap and cave my face in, or walk out of his office with a shotgun and

pollute our environment with countless amounts of lead. He was obviously having some difficulty keeping his composure in check. His hands were trembling, and his elongated forehead was sprouting fresh beads of sweat.

"Oh yeah," I said. "A fantastic performance. Have you ever considered making a career out of it? I mean, your scrotum is incredibly camera friendly."

Alternating flashes of anger and shame rushed through his eyes as he leaned in closer to me with a quivering bottom lip.

"You... You prick!" he snapped. "I'll have your head on a stake for this! How dare you embarrass me, you little shit! I'll find something, Mickey, and I... I'll have you crucified for it!"

I smiled rather pleasantly, all the while knowing in the back of my mind that once our little confrontation was over with, I would have no other choice but to spend an unconscionable amount of time searching the web for those videos in the name of insurance–and mostly to satisfy a demented human curiosity.

"I doubt it, Grant. You're fucked mister, and in a way that you can't put on the internet because it's just not as entertaining."

His demeanor shifted again. He quickly abandoned his murderous rage and replaced it with a sense of utter despair. He dropped his clipboard onto my desk and whispered quietly, mindful of the wandering ears around us.

"Pl... Please, Mi... Mickey," he stuttered. "Don't do this to me. All I have is this job."

"Is that why you're always here? Jesus, get a fucking life, man. Live a little."

"Please!" he slammed his hand against my desk. "Please. I'll do anything. Just don't say anything. I'll do whatever you want."

"Yeah," I said. "That's kind of creepy, Grant. I know you'd do anything. I mean... Yahoo."

He had the look of a man who was desperately trying to fend off an oncoming menace that would cripple him forever, however, he was quite unsure of what to do next.

"All right, Grant," I continued. "Here's what we're going to do. From now on, I want you to stay the hell away from me. I don't want to be bothered by all of these silly complaints you constantly annoy me with."

"You got it... Nothing more," he replied.

"Oh, and I want you to make an effort every morning to get up from your desk and say hello to me."

"Yes."

"Every morning, Grant!"

"Yes."

"And protect my job, Grant. No more of this mindless jibber jabber. Just leave me the fuck alone, all right?"

He nodded quickly in agreement.

"If you can do that, then I promise I won't reveal you. But I'm warning you, one slip and I'll email the links to every person in this goddamned company, got it?"

"Yes, yes. Th... Thank you, Mickey. Thank you. You got it. Anything you want."

He nervously stood over me like a child waiting to be dismissed.

"Now," I said. "If you'll excuse me, I have some important business to tend to. It's Friday afternoon."

"Ye... Yes," he said. "Of course, Mickey. Have a good weekend. I'll see you on Monday."

"See ya, Grant. Your secret is safe with me!"

I sat back in my chair, stunned. I couldn't believe it. Somehow, one of my twisted ideas had actually worked to my benefit for once. Incredible. I felt great! Once again roaming freely in my controlled environment, until another voice suddenly cried out from behind me, disturbing my early attempts at matching Grant's features to the moaning, pain-pleasured faces up on my screen.

"*Mickey!*" I turned quickly and noticed that her face was framed with thick streaks of black tears. Her nose red, and her eyelids puffy.

"Whoa," I said. "What's wrong?"

"*Ugh!*" she cried. "Davie just called and screamed at me. He says it's over," she tried containing her anger. "Do you, do you have time to talk or something? I really need to talk to someone."

Alice was one of the few people I truly liked at my job, however, I did tend to agree with her boyfriend's opinion of her. It wasn't that she was an evil fear mongering bitch, she was just an incredible flirt. The type of girl who always laughed at your stupid jokes and wasn't afraid of breaking touch barriers. Many times I have wanted to pounce and ravage her against the water cooler in the lunch room, or now, right on top of Grant's desk, while his camera hovered feverishly around us. *"Louder! Moan louder! Okay, now flip her around."*

"Ah... Sure," I said. "Where do you want to go?" "I just want to get away from here."

"Okay. Sure," I said. "So, what's going on?" "Ah," she said, frustrated. "Davie's an asshole! He says I flirt too much and that I don't love him. And you know what? He's right. Screw him. I'm through with him, and this time I'm not letting him crawl back with his tail between his legs."

"Yeah," I said. "Of course not." I had no idea what to say. What the hell did I know about relationships? Ask me about drunken one night stands or about girls with more looks than brains. Those were my gigs. This was uncharted territory.

"Can you give me a ride home?" she asked. "I just, I just want to go home."

"Sure," I said. "Why not?" "Perfect. Thank you so much, Mickey. You're such a nice guy."

It wasn't a long drive from work to her apartment complex, but by the time we arrived she was already in a noticeably better mood. Her smiles were wide, her eyes bright, and her laughter infectious. I shifted the transmission into park, and she sat in silence for a moment, pensively staring at the dashboard before speaking again, smiling shyly.

"Do you want to come up for a while? I could use

some company."

"Ah... Sure," I said, but I was feeling rather wary. "Davie won't be there, will he?"

"Davie?" she said. "Screw him! He doesn't live here. This is my apartment and my life. He has nothing to do with it anymore."

"Right," I said. "Cool."

I followed her into the marble slabbed lobby of the building and into the elevator. With the ring of the bell, the doors slid open, revealing the fourth floor hallway. Turning left, I followed her past a series of doors until we reached hers. Once inside, I took a moment to note her apartment's elegant style.

"Wow!" I said. "My apartment looks like shit compared to yours."

"Of course it does," she chuckled. "You're a guy."

"Yeah, my idea of decorating involves empty beer cans, overflowing ashtrays, and a beautiful blanket nailed over my bedroom window."

"Well, it's all about accessorizing," she laughed and offered me a beer, inviting me to sit on the sofa. I did, and she sat next to me, sipping on her own beer.

"So, thanks again for driving me home," she said, smiling shyly. "And I'm sorry for dumping this all on you, it's just, my life has been strange lately. It feels like everything is suddenly falling apart."

"No problem at all. Everyone needs to talk sometimes. I hope you're feeling better."

"I am," she smiled crookedly and had a healthy drink of her beer. "I'm just feeling a little lost lately, you know? I've always wanted to do something different with my life, but it's almost as if I'm just wandering through it, unable to make the connections I want, or get the opportunities I need to get ahead. I've always wanted to set my life to the wind, you know, backpack Australia, or South Asia, but it never seems like a good time to do any of it, and when it could be, I'm always too damn poor to do anything of meaning," She stopped and lowered her eyes, smiling shyly. "I'm sorry, I'm not boring you am I?"

"Absolutely not. And don't feel bad about it, it's the same for most people these days. It's a broken world we live in. The middle class is really just a different word for slave."

"Ha, ha, I guess," she replied.

"It's true," I said, and had another drink of my beer before continuing. "Just look at the system we are all forced to follow. We can go to school, but only for obscene amounts of money, because it then forces us to begin working immediately after our education whether it's in our field of study or not, nobody cares as long as we're paying back the loans at grossly inflated interests. And then we'll need things like vehicles, and houses, and all of the basic things our expensive little diplomas still won't allow us to afford–but wait–there's a solution. Since our loans are being paid, here's some credit. There is no real or even logical reason for a vehicle to cost seventy thousand dollars, but some do, because our values today are dictated by advertisers, not logic. It's what the other guy has and you don't that matters, not what makes sense. The price of houses, oil, food, and other necessities have nothing to do with anything as elegant as supply and demand–those are based on the speculation of millionaires–billionaires who couldn't care less about gasoline at four dollars per gallon, their stocks are up because of it. They laugh and gloat over the middle class because they are the ultimate benefactors, and we are not. That's the reality of the world we live in, and the best part of it all is that the middle class illusion goes completely unnoticed by most. You got the shiny car, and the big house, and the toys you wanted, don't you feel properly rewarded? Put a smile on, chalk it up to *that's life*, and get back to work, make us some money. You and I live in a time when our entire economic system is based on things so grossly disconnected from anything real or even natural, it truly is flabbergasting. We suck, and most likely, we always will, because we are part of a herd mentality that never notices the elusive shepherds employing their cunning tricks."

"That's true!" she replied, her eyebrows arched high. "I've never thought about it like that before. I think we're addicted to shopping, we spend so much on so little."

"Ha, ha, yeah," I said. "I didn't mean to get all philosophical on you, but that's the basic idea. What we tend to consider valuable most often has no real value to us, they are valuable to the other guy. I mean, even most of the popular TV shows feature characters that either live at work, or lead completely unrealistic lifestyles, or need six takes to film a scene of a so-called "reality." It's all superficial, and it truly is what dictates our behaviors. It's what tells people what's cool and what's not, what they should believe in and what they should be caring about, what their goals should be, and it makes them feel inferior to its expectations. It's a terrible world we live in when even our values are manufactured."

"Ha, ha, you're right," she said, smiling widely. "And passionate," she rubbed my shoulder with her hand. "And I think I need to get my hair done, ha, ha."

"And I need four hundred dollar shoes, million dollar houses, and some bitches! Ha, ha."

We laughed and each had another drink from our beer; an awkward silence followed. She bit her bottom lip and lowered her eyes apprehensively. I was unsure of what was happening, the mood had changed, but I was having trouble wrapping my head around it. I finished my beer and considered making an exit, but she quickly broke the looming silence.

"Do you want to smoke a joint?" she asked, smiling deviously.

"Can you handle it?" I replied. "I've been stoned with you before, at the Christmas party–you get a little loopy. You're scary when you're high."

"I am not!" she defended with a smile. "I was really drunk, all right?"

"Okay, I'll do it," I teased. "But at the first sign of loopiness, I'm outta here, ha, ha."

"Deal," she said. "I'll be right back."

"No need," I interrupted. "As luck would have it, I happen to have a joint right here in my pocket. The silly things we kids carry around with us these days. Here," I said and handed her the joint. "Light this and be prepared to take the trip, but be careful."

She lit the tip and a thick puff of smoke momentarily encased her head.

"Careful of what?" she asked, exhaling.
"Well," I said. "I secretly laced the joint with crack, so I'm sorry but from this day forward you will forever be a depraved dope fiend."

"Are you trying to turn me into a crack head?" she laughed.

"What?" I said, as if shocked. "I thought, I mean, you're not already a crack head?"

"Oh screw you," she said. "I'm just a lost little girl. Don't judge me."

There was considerable tension rising in the room, our chemistry was changing, our courage mounting. This girl, she was suddenly tantalizing, and irresistible. We smoked the joint and then erupted into bouts of laughter–until–the laughter suddenly stopped, and the mood changed drastically. She attacked me in a fit of lust! Like an animal. Instantly, I followed the loss of control, and together we reverted to ancient, primal instinct. We hurried to her bedroom, frantically dodging obstacles and smacking into walls.

I felt like a million bucks! There is nothing sweeter than a woman you've only ever dreamed about. I let it all go in the moment. All of it. I felt the euphoric rush of success, of conquer, of–all at once, I suddenly felt a rush of air flow through the room, and then noticed a figure standing next to us, screaming wild gibberish. In surprise, she pulled away and left me with hot convulsions rushing through my body. It was too late. A projectile was launched, and a t-shirt soiled. There was a moment of disbelief which quickly deteriorated into a terrible reality. The figure mutely stared down at his chest, allowing the insane realization flash wildly through his mind. He suddenly shrieked like a foiled medieval warrior after having found his family slaughtered by his enemy–he was very dramatic about the whole thing.

"I'm gonna fucking kill you!" he roared.

I had no formal training in performing such a feat, but it had happened anyway. A macabre money shot that would forever haunt this man. I had officially ruined his life.

Naturally, my quick quips of laughter contributed absolutely nothing productive to the situation. With murder in his eyes, he lunged for me, grinding his teeth in rage. I rushed backwards as quickly as I could and made an attempt to escape. I circled the beast and lunged for the door. "Call me!" I yelled and ran down the hall, still completely nude. Nothing but a bundle of clothes in my hands like a misunderstood gift basket.

With my hunter quickly closing in, there was no time for the elevator. I frantically searched for the door to the stairs, and found it! I pulled on my underwear and rushed down the stairs at a dangerous pace. I got to the main floor and ran out to my car, throwing the mess of clothes in and peeling out of the lot like a bank robber. But it didn't end there. Rightfully so, I suppose, the poor fool jumped into his car and gave chase. It's one thing to sleep with another man's girlfriend, but it is quite another to soil him with undeniable evidence of it.

I stomped on the accelerator and picked up speed at a sickening pace. I had the impression that he would eventually tire of my relentless speed and give up the chase; perhaps to stop at a bar, drink himself stupid, and get into a fight with men that were far too powerful for him to handle. Anything to relieve the rage that bubbled inside of his every molecule. Of course, he would need a new shirt first.

I screamed in laughter at the thought of it. I was no fool, nor was I a stranger to high speed driving. I grew up pushing man made machines to their limits; until they either crippled under the pressure and killed me instantly, or lived up to their highly held testament of quality made manufacturing principles. The only problem was that I knew nothing of my pursuer. Had he the experience under his belt? Had he felt the incredible rush of near death and dealt with it dashingly? I would soon find out.

I swerved wildly through city streets, pushing my

vehicle to its limit. I turned up the stereo and screamed, "Come and get me, fucker! Woo!" To the right, then to the left, then back to the right, I cut through traffic like a high speed jet–and still–he followed.

I swerved around a corner with the brakes locked, when the front rim on the passenger side hit the asphalt and sent a massive tail of sparks flying from the side of the car. A perfect example of piece of shit manufacturing principles! No sooner had I made this sickening realization, did I also notice that the vehicle was suddenly at the mercy of the all-encompassing laws of physics. The ugly mass of steel slid sideways, and then a monstrous force flipped me upside down with a bang, sending me flying through the air.

Once fully assaulted with flying shards of glass, I realized my situation–the bastard had hit me at full speed from the side. He could have at least attempted to slow down. Prick. I snatched my knife from the glove compartment and made my exit, still wearing nothing but underwear. I stomped hastily toward him with a look of pure insanity in my eyes. It was my turn to unleash!

I was furious, and he was now terrified of the entire situation, especially of the transmogrified beast heading his way with a shiny blade in hand. He quickly stepped out with his hands up in front of him, a sign that meant, *I'm sorry! I didn't mean it! Please don't stab me 86 times in the middle of the street!*

"Oh, my god, man!" he yelled. "Are you all right? Are you–are you okay?"

I grabbed him by the collar of his defiled shirt and slammed him hard against his car, holding the stainless steel blade tightly against his throat.

"You are a cockroach!" I snarled. "I should cut you on principle alone."

"I'm... I'm..."

"Shut up!" I snapped. "You're really pushing my last nerve here." His face was pale, a cold mask of terror. "You destroyed my car, goddamn it!" I yelled.

"I... I'm"

"Shut up!" I snapped again. "From now on, you stay away from Alice, or else I'll come back and I will hurt you, got it?"

He nodded quickly, his eyes wild, trying to pull away from the blade.

"Now get your ass out of here before the police get here. Goddamn it! Now I have to deal with the fucking police. Those bastards have never fully understood me."

He stared at me strangely, wondering if he could actually leave.

"Just get in your car and drive away, man. Forget about all of this. Just fuck off!"

He hopped into his car and began pulling away, but I stopped him once again.

"Wait! Wait!" I yelled.
He stopped quickly and I ran up to his window.

"Here, take this," I said, and threw the knife into his vehicle. "Pigs don't like me and weapons. Now go! Drive!"

He took off in a hurry and I slowly lowered my numb, shaking body onto the curb. I was beginning to feel the full brunt of the physical assault I had endured.

"Jesus," I mumbled to myself. "That was intense." I had let my exceptional temper get the better of me. I could hear emergency sirens approaching, and noticed a large crowd of people gathering around me, asking me if I was all right, and placing a warm blanket over my half naked body.

"I'm fine. Thank you," I responded, and sighed. "I'm just fucking great."

For a long time, this type of behavior was what I called my life.

CHAPTER 2

The police had no explanation for the carnage. There was too much craziness to make any real sense of it, so they did what all responsible authoritative bodies do in such a case–they slapped me with a hefty fine for reckless driving, and they did it right through my wild ranting about potholes, and calling the media about it.

"This is bullshit!" I screamed. "I could've died a horrible death because of this city! This isn't the last you'll hear from me! You sorry saps are going to have me and my lawyers on your hands for so long your kids will call us uncle, and then I'll sell them weed!"

Of course, none of it was true. I certainly didn't have the money to hire a lawyer, and I didn't even necessarily like kids. I was angry over having wrecked my car, but I did find solace in the fact that I was still alive, and that in the ensuing melee, I had actually taken the time to rip one last piece of scornful abuse on poor old Davie boy. A man I had never met before this event, and one I would probably never forget. Definitely vice versa. He had an ex-girlfriend I had savagely defiled, a T-shirt stained with my forensics, and even the very knife I had threatened to slit his throat with. An impressive list of vileness jammed into the span of only a few minutes, and a story that seemed so ridiculously blown out of proportion, it would be utterly embarrassing to retell.

It's funny how your life can crumble and change with such speed that it leaves your head spinning for years afterward. I could picture him trapped in a situation he despised in the future–perhaps with a wife he hated, six delinquent children, and a dilapidated suburban home with far too many bills–only to realize in his wallowing misery that the true source of his anguished feelings about life somehow stemmed from the events of a single day. "Goddamn you, Mickey!" he would curse at the sky. "Wherever you are, goddamn you!"

I was comfortable with that. It's been my experience that some events simply cannot be helped no matter what you do. As always, it was partly my fault, and partly the fault of the winds of fate. No use in sulking over it.

The police took my ranting statement of threats while 2 paramedics checked me out. I was fine, refused a hospital visit, and grabbed a cab to drive me home. My muscles pulsed in agony, my limbs stiff and sore. Every bump in the road resonated with solid bursts of pain blasting through my head. I lit a well deserved cigarette on the way, despite the driver's complaining.

"No smoking!" he immediately barked. "No smoking! Read Sign! No smoking, buddy!"

"Listen!" I said. "I've had one hell of a night. Bad things happen all around me. If I were you, I would worry about what kind of unexpected disaster is coming your way just for being in my presence. That will kill you faster than my goddamn cigarette. Besides, we're almost there anyway."

"Stupid Americans!" he snarled.
"All right," I replied. "Maybe you're right. Maybe my cigarette will kill you–once I ram it down your fucking throat!"

He sighed and dealt with it, shaking his head. I was irritated and tired. Broke and car-less. Tired. I was tired.

In the parking lot of my apartment building, I exited the cab and handed the driver a crumpled mess of bills. I shuffled slowly through the main entrance, taking the elevator up to the 16th floor, down the hallway and over the homeless drunk on the floor who momentarily came to consciousness, muttering nonsense.

"I've... I... Had some–where's my? Hey, what's up Gibralto?"

"You wasted fool," I said. "Have the women in here been feeding you? Is that why you're always here?"

"Hey... Hey," he said, slurring his words as he sat up,

clenching the butt of a cigarette in his lips. "You gotta light?"

I sighed and lit his cigarette.

"Here," I said. "Don't make this a habit. I'd just as soon throw you down the garbage chute on principle alone."

"Thanks kid, you're good shit," he slurred, and began singing a crude version of Me and Bobby McGee as if he were alone in the shower. It was an alcohol inspired, talentless mess.

"Don't waste too much time singing, old man. And watch out for that evil Mrs. Greene. She'll cut you up and eat you for dinner. She has no children you know, and she'll probably keep you hostage in a baby crib. Of course, you'd probably like that, wouldn't you? Of course you would, you filthy bastard."

He was no longer paying any attention to me. His awareness was failing, his tune slowing as he passed back to a land of dreams, away from the nightmare of reality.

I opened the door to my filthy apartment and grabbed a beer from the refrigerator, which truthfully, held little more. Sitting on my sofa, I let out a wearied sigh and lit a cigarette. I wondered why it was, exactly, I always seemed to attract so much trouble to myself. It was like I was some sort of demented magnet. As though the universe was quite unhappy with my ability to make a decision of any kind. Anything I tried, it seemed, I eventually found myself haunted by. Why was that? Could it really be bad luck? Could it be attitude? With something so simple as the way in which I perceived life, was I truly succeeding at nothing else except setting myself up for disaster with every decision? Every action? Every thought? In light of recent events, I'd say so.

I quickly finished my beer and returned to the refrigerator for a fresh one. I was zoned into an uncomfortable fatigue. Tired, yet horribly aware. I wondered if maybe I was pre-programmed to fail. If not, then why this constant urge to do things simply for the thrill of sabotaging my own life? I put on a brave face and pranced around calling it fun, but seriously, what was I doing? I no longer had a car, my job was a joke, and my apartment sucked. My "outside personality" was nothing more than an attitude I had created–an alter ego–but when I was alone, after a car accident, or after having just finished destroying someone else's life and washing my hands before dinner, I was really just scared. I said I didn't care, but that had to get old eventually, didn't it?

CHAPTER 3

I fell asleep after having far too many beers and woke up in a panic to the sound of my cell phone screaming its annoying tune, the television flashing brightly with some weird anime cartoon, and a horrible, rancid stench hovering in the air. For a moment, I stared in disbelief through the haze of my slowly recovering vision at the foot of the sofa I had drunkenly spent the night on. In the carpet was a huge black crater, a massive burn that should have turned me and the other tenants lodged in the rat infested building to ashes. How could it be? Luck–perhaps it was already improving.

The screaming ringtone seized my attention again. How long had it been ringing? Forcefully, I struggled through my dreary, mind altering hangover for the phone and knocked over half a can of beer onto the coffee table.

"Shit! Hello?"

"Mickey?" the tiny voice screeched.

"Yeah," I cleared my throat. "Who is this? What do you want?" I could feel every muscle in my body searing with pain. My thumping, pulsating head was excruciating. I felt like my eyeballs were about to fall out.

"It's Alice."

It sent another shock through me. Alice. Of course. Why not?

"Alice," I said, my voice harsh and dry. "Hey–ah, how's it going?"

"Tell me what happened!" she demanded, the tears audible in her voice. She was angry, and worried.

"How do you mean?" I said. "Oh, with Davie? Nothing, it's all fine. He chased me and I lost him; I'm sure we're on good terms now."

"I'm serious!" she cried. "Tell me, Mickey."

"Haven't you spoken to him?"

"I tried," she sniffled. "He wouldn't return my calls, and when he finally picked up, he said he didn't want to talk about it."

Well of course not, I thought. What could he say? *Sweetie, you know the man you had sex with barely an hour after our fight, the same one who ruined my favorite shirt? Well, I hit him with my car and totalled his, only to have him threaten to slit my throat in the middle of the street if I ever came near you again. So that about covers my evening. I lost. By the way, I'm really sorry and stuff.*

Foolish.

And what could I tell her–the truth? She was a decent person, how would she react to those crazy words? *You know the dude who chased me? I threatened to gut him like a pig if he ever came near you again–so you're welcome and all that.*

"Seriously," I said. "Nothing happened with us. I lost him."

There was a long pause. I didn't feel as though she believed me, but I certainly wasn't offering any more in my defense to solidify the doubt.

"Whatever," she finally said. "I... I just wanted to say that I'm sorry. I'm so pissed right now."

"It's fine," I said. "No harm done. I had fun."

Shit!

"I had a great time too," she quickly replied, and my head exploded again. "I mean–you're awesome, Mickey. You really are."

Crap.

"Well, Alice, you're pretty great too, but–listen–I was just a rebound guy. You were angry, I understand."

"You're not just a rebound, Mickey. Do you know how long I've had a crush on you? Pretty much ever since we've met. I don't love Davie, I love you."

Oh no. Not this. Not now.

"Alice,"

"I hate Davie!" she snapped. "He's such an asshole!"

Uh oh.

There was nothing to say. The only thing I really knew about the guy was that he appeared to be terrified of sharp objects and he was probably abused as a child, nothing else.

"Alice, you're my friend."

"No!" she snapped. "Don't give me the friend speech, you asshole! Listen to me, Mickey. I'm in love with you, and I am willing to at least try and see where it leads us."

Silence. I wasn't ready for this. A girlfriend? I was... Comfortable. I was happy. I told myself that every day. *You're happy, you prick, now smile!*

"Listen," I said. "I'm–we're... friends, right? I'm just trying to be honest. I'm... Ah..." I was stumped. What could I– "I don't think I'm ready for this," I blurted out, and suddenly, the silence felt offensive. My head was pounding and my stomach was in knots. "Alice, I'm... I'm really sick right now."

"You're sick?" her tone suggested that she was highly unimpressed.

"Hungover," I said. "I got really drunk. I'm still, kind of drunk. I'm sorry, but I can't do this right now. I'm going to be sick."

"Well, can you–"

I hung up. Screw it. I was in no mood or condition for any of it. She loved me? Of course she did. My untrustable male instinct had once again failed me horribly. Blind to emotion. Ignorant to undertones. Everything taken at face value. *Idiot!*

I'd been an idiot. I was always an idiot. I wasn't sure of how I should handle the situation with Alice, but for the moment, it didn't matter. The pain was pounding in the back of my eyes, slashing through my skull in alternating blunt and sharp jabs. Unbearable. My thoughts were too unfocussed to care about anything else. I needed relief. I needed a shower, and some food, and–my eyes were getting heavy. I thought of Alice. I thought of my car. I passed through the darkness and into a land of dreams.

***

Frantically, I searched for the golden key that would open the door in the side of the mountain, when a terrible roar ripped through the sky. Loud, and ominous, causing the sky to darken above me and the air to cool enough to make me shiver. What was it?

My eyelids snapped open and I sat in unmitigated confusion. What was happening? The stench of the room quickly returned to prominence, causing my gag reflex to engage, but the roar, it was still so loud. It was–the intercom in my apartment! I sprung from the sofa, weary and dizzy, racing for the recessed box in the wall, when a terrible fear suddenly tore through me.

What if it was Alice?
Hesitantly, I brought my finger to the button marked "talk" and pressed on it.

"Hello?" my voice was harsh. I desperately needed hydration.

"It's Steve," the voice said. "Let me up."
Thank Christ! I hit the button to unlock the door and ran a shaky hand through my hair, staring at the clock on the wall. 6:00 p.m. I had wasted a full day. The brunt of the previous night felt horribly exaggerated. My neck and arms were stiff and tender, every action a small torture.

Three quick knocks on the door preceded a quick entrance by Steve, his face bright, and his gait carrying a sense of urgency that seemed hardwired into him at all times.

"Hey, buddy," he said quickly, smiling. "What's happening?"

"Hey, man," I said. "Come on in. Do you want a beer?"

"Do I want a beer?" he questioned as though I had offended him. "No, a lemon water and a pacifier will do just fine to compliment the 60 fucking bong rips we're about to do–of course I want a goddamn beer."

I chuckled and threw him a can, which he caught, but then seemed perplexed with me, the can lingering in his hand unopened.

"Jesus," he finally said. "You look like shit."

"Yeah," I said. "Rough night. I totalled my car."

"No shit!" he exclaimed. "What happened?"

I told him the story, mostly through bursts of laughter and smiles that portrayed wordless responses like, "Atta boy!" followed by, "There's no goddamn way that happened!" and finally ending with, "From this day forward, you, sir, are my hero!"

"Well," he said. "At least that motherfucker won't screw with you if you do end up dating that chick."

"Yeah," I replied, but I had nothing else to add really. Telling him the story had only amplified my discontentment with life. What was I doing? Where was I going? What now, without a car, and without any ambition? What now, with Alice? Goddamn it. I could tell that he sensed the disturbance washing through me, but in the true spirit of male machismo, he said nothing about it.

"You know what we need to do?" he said, squinting his eyes and nodding his head. "We need to get drunk!"

My stomach churned. Yuck. My head was still spinning with alcoholic residue, I was hardly prepared for another night of hard abuse. Unfortunately for me, Steve was an extremely persuasive individual. Sensing the resistance, he immediately jumped into salesman mode before I could even say a word in protest.

"Fuck you," (his speeches usually started in this fashion.) "Don't be a bitch."

"I was in a car accident, man," I replied.

"Oh, cry me a fucking river," he said. "You've been sleeping all day, you're fine, there's no need for this big dramatic show of resistance. Don't you understand? Out there, under bright lights contrasting dark walls, there are women, and alcohol, and all kinds of fantastic whims just happening right now while you miss it sitting here feeling sorry, and worried, and whatever else you're feeling because you crashed your car and shit. Well fuck that; that's what insurance is for, dumbass. Get your fucking ass in the shower and clean yourself up."

I shook my head, "I don't know, man." My neck felt like it was trapped in a vise, my temples about to explode.

He stared at me icily, extending his arm toward the bathroom, "Now, motherfucker."

I wasn't getting out of it. As stupid as it sounded even to myself, I was going out drinking.

***

It seemed as though my body was taking note of every sip of alcohol, fully prepared to punish me for being an idiot. My head was already swimming, trying to find a balance between the crap music, the festering crowd, and the heat. I couldn't concentrate. I should have stayed home in bed, suffering, and feeling sorry for myself.

I downed my drink and glanced over the crowd, looking for Steve. He had gone to the washroom 20 minutes ago–typical. As good of a friend as he was, he was a complete whore. A cowboy in his own right, fearless of the ever looming threats of community fucking, and a great lover of a vast array of abusive substances. In places like these, with the swirling lights and the stench of sweat coursing through the air, he was a lurking, lust filled animal roaming the edges of the place like a hyena hunting for willing participants; or just the left overs. The one thing he was not, was picky. He didn't see the naive kids and the drunken perverts commingling in bathroom drug deals, or the sexual partners that one could instantly tell, indeed needed bug spray. All he saw, was potential.

"Can I get you anything?" a stern faced bartender yelled, his words drowned out by the assault of the music and the cackling voices around us.

"Whisky," I yelled back. He nodded and poured me a drink.

"Six fifty," he said. I paid him and held the drink while leaning against the bar, determined to make it last at least an hour before ordering another one. I peered through

the crowd. There were groups of dancing girls and huddles
of manufactured tough guys; drinking, stinking, laughing
and petting. My stomach was still rather unsettled, and the
drinks weren't helping. Where the hell was Steve?

I was just about to leave and search for him, when
a girl caught my eye. She was sitting alone at a table by the
far wall nursing a colorful drink, and staring right at me. She
quickly looked away when our eyes met, but I could tell that
her gaze was aimless. She was trying to be inconspicuous.
I looked away from her, moving my eyes against the sea of
jittering, nervous youths, only to quickly return my attention
in her direction and–she was still looking at me. I smiled
and nodded my head, raising my drink in the air. She smiled
back; some things never need to be said. I pushed my way
through the crowd toward her, swishing my drink around the
inconsiderate bodies hustling about. I made it without spilling a drop and stood there, suddenly unsure of what to say,
how to start.

"Hi," I said.
"Hi," she smiled. "You look bored over there."

"Me?" I questioned. "Well, this isn't really my thing.
Too many idiots. Plus, I lost my buddy," I momentarily
glanced behind me. He was still missing in action. "Are you
here alone?" I asked.

"Well," she said. "I wasn't. I was here with my
friend, but she took off with some guy."

"She ditched you?"
"Yeah," she chuckled. "But it's okay, I don't need her. I'm a
big girl."

I smiled, suddenly nervous. I was never one to be
intimidated by women, but this one had something different
in her eyes. An attitude we seemingly both understood, and
identified with. Something arcane, yet hard to define with
words.

"Can I buy you a drink?"
"Sure," she said, and just like that, an arduous interaction
filled with horrible amounts of potent liquids began. To
hell with my stomach, it was too late anyhow. We poured

shooters down our throats and talked as though we were old friends finally reunited. Suddenly, nothing else mattered. We were having fun.

Before long, with our heads spinning and our words slurred, we found ourselves extremely drunk, and kissing. Helplessly so. She giggled hysterically while we competed over who knew the dumbest jokes–when Steve suddenly manifested next to us.

"Hey, man," he said, his eyeballs wrecked and red, his smile wide, and his hair soaked with sweat. "Where the fuck were you?"

"Where was I?" I said.

"I'm just kidding," he smiled. "I had a date with a girl in the bathroom–and then a car–and then a... Hey," he stared at the drunken girl next to me, noticing her for the first time. "How's it going? I'm Steve."

"I'm Polaris," she replied and smiled sweetly.

"Polaris, huh?" he said, and winked at me. "See? Good thing I told you not to be a little bitch. This place is great."

I wasn't so sure about the place, but this girl, Polaris, was tantalizing. Exciting. The lot of us were horribly drunk, and sweating profusely. It was so hot, and humid with human grease.

"What time is it anyway?" Steve asked.

"It's like–a quarter to two," Polaris answered, squinting her glassy eyes in order to see her watch properly.

"Shit," he said. "Let's get out of–"

A girl suddenly threw her arms around his neck from behind him, surprising us all.

"There you are!" she declared. "Were you running away from me?"

"Hell no," he said, but I was his best friend, he most definitely was. "I was just looking for you. These are my friends, Mickey, and Polaris. Do you want to get out of here?"

She smiled big, her bloodshot eyes wide, "Sure."

I looked at Polaris. There were no words needed. She was going to follow. Somehow, I felt like I really liked this girl.

That, or the alcohol did; either way, we had connected on a level yet to be identified.

We stood and locked arms, supporting each other while we pushed through the thick crowd of wobbly bodies. We made it to the door and I lit a cigarette once outside. Polaris did the same. Steve's date, whatever her name was, was cackling away about cats and the weird ways they mated. Even with the heavy bog of alcohol pressing down on my mind, I had to laugh. Steve was the kind of demented sex fiend who revelled in phrases like, "Go to your happy place," or "Close your eyes, this may hurt a lot," but who was she? Talking about cat penises and feline foreplay; she was right up his alley. I, on the other hand, had this girl, or at least, through the drunken delirium, I was fully convinced that I was really quite fond of this Polaris person. She was exciting for reasons I couldn't necessarily explain. They were undertones. Understanding. Drunken hormones.

Moments later, Steve acted as though calling a cab was a personal attack on his status as a man, and insisted on driving. After a long procession of arguments and protests, we eventually, stupidly, boarded the suicide machine. He was wild and straddling his date, spending more time on molesting her than on paying attention to where he was going. We jumped curbs with incredible speed and sickeningly swerved across lanes of mostly empty streets. Yet, despite the occasional shock of fear, the mood was still somehow high with excitement. Demented exhilaration. A comfort found in decadence, but none of it lasted long.

I suddenly felt a distraction from it all as a rude, vicious reality slithered its way into my mind. I was suddenly focussed on Alice, on my car, on my–on my empty existence. Why was I alive? What purpose did I serve? This life I was living, these things I did, why was I doing them? Were any of them good for me? Sitting in a car, drunk as shit and flying down dimly lit avenues while straddling complete strangers as if we were entitled to ignore all of the possible dangers of the world–was any of that advancing my life in any way?

Polaris took my face into her hands and stared deeply into my eyes, but said nothing. She kissed me, and I forgot my feelings of doom.

CHAPTER 4

She sat on the edge of the bed and stared at me like a stalking animal, smiling like a drunken beauty. I stood before her, feebly maintaining my balance, and stared back while the tension rose in my body. She was mysterious, mystical. I felt like she was in tune with reality in the same way I was. I didn't know her, but somehow, we knew each other. Somehow.

To my great relief, Steve had let us out of his car with all limbs still attached and no one killed on the way. Having just survived a serious accident the night before, his driving had given me a bad jolt. Stupid. As always, I was being an idiot, which I was usually okay with, but lately it seemed to be losing its flavor. Nevertheless, Polaris and I were consumed with each other, trying desperately to keep our clothes on in the elevator. She had followed me down the hall, over the drunk passed out against someone's door, and into my apartment. I had forgotten about the smell, the burnt carpet, the disaster I called my home, until we were right in the thick of it, but she had nothing to say in response to any of it. The drunken urges were far too powerful.

She sat on the bed, still dressed, just staring at me with her eyes squinted and her elbows resting on her lap, supporting her face with a hand on each side, smiling. Malicious, and sexual. I smiled back, curious about this strange mind I'd brought home. We were no longer petting for the moment, but the tension was still rising steadily.

Suddenly, as though it was the start of a race, she said, "Come here."

Without hesitation, I pounced on her like a beast, ready to devour, to conquer, to decimate. With urgency, we peeled away our clothes and wrestled around the bed. She smelled like heaven, and felt like a drug. Infatuating. Irresistible. She arched her back and moaned, digging her nails into the flesh of my back. We rolled over, her on top, then rolled again, the beast on the conquer. Despite having been with Alice barely 24 hours before, I felt as though I hadn't been with a woman in 10 years. I wondered why Polaris excited such primal instincts in me. Why was she so tempting? Pleasing. I wrapped my arms around her and held her tight, her face pressed up against mine, our bodies grinding. We were covered in sweat, tense and aggressive all at once, heading for the ultimate prize.

She kept her eyes closed, her chin up while she moaned, smiling and giggling. We were close now, together, meshed. The infatuating point of no return was at hand.

"Faster," she demanded.

I kicked it up a notch, breathing heavily, and feeling beads of sweat stream down my forehead. So close. She dug her fingers into the tops of my shoulders, pulling her weight against mine, her face contorted in emotion, and then–

"Choke me!" she commanded.

I stopped. I couldn't move. Was she serious?

"Don't stop!" she pleaded. "Please."

I had no idea how to handle it. It was obscene, and exciting. Dangerous. She clamped her hands around my wrists and brought them to her slender throat, pressing them down and inward. Squeeze. I did, but it was apparently not enough.

"Harder," she said, her eyes swelling with tears.

I clamped down harder, and harder, and harder, until I suddenly felt like I wanted to kill her, strangle her in rabid urges and misguided instincts. Smother her like a demented sex fiend unable to control his fetishes. The climax nearly crippled me. A fantastic wave of euphoria tickled my skin like electric convulsions. She moaned, incomprehensibly satisfied with the horrid scene.

"Ah, man," I panted. "What the... What the fuck?"

"Ha! Ha! Ha! Are you okay?" she asked.

"Yeah," I said. "But I've never choked anyone before."

"Well," she replied. "It worked. Thanks."
"Yeah?" I said. "Why do like that?"

"It's not really that I like it, well, I do, but... I don't know," she said. "It's like, it makes me feel alive. Like the only way I feel alive and human is when I feel death closing in and threatening it all."

I supposed I could relate to that, perhaps not in such extreme fashion, but I could understand. Life was often an oppressive thing, a choking sensation–why not beat it to the punch? I guessed it partly explained a big part of my own personality.

"I hope I didn't freak you out too much," she said.
"No, of course not," I replied. "Actually, what you're saying is helping me. Mentally, I mean. You know, a shred of under-standing about the collective human mind."

I suddenly found myself fascinated with her strange fetish. It was as though the answers to life were held in simply being choked. This girl, even beyond the heavy abuse of alcohol, was pulling out all the punches. There was definitely some wild, unexplained connection between us; something that trumped simple infatuation.

She swung herself out of bed, heading for the bathroom. A beautiful girl, but I could suddenly see the track marks of the reality she embodied. She was covered with obvious signs of a very crude and painful emotional past. A victim succumbed to her own twisted mind. Her arms were covered with ancient scar tissue from razor blade induced pain. The very sight of her spelled trouble, and I probably should have been thinking about escaping her savage past, but as always, her degraded way of dealing with life was mostly responsible for the attraction.

"Do you want to do it again?" she asked, and a weird excitement suddenly came over me.
"Come here."

CHAPTER 5

When I opened my eyes, a sharp, potent rush of pain crushed my head. I exhaled a labored breath, trying to cope with the squalid feeling that my brain had swollen to three times the size of my skull. I was a fool. Too much abuse. The room was bright, too bright, and the air too dry. I gingerly pulled back the covers and sat on the edge of the bed, my pounding head hanging low against my chest. Goddamn.

I looked to the other side of the bed, feeling the muscles of my neck resist the action with all of their might, and suddenly felt a deep, satisfying happiness. She was still breathing! Despite having no previous experience with recent events, I was fully confident that the very last thing anyone wants, or needs, is to kill a sexual prowess caught in the grips of a mad fetish. It had been an incredible night, no question, but I soon found myself wondering about my neighbors. Had they been as fascinated as I was, staying up late into the strange night with ears pressed tightly against the adjacent walls, saying things like, "Honey. Honey, listen. Do you hear that? That woman keeps screaming that she wants to be choked. What the hell?" It brought a smile to my face. I felt a weird, decadent satisfaction with the knowledge that I'd experienced things they probably never would. Arcane.

I stood, my head dizzy and my body weak, and headed for the bathroom. I trudged through the room pressing the palms of my hands against my temples with only one thing on my mind. Painkillers. Powerful, beautiful painkillers, mainly produced and manufactured for idiots like myself. I couldn't spin the top from the bottle fast enough. I downed a bunch of pills and sucked at the water coming from the faucet. Too much.

I snuck out of the room with Polaris still sound asleep, and left the door slightly ajar behind me. Black coffee and cigarettes; the time had finally come! I made the coffee and sat on the sofa, lighting a cigarette and taking a long, slow drag. I was having trouble properly assessing my weekend. Had it been good, or inherently bad? It was hard to tell. I had never wanted to be the same boring masochist as everyone else. I wanted nothing to do with normal–no nice home or happy family, no regular job to slave away at day after day like my parents had done, and their parents before them–but where do you draw the line? How far does one go before it is deemed too far? Deep down I knew, as we all do I suppose, that the distance between what we want and what we get is often measured in light years. I, like most people, wanted the experience of life cranked up to the fullest extent. Real living. Real excitement. Full flavored, and believing with complete conviction that what was real, what was worth it, was somehow deeply rooted in taboos. My generation seemed to carry this heavy belief; it was forever lurking beneath the shining civility we all pretended to uphold.

She startled me when she came through the door, still naked, immaculate despite the self-mutilations of her past. Her head was also pounding, what with the lack of oxygen to the brain and all, so I shared my painkillers and she had a shower. Out of the shower, she smelled of sweet artificial chemicals while sipping on her coffee, making conversation. Aside from her name, which could very well have been a stripper name, I knew nothing about her. Not her age, or home, or family, or even interests–but I was careful not to ask too much, fearing that perhaps too much knowledge about such a person would wind up ruining the excitement of being with her. I wanted her to remain a stranger. I wanted her to remain my taboo.

A few cups later, she apologized, but had to leave for home, and then work in a few hours.

"Well," I said. "I'd give you a ride, but I totaled my car."

"It's fine," she smiled. "I'll cab it."
Her eyes were unwaveringly intent on me. I led her to the
entrance, but once there, we awkwardly stared at each other,
unsure of what to say next.

"I want to see you again," she finally said. "I really
hope to. I haven't had this much fun in a long time."

"Neither have I," I replied. "I do like you a lot."
She asked for my phone, which I handed to her and watched
as she punched in her number under the contact name,
"Choke."

"If you really do want to see me again, just call me."
"I'll call you," I replied. "I swear. I like you."

She smiled, "Bye magic hands."
I smiled and watched her stroll down the hall before shut-
ting the door. Polaris, what a strange, unexpected addition
to my life. She excited something inside of me I couldn't
quite understand, but I was enjoying it. It was a connection,
something obscure and almost intangible, but it was there
nonetheless. I was suddenly faced with a startling realization,
standing there with the painkillers overtaking the hangover
and my mind reeling with the events of the night before. It
was that no matter how hard we may try, or how much we
may pretend, there will always be parts of ourselves that we
will never understand. The worst thing anyone could do was
fear the unknown.

CHAPTER 6

If there's one thing I've learned, it's that you can easily get away with blackmailing your boss for total immunity by holding his supposed decency hostage, but when you walk through the doors expecting a happy, polite hello, and you are instead met with a hawk faced conservative knob in town from head office, things begin to change.

The very sight of his balding head and wire framed glasses repulsed me. The expensive suit, immaculately pressed and free of defects, spoke volumes about this geek. He was weak, and I was in no mood to put up with any of it.

"Mr. Tyler?" he asked with a squeaky, weasel-like voice.

"What?" I said, already annoyed. "Who the hell are you?"

"I, am Mr. Holmes, thank you very much," he said, reflecting my tone. "Senior V.P. of Operations, and I am here to try and turn our operations around one branch at a time. There are some new corporate policies coming into effect as of today, and starting, with this location."

I could see the frailness in his eyes. He was a man who clearly held zero confidence outside of a corporate setting.

"Really?" I said. "You know, Holmes..."

"Mr. Holmes!" he snapped.

"All right, Mr. Holmes. It's Monday morning. I've had one hell of a weekend and I haven't even had my first coffee yet. Can we do this later, when I feel like talking to my father?"

"I am not your father!" he snapped.

"M...Mickey," Grant said from behind the fool. He was obviously perturbed, and sweating profusely. He was terrified, and I suddenly found myself feeling sorry for him.

"H.. Hi Mickey," he said with a sudden pleasant smile.

"Hello, Grant. Nice weekend I hope?"

"Yes, Mickey. N...Nice and quiet."

I could tell that he expected me to expose him at any moment to the Gestapo looking fool in front of me, but as luck would have it, I already hated this Mr. Holmes more than anyone I had ever met. That, and in lieu of my own new found excitement with Polaris, I felt that I somehow understood some of Grant's motivations. I would never tell a soul. Indulge in your fetishes freely. Being human, it seems, is to be a sexual beast.

"M...Mickey," Grant continued. "Mr. Holmes is here to help the company impose some new policies for a more streamlined service to our customers, and–"

"That's right!" Holmes interrupted. "We want to make sure that all of our employees are giving the company absolutely everything they have to offer."

I eyed him suspiciously, filled with an intrinsic rage I couldn't quite explain, forming involuntary fists.

"That was very rude of you, Holmes," I said.

"Mr. Holmes!" he snapped again.

"Grant was speaking to me–" I started my protest, but he interrupted, bringing his scowling face inches away from mine, his breath confirming that he did, in fact, eat deep fried dog shit for breakfast.

"Now you listen to me!" he demanded in a harsh whisper filled with suppressed rage. Probably a sexual problem. I thought of perhaps strangling him, setting all of that weird energy free. "Get to your desk and get to work. I'm doing inspections today, please have your things in order by the time I get to you," he smiled like the cocksucking asshole he appeared to be. "I'm watching you, Mickey Tyler. You're on very thin ice already and it's not even 9 a.m. Fantastic first impression, by the way."

I desperately bit my tongue–literally bit into it until

a sharp pain engulfed my face. I was trying to maintain my composure against the monstrous fit of rage erupting inside of me. I stared at Grant, standing behind the pig fucker, shaking noticeably and soaked with sweat, fiercely fighting the urge to collapse. I decided to say nothing and quietly, calmly, proceeded to my desk with the battle lost, but the rage unabated.

I brushed past his pretentious smile and his hillpeople-like, simpleton stare, and walked to my desk, seething with the urge to break something. Anything. Fuck!

I dropped into my chair and tried calming my heart rate, but to no avail. The scene had sunk me into a grotesque, morbid mood, and one made no better by the background disturbance of Holmes's voice roaring through the large room, belittling employees for improper reports filed and a general lack of ambition for success of the company as a whole. Disgusting. No one could ever ask me to be so pathetic.

I heard him tell some girl that a monkey could do her job, and suddenly, it dawned on me–this was my life. This was real. This oppressive, depleted sense of reality–it was real. It was being mass produced by the gallon by Pig Fucker's weasel-like voice and his manufactured tyranny still not making up for the obvious downfalls of his personal life. My apartment, my car, my empty bank account, it was all real. Polaris, she was real. She was exciting. She understood. And–Alice. *Shit!* I suddenly ducked my head down closer to my desk as if someone was popping shots off in my direction. What would I tell her? What could I? Christ. All of this was real! Why? Why was I always so hellbent on stupidity?

Grant's voice suddenly snapped me out of my mini anxiety attack, but he wasn't speaking to me, he was a row away stammering some gibberish in response to a mindless barrage of questions from Holmes. I could see them from my seat; Grant, his shirt soaked in sweat, his legs jittery and unstable, his balance swaying uncertainly, and Holmes, towering above him, his arms slashing through the air, his voice roaring hoarsely about an unacceptable lack of toner in the office and too much damn paper wasted. He was threatening to fire him, actively belittling and destroying him in front of the very staff he was charged with overseeing. A show. I felt bad for Grant. Holmes was making his life hell, causing his heart to pump unnaturally, and his mind to swoon with unfocussed thoughts. It was all highly unnecessary.

I tried doing some work, concentrating on weaning off the rage, but my hands were trembling uncontrollably. Suddenly, I felt as though if I did happen to see Alice, I would probably break down in tears. It would all be far too much for one simple morning. Why was my life so complicated?

"No smiling! Why are people smiling?" his voice roared from only a row away, causing me to twitch and grind my teeth. There was no need for such behavior. It was as though all of the various problems that plagued each one of our pathetic little lives had suddenly transmogrified into a single balding, beady eyed, weak little man whose only sense of importance lay in wielding a feeble, delusional corporate whip.

I couldn't concentrate. I needed a walk. I needed a chance to stow the spastic, relentless tension that was–

"Mr. Tyler!" his voice caused every muscle in my body to contract into a hard, solid mass. I tried to breathe while assessing the situation from the corner of my eye. From that angle, I could see Grant's legs trembling, his body about to burst from the unwanted confrontation, and next to him, an ugly silhouette towered above me; the stench of him was making my eyes water, and my fists tighten, and my breath shallow. Slowly, and with the eyes of an offended lion, I turned and stared at him as if I was in total disbelief that anyone was stupid enough to have wandered into my territory.

He smiled maliciously, like a tyrant, like a prick. "I want to see your time sheets, your APB reports, and your claims spreadsheets immediately!" he demanded, his eyebrows twitching unnaturally with every feeble attempt at authority.

"What?" I replied arrogantly. I was furious.
"Give me your reports, you blistering moron!" he snapped,
and the reaction that flowed through me was unintentional,
but fully motivated. An ugly, manic rush of psychosis
overwhelmed me. I was to my feet in a flash, my face inches
away from the pretentious prick's, my blood boiling.

"What did you just call me?" I snarled, and his eyes
grew wide with surprise, disbelief. A crooked, nervous smile
spread across his face.

"Your reports!" he screamed.
"Don't avoid the question!" I screamed back, fighting the
express urge to crush his nose under the force of my fists.
"Who the fuck do you think you are?"

His eyes were suddenly clouded and wandered aimlessly about the room. I wondered if he was thinking back
to some mindless managers seminar he had been forced to
attend over the course of his career. I reveled in that thought
for a moment, imagining the gears in his unstable mind racing furiously to dissect the situation and devise the proper
course of action to deal with it while repeating to himself
over and over again, "Stay calm! Be professional! Stay calm!
Be professional!' Unfortunately, what they don't teach you in
those assemblies is that if your personality is dependent on a
job title, perhaps you could also benefit from a CAT scan.

"I... I," he was stumped. "I am your boss, and you
will show me some respect!"

And then it hit me. My job, my life, and the way I've
been feeling about it all–I had no real control over any of it.
I was trapped. This man, this pathetic excuse for a human
being, he had more control over my life than I did. He could
make me feel inferior, or worried, or defeated with minimal
effort. I, we, had no real control.

Enough! It was unacceptable.
My attention faded back to his cackling face, red with rage,
and screaming things that were only slowly beginning to
register with me once again. I caught the end of a sentence,
"... I am your superior!"

I smiled, focussing my eyes on Grant's flushed face
for a moment, watching as he fought with himself to stand
up straight and not collapse. I felt bad for him. I felt bad for
everyone around me, and especially, for Mr. Holmes here.

"Take it easy, you Nazi pig!" I said, still holding my
smile. "You're a sad man, you know that? Here you are, a
mid-fifties momma's boy, trying like a big boy to feel like
someone important. Well you're not, Holmes. You are sad.
You are scared, and you are absolutely not fooling anybody. I see right through your little show here, yelling and
screaming as if everyone should bow to your every wish just
because you sucked enough cocks to get a title."

His hand flew up into the air, his mouth gaped open,
just about to interrupt, but I would have none of it.

"I know, I know," I said. "Incest is a difficult thing
to recover from, especially since the last sweet piece of mom
pussy was just last night before leaving, or wait–no–she's
waiting at the hotel room right now, isn't she? Ah, Holmes,
you're not fooling anybody. You can kiss my ass and stick
my reports straight up your fucking cunt. I quit, you fucking
clown."

He seemed to be holding his breath, his eyes were
bulging and red, his face was drenched with sweat. He
snarled his teeth like a dog defending his food, ready to
pounce. His pupils dilated, his eyeballs glossy, he lunged
forward, pushing me back into my chair. It was official, the
beast had been unleashed in full alpha mode. I let a loud
packing sound echo through the stunned room. He flew
backward and landed on the ground with a thump, blood
gushing from his nose.

"You broke my nose!" he screamed, but no one
moved. I looked at Grant, his face suspended in disbelief, his
breathing non-existent. I swore, somewhere underneath his
anxiety-fueled catatonia, deep inside, he was smiling with
vicarious pleasure.

"Grant," I said, speaking over the moaning baby
on the floor. "Grow some balls and tell this guy to go screw
himself. Don't let him do this to you, any of you. Life's way

too short for this shit."

"Call the police!" Holmes screamed from the floor, his body squirming like a bug, but no one heeded his demands. The repulsion was unanimous. I nodded to Grant before stepping over Holmes and walking away, feeling amazing. I hated that goddamned job with its ridiculous office politics and huddled cliques of gossiping degenerates. I hated many things about my life, but none quite so deeply as my job. It was over. Finally.

I felt like a million bucks. I was free to throw myself in any direction, attempt any job or hobby. It felt exciting. It felt like living! I was alive, and I was wasting my precious time filing insignificant reports and counting the seconds until the end of the day, doing anything to get through the disheartening torture of it all for only a few more hours. Screw it, I was done. This was opportunity; possibilities at every angle.

I waited at the bus stop barely a minute before helping an old lady with paper thin skin get aboard and seated. I nodded hello to anyone who dared glance in my general direction. I loved myself, ready to take on the world and any stealthy curve ball it threw at me–and then my phone rang, destroying my swollen sense of euphoria, and changing my life forever.

CHAPTER 7

My auditory cortex was receiving the frantic voice screeching loudly through the phone, I was getting the message, but the rest of the receiving neurons were caught in a fit of confused misfires.

"What?" I yelled into the microphone. "What?"

"I'm so sorry, Mickey! Jerry died!" she said, the crushing tears audible in her voice.

"What? What happened?"

"He–he's dead, Mickey! He's dead!" was all she could say.

"Okay," I said. "Okay. Just breathe. Just breathe. Are you home? Stacy? Are you–I'm coming over! I'll be right there!"

I hopped off the bus and hailed a cab, feeling an overwhelming sense of unease. My hands were cold, my stomach tied in hopeless knots. Too shocked to think. The cab came to a sudden stop at the curb, the driver obviously sensing the overtones of panic in my demeanor. I threw him a bunch of bills and ran toward the front door of the house, banging on it wildly.

"Stacy! Stacy, it's me! Open the door!"

The door swung open and revealed a shattered soul. Her face was swollen with painful emotions, her body shaking uncontrollably. I quickly threw my arms around her shoulders, caressing her tightly.

"Shh," I said. "Shh. It's okay. It's okay."

"He's gone!" she cried, her fingers digging into my back. "Ahuh huh huh huh!"

"It's okay," I tried consoling her. "Come on, let's go sit down."

I led her to the living room and sat on the sofa, still

caressing her slender torso in my arms. She said nothing, and cried; I simply waited with ragged breaths, giving her the time to mourn and let it all out while in comforting arms. I hugged her tightly and swayed her back and forth, gently rubbing her back with my hand. I felt terrible. I felt numb. The tortured soul I held in my arms, she was Jerry's sister, and Jerry was one of my childhood friends. He, along with Steve, Stacy, and I, had made the big move from our quaint little hometown nestled neatly somewhere in the valleys of the Colorado Rockies, to the big city life of Los Angeles with hope in our eyes and naive courage in our hearts. That was 7 years ago already. But we were still young, relatively healthy, and–surviving. Struggling, truthfully, but alive. How could he be gone? Here yesterday, gone today. It was brutal. It was foul. It was real.

My heart sank. Goddamn. I had no idea what to do. My life suddenly felt threatened, and doomed. The thought of a future was intangible, and fake. I could feel Stacy's body convulsing in sobs, causing my throat to clamp shut, and my head to spin lightly. How could it happen? I didn't know, but I wasn't about to press for the information just yet; the poor girl was decimated.

Eventually, she lifted her head, her eyes were red and puffy. Her face and shirt were black with eye liner, soaked with tears. She stared into my eyes intently, searching for answers, searching for confirmation that it wasn't real, it wasn't happening.

"Thanks for coming," she said, and rubbed her forehead with her hand. "I'm sorry–"

"It's all right, Stacy," I said, and hugged her again, "It's okay. It's no one's fault."

She slowly pulled away from me, her hair tangled, stuck to her cheeks. She swallowed laboriously, frowning, and then cleared her throat. "Do you want something to drink?"

"I'm fine," I replied. "Just take your time, there's no rush."

She nodded, squinting her eyes under arched eyebrows, and slowly returned her head to my shoulder, exhaling a sigh.

"He–oh, God," she choked. "I can't believe it! He was hit by a bus! How the fuck does that happen?"

"A bus?" I frowned, sharing in her disbelief. How could that be? "Where?" I asked.

She rubbed her nose vigorously with the back of her hand, sending a flurry of tears down her face. "At the university, I guess he just–he just..." she broke down in convulsions, her shoulders heaving nastily up and down. I held her tightly in my arms once again, stunned and fiercely fighting against the vast array of ugly emotions that were threatening to erupt in physical manifestations. It seemed so ridiculous. A bus. A goddamn bus had done it. What the hell?

She lifted her head from my shoulder once again, her face devastated, her eyes wrecked. "He–the bus driver, the police said he had a heart attack and lost control," she licked her lips helplessly. "I don't know what to say, I'm sorry."

I had no physical reaction. My face remained void of emotion, cold, terrified, but inside, deep inside, an ugly wave of soul crushing emotions washed through me. It was such a stupid way to die. Unfair, and made even worse by the fact that Jerry, my childhood friend, was a 3rd year student of cardiovascular sciences. I could see the headline now. ***Cardiology student killed by bus driver suffering a heart attack.*** Fuck sakes. How could it be? One minute you're living your life, the universe in harmony, and the next, a fucking bus runs you over. Ridiculous.

She stood up from the sofa, excusing herself to the washroom, and left me with an empty silence that felt far more menacing than anything I had ever experienced. Breathtaking. Ugly. I felt helpless. What could I do? What could anyone do? It was done. I took a deep breath and shook my head, letting the reality of it sink in. Jerry was dead. He was gone.

He was gone.

Stacy returned, her eyelids puffy and red, but her tears seemed to be under control. She crossed her arms, squeezing tightly as if giving herself a comforting hug, and gave me a sad, crooked smile.

"Thank you for coming, Mickey," she said.
"Of course," I said, still sitting. "I'm really sorry, Stacy."

She nodded, but said nothing, pursing her lips tightly. "Are you sure you don't want a drink or something?"

"No, I'm okay, thanks," I checked my watch, not really sure why. I felt like my skin was about to burst, the anxiety too much to handle. "I, ah–I should get going–unless you need me to stay. I can stay."

She smiled and shook her head, her eyes closed for a deep breath. "I'll be okay," she said. "It's just, hard. But I have to deal with it, and so do you, Mickey. Thank you." She sat next to me, rubbing my arm in consolation. I stared at her, involuntarily holding my breath, not blinking, and wondering what I should do, where I should go. Jerry was dead.

"Yeah," I finally said, exhaling. "You can call me at any time, okay?" She nodded. "Any time," I said, and stood up from the sofa, straightening out my shirt, and looking at her tiny body balled up on the sofa.

"I'll call you," she said. "Even if it's just to talk."
"Any time," I smiled crookedly, fakely. "And take good care of yourself, okay? Make sure you eat and stuff, promise?"

"I promise," she smiled. "Thanks again, Mickey. I'll talk to you later."

I bent over and gave her a final, comforting hug. "Okay, talk to you later," I said, and headed for the door with a heavy pressure building in my chest. I couldn't breathe. I couldn't think. I made my way outside and ran my fingers through my hair, not really sure of where to go, or what to do. I took a deep breath and held the back of my hand pressed tightly against my mouth to keep from screaming. I felt savaged, and despaired, trying to deal with the bubbling rage, and–and–I felt myself gasp. Tears suddenly distorted my vision. The reality was too foul, too surreal. How could it be?

I looked around aimlessly, searching for answers, for a direction, for–I plunged my hand into my pocket, pulled out my phone, and impatiently searched my contacts list. I found the number and dialed. It rang once, twice...

"Hello?"

"Polaris?"

CHAPTER 8

Her eyes were red and bulging, as though she could cry blood. The result of an intense session of lustful asphyxia. I fell over beside her, still caught in a wave of euphoria while she gasped for air with a wide, consuming smile on her face. Sick with lust. Lusting the sick.

"Ah, God!" she exclaimed. "Jesus, that was great! Ah, hahahaha."

"Yeah," I panted. "That was incredible."

I stared at the plaster ceiling, letting the rush of ecstasy wash through me while she rolled over and lit a cigarette. I felt good in that moment, lost in the fact that I couldn't understand why I suddenly liked this girl and her primal urges so much. I took a deep breath and felt the euphoria dissipate, and the sadness overtake it. I suppose she could feel it emanating from me.

"Are you all right over there, strangler?"

"Ah," I replied. "I'm okay I guess. Why?"

"Well," she smiled. "You went somewhere just now. Lost yourself in the moment, did you? There were some real emotions there."

I sighed loudly.

"Yeah, did I hurt you?"

"Well, yeah, but that's kind of the point, remember?"

"Yeah," I said. "Sorry. I ah, I just found out that one of my best friends died."

"Oh, my God!" she exclaimed, staring intently. "What happened?"

"He, ah–he was hit by a bus," I shook my head, still not fully believing it.

"Jesus," she said, arching her eyebrows. "Can that happen?"

"Well, it did," I said, staring at her strangely. "What's wrong with you?"

"Sorry, It's just–that's like, stuff that happens in the movies. I'm sorry, Mickey. You must be feeling pretty rough. I can leave if you want me to, I mean–if you want..."

"It's all right," I replied. "I mean, I guess this kind of thing happens, but what the hell? It just seems so simple, and morbid." She didn't say anything and stared at me with a saddened face. I sighed again, still feeling the incredible pressure in my chest, the anxiety, the reality. "And I don't want you to leave," I spoke again. "I mean, I don't know why, or how, but you just, you help me, somehow."

She continued staring for a moment, her face slightly contorted, and then she spoke, suddenly grinning oddly.

"Ditto," she said.

I returned her smile, suspending the silence, thinking.

"You know what else? I quit my job yesterday."

"Really?" she suddenly sat up with excitement flashing through her eyes. "That's so cool. Why did you quit?"

"Why? Because it's a soul raping establishment that keeps me from doing the things I love to do in life. It's depressing, and it feels wrong. Life's too short."

I thought of Jerry again, my breath suddenly shallow. Life was too short. Too short to spend day after day being beaten and belittled by a soulless corporation. Too short to take unreasonable orders, or to heed to other people's pretentious tyranny, or to waste a single second more than necessary on things you don't want to do. It was too short, and too precious to not be doing what you thought was right for your life. To hell with everyone else, they just couldn't help but try to ruin your experience.

"God, I wish I could quit my job too," she said. "That would be so awesome," she smiled, but her face was still suspended in sadness, empathy. "So, what now? I mean, what is it that you love to do in life?"

"Well–I don't know," I said, and grinned. "But I'm

sure it'll come to me eventually."

"Yeah," she chuckled. "You're right, you know. Surviving in the world today is depressing, and unfair. We're basically forced and brainwashed into becoming a herd of young dreamers, humping the American dream, until one day, it dawns on us that it's the one that's been humping us the whole time."

"People would be happier if they just choked it," I said.

"Yeah?" she smiled. "You think so?"
"I do," I said. "I'm happy again–mostly."

"You have a special talent for it." she rubbed my arm with her hand, a crooked half-smile on her face.

"Yeah," I sighed. "I don't know–maybe I should get some counseling or something." The room fell silent after that. I lit my own cigarette and continued staring at the ceiling, suddenly thinking about how great it was to be with this near complete stranger and not feel a shred of shame or embarrassment. Why was that? Who was this girl suddenly making my life so exciting? What did she mean to me? She felt comfortable, mystical, even. She made me feel better about the world around me. My lack of work. The death of my good friend. The unending pressures of modern survival. She made it all easier, somehow.

"So," I broke the silence. "Would you like to be my date?"

"For what?" she asked softly, puffing on her cigarette before crushing it in the ashtray.

"The funeral."

CHAPTER 9

There aren't many things in life able to make you feel more helpless, hateful, and empty as having to attend the funeral of a good friend who has died far too young, and in much too savage a way to be acceptable. You enter the room with a feeling of doom crawling under your skin while facing all of your old highschool friends, their faces sagging, their eyes trapped in sorrow. You watch everyone hug, and cry, and wipe watery snot from their noses. You see the crushed family, the emotionally annihilated mother, the ugly, dark flowers accentuated with lighter toned ones, all of it, screaming of death. The picture next to the casket; an absent, smiling face. Goddamn it. It becomes too real.

Unknown faces shake hands and extend condolences, words devoid of hope, but filled with empty encouragement. The air hangs thick, and stagnant, and marinated with the perfume of old ladies. In the back, a huddle of old folks sit together drinking bad tea, spewing out horrible stories about how other people they have known had died; all of them competing for the better story. "*He fell off the ladder and was decapitated by his chainsaw, it was very sad.*"

Upon entering the room, I was stunned, paralyzed. Jerry. How could Jerry be dead? How could this have happened? I felt no particular interest in speaking to anyone, much less with the now complete strangers I once attended highschool with. Polaris clung to my arm, but she was mindful of my emotional rush, careful not to hurry, or even console me. I just wanted to be left alone. I wanted to be somewhere else.

We were back home, in the Colorado Rockies, but without any of the usual excitement of coming home. It was foul. Steve and Stacy had made the trip back with Polaris and I, and Steve was already in full mingle, enjoying the reunion of nearly 30 year old teenagers. I wanted nothing to do with it. I just wanted to get it over with and get back to Los Angeles, and–well–I didn't know, but anywhere seemed better than a goddamned funeral for someone you loved.

"Oh, my God!" the exclamations of overexcited women broke in. Old friends. Old faces. Death. I played nice and even smiled while greeting them, but not without a growing sense of chagrin getting deeper, and stronger inside of me with each one that recognized my face. It only served to magnify the situation I was in; it magnified the doom, widespread, and crawling its way into every facet of my life. I suddenly felt as though I was losing control. I had failed. Surrendered. The kids I used to make fun of, they were now well adjusted citizens, or at least appeared to be while boasting claims of good jobs, and displays of good hair and teeth, and wives that belonged on the covers of magazines, certainly not in the arms of pretentious little geeks. They extended firm handshakes, complimented with belittling smiles – vengeance. Were it not for Polaris, I might have swung a fist or two in rage; Jerry didn't like these people, they were superficial, and shallow, and sardonic. But Polaris was a professional, a natural born people person, and acted as though the life we led in Los Angeles was nothing short of glamorous, even lacing it with undertones of, "*I can't believe you've never left your hometown, you sheltered little pricks.*" It was beautiful, and calming, and with every day, every hour it seemed, I was feeling something rather drastic for her. I was hopelessly attracted. Infatuated. Stunned. Where had she come from? What was happening?

"Oh, Mickey!" I turned, and held my breath. It was Jerry's mother, Annie, with tears streaming from her eyes, and her arms up in the air in embrace. She clutched my face with shaky hands before caressing me tightly, lovingly, genuinely. "Oh, God. How are you, Mickey?"

"I'm okay, I guess," I said. "I'm ah–how are you holding up, Mrs. Harvey. Is there anything I can do? I'm–

I'm so sorry," I wrapped my arms around her and pressed her tightly against me. She was like my second mother. She had fed me throughout my highschool years. She broke down and sobbed on my shoulder while I stared at Stacy's crying face standing next to us, fighting to stop the tears. I didn't want to cry. Not yet.

"The good Lord wanted him," she said from my shoulder. "I guess it was just his time, but it's–it's so hard." I held her while she cried; she felt fragile, devastated.

"Yeah," I said, not really knowing what to say. Jerry was dead. It was fucking bullshit. End of story.

She was eventually able to stand of her own accord, and frailly clutched to Stacy's arm, fighting the urge to break down and just give up. I looked to Polaris, still standing next to me. She was crying. She wiped her eyes with a tissue and smiled at me. I smiled back, barely, and gave her a hug.

"Of course," I said, returning my attention to Jerry's mother. "Mrs. Harvey, this is Polaris. Polaris, meet Mrs. Harvey."

"Hello dear," Mrs. Harvey said, and Polaris greeted her with a quick hug, a gesture the shattered mother appreciated. Any comfort would do. "Did you know my Jerry?" she asked, her voice shaky, and hoarse.

Polaris pursed her lips in regret. "I never had the opportunity," she said. "But I hear good things about him. He was a good man, and a good friend."

"And a good son," Mrs. Harvey finished, bowing her head as her eyes welled up, excusing herself for the emotional barrage she was suffering. She recovered, painfully smiling at Polaris, then to me. "Have you seen him yet?"

I shook my head, staring at the floor, feeling terror explode inside of me. Did I want to see him? I didn't. I took a deep breath, shaking my head again, unable to find anything to say.

"Come on," Polaris said softly, tugging at my elbow. "I'm here with you." She led me past the wrecked mother, and the crushed sister, toward the casket. I couldn't see him on our approach, I tried avoiding it until the very last moment–and there he was. I just stood there, numb and heavy, as though more gravity was pulling on my body, as though– as though the floor was about to swallow me whole. It was Jerry, his face unnaturally white, and his hands appearing stiff, and–dead. He was dead. I felt my face droop as disgust overtook me and clamped my throat shut, forbidding my lungs a breath of oxygen. I felt dizzy, and scared as the room around me pulsated surreally. How could this have happened?

"He looks like he was a nice guy," Polaris broke the silence, perhaps even sensing my desperate attempt at keeping my composure for as long as I possibly could. "He looks friendly, and confident."

"Yeah," I said, arching my eyebrows as my eyelids grew heavy. "He was–he was awesome. Definitely one of the nicest people I've ever met. What a waste." I shook my head in despair; Polaris squeezed my hand tightly. I worked up the courage to place my hand over his, perhaps only for confirmation, but I was only further shocked by how fake it felt. Cold, and absent.

It was more difficult than anything I could ever remember doing, but it had to be done. I had to say goodbye, forever. Son of a bitch. "Take care, buddy," I whispered, my esophagus convulsing, my breath uncontrollable. I swallowed hard and nodded. "You were the best, man. I'm gonna fucking miss you." I felt tears rush down my cheeks, but I didn't attempt to wipe them away. This was bullshit!

Eventually, I managed to pry myself away from the casket, still choked and barely breathing, searching for a place to sit as far away from the empty shell of my best friend as possible. We kindly pushed our way through a crowd of broken eyes and leaky noses, heading for the back of the room, or anywhere the crowds were less dense. Near the back, I could see Steve with his arm around a girl I barely remembered from highschool; she was giggling stupidly, and hugging him closely. There was no stopping that idiot. We sat next to him, to them, I suppose, and tried avoiding the skeletons from my past. The millionaire geeks.

The philanthropists. The business executives. The trophy wives. And over in this corner, the sullen, broken, erotically choked failures still frantically gasping for a breath of fresh air. I wanted to leave. I'd had enough already.

I managed to organize my thoughts and ignore the past made present, returning my mind to Jerry. Damn it! I shook my head and looked at Polaris. She smiled crookedly, sympathetically. I pursed my lips and nodded.

"When we were about nineteen years old," I said softly. "Jerry and I had an apartment together. Well–honestly, it was just a fucking pig sty with shit all over the floors and walls, because all we ever did was party," I smiled again, enjoying the memory. "It was great. We were young, and free, and really, really stupid." Polaris smiled widely. "Anyway, this one night, we had a huge party at our place, and way more people than we had invited showed up, so things got a little out of hand, and Jerry and I ended up doing acid that night, so the details are pretty untrustable. But the next morning, we both woke up on the living room floor surrounded by complete strangers, and suddenly, we could hear escalating noises coming from one of the bedrooms. Some people were going at it pretty hard, and the girl was screaming, and moaning, and then screaming even louder, sometimes almost panicked. We laughed, despite our chemically cooked brains, and were suddenly curious as to who the culprits were. We found our clothes and got dressed, then crept up to the door to find out. Inside, we found our friend, Fat Tim. Now, Fat Tim got his name because, well, he's fat. A solid 350 pounds, violently giving it to this girl, the headboard smashing into the wall, her voice tearing through the walls, wailing. We laughed again, the boy wasn't exactly a ladies man, so we were proud of him, you know."

Polaris chuckled. "Boys," she said.
I even managed a chuckle. "Yeah," I said. "But then, he finishes and rolls off of her, panting, gasping for breath, and the girl just kept saying, 'Oh, my god. Oh, my god.' Trying to catch her breath. Fat Tim was obviously proud of himself and he was staring at her with a big smile on his face before

saying, "Yeah, I have a big dick, don't I?" And the girl sits up, her face enraged, her eyes wide, and she screams at him, 'No, you asshole! You were squishing me!'"

Polaris burst out laughing, and quickly covered her mouth with her hand in slight humiliation. "That's pretty funny," she said, smiling widely.

"Yeah," I laughed. "Well, Jerry doubled over in laughter, and Fat Tim heard us outside the door and threw a fit, but there was no stopping it. Jerry couldn't stop saying it, 'You're squishing me! Ha! Ha! Ha! You're squishing me!' It was his favorite story. After that, even years later, we would be hanging out and he would just blurt it out of nowhere; 'You were squishing me!' and we'd laugh hysterically." I took a long, deep breath. "Fuck," I said. "I'm gonna miss that little fucker."

Polaris leaned over and gave me a hug, tight, and full of care. I hugged her back, but stared at the floor, suddenly in a macabre mood. What the hell was I going to do after we left the funeral home? I had nothing left in Los Angeles, nothing except this weirdly attractive girl. I felt like my chest was going to implode. Doom. All I felt was doom.

CHAPTER 10

In the mirror, I could see the veins in my arms and forehead bulging while I squeezed her from the back. Her blueish lips. Her white fingernails. Her gasping breath. The loud packing sounds, probably a source of slight concern for the other passengers at forty thousand feet in the air. There was a biological explosion, followed by the doubling over of two bodies, numb with ecstasy, ravaged by weird lust. For seconds, I felt much better. For seconds.

"Jesus," I panted, the powerful rush of dopamine rendering my limbs numb, useless. It was hot in the tiny bathroom; the sweat stung my eyes while I stared at Polaris, her head leaned against the wall, her face glowing, her smile genuine. I felt better, but it was superficial. It was fake, as so many whims in life often are.

"Are you all right?" she asked, wiping the beads of sweat from her forehead with the back of her forearm, still panting heavily.

"Yeah," I said, not really convinced that she believed it, but not really caring either. "Are you?"

She nodded yes, licking her lips and stretching her neck. "Well," she said. "We better hurry before we get in trouble." I nodded, my limbs returning to normal functionality, my thoughts organized, the doom prominent. She fastened her pants back around her hips, tightening her belt, smiling. "I'll see you in a few minutes," she said, and left the tiny bathroom first, closing the door behind her quietly, trying to be inconspicuous despite having been quite loud only moments before. I locked the door and took a moment to straighten out my clothes and stare into the mirror, suddenly feeling as though I didn't recognize my own eyes. They appeared cold, and–disconnected. Scared. I took a deep breath and ignored them. I unlocked the door and was suddenly face to face with a line up of kids and parents all waiting for the facilities. How long had they been waiting? Why were they looking at me? I smiled shyly; a woman's voice screaming *choke me!* isn't always the most acceptable of all situations. Probably less so on an airplane with kids standing at the door, asking their parents why someone was killing a woman in the bathroom and everyone seemed angry about having to wait longer for him to be done instead of being alarmed.

I made it to my seat next to Polaris, feeling exhausted. Emotionally exhausted. I wanted a different life. I wanted something new, and exciting, something that made me feel like I had a purpose to be alive and making decisions. To take risks. To succeed. A reason. I looked at Polaris, catching her eyes, her smile. She seemed happy. She was exciting to me. She made me feel something I still couldn't define, but it was something strong, and it was getting stronger. She was a risk, somehow. She felt risky, and I was starting to like it, a lot. I was starting to like her, a lot. I smiled and kissed her forehead, suddenly noticing the smell of her hair. How did these things happen?

Forty five minutes later, we landed in the heavy, humid air of Los Angeles. It was blazing hot out, but cabs were abundant. Polaris and I hopped into one, and Steve and Stacy in another, all rather desperate to get home. The trip had been exhausting, and I suddenly had a whole life to re-organize. I was tired. We dropped Polaris off first; I thanked her for coming with me, but explained the need to be alone and think, and maybe even cry. Goddamn it. She understood. The rest of the ride home felt like hours, the wait accentuated by the silence of the cab, the smell of it, and the goddamned lunatic at the wheel. After what seemed like 200 miles of blaring, screaming, and obscene rush hour traffic, I was finally at my destination. Home. The place I would probably lose in the near future, and I didn't even have a car to live in anymore. I felt screwed. I missed Jerry.

I made it to the 16th floor, over the homeless drunk
still passively holding some old lady's door hostage, and
into my apartment. The smell was repugnant. The carpet
had become a festering, rancid sore in my floor, in my life.
The only proof of good luck I had seen in months; maybe
years. I had a shower, the water providing a temporary sense
of comfort. Home. I dried off and then sat on the sofa with
a beer, my mind still racing, incapable of making any sense
of the kaleidoscope of worries. Too much. I was restless,
and squirmy. I felt itchy, and gross. I felt trapped. I ran my
fingers through my hair and took a deep breath. I needed a
walk. I needed to clear my mind.

I made my way back outside and decided to stroll
the sidewalks of the busy shops a few blocks away. I
watched people bustling about with a certain motivation
behind their actions. What was it? Where had they found
it? Why was I so different? Or was I? I had no job, and no
money; Jerry was dead, and Polaris was–something powerful. What was I supposed to do? The possiblities, where were
they? The American Dream, what did that even mean?

I wondered who these people were. For some-
one coming from the quaint safety of a small city nestled
amongst the Rocky Mountains, the move to a big city comes
as a shock. For someone used to seeing bears and bobcats
in place of crack heads and prostitutes, it's surreal. A living movie caught in a loop. A blur. The whole city is on fast
forward, in a hurry to arrive at no particular destination, but
feeling entitled nonetheless. It is unrivaled madness. Up
ahead of me, by the bus station, dancing fools clogged the
busy street corners for reasons unexplained. Boredom. And
then the bus station itself, the perpetual breeding ground for
freaks and geeks, dope fiends and wannabes, panhandlers
mooching change with a knife against your throat. Foul.

Farther down, more shops, more strangers, more
motivation. I hated feeling so helpless. I needed a change of
pace, a change of mood. I needed to clear my mind. I trudged
the sidewalk like a stalking vampire, avoiding interaction. I
just wanted to be alone with my thoughts, and my hope that

perhaps just around the next corner, a small piece of understanding was waiting for me. A decision. An initial spark of
ambition from something unknown. Anything. Perhaps it
had been the visit home, but suddenly, this city seemed to
weigh heavily on me. The thought of it, the rush of it, the
noise–I just wanted to get out and away from the endless
supply of douchebags and wannabe thugs, the petty thieves
and the failed con-men. The screaming sirens at all hours of
the night, and the immigrant couples fighting in unknown
languages. The car accidents and the desperate hookers wallowing in the gutters. The pimps and the police. Too much of
it all. There was no room for intimacy anywhere. No room
for friends in a place where your neighbor might say hello
to you one day, and rip you off the next, or slash your tires,
or shoot you in the face in retaliation for your television being too loud. No room, in a place where women gasp to be
choked harder, and good people are erased by busses. It was
all just–overwhelming. It's a wonder everybody doesn't just
kill each other.

I'd had enough, I was going home, no matter how
restless. I turned and sped up my pace, passing the same
crawling bus station, the same dancing fools. I was soon in
my elevator, heading to the 16th floor, when I was suddenly
caught in a fit of tears. I couldn't control it. I gasped and
choked, trying to recover, trying to stop it. The bell rung,
preceding the opening doors, and I wiped the tears from my
face, desperate to show no weakness, especially to myself.
I passed through the doors and found myself facing the old
drunk on the floor, but he wasn't sleeping, he was staring at
me. I looked away quickly, hustling to pass him and avoid a
conversation.

"You look like you're crying," he said. *Shit!* "Don't
you live here?" I stopped, reluctantly, and slowly turned to
face him again. I nodded my confirmation, but said nothing.

"Well then, what the hell are crying about?" he
said. "Here, come over here. Come on, I never did anything
wrong, get over here, I want to tell you something."

"I'm not in the mood for drunken tales, old man," I

said, yet still approached him. "Don't waste my time."

He simply continued to gesture with his hand for me to approach. "Sit," he said. I snorted, uncertain, but then shrugged and sat down on the floor, my back leaned against the opposite wall. He smiled and seemed to wink at me, his eyes glossy and wavering; he was smashed. He twisted the top off a whisky bottle and held it in my direction. I smiled, and accepted, taking a long drink of the golden liquid. I stared at him, feeling the delicious sting of the drink in my stomach.

"Who are you, old man?" I asked, and swiftly followed the last drink with another. He smiled, his eyelids barely opened, his face droopy.

"I'm Jack," he said, slurring his own name. "Jack Shifton. Nice to meet you." I shook his hand, but he had no grip, the alcohol had rendered him numb for how many years?

"I'm Mickey," I said. "Mickey Tyler." I had another sip of the whisky and passed the bottle back to him. "So, how come you're always out here, man? Doesn't anyone ever call the cops?"

"Nah!" he boasted. "I'm a nice guy, I swear. So I like a few social drinks here and there, it doesn't matter if the others aren't drinking on the other side of the walls, does it?"

I smiled. "You're a funny old man. What did you want to tell me?"

He had a swig from the bottle and savored the taste of his personal poison, licking his lips while he passed it back to me.

"Frankly," he said. "I don't remember." He chuckled loudly, amused with himself. "But seriously, listen, stop making me go off topic. Why are you being such a baby? And where's that girl from the other night? She was a nice catch, huh? Reminds me of my ex-wife. Maybe you'll be lucky enough to have her be your ex-wife someday."

"What?" I said. "What are you talking about? Are you spying on people, old man? That's not cool, man."

"Nah!" he scoffed, pushing the issue aside with

drunken friendliness. "It's all good, man, relax. It's my– it's my job." I had another drink and passed him the bottle.

"What do you mean, your job?"

"Do I look like a jobless bum to you?" he smiled before taking a long drink.

"Absolutely," I said. "You live in a hallway, drinking your life away."

"Yes, but it is my choice, that's the difference."

I arched my eyebrows and pursed my lips. "So you chose to be a drunk?"

"Of course," he smiled, and had another drink, passing it back to me. "We are all responsible for who we are, aren't we? Is it your fault that I'm a drunk?"

"Really?" I said, feeling suspicious. Here we go with the drunken tales.

"I used to be a banking executive," he slurred. "For real. And I was good at it, too. I made a ton of money, sure, but what for? Really? I had the houses, and the toys, and the wealth, and what did it get me? It got me lonely, that's what it got me. There was no time for anything. No time for love. No time for life. I look back now, and those were the worst days of my life, and these now, are the best. I'm free, don't you see? If I want to be a drunk, I can be a drunk, end of story. It's my life, and I am the one who has to live it, and the same goes for everyone else. If you want to do something, you do it. Life passes much too quickly to not do the things you want to do, the rest is all superficial."

I stared at him, still suspicious. "What are you, like, some drunken hobo guru? Jesus, old man."

"I have lived my life. I am living my life," he said. "That's my point. There's no time to cry about the things you don't like in your life, because you always have a choice. All you need is the guts to make a decision and force yourself into some discipline, the rest are all excuses. Hard work toward something you love is the only way to find your purpose in life–of course, personally, at this point in my life, I'm sick of it, so fuck it, have a drink! You only live once."

Somehow, he was right. This old man, this drunken

fool, despite the slurring babble that spilled from his mouth, some kind of philosophical truth had made its appearance.

"So–" I shook my head. "What the fuck, then? Why are you here?"

"Because I want to be. I have an endless stream of money, kid, and an awful loathing for materialistic pricks and superficial friends. This is what I choose to do. It is my life, and you have your life. Whatever you're crying about, quit being a pussy about it and find your balls. Goddamn kids these days."

I smiled and had one last gulp from the bottle, feeling the booze swim through my perception of reality. I was feeling good, and this old man–this old man was good shit too. I was responsible for me. It was true, he was right, but it was difficult. I passed him the bottle and sluggishly used the wall to stand myself back up, feeling light headed, and careless. "You have a good night, old man. You're good shit. I like you."

He smiled and held the bottle up in the air, toasting. "Man up," he said, and drank the quarter bottle left of whiskey clean, the effect on his eyes was almost instantaneous. I chuckled and walked to my door, fumbling with my keys to get in. I managed and made my way through the stink toward the sofa. I laid down and took a long breath, closing my eyes. Life, it was such a strange thing. Unforgiving and void of empathy, but capable of a vast spectrum of experiences, from bad to worse, and good to better. Possibilities. Possibilities. Where were they? What was I supposed to do?

CHAPTER 11

I was a wasted, exhausted hunk of flesh sluggishly tossing one way, and then another, and then another. I woke up in a panic, my hands flailing through the air in search of my phone, frantic to call in to work and make up an excuse–when I realized I didn't have to. Shocking. It was both liberating and frightening. Euphoric and terrifying. Since then, however, my tired mind wouldn't quit. Not ever. The pain pounding in my head was bad, but the emotions were far worse. They were raw and horribly unfocussed like a tortuous kaleidoscope ranging from happy, to sad, to angry, and everything in between. Breathtaking. I kept my eyes focussed on the hole in the carpet, suddenly feeling an emotional connection to it; as though it had been blessed with the ability to understand me. The real me.

Physically, I was sore, and weak, and rather ill. My body had taken a mean beating over the course of the week, and it wasn't about to let me forget about it so soon. I felt old. I felt like shit. No position could offer me rest, no amount of deep breathing resulted in calm, I was bursting with anxiety. I sat up quickly, hating the air around me, and lit a cigarette. I rubbed my eyes with a fist and sorely, tenderly, stretched out my tense limbs, my neck and back. I stared at the burn again, wondering about it still, not fully believing it. Was that luck? It disturbed me, scared me. Luck, was it even real?

I looked at the clock on the wall, it was 3:15 p.m. I should have been out looking for work. I should have been harnessing my talents and striving for advancement despite the obstacles. I should have been listening to the desperate commercials on TV telling me that my couch was not my friend, that I should be going back to school, learning to be a better slave, a valuable employee, a contributing member of society. Fuck them all. It was depressing, what other options did I have, did anyone have? I saw the rich celebrities on TV, the wealthy business tycoons and the self-made millionaires and I wondered what the difference was. What was it that made me different from any one of them? Was life really just some dude's sick idea of a lottery? Was I not chosen, therefore, fuck me? How else could anyone explain it? It just felt like a big joke. A carrot dangling in front of my face, and I kept falling for it every time.

I stood up, heading for the door to the balcony and stepped outside, staring at what I could see of the sprawling city. The smog was thick and heavy, doomish. I was suddenly thinking about the old man. That drunken fool, he had said that he chose to be a drunk. Was that true? Why? Had he managed to tap into some arcane force of humanity I wasn't even aware of? Did he feel something different, something indestructible–something stable? He said he had money, did he? He always did have a bottle, come to think of it, and he was rather careless in spirit, nonchalant and almost, damn it, he was happy. Content. Something far beyond the alcohol. Something deep. How was that possible?

I wasn't even sure of what any of it meant to me, really. It felt like the destruction of my life was nearly complete; all that was left was for something erratic to happen, like Alice calling, to provide the final push I needed to jump off the ledge punching myself in the scrotum on the way down. Fuck it.

I shook my head. Alice. My mind was miles away from Alice, it was focussed on Polaris. Damn. Polaris, the star, the only excitement in my life. Alice was a nice girl, but Polaris was–she was–Polaris. That meant something to me, somehow. It was undefinable, but the reaction was undeniable. I was plugged into her, on her wavelength, on her excitement. My escape. Was that love? Did I need that right now? What did it mean?

I shook my head; enough with the wandering

thoughts. I had to get myself together, get a grip on the situation at hand and decide on what needed to be done. The old man had been right, even on a sober day; I was my responsibility. It was my choice, my decision, my life. This was supposed to be an opportunity to prove to myself that I could do anything I wanted. I didn't have to slave away like a fool, barely surviving from one paycheck to the next with an irrational dream of winning the lottery being my only honest hope for the control of my life back. Pathetic. I had the potential, and the temporary blind confidence to believe in it, but what could I do? Start a business? I knew the basics, and I was also fully qualified to mock my past managers and decision makers, but could I make it real? Could I survive off of my very own hard work, with no middle men standing in my way, reluctantly dropping coins in my direction, staring at me as though I should act like a child being spoiled with the newest greatest thing ever made, ever? Disgusting. I wanted something new, something real and tangible, something to be proud of. Yes! That's what I wanted in my life, it's what I needed. Something to be proud of. Something I could look upon and smile while absolute satisfaction washed through me. Could that be? Why not? It was all over the television. Millions of dollars were given to the dumbest, biggest piece of shit fucking idiots on the planet, and for reasons so ridiculous, it couldn't possibly be real–but it was. Goddamn it, it was! In this city, where I lived, people were being paid enormous amounts of money to achieve new lows in stupidity while the rest of the world worked their asses off, honestly, righteously, for fractions of profits; only to go home and be battered by the dumbing down process by the same rich, lazy bastards cashing on their stupidity. Fair–there was no such thing in the world. It was eat or be eaten. Take or be taken. Einstein once said that the definition of insanity was doing the same thing over and over again and expecting a different result. That was powerful thinking. That was what I needed. Powerful, focussed thinking. Getting another job was counterproductive. It was doing the same thing. It was staying safe and comfortable when that was partly what was bothering me in the first place. It was pure insanity. I could do anything I set my mind to. I could do it. I could fight for it, stay with it, and force it through to the top of the chain– but what? What could I possibly do? Aside from choking Polaris half to death, I wasn't really good at anything. I could do porn. I wasn't anything but average, but who cares when you know the exact moment you should probably take your hands away from her throat? Ridiculous. I needed a business idea. I needed financial freedom, investments and all that crap. I could do it. I just needed an idea.

My phone was ringing, tearing my train of thought away. I hopped back into the living room and answered it.

"Hey, it's Polaris."

"Hey," I said, suddenly thankful for the lack of Alice's voice on the other end. I hadn't even thought about it. The possible horror. "How's it going?"

"I'm okay. How are you feeling?" She sounded concerned; it even made me smile. Did I need this? "You sounded pretty down on yourself yesterday."

"Yeah," I said. "Sorry. There's just a lot of stuff going on right now, just, all at the same time. My life is drastically different from last week's boring same old, same old."

"I know," she said sweetly. "But you sound better today. I hope you feel better, everything will work itself out. What else is it going to do?"

"Yeah, I know. Until then though–well, you know– life and shit. She's a bitch."

"She is," she replied. "So, um, I get off work at five and was wondering if you were up for a movie or something tonight? If you're up to it, I understand if you just want to be alone again tonight. I won't be offended."

"Nonsense," I said, almost confidently. "I would actually really like to see you tonight. I could use the company, I think."

"Okay," she said, her smile audible. "Well, I'll just head home and shower and stuff and I'll be over around seven-ish?"

"Sounds good," I said. "See you then."

I hung up and suddenly found myself staring at the wall thinking about her. Polaris, why her? Why now? Right now, in the middle of the dismantling of my life, she seemed like a solid post. Weird, but solid, and highly enjoyable. Desirable.

I needed a shower.

***

She was cuddling a blanket on the couch, her face smooth in the pale blue glare of the television, watching me with eyes that were difficult to define, but carried a sense of satisfaction. It was already 10 p.m. Three hours had passed, and this was basically the first conversation thus far that didn't involve screaming words like God, and fuck, and choke. My arms were still numb, my legs weak, but somehow, I felt happy. I felt intrigued. She made me feel different and oblivious of everything else. I was screwed. I liked her.

"You look like you're scheming something," she said, smiling.

"You know the old man in the hallway? I had a drink with him last night."

"What?" she chuckled. "In the hallway?"
"Yeah," I said. "I just sat on the floor and we shared his whiskey bottle."

"You drank a homeless guy's booze? It probably took the poor guy a week to save up for it."

"But that's just it, he says that he has tons of money, and that he chooses to live that way. He likes to drink, so he drinks, to hell with everyone else, that's what he said to me."

She shook her head, an uncertain smile gracing her face. "I don't think so," she said. "Why would anyone do that? If you have money, you buy a house, and cars, and whatever, you don't loiter in hallways, wasted and nonsensical."

"I'm just saying–he says he does. And even worse, I actually believe him."

"What? Why would you believe him? He was probably just trying to impress you."

"Impress me for what? Seriously, it's in his eyes. The guy is happy, and not just drunk happy, he's life happy."

"Life happy, huh?"

"Yeah," I replied. "He said he was a banker, a good one, and that he was rich but didn't like being around other rich assholes all day or worrying about materialistic gains. He said he liked to drink, so he drinks, end of story. There's something beautiful about that somehow."

"Beautiful about being an alcoholic? I don't think so."

"No, no," I said. "Not so literal. I mean, he just does whatever he wants. Says he always has. If that's true, despite what outsiders may happen to think, he's the happiest person I have ever met in my life. He understands freedom, I think. The type of freedom that is invincible to outside stimuli, because none of it really matters, only what's going on inside does." That was it. I understood what he had been trying to tell me. What he was feeling was freedom. It was an inner peace that came from knowing that he would only ever regret the things he had done, instead of those he hadn't. It was cliche, but it was right.

"Maybe," she said. "I don't know. Alcoholism is a horrible addiction."

"Right, but his point is that it's only horrible to you, the non-alcoholic, the non-experienced, the safe." Bingo. I had to find something to get my life going again. Something new. Something big and daring and bold.

"I guess," she said, shrugging her shoulders. "You sure are in a different mood tonight."

"I've done a lot of thinking," I said, smiling. She smiled back, squinting her eyes, happy. Adorable. Her attention turned to the television, causing mine to follow. It was breaking news,

"*...Police are asking the public for help in this afternoon's daring armed kidnapping of a man outside the luxurious Pantheon restaurant. The victim is rumored to be Mr. Ronald Essex, chairman of the board of Worldsafe, a hedge*

*fund with an operating capital of over 13 billion dollars.
A security guard was shot in the melee, but his condition
remains unknown at this time. We will bring you more details
as we receive them."*

The screen flashed with emergency lights and broken glass, a security guard being hauled into an ambulance on a gurney. Polaris lit a cigarette and stared, furrowing her brow and sending a cloud of smoke dancing against the light. Her mind was somewhere else. She took another puff and exhaled it, angling her mouth oddly toward the ceiling.

"That would be so awesome," she said.
I looked at her, confused, "What would? Getting shot?"

"No, no," she said. "Getting kidnapped."
"Kidnapped?" I said, and something drastic suddenly happened in my mind. I couldn't explain why, but I was enthralled. Fascinated. That felt risky. It felt exciting and heart pumping–but why? I couldn't put my finger on it, but it meant something to me. Somehow. It made me feel–electrified.

"Yeah," she said. "Imagine the rush. It would probably change your life in some way."

That was it! Imagine the rush. The rush. Possibilities. Where were they? What were they? Was this what opportunity felt like?

Imagine the rush of changing your life.

CHAPTER 12

Jerry's death wasn't meant to destroy me, it was meant to wake me up. That was the thought suspended in my mind, emblazoned in my spirit. It had become my motivation. Life was too short, move your ass. Find something, focus on it, and start pushing. Never give up. Never. Take the sucker punches, the unexpected kicks, the abuse, and come out smiling on the other side, a survivor. Proud.

I needed a shower, two days ago, and my stomach was grumbling horribly, desperate for nutrition, but my mind was in full gear and racing toward something that felt big, but still without any real direction. I was relying on my instinct. What could I put together and throw myself behind full-heartedly? What could I be proud of? Where was my rush?

I tore through the internet looking for answers, clues, ideas–a shock that would cause something inside of me to move and never let it stop. Something like Polaris. She made something inside of me move. She made it come to attention, determined, and confident. How could I make that feeling the center of my life?

There was something magical about researching an obscure idea. It was more like searching for an emotion rather than an action. A hidden truth, instead of a blatant announcement. I rushed through the videos, and the articles, and the stories. Kidnapping was an odd thing. It was taking people for money, blackmailing with emotions, threatening violence–murder. Exciting. I wrote these things down, everything that came to my mind, trying to make a connection between the ideas, trying to put the puzzle together and come out with a plan, a direction. Maybe. What could it be?

How? What could my connection to kidnapping be, and why did the idea seem to excite me so much? Was I about to start taking random people, demanding ransoms, and threatening death? Probably not. That was a first class felony, a direct ticket to life in prison, or even death if anything went wrong. It was too risky, but was there a balance between that and some acceptable form of it?

I shook my head and licked my lips, passing my fingers through my hair. Why had Polaris's comment struck me with such force? Kidnapping–that would be so awesome. Imagine the rush. It would change your life. Yeah, it would change your life forever. If even in a small way, did that make it worth it? A drastic action in exchange for a small but permanent reaction. A rush. A change. It was something that seemed hard wired into our minds, somewhere, but it was there. The constant search for a rush. The existential orgasm. The ability to push your life so far beyond your comforts that something had to change, forever. To backpack a foreign country, or experience the kick of far too powerful drugs, or choke somebody–get kidnapped. Yeah–how would that work? I didn't know, exactly, but I felt fairly confident in saying that my goals in life had drastically changed. My future, the one I had forever branded into my mind, the boring one with the grossly overpriced house in suburbia, the 5 star rated piece of shit on wheels, and my uptight, overly worried little wife lying like a corpse until my deeds were done–it was all gone. It felt like it was time for something new, something wild. Why not? You only live once, in the words of a drunken old man. No time to waste on not finding that one thing in your life that causes you to look into the mirror and say, "You know what? I don't give a fuck." That was living! That was what freedom felt like. Nonchalance. Indifference. Peace.

I continued my search, scouring through obscure and famous websites alike, looking for a common thread, a trend, anything that would help me define what I was feeling, what my instinct knew was there, but my conscious did not. I lit a cigarette, unconsciously letting my eyes scan over the headlines on the computer screen, waiting. Just waiting. I clicked on a link which lead me to a video some idiots made, pulling a prank on an unsuspecting friend, and it felt frustrating. Stupid. These goddamn idiots clogged the net with their stupid fucking ideas of what they thought was funny and–wait! I felt something changing inside of me, like a wall collapsing and releasing rabid thoughts through the fog, making them clear. That was it. The prank. The idea of the prank. The excitement of it. I thought about Polaris and her fetish. Our fetish. The rush of fetishes and pranks. Marry them, and what would you have? You'd have–what? I was so close I could taste it. I could feel it throughout my numbing limbs, and my frowning forehead. My eyes were frozen in a blind twenty yard stare. You would have–kidnapping for hire? Kidnapping for hire!

It felt like my innards had ruptured. Was that it? Was that asinine? I couldn't tell really, but who ever could? People loved to tell others what would fail without any proof whatsoever. The computer, the fax machine, the xerox machine, internet pornography, they were all stupid ideas that would never work. Luckily, I already knew that the majority of people were completely fucking retarded, so I couldn't care less about what anyone thought, I had better things to do. The truth was that people were into all kinds of weird and crazy shit, the proof was all over the internet. I typed in kidnapping and got a vast spectrum of things spanning from legitimate reports, to hoaxes, to fantasies, to hardcore bondage porn. The rush of a fetish.

It was a powerful form of psychology. Using the primal, arcane urge to push yourself faster, further, stronger, and for what? It was for the rush. People would buy into being kidnapped for the exact same reasons they jumped off of bridges with an elastic band around their ankles, or leapt off cliffs, or fucked 57 strangers on camera for free. The rush. Why wouldn't they be interested in pushing their limits in a new, intense way? The key to it was in the marketing, in the way the idea was presented to the people, that was what made the difference between being perceived as either cool or stupid. It was a fine line, but it could be negotiated. For the first time ever, I was confident that I could do it. I had to.

The rush. Thank you, Jerry.

It suddenly felt like a new day. Brighter outside. Inside. Did it make any sense? Would anyone actually pay to be kidnapped? What would I have to promise them? What kind of limits should be imposed? What would I call it? I took a writing pad and walked back to the living room, to the sofa, crushing my cigarette in the ashtray and lighting another. I started writing everything that was coming to me, a difficult task because not all of it made much sense, and most thoughts were replaced by another one zooming through it before any understanding could be had. I had no choice but to mull it over. It was too big to figure out in one day, but I would try.

Think! You could kidnap people right off the street, in public, day or night–unexpectedly. Would people pay for that? Why not? To be on a dinner date, a business lunch, or a simple walk down the street, only to be snatched up by force and thrown into the back of a van with a hood over your head, the sound of a revving engine in your ears–fear, exhilaration–a thrill.

It felt like the beginning of an astounding revelation, but the harsh reality quickly sunk in; before I could do anything, I would need some cash. Naturally, the banks were out of the question. *"Yes, hello. I would like a loan so I could set up a little business and perhaps even kidnap your child one day. It would be to our mutual benefit, you know."* No, I would have to resort to more sinister sources, but that was something I could figure out in the future. First, there was another thing I would need. I would need people, help. Kidnapping could hardly be effective as a one man operation, there were too many variables, too many threats. I would need Polaris, and Steve, at least. Three people had a fighting chance. Three minds analyzing the same situations, offering different solutions and opinions, that was a good thing, and a thing I would be happy to share with those I cared about. We could make it work–but how would I convince them, and make them feel the same things I was feeling? Possibilities. Finally. But it felt personal, and hard to convey to others. It had to be felt independently in order to be understood. I thought that Polaris could handle it. She was a free spirit, a thrill seeker, but with intelligence thrown into the mix. Steve was the same, except for one difference–he was quite often a loose cannon. We all liked to have fun and let loose, sure, but Steve was an avid partier. It was nothing for him to disappear for days into some weird haze of drugs, and booze, and women, only to reappear suddenly rather serious and feeling shameful, but the shame was what gave him the rush he had grown to love. It was part of his DNA. Decadence. Compulsiveness.

Could I trust him? He was my best friend and I loved the man, but what I wanted to do was serious. It was real, and I was dedicated to it. The difference in focus between business partners was what ended relationships for good. Polaris, I had just met, but Steve, I had known since childhood. Did I want to test our relationship like that? With age came habit, and a personal, ironclad mind-set that wasn't easily changed without a fight. It would hurt far more to lose a genuine friend than it would to lose Polaris, but what other choices did I have? I had other friends, sure, but none that I trusted with my life. Most were acquaintances at best, people I knew from here and there, not people I wanted to drag into something weird and unheard of, searching for the limit to something we couldn't explain, but had to find. I needed Steve. We could do it. Together, we could do it. I only had to explain it to them.

***

"Wait. You're actually serious about this? Is it even legal?"

"I am," I said, my face stern. "And I don't know, legal or not, I'm sure we can make this work."

He ran his palm across his face, taking in a deep breath, trying to decide whether I meant it or not. He looked to Polaris, trying to gauge her reaction to my proposal. She stared back at him, and then to me, her face pale and serious. The room was deafeningly silent. I had just finished telling them about the fetish psychology, the urge, the thing we needed to awake in people in order to make them buy into our cause. They would want it, they would need it, but I couldn't do it alone. I could take care of the money, the setup, and everything else, but I needed help to execute the promises I made, otherwise, it would never work. It would fail before I ever even started. It was their choice, and I would never hold it against either one of them, but I would much rather have them by my side than people I didn't trust. Regardless of their answer, I was going forward with it.

"I don't know," Steve said. "How can that even be legal? I mean, if you take people off the street, other people are going to flip the fuck out and call the cops. And even if it's not illegal because they paid for it, you'll be charged for constantly wasting the cops' time. I don't know, it doesn't seem plausible. At least, not forever."

"Who cares?" I said. "At least we can say that we had the balls to do it. Do you know what I mean? We did something crazy, unheard of, completely insane, and it was fucking fantastic, regardless of the consequences. It's why people do the things they do. Compulsion. Urge. The rush. And that's exactly how the people who take part in it are going to feel too. It's weird, and it's fucked up, and it's great to brag about. *Hey, what happened to you last night? I was fucking kidnapped!* Imagine that. Are you telling me that in the 21st century, in this very city, the epicenter of psychotic self-indulgence, people won't buy into a rush like that? Goddamn it man, you're the biggest thrill seeker I know, you fucking lunatic."

He smiled, Polaris too, and I stared back at them alternately, grinning, and truly believing every exaggerated word that left my mouth. I had conviction, motivation. I was locked in until the end, void of any thoughts concerning consequences, none of it mattered. This was beyond the sheltered social system. This was living on a different level.

Living.

"Jesus Christ," he said. "You're fucking impossible, man. You're my best friend, what else am I supposed to say, no? Fuck you, you piece of shit, I'll help your stupid ass." He shoved me back, like best friends do, and I smiled, ready to punch him in the shoulder, a show of affection. I landed my fist and he yelped before returning a fist to my stomach. Bastard. Polaris was shaking her head, a smile plastered to her face.

"Boys," she said. "Always so violent."

"Are you in?" I asked, finally getting the upper hand with Steve in a headlock. I twisted hard, toward the inside, feeling his neck stretch and his fist pummeling me in the thighs. He suddenly grabbed hold of my legs and lifted, sending both of us crashing through the coffee table, glass flying everywhere. Polaris was on the couch with her legs up, her hand to her mouth, laughing in disbelief. I laid there, my back supported by scattered debris, trying to catch my breath, smiling.

"I'm in," she said suddenly. "We're both in, but how are we supposed to get started? We can't kidnap anyone with a car, not efficiently, anyway. We're going to need things like a van, where are we going to get the money from?"

"Don't worry about the money," I said from the floor, my voice relaxed, my mood perfect. "I have some ideas, and neither of you have to take on any risk or debt. I'll take it on, I just needed your help."

It was set. We were going forward, head first and with fists swinging. We were going to take control of our lives and completely ignore what other people tried to tell us we should be doing. It was our lives, and for the first time ever, we were going to take a risk.

CHAPTER 13

Final notice–Account past due–14 days until notice of eviction.

The nearly transparent yellow page taped to my door should have awoken feelings of despair in the gallows of my mind. It should have scared me and caused me to hunker down and race against time to find a solution. I should have been desperately looking for a job, ready to accept any mindless slave pay I could accrue, but I wasn't. In fact, I was smiling. I wasn't sure of how I would manage to pull it all off, but there had to be a way. The will was there, the way was somewhere too. It had to be. I took the paper from the door, folded it, and put it in my pocket, intending to keep it as a memento. A piece of my life that I would later look back on and glorify as a defining point. A change. A rush.

For weeks I came up empty. Money was everywhere, passing from one hand to another, making things move, propelling careers forward, ending lives, turning the world–but it was nowhere near me. I had ideas about where to get it, and naturally, I attempted to exhaust the easiest sources first, but they wanted nothing to do with me. Most of these sources, these shady underground bankers I met with in obscure restaurants, agreeing on definite terms, unfavorable interest rates, and unsavory payment plans–they wanted to know what the money was going to be used for. Kidnapping. The reactions were hilarious. Fat mouths sucking back the insides of lobster shells remained suspended in mid-chew, beads of sweat building on creased foreheads, voices forced through coughing fits, "Are you fucking crazy or something?" It was unheard of, and perhaps even stupid, but stupid never stopped things from catching on in the world.

In fact, some days it seemed as though stupid was the only thing that ever truly did catch on. This had a fighting chance.

I went through the loan sharks, the buddies, the far-away and well off uncles, but none of them seemed capable wrapping their heads around what I was trying to tell them. They were businessmen, after all, and despite the fact that most of them already dealt in unsavory and even illegal business prospects, I suppose I couldn't necessarily blame them for the suspicious eyes and the shaking heads. These fools were used to a common lingo, a simple one, where all that was needed was the correct answer to a few questions before passing the test and investments were granted. Questions like, "What's my return on investment, and how long?" and, "How many points are you looking to pay?" and then the clincher, "What will you be using it for, exactly? What does your business plan entail?"

Business plan. I had no such thing other than in the most literal sense. You pay me, I kidnap you, the end. But none of that was good enough to cause the arching eyebrows to lower, or the squinting eyes to be less suspicious, or the bellowing laughs to be any less bludgeoning; most of them thought I was messing around. A lunatic. A cowboy. Stupid. But none of it daunted me. I was determined to go ahead and chase after whatever crazy dream was bouncing around in my head. Wasn't that what people called the American dream in the first place? The freedom to run after anything we fancied no matter how crazy or obscene anyone else might think it was. It guaranteed no success, as nothing ever did, but it sure was a comfortable illusion. Success. Wild dreams. The rush.

I made my way into my apartment, pensive, and slightly battered, but no worse for the cause. There was always a way. I sat on the couch and opened a fresh beer. I stared at the wall, wondering about what I could do. There was one possibility that was almost guaranteed, and no questions would ever be asked about what the money was for, because it didn't matter. What mattered, was getting it back on time, every cent of it, or else settle the debt with something drastic, like a testicle, or a limb, depending on how much was left outstanding from the balance. Did I want to go that route? Was I brave enough to delve into that world? I felt as though I had no other options left. The last fool I had met with had been bewildered and quite belligerent about the whole thing. He had tested my patience with his pretentious lectures and boastful antics, causing me to wring my hands tightly together, fighting the urge to beat his sardonic little sense of judgement clean out of his skull with my boot. Cocksucker. He had tried to make a joke out of me, just like the others, not understanding my determination, my urge to get these things done and working just as cleanly and efficiently as any other business. It could be done, but visionaries, it seemed, needed other visionaries to back them, or else they were shit out of luck. I needed a visionary, someone with guts and a fondness for things they could not fully understand, but still bet on purely on its potential. I had one more option, but he was not so much a visionary as he was a brutal, balls out business monster with little interest in excuses. It was do or be done. Simple nuts and bolts kind of stuff. He would lend me the money and he wouldn't even ask why, but it frightened me. Would I be prepared to give my life, or a limb, or my freedom if things didn't work out? I didn't know. What was worth that? Money was one thing; it came and went, you gained and lost, it was all more of an illusion than anything real or concrete. Money was nothing more than an idea attached to a worthless piece of paper, but this was a whole other animal. Was I prepared for that kind of debt?

I took a drag from my cigarette and exhaled a cloud of smoke slowly, staring pensively at the wall. I pursed my lips, realizing that I truly had run through all of my options. This was it, the one big decision. I was confident, sure, but was I confident enough to assume bodily harm as collateral? How badly did I want this? How much did it mean to me? Before I made the call, before I did anything even remotely close to making the call, the biggest decision of my life had to be settled. I was trapped in the one question that all conscious beings have asked themselves since the dawn of time before taking a big risk.

    Should I?

CHAPTER 14

Andy "The Terror" Labelle, was a gangster; a ruthless, unforgiving criminal, originally from Montreal. He relocated to Los Angeles some years ago, deciding that the movie production business was a damn fine way to make a living, launder money, and make very powerful, very wealthy business contacts. He had forced his way into the city's underground, snatching up business prospects, and pushing lesser criminals out of his way like a bully, gladly offering proof to anyone who questioned why his reputation mandated the need for his nickname, The Terror. He was relentless and aggressive. Within months of his arrival in Los Angeles, he was siphoning out vast contributions to his bottom line from a network of the filthiest, most degraded forms of enterprise known to man. He was strategic, and dangerous, and unstoppable–and he was my final option.

I didn't know the man, per se, but I'd had the misfortune of meeting him in person once before, which had honestly felt like an honor. Terrifying, of course, but quite in line with his legend. The Terror. I had been walking home following a path of back alleys, when a black SUV suddenly swerved into the lane before me, hot on the tail of a shabby looking man running for dear life from the threat of the bumper. The man had tripped and fallen flat on his face, causing the vehicle to come to an abrupt halt. Four giant men in expensive suits stepped out, guns in hand, threatening. I stood, not at a comfortable distance away at all, frozen stiff in place by the scene unfolding before me. I had no idea what was happening, or what I should do. If I ran, would they kill me? And what if I stayed, would they kill me? I was terrified, itchy with anxiety, dizzy, and undecided. One of the men lifted his weapon, aiming for the shabby man squirming against the asphalt like a bug in panic, and shot two quick blasts, hitting the fool in the knee caps. My legs were numb, stiff, unmovable. I stared in disbelief, fully expecting to be killed next.

The other three men proceeded to beat the bleeding man into a useless lump of ground meat. There was nowhere for me to hide; it was too late. The shooter had already turned around, his eyes riveted on me, his face devoid of emotion, unreadable. I couldn't tell if I was shaking, I couldn't feel anything except my heart beating brutally against my rib cage, my eyes unblinking, my mind reeling. What could I do? There was nothing to do but stare back, hoping to live on for at least a little bit longer. Before I could even make sense of the situation, the shooter was already standing in front of me, his face stern, his eyes cold. He stared at me intently. I couldn't remember ever being so scared. He flashed his gun, ensuring my full cooperation.

"What happened here?" he asked, and his accent had been enough to confirm his identity. It was The Terror, himself. The French Canadian monster. He was as famous in the mainstream as he was underground, and his trademarks were quite undeniable.

"I don't know, officer," I replied, my lips quivering, my balance uncertain. "The guy was crazy, he called a gang of thugs wetbacks, it was stupid. They beat the shit out of him–rightfully so, I suppose."

He smiled, and his eyes relaxed a little. He nodded and turned back to look at his thugs for a moment before returning his gaze to me.

"*C'est vrai, tabarnacle!*" He suddenly exclaimed, but I had no idea what it meant. I didn't speak French, and there was strong conviction behind his words regardless of our respective language barriers. I thought he was about to have me killed, but then he smiled. "Very good," he said, and suddenly reached into the inner breast pocket of his jacket, causing my body to somehow grow stiffer. I expected a shiny blade to slash my throat open at any moment. Slowly, he pulled his hand out and extended it toward me, still smiling, his eyes glistening.

Eventually, with a growing sense of trust, I allowed my eyes to look down at his hand–it wasn't a blade, or a gun, it was–a card. A business card. I raised my shaking hand to his and accepted the offer gratefully. I tried smiling, but I wasn't sure I could move my face, let alone my legs. I stared at it, frowning, trying to understand. "Andy Labelle – 800-555-5545."

"If you ever need anything," he said. "Just give me a call." He turned his head, staring back at the bleeding, beaten man on the ground. "I'm pretty sure I don't have to go through the ceremony of telling you the consequences of trying to fuck me, do I?"

I nodded no, quickly, panicked.
"No," he said, his eyes staring deeply into mine. "I am a businessman," he continued. "And business truly is a very simple matter. Be honest, be on time, and there are no prob-lems." He lifted his hand, causing me to shudder, fighting with every ounce of energy I had not to burst out screaming, or crying. He tapped my cheek, the way an older uncle might do, and winked. "Take care, kid," and just like that, he turned and headed back toward his goons. "Two days, David!" he yelled at the barely conscious man on the asphalt, and then kicked him in the side, the man's yelp was barely audible. "Two days to pay, or else I'll have your ears deep fried for dinner. *Crisse de borien! Venez vous en!*" he motioned for his monsters to get back in the vehicle, but he stopped before getting in, once again facing my direction. "Oh," he said. "Don't help him." He pointed to the bloodied fool. "I don't want to have to cut you up into rat food. You seem like a good kid. Stay that way."

I nodded yes, of course not, what the fuck was hap-pening? I watched the SUV scream out of the alley, leaving me behind, bewildered and wondering if my limbs would ever function properly again. And then I heard him, distant, even though he wasn't actually all that far away. "Please... Man," the injured man, David, moaned in a hoarse whisper.

"Please. Help me."

I could only stare, feeling the weight of the business card still clutched tightly in my hand. It felt threatening, as though The Terror could hear everything I said, see everything I did as long as I was still in possession of the card. Terrifying. There were no other words to describe a man who beamed with supreme confidence and carried an arrogant threat of violence that could be sensed without a single word being spoken. He hadn't threatened me in any way, but I was still fairly sure that puking was inevitable.

The man squirmed again, moaning gibberish, crying. "Please," he forced out. "I need..." But what could I do? I was still stunned, almost rendered euphoric through fear, numb. I shook my head, the muscles in my neck tight and rigid with resistance. I took a deep breath.

"I'm sorry, man," I said gently, almost whispered to myself. "I can't. You don't fuck with a guy like that. I'm not getting fed to rats, I'm sorry, but you shouldn't have fucked up–whatever it is that you did."

It was a harsh response, sure, but what was happening inside of me now made that day, that response, more terrifying than anything I could remember. Not the violence, but the man. I still had the card. I was staring at it, remembering how I had purposely protected it since our meeting. At the very least, it made for a triumphant party story that was unrivaled by anyone. *"Yes, that's right. The Terror shoved his gun into my face and told me he was going to cut me up and feed me to rats."*

"Oh, my God. That's so cool."
The card had become a trophy of sorts, a memento, like an autographed poster of your favorite rock star. I never expected to need anything from him, at the time I was still just some stoner kid who liked to jerk off to literally any type of weird ass porn and play video games, what the fuck would I ever need The Terror for? Yet, here it was. The need. The rush. I needed his help.

I lit a cigarette, staring at the card in my shaking hand, unable to get the full surge of confidence I needed in order to call the number. My stomach grumbled and twisted in pain. The years since our meeting seemed to make it all even worse; there were so many possibilities. What if the number had changed? What if it hadn't? What would I say? What could I? I couldn't expect him to remember me in any way, it had already been three, maybe even four years ago. My cigarettes suddenly seemed to be burning too quickly. I crushed mine out and quickly lit another, straightening out my back and neck, trying to stave off the badgering anxiety. Fear was always worse when the source was imaginary and irrational, but possibly still right. Goddamn it.

I stood up from the couch, pacing the living room, avoiding the hole in the carpet, desperate to make the call, but too scared to start dialing. I returned to the couch, sat down, and after taking a deep breath, decided to do it. I could do it. I had to do it. It was this or another dead end job. *This or another job, come on, man. This or another job.* I was dialing, not slowing down to think about it. I hit the last 5 and slowly brought the phone to my ear, taking in another deep breath, concentrating on concentrating. The wait felt menacing, tense. It was–

"Good afternoon, Wallace and Greene," the peppy female voice answered."

"Oh–" I stuttered. "Ah–sorry, I think I–"
"Who are you looking for, sir?" she interrupted. I thought about it, who did I want? Was it Mr. Terror? Mr. Labelle? Was this the right number? "Hello?"

"Yeah," I said. "Ah–Mr. Labelle, please."
Silence.

My heart rate suddenly rose, sweat poured from my palms, my phone slippery and unmanageable.

"Are you in law enforcement?" she asked.
"What? No. Why?" I said.

"Why did you call here?" she asked.
"I um–well, I wanted to see if I could speak with Mr. Labelle regarding a business proposal," I said, and it was followed by a long pause on the line.

"One moment, please."

Elevator music came on, not helping me pull myself together.

"What?" a harsh, deep voice asked.

"Hi," I said.

"Yes, yes, hello, how are you?" he said sarcastically, "Are you satisfied now? What can I do for you, Mister..."

"Tyler," I said. "Mickey Tyler." Silence. "Ah–I need to speak with The Ter– Mr. Labelle, please."

"About what?" was his response.

"A loan," I said, biting my bottom lip nervously. I was running out of cigarettes. There was a pause.

"Mickey Tyler? Is that right?"

"Yes."

"All right," he said. "Hang on."

Seconds turned into minutes, and minutes into a quarter hour, until halfway through another quarter, when I was ready to puke all over myself while sitting up against the wall to keep from passing out, the dead line was revived, but the hoarse voice was gone and replaced by one that was calculated, haunting with its trademarked accent.

"Who is this?" he asked.

"It's, Mickey Tyler, sir."

"Yes, we know this much already, but who are you? And how did you get this number?"

"I'm–I'm just a guy," I said, suddenly panicked and unable to express myself in a coherent way. "I'm nobody–and, you gave me this card, sir, although, it was a few years ago."

"Refresh my memory," he said.

"In an alley," I said quickly. "Some guy, he called a bunch of guys wetbacks and got his ass kicked; rightfully so, sir."

"Right," he said. "I remember. And you have kept the card for so long, why?"

"Well–" I stammered. "You're famous, sir."

"You can suck my dick later," he said, but I was too distraught to detect any sarcasm, was he joking? Come on. "Answer these questions. Are you recording this conversation?"

"No, sir."

"Are you a member of any type of legal organization that could jeopardize my organization in any way?"

"No, sir."

"Are you on probation, and, or, have you ever been arrested for a serious crime and incarcerated? If so, for what, and for how long?"

"Nothing, sir."

"I'll check," he said sternly. "If I find out you lied to me, I'll cut your fucking arm off and use it to beat the shit out of you, understand?"

"Yes, sir. I–"

"Meet me tonight," he cut me off. "Do you know where *Les Anges* strip club is?"

"I'll find it on my phone," I said.

"You kids and your goddamn phones," he said sharply. I had no reply. "Meet me at eight, sharp. I don't tolerate tardiness, Mr. Tyler. On time, or fuck you."

"I understand," I said, physically nodding alone in my living room. "And thank you–" The line was dead. Astonishing. The man was nothing short of intimidating. It was official. The idea, the risk–it was all real now. I stared vacantly at the phone, not sure of how to react. It was bitter sweet. It was real, and then, it was fucking real. No room for bullshit. No excuses. I stood up from the couch, feeling my stomach churn sickeningly, sending me racing for the bathroom, trying to beat the erupting vomit.

It was too real. What the hell had I just done?

***

7:30p.m. The cab pulled into the packed parking lot of *Les Anges*, but these weren't the common vehicles one typically found at the strip club. There were no half-broken, rusted pieces of shit drunkenly parked diagonally across two spots by some guy with four little kids at home while he spent the last of the grocery money on tattoos and strippers. No bouncing suspensions from parked cars. This was a classy lot. Rich, rather. Cars I would never drive, let alone own. Not unless I could pull off some kind of miracle and actually make this work out.

I was ill, physically, mentally. What was I doing? This was dangerous, and suddenly, as quickly as the conviction had appeared, my ideas felt stupid, and juvenile, and just plain fucking retarded. I wondered if I had some kind of cryptic mental disease. Was there something wrong with me? I was meeting with The Terror! The Terror. I was completely insane. I suddenly didn't want this so much, but I was already there. It was within my reach, only a few more steps, a few more minutes, and it was mine if I wanted it. *This or another job. This or another job. Just take a risk for once.*

I walked on numb, stiff stumps for legs and headed toward the door, awkwardly approaching two enormous bouncers blocking the way, muscles testing the seams of their black shirts.

"Hi," I said, smiling nervously.
"Name?" was the stern response.

"Mickey Tyler."
He checked the list, found my name, and let me through without hassle. I nodded and nudged past them, pursing my lips in appreciation, and passed through the gold-plated doors. It was stunning. The Terror's "strip club" was more of a rich pervert's fantasy come to life than anything else. It carried none of the general junkie bathroom atmosphere I was privy to. Those providing the entertainment were sculpted, their bodies hard, and perfectly toned. Impossibly, at times. Son of a bitch. The bartenders wore tuxedos, and the bouncers were friendly and polite, and even the furniture, the tables and chairs, were made of nothing but the highest quality of materials and craftsmanship. The Terror had style, and I was completely under dressed in ratty jeans and an old t-shirt, not expecting such a classy setting. Not expecting to attract such unwanted attention from other patrons.

I walked toward the long marble bar, keeping my eyes to the floor, and quietly, gently, sat and ordered a drink from the bartender. Steve would never make it in such a place. There was zero tolerance for fools of any kind. No screaming maniacs or disruptive goons, and any who dared were probably led out to the back with a barrel pressed against their medulla.

I sipped on my drink, avoiding eye contact with most around me, constantly checking my watch, wondering if I should ask for the big boss or simply wait and see what would happen. The deadline was coming, and no tardiness would be tolerated. I was ready, but where was he? I suddenly felt a hand gently tapping my shoulder, a bear paw sized palm. I turned and was face to face with a bald headed beast, but a smiling and well dressed beast, nonetheless.

"Mr. Labelle will see you now," the bouncer said. I smiled, glancing about the room, still not seeing him. "Right this way, sir."

I left the remainder of my drink and followed the bouncer toward the back of the vast room, through protected doors, up a stairwell, down a hall, through another set of protected doors, and into a rich man's dream. A high priced environment set for a ruthless business machine. It was an elegant space of marble, gold, and brass-plated things all around me. A personal bar stretched across the back of the room, a water wall behind it, and expensive leather sofas covered the hardwood floors here and there. On one of them sat The Terror, grinning almost maliciously, sizing me up, and letting me feel the uncertain tension that wafted through the room. He eventually stood and extended his hand to me, true gentleman killer that he was, and shook my hand.

"Welcome, Mickey," he said. "Please, have a seat." "Thank you," I said, appreciatively, apprehensively, and complied, sitting on the sofa nearest me. He returned to his seat, sipping a drink, staring at me.

"How do you like the place?" he asked. "It's amazing," I said. "An amusement park."

"*Bien oui, calice!*" he said, smiling big. "It's true, an amusement park for rich perverts. I like it," he winked. "Might even attract more members with that slogan. Thank you, Mickey."

I nodded with pursed lips, nervous. He offered me a

drink, which I accepted, of course, and once the procession was over with, he immediately returned to business mode.

"So," he said, his accent thick, yet clearly understandable. "I checked you out, boy. So far, you have nothing to worry about. Now that we are all acquainted, what is it that I can do for you, Mr. Tyler?"

"Well," I was suddenly crippled with anxiety. "I was looking for a loan."

"How much?"

"Thirty thousand," I said, hesitantly at best.

"No more than that?" he frowned, staring at me like a predator, feeding off of my fear. If he were a wolf, my throat would already be clutched in his jaws.

"No, sir," I replied, wringing my hands tightly. "That should be enough."

He nodded. "When do you need it?"

"Ah–as soon as possible, sir."

"Is this for a bad debt?"

"No, sir," I replied tensely. "Honestly, my credit is shit from when I was a kid, but–"

"Right," he said, waving it off with his hand. "How long?"

"I'm sorry?" I asked.

He nodded again, obviously sensing that I had no idea of what in the hell I was doing. "I'll tell you what, kid. I'll let you carry it for six months, free of payments, after which, you will pay me in installments of two thousand dollars per month, until a full payment of forty thousand dollars has been reached. After that, you are off the hook and owe me nothing. How does that sound?"

"Ah, that sounds perfect, sir," I was bewildered. He spoke like a financial advisor.

"Understand," he said. "Normally, I would give you 6 months to pay the forty thousand, or I'd stab you in the face fifty times with a fork, but I like you." He squinted his eyes, staring at me intently. "You remind me of my younger brother, *pauvre jeune*."

I nodded, not really sure of how to react, the man's

presence was something intense, something I had never experienced before.

"But you understand, don't you?" he asked. "If you happen to falter on your debt, I'll cut off your little balls and you'll choke on the right one, and your mother on the left. I do not fuck around."

I nodded gravely. "Yes, sir."

"It's nothing personal, Mickey. It's just business. I am not a bank, and I do not believe in calling creditors. I like to settle my own scores. My money, is my money, and no one gets a chunk of it without contributing back to my bottom line."

"I understand," I mumbled, trying to stop the shaking.

"*Très bien*," he said. "Now have your drink, man. You haven't even touched it yet."

I took a long drink from a shaky glass, desperate to maintain my composure.

"Is there anything else I can help you with, Mr. Tyler?" his customer service skills were impeccable, especially in the face of his ruthless legend. It threw me off guard, but there was something else I needed. I needed a headquarter, a base of operation. The neighbors would put up with blood-curdling screams for only so long before having my operation shut down. I was in need of privacy, and secrecy. What better source could I possibly come into contact with than a gangster? Secrecy was his specialty.

"Actually," I said, timidly, smiling crookedly. "I could use a space."

"Space?" he cocked his head slightly to the side. "*Quel sorte?*–I mean," he smiled. "What kind of space are you looking for?"

"Well," I sighed, the crushing anxiety unabated. "I don't know, maybe like a small warehouse or something? Something quiet, away from residential areas, listening ears, and peering eyes."

Quickly, The Terror turned his head, calling for his assistant. "*Claude*," he said, and like a machine, a well dressed, straight postured man stepped in closer to The Ter-

ror. "*La place dans le parc, est-elle occupée?*" the assistant
shook his head. "*Crisse de jeune vas peut être nous faire
un sou ou deux après tout.*" He turned back to me, his eyes
glowing, but serious. "I have a place," he said, and I reposi-
tioned myself in my seat, listening intently to the offer. "It's
a warehouse in an industrial park, away, as you've requested.
The previous owner died in an unfortunate car explosion. I'll
rent it to you for a very reasonable price."

I nodded. "Okay, how much?"
"Six hundred dollars per month," he said. "If you're willing
to sign a leasing contract stating that you pay three thousand
per month. The IRS needs to see how much of a terrible
hole I make with the place, those cocksuckers can't have my
taxes."

I was hesitant, but I had to ask, it was too stupid not
too, "I'm sorry, Mr. Labelle. No offense intended in any way,
but what's the catch?"

"No catch," he said, his index finger pointed to the
ceiling, his lips pursed. "It's only for my personal benefit to
have that contract signed. A favor, for a favor, let's say."

"Really," I mumbled to myself. There had to be a
catch, but I was desperate, and nervous, and out of options.
If this was to happen, this man was to be the sole supporter
of it. He was giving me money and a place to work out of,
it was far more than I had expected on my way in, with my
stomach tied in knots and my gag reflex kicking in at random. I stared at The Terror, frowning, serious. "Six months?"
I asked.

He nodded, but said nothing, the posture of his body
was enough to flash an obvious unspoken message that
beamed somewhere along the lines of, *I don't fuck around*.
"You can call my assistant here, Mr. Gordon, when you are
ready to see the building, and he will take care of everything."

I nodded in agreement, ready to leave, ready for a
cigarette, or twelve. "Thank you, Mr. Labelle," I said.

He cocked his head quickly to the side, a gesture
conveying his satisfaction with the ease with which the

negotiations had happened, and then straightened up in his seat. "*Claude,*" he said, speaking to his assistant. "*Appelle la fille, trentre mille dans une enveloppe, s'il-vous-plaît.*" The assistant nodded and pulled out his phone, dialed a number and whispered in French into the speaker. Seconds later, he replaced the phone in his pocket and stood at attention once again. The Terror said nothing and stared at me, smiling, friendly, calm. A young woman suddenly came through the doors, her face bright and her eyes happy to see The Terror. She made her way toward him, handing him an envelope, and just as quickly as she had appeared, she was gone. He felt the weight of it, as if he could tell the amount by touch alone, which for all I knew, he could, and then handed it to me without opening it.

"There you are," he said. "You have six months to the day to get back in touch with me. Otherwise, well, you know what happens when people try to fuck me without a kiss."

I nodded yes, of course, I would never. "Yes, sir. Of course, I know the rules."

"Good," he said, relaxing in his seat again and finishing the rest of his drink. He held the empty glass in the air, toward me. "Would you like another drink?" he asked politely. "You can stay for a while if you like. See the sights, get drunk, try on one of my girls?"

"Ah–no thank you, sir," I said, as humbly as anything I'd ever said in my life. "I have to get going. Lots of work to do, plans to set in motion." I was gawking now, making a fool of myself. I was such a goddamned weakling. These men, they were men. They took no shit, no threats, and certainly no trouble from anyone, no matter who they thought they were. The Terror had his ways of setting fools straight. I had to get out of there.

"Good," he said, matter of factly. "I respect the hard working, and despise the entitled. *Les tabarnacle de calise!*" he swore quickly, suddenly caught in a personal sort of rage, not directed at anyone in the room. "Anyway," he recovered. "I wish you good luck, kid. Work hard, stay disciplined, and you will always find success. See you in six months."

"No tolerance for tardiness," I said, and he smiled in response, amused. "Thank you, again." I nodded and headed for the door, but before I could reach it, Mr. Gordon, The Terror's assistant, called after me. I stopped dead in my tracks, wondering if there was a gun suddenly pointed at me. Was this it? The idiot who had been swindled and then executed? A little game they liked to play. Motherfucker. My body was stiff again, rigid, and resistant, but I managed to turn around, forcing myself to keep my eyes open. Mr. Gordon's hand was extended, but it wasn't a gun he was wielding; just like The Terror before him, it was a business card. He smiled, very politely, professionally. "The number to call when you are ready to see the property, sir." He bowed his head slightly, the entire professionalism of The Terror's operation was stifling, and completely unexpected. He was a businessman like any other, only with a dangerous temper, and the will to allow it to be unleashed.

I accepted the card, my hand trembling visibly, and I nodded politely in response to his bow. "Thank you," I said. "I was thinking maybe we could meet on Wednesday?"

He shrugged nonchalantly, suspending his shoulders in the air as though puppet strings were attached to them. "I appreciate receiving requests no more than 24 hours in advance, everything else is kosher. It was a pleasure to meet you, Mr. Tyler. Good luck, and I hope to speak with you soon."

Wow. This was the greatest company on the planet. Imagine if customer service was always this close to its definition. I smiled widely, accepting Mr. Gordon's hand once again, and nodding to The Terror with more respect than I had ever offered anyone in my life–known murdering, extorting, drug dealing monster or not–there was something decent about the man. He understood what it meant to have balls in life, to go for it with guns blazing, fuck it. Of all the people I had ever known, the criminal was by far the most honest. He made no illusions about who he was, he owned it and to hell with what anyone happened to think about it.

He didn't run his mouth, he showed, he took action. It was brutal, but righteous. Ironic.

It was done; it was real. The money was in my hands, clutched tightly against my body like it was an essential organ I desperately needed for an operation I was late for. It was so–surreal. I had done it. I was completely insane.

CHAPTER 15

The room was quiet while the three of us sat staring at the surprisingly tiny stack of bills in the center of the table. Thirty thousand dollars. Amazing. It didn't even feel real. I had met The Terror in person. I had conducted, blatantly partook, in business negotiations with the man himself. Who would have thought? I suddenly felt better about myself, my ego inflating with each reminder that it was, in fact, real; the proof was right there in the middle of the table, stacked neatly, and commanding hard stares from all of us. No one present had ever held that much cash before; at least not any that didn't have to be handed over to someone else in a matter of minutes.

I lit a cigarette, offering one to the others, which they accepted, but still, no one spoke. Money–why did it induce such an intense reaction in the human brain? It was incredibly powerful, and yet, it was nothing but paper. The idea. The rush. Possibilities.

I decided to break the silence first, "So? What do you guys think?"

"It's not counterfeit or anything?" Steve asked, his eyebrows perched high up on his forehead, suspicious. But Polaris remained silent, and staring.

"It's not fake," I said. "It came from The Terror, and believe me, the man does not fuck around. He respects loyalty, and he knows the value of a good business relationship no matter how big or small; an opportunity is an opportunity. Oddly enough, he's an honest man." What was happening to me? I wasn't sounding like myself anymore, but I sort of liked it. That was the point, after all. Why else was I doing this, to keep doing the same thing over and over again, remaining the same forever? No. It was time to challenge myself. *This or another job. This or another job. Do it. Quit being a pussy. Take control, goddamn it!*

I had cancelled the options and put all of my eggs into one basket. Success or fifty stab wounds to the face with a fork, take your choice. Failure wasn't an option. Failure was now on par with death as far as I was concerned. Success. The rush. I was going for it, guns blazing.

"What do you think?" I asked Polaris.
She shrugged. "I think it's good," she said, but still offered no physical reaction. "I just–maybe you shouldn't have gone to see The Terror, I mean–he's dangerous, you know that, right?"

I nodded, politely, and stared into her eyes. She was afraid, and worried, but I didn't get the sense that she would back out. "I know," I said. "But I had no choice. He was literally my last resort. I had to make a decision–there it is." I gestured to the money. "I understand if you guys don't feel comfortable with it anymore, or if you just want to back out. I won't be offended, and it won't affect our relationship in any way. I just thought I should give you guys a chance to reassess your decision now that The Terror is involved."

They stared at each other, both serious, almost neutral, trying to find some kind of team approval within each others eyes, an outer boost of confidence. They nodded to each other, and then to me. Confirmation.

"Okay," Steve said. "It doesn't matter. I mean, I know it's a crazy idea, it's completely insane is what it is, but somehow, I think it just might work. Especially the way you explained it; people just might go for that."

He saw the rush, the appeal of it. It made me smile. Polaris was still nodding absently, staring at the pile of money.

"Yeah," she said. "I think so too. I think we can do this."

"We have to," I said, scratching the back of my neck, ignoring the ugly possibilities trying to bubble up to the forefront of my mind. "We can," I said. "And I haven't even told

you guys about the best part yet, he also agreed to rent me a
warehouse at six hundred dollars per month."

"A warehouse?" Polaris questioned.

I shrugged in response. "Why not? We can't bring people
here, I'm not even paying my rent anymore, I'll have to
leave eventually. It's in an industrial park, far away from
residents and curious eyes, easy to get in and out of in a
hurry, and it's ours."

"Have you even seen it?" Steve asked.

"Not yet," I said. "I wanted you guys to come with me. We
can go anytime it works, as long as I give him twenty four
hours notice." Eyes glanced from one face to another, almost
perpetually, trying to sort out our emotions. "What about
Wednesday?" I asked.

It was unanimous. On Wednesday, a new world
of possibilities would open for us all. New ways of thinking about things, but most importantly, new things to think
about, period. I would call Mr. Gordon and set up the appointment. In the meantime, I would need more cigarettes,
and some weed. Waiting–it fucking took forever.

***

The air over the city was brown and thick with swel-
tering humidity, suffocating. A heat wave was moving in,
bringing with it a sense of general irritation, and an increase
in road rage. The traffic was heavy. The traffic was always
heavy in this city. Day or night, unending lines of blinking
lights, red and white, converged together to form a veritable
migration of angry fools to destinations unknown and most
likely, unimportant. The rush.

Steve brought his car to a stop before a half-di-
lapidated building, the exterior faded blue, battered by the
elements. It was set in the middle of a vast parking lot that
surrounded it like a paved moat, keeping the line of sight to
the perimeter clear, the unexpected arrivals to a minimum. It
was perfect. It was incredibly quiet, with nothing for miles

aside from industrial plants, manufacturing facilities, and, well, shady activity. A facet I was hoping to contribute to in the very near future. Mr. Gordon was already waiting for us, standing there like a token of discipline, his arms crossed powerfully across his chest, two huge bodyguards standing behind him at the ready, monitoring the perimeter, watching for any indication of trouble. He wore a custom tailored suit, his hair combed back perfectly, a healthy mixture of grey and black, his posture straight and rigid, radiating with an aura of pure business. He greeted us gracefully, smiling, and polite. He was the most professional man I had ever dealt with.

"Welcome," he smiled, his French accent also show-ing, but diminished from the years of living in Los Angeles.

"Hello," I said. "Thank you. This is Polaris, and Steve."

"Yes, very nice to meet you," he smiled. "Are you ready to see the property?"

"Yes, of course," I replied.
"Good," he nodded. "Follow me, please."

We followed him into the building, the two guards trailing behind us, the excitement highly evident in the three pairs of eyes before them. The first half was all office space, an ancient relic of some long ago defunct operation. Spider webs covered the corners where the ceiling met the walls. The air dusty, and stagnant. Mr. Gordon turned the lights on, half weren't working, and those that were barely shone through the accumulated dust of—who knew how long? It was inconsequential. I was excited, and happy, and bewil-dered all at once. This was real. The building, the money, the arrangements, they were all real. My life, my dream of doing something different, it was all in action. It was amazing.

"I don't know what you're up to," Mr. Gordon said. "If you'll need this space or not, I mean, but it's here." He shrugged his shoulders, his hands suspended in the air, show-casing the dirty, foul, dusty, but absolutely perfect space. "But this is only the front, back here is the actual warehous-ing space." We followed him through a set of double doors and into a dark, empty space. "Mario," Mr. Gordon said, and one of the guards turned on the light switch, grimly illuminating the vast, echoing space. Even with them on, the overall ambience was industrial, and filthy with years of unmoved dust. It was gray, and cold. Humid, and damp. Perfect. The old fluorescent bulbs barely pushed the artificial photons through the caked on dust, but it was enough to fill the empty air around us with dingy light and an audible hum of electricity. The space was far bigger than anything I had thought of ever needing, but space was space, and it was always better to have too much of it at your disposal than not enough. Who ever knows where plans will lead? The simplest of plans have often turned into the most monumental undertakings without warning. The place would do just fine.

"Over here is another office," Mr. Gordon said, his hand extended to his left toward a closed door in the wall nearest us. "Bathroom around the corner. A lunch room, and upstairs," We all looked up, staring at a long row of windows overlooking the space from a height. "More offices," he said. "Two other bathrooms, another lunch room, you know, the usual industrial layout. Do you think this will suit your needs?"

I looked at Steve, and then Polaris. Their eyes were wide and bright against the grimy ambience. Polaris's arms were covered in goosebumps despite the overwhelming heat outside.

"It's perfect," I replied, smiling.
"Good," Mr. Gordon said. "Shall we sign the papers?"

I nodded yes, of course, an agreement with The Terror was the last agreement I would ever break. Give me a pen. Where the fuck do I sign? I signed the papers excitedly, elated. Mr. Gordon nodded and handed me the keys to the place with a wide smile on his face.

"On behalf of Mr. Labelle and myself," he said. "We wish you the best of luck with your undertaking, and as always, if you need anything else, please do not hesitate to contact us."

"Thank you," I said, accepting the keys. It was official. I was at the mercy of a lunatic, desperately attempting to claw my way out of debt before the deadline. At any cost, my name had to be erased from The Terror's overinflated books. Shortly thereafter, Mr. Gordon and his goons left, hurrying to another appointment, and leaving the three of us staring around, bewildered, and silent. It was done. Mental plans had been turned into reality. Weird. I was happy, but I already felt the strong urge to get things moving. Get them flowing and in our favor as quickly as possible. No mistakes, no wasted time. Things needed to happen, or it was my testicles that would be sacrificed, and no one else's. It was time to get to work.

CHAPTER 16

Salespeople, especially the overly professional type, tend to react strangely to customers who come in teeming with excessive paranoia, suspicious of every word being pitched, and in turn insinuating some kind of vile, highly illegal, and dangerous intention as a result of completing the transaction. The salesperson's voice cracks while their imagination is sent on a wild ride of weird suspicion and bad confusion. Sweat beads form just below their hairline, their breath becomes shallow, and causes their entire demeanor to feel alien even to themselves, never mind the customer. They may begin to shake lightly and wave it off as too much caffeine, desperately fighting against a creeping swoon; never give the indication that the customer is making you uncomfortable, just focus on the deal. The deal is what feeds your kids. The deal is your life!

This was the kind of thing that was happening to our salesman, Mr. Crowler. Poor Mr. Crowler, standing in front of us, his back straightened unnaturally, awkwardly, his eyes darting unpredictably, trying to keep his shit together. This reaction was in response to the curious questions we demanded answers to. Things like, "The average size of a body, would it fit in there?" He had lost control of his flapping lips, unable to say anything. "What about Asians? They are slightly smaller on the average, how many?"

I was a different person. I was thinking differently, changing my habits. My confidence level was at an all time high. If I could successfully deal with The Terror, then who the hell were you? I was doing something with my life. I was taking a risk, betting it all on a gut feeling, the ultimate rush. I was the king of my life, no one else, and right now, with our shivering salesman literally sweating for a buck, I was in the mood to screw with the man and hope for an awesome deal.

"Is the undercarriage waterproof?" I asked quickly, pointing my chin to him.

"Of course, sir," he nodded nervously. "Nothing will ever splash into the vehicle, it's completely insulated with–"

"No, no," I interrupted. "I mean, from the inside out."

He stared weirdly, absently. The folds in his forehead seemed to bog his face down. "I–I suppose so. I mean, if–"

"What about the fuselage, is it soundproof? We'd need that."

"Sir," he said quietly, suddenly leaning in closer to me so as not to hurt my feelings. "The fuselage is the body of an airplane."

"Yes, well, I plan on driving very fast, what's it to you?" I replied. "So what about it? Soundproof or not?"

He smiled uncomfortably. "You won't ever hear the road, sir."

"What about screams?" Steve suddenly broke in from the side. The salesman cringed in surprise.

"Ah–" he stammered. "Well–I don't think that–" he was at a loss for words as his mind raced feverishly to figure out what in the hell was going on; was this serious?

We watched as Steve suddenly broke away from us in a hurry, heading for the driver side door of the van like he was going to steal it. He jumped into the vehicle, slammed the door behind him, and then screamed at the top of his lungs. Bloodcurdling wails, horrible. He thrashed himself wildly against the seats, his head bashing into the dashboard before launching himself into the back of the vehicle, behind the cloak of tinted windows. He thumped hard against the van walls with his full weight, still screaming wildly while we watching the vehicle's suspension compensate for the shifting weight inside, rocking it side to side, and sud-denly–stopping–as though the deed was done, and all that remained was a two hundred dollar detailing job. When the motion stopped, something cryptic seemed to happen to Mr. Crowler. He began shaking and sweating despite the fact that he seemed rather cold. He began laughing nervously and stuttering his words, trapped in tongue twisters.

Steve suddenly reappeared, his eyes bright, but still in full character. This was the greatest prank we had never had enough money to pull off. "How was that?" he asked, very seriously.

"Excellent," I declared. "A good selling feature, Mr. Crow."

"It's Crowler, sir," he managed.
"Yes, well, Mr. Crow, I was thinking," I walked around the man, demanding his attention, when I suddenly tripped on a concrete curb. I fell to the ground, unintentionally, but it was completely favorable to my plans. I clamored back to my feet quickly, my balance uncertain, and forcefully clung to the salesman's arm.

"Good God!" he exclaimed, grabbing at my elbows to help steady me. "Are you all right?"

I stood normally once again, as though nothing had happened, my eyes riveted on the salesman. "I'm fine," I said. "How about a test drive?"

His face turned red, heavy with painful anxiety. He stared at me apprehensively. "Sir, um–please excuse me, but–are you drunk?" He was desperate not to offend, but knew that an intoxicated test drive would probably cost him his job.

"Drunk? I have a physical condition!" I declared, causing his eyebrows to arch high on his forehead. "A chemical imbalance, I think. I need more, or something like that. I don't know, my doctor is a moron."

His instincts were flying in the face of all those selling seminars and professional books he'd read throughout his life. I doubted any of them included a module on how to deal with unruly, seemingly intoxicated, and perhaps even psychopathic customers.

"Sir," he finally managed, but with very little conviction behind his words. "I–I'm afraid I may not be able to sell you this vehicle."

"What?" I asked, completely offended, and suddenly, Steve was standing next to me with threatening body language in full force. "Is this because of the color of our skin? Are you a racist?"

"But, you're white, sir," he stammered in surprise, his eyes unfocussed, his palms held out in front of him.

"So?" Steve replied gruffly. "Do have anything against white people?"

"But–I'm white too," he pleaded. "This is absurd, guys. Surely we can work something out, I'll just need to speak with my manager first." Our eyes remained riveted on him like truly offended patrons.

"All right," I turned to Steve, as if trying to calm his racial anger. "It's okay. He's okay. I'll give you fifteen for it," I said, turning back to the bewildered salesman.

"But, it's a twenty thousand dollar vehicle," he replied. "I can't just give it to you."

"Why not?" I said. "I heard screams coming from the inside. It's not to our exact specifications, but it will probably do for now–at least until they catch up to us." I mumbled just loudly enough to cause a new reaction in the man.

"Ah–I–" He was speechless once again, a terrible salesman.

"Listen," I said. "I'll give you sixteen for it, final offer, and you throw in some of that powerful carpet stain remover you use here. We'll need some of that industrial strength shit. I don't really need a test drive. I'm sure it's very fast."

Finally, as if fearing for his life, or at the very least his sanity, he retorted with an offer, "Okay, sixteen five, and it's yours."

"And the stain remover?" I asked.
"Done."

"You've made a wise choice," I said, my face stern. "You're a good man, Crow. A good man, with good instincts." I smiled.

"Thank you," he replied, confused. "Good, then I suppose we should get the paperwork out of the way."

I nodded with a smile, and followed him back to his office where Steve and I sat quietly, our eyes inspecting every little scrap of paper on his desk, making our salesman visibly uncomfortable. He was anxious to finish the deal, collect his hard earned commission, and then perhaps go home for the day and allow his frayed nerves to rest. I took a business card from the holder on the corner of his desk.

"Derek Crow," I said, mistaking his name once again.

"Ah–It's Crowler, sir," he repeated, his face ansy. "Yes," I nodded. "Have you been working here for long, Mr. Crow?"

"Derek is fine," he said, giving up. "I've been here five years already."

"Five years," I repeated, my eyebrows high on my forehead. "Well, you're pretty good at your job."

"Thank you, sir," he replied plainly, shifting uncomfortably in his seat while shuffling through a stack of forms. "Would you like to purchase the extended warranty? It covers everything from–"

"No thanks," I interrupted. "We're in a hurry, she'll be home at three thirty."

"I'm sorry?" he frowned.

"Oh, nothing," I replied. "Just speaking to myself. Where do I sign?"

He pursed his lips and tried ignoring the deep sense of ridicule he was feeling. Steve had remained rather quiet in the chair next to me, inspecting every inch of the man's office with the intensity of a detective looking to solve a crime by connecting obscure dots. I began filling out the forms, but no further in than my name, without a word, Steve suddenly stood and left the office, prancing across the vast showroom floor. The salesman and I were confused at first, until I saw the reason for his speechless departure; there was a wide eyed blonde across the way, merely glancing in our direction from her desk. Good enough for Steve. I could hear his voice

from Mr. Crowler's office, but not quite what he was saying.
Something perverted, I was sure.

"Hot," I said to the salesman, nodding my head
toward the blonde.

"Yeah," he replied uncomfortably. "That's actually
my girlfriend." He smiled awkwardly, nervously, and nearly
insulted.

"Your girlfriend?" I replied. "Jesus, you should
probably hurry this up or else she'll be leaving with that
idiot. You saw how that van swung a little while ago–"

"Please!" he snapped, but quickly attempted to
recover. "Sir," His eyes were suddenly unfocussed, his mind
disturbed by irrational images of a swaying van with his
screaming girlfriend inside. He placed more forms in front of
me and said, "Sign here, here, here, and here, please. I will
be right back."

I smiled. "You better hurry."
He ignored my comment and swiftly left his office, head-
ing across the showroom floor toward Steve and the blonde.
"Sir? Excuse me, sir?"

I remained in his office, preferring to watch the
entertainment rather than get involved. Steve was raising his
voice at him and throwing his arms up in the air. "She can
fuck who she wants!" he snarled.

He was drawing a crowd from all angles. Curious
eyes searched for the source of the disturbance, but they
were also getting excited, and ready to call the police on
Steve and his increasingly dominant behavior over poor Mr.
Crowler's girlfriend. I decided to intervene. We had the van,
and Steve had had his fun. It was time to go, enough with the
bimbos already. No use in getting arrested before actually
succeeding in kidnapping anyone. I left the salesman's office
and quickly strutted toward the escalating scene with a stack
of forms clutched in my hand.

"Here," I said, handing the papers back to Mr.
Crowler, smiling. "All done. Where are the keys?"

The rage masking his face began dissipating. His
eyes shifted from me, to Steve, to his supposed girlfriend,

and then back to me, trying to calm down and return to his professional demeanor. He pursed his lips, trying his best to ignore Steve's alpha behavior, and nodded, indicating that he would complete the deal despite the disturbance. I turned and grabbed Steve by the arm, leaning in closer to him, whispering.

"Come on, goddamn it," I said. "These bastards will have us arrested for this shit. We got the van, let's go."

He stared at me absently, angrily. I could tell by his face that if I hadn't intervened, fists would probably have been swung by now, rendering our negotiation efforts futile. He finally agreed to leave the blonde, but not before writing his number on her business card.

"Call me when you want a real man," he said, and winked, and strangely enough, she seemed to respond to his advance.

"Goddamn whores," I whispered under my breath. "Come on, Don Juan." I tugged at Steve's arm. He came with me, passing the angry salesman now scowling at his girlfriend.

"Cocksucker," Steve snarled as he passed by him, making his distaste for him quite clear.

Eventually, we made it back to his office with the forms signed, the individual angers calmed, and the keys exchanged. He smiled uncomfortably, his eyes screaming for us to get the hell away from him, unwilling to deal with us any further.

"All right," he said, nodding his head. "Congratulations, sir. You are now the owner of a new van. Thank you very much for choosing us as your dealership, and please have a wonderful day."

"Oh, we will, Mr. Crow," I replied. "A brand new, sound proof, leak proof, totally unmarked van."

"Yes, well, good luck," he replied, shrugging his shoulders impatiently, avoiding eye contact with Steve, his new mortal enemy.

"Oh, shit," I said. "I almost forgot. I'll need that high powered carpet cleaner."

He seemed to tense up once again. "Yes," he said. "Of course." He left us in his office for a moment, and Steve stared incessantly at his blonde conquest. I was getting excited to leave, not trusting my friend's incredible lust at the cost of common sense. Our salesman returned clutching a can of chemical spray I would probably never use, and handed it to me.

"Here you go, guys," he said, attempting a fake smile. "Again, thanks a lot."

"No!" I said very loudly, causing his body to shudder nervously. "Thank you, Mr. Crow. You have yourself a wonderful day."

"Okay, bye," he replied, the relief in his voice apparent, probably thinking about going home to recover from the savage abuse his nervous system had just been submitted to.

"Bye, tits," Steve yelled across the showroom and waived, causing offended faces to glare back at us from every angle, and still, the girl waved back! Incredible.

"You fucking maniac!" I said once outside. "Haha, that guy looked like he was going to kill you."

Aside from a smile, "Fuck him," was his only reply. He didn't care. He was an opportunist, and when opportunity knocked, Steve humped. It was a simple existence.

We hopped into the van, looking over the various dials, and buttons, and unexplained lights, when a realization came to me. This was it. I had the money, and the van, and the location. Before I could even comprehend how, exactly, it was done. All the pieces were falling into place as though they were predestined. A strange sensation indeed, especially for something seemingly so wild. Only a few more supplies left to take care of, a few more ideas to organize, and this thing would come alive. My very own monster, designed and made to live purely from my own will. Life was a strange thing. I had willed it to happen and it was happening right in front of my eyes, like magic. Amazing. Just a little more work and I would feel extremely confident that the face my mother loved so much would not be spoiled by a wielded fork. It was time to pump life into the idea and captivate people's attention.

CHAPTER 17

I moved out of my filth ridden, burnt carpet, foul smelling apartment, and moved into my dilapidating, highly secretive, tucked away from everything, warehouse. As good a place as any really, and there was no longer a need to waste any more money on rent for a place that did nothing but heighten my sense of depression in life. The apartment acted like a giant magnifying glass, enhancing the foul failures of my life, throwing it back into my face until I wanted to jump into the black hole in the carpet and disappear forever. I was sick and tired of it. It was time for a change. The warehouse, the van, the money, the wild ideas rushing through my mind at a million miles per hour–those things now defined my life, nothing else. Focus. I needed to focus.

I made my room upstairs in one of the offices, feeling rather proud of myself for a change. It was gratifying to mull over the recent events that had led me to the position I now found myself in. I had made them happen, I had pushed them forward, in reality, and yet, nothing else felt more unreal. It was weird. I felt as though I had to thank Jerry under my breath, allowing a bitter sweet sensation to flow through me. I missed the man, my friend, my hero at times, but without his death in one of the most random, devastating ways I had ever heard of, I would still be no one, doing nothing aside from watching the hands pass by the minutes until my heart stopped beating and I suddenly felt a deep regret for all of the things I should have done, I could have done, I would have done, but I never did. Depressing.

The death of my friend had been a blessing in disguise. An evil, unwarranted reality that had somehow succeeded in getting me off of my lazy ass and doing something useful for myself. The time had come to take the oppressing, soul crushing rat race by the throat, and squash it's pretentious little head into the ground. For Polaris, Steve, and I, it was time to break free and live our lives. Success or failure didn't really matter; at least we'd had the balls to go for it, and no one could ever take that away from us. Those who tried were the failures, the gut-less, no matter how comfortable they happened to appear. Suburbia–it was all just a massive, widespread illusion. I wanted no part of it. I wanted something new, and this–this was new. It was fresh and exciting. It was life, my life, and I was ready to live the hell out of it! The excitement was electrifying, elating, and frustrating all at once. I passed from moments of unrivaled confidence, ready to take over the world like I was a high powered dozer, only for it to pass and leave me caught in flat out terror, petrified, and convinced that I was completely insane. I was insane, but I was unsure of whether or not it even mattered. Plenty of people were clearly insane in the world, and all they did was stir up the insanity of others, attracting them, leading them, becoming a force. I needed to use my insanity. I needed to identify with others. I needed to deliver an experience that no one would ever dare forget.

      Shortly after moving in, it was time to design the experience. The warehouse, a vast and gritty space of humidity and stagnant emptiness, needed to be molded and shaped into the ultimate psychological experience. With little work, we made the place look like a doom cult had murdered all of its followers and left their mindless propaganda forever plastered to the walls in spray paint and crude, half destroyed posters. The multicolored LED lights we attached to the walls and strewed across the ceiling in chaotic patterns weren't enough to illuminate the dark space, but they were enough to accentuate the dismal atmosphere we were looking for. It became a dark, gritty safe haven for the downtrodden and the depleted hopefuls to converge inside. A beautifully crafted environment that seemed more fitting for junkies to hunker down in and wait for the rush to pass than for a bunch of shady business virgins on the verge of–something. We were close, all that was left, was attracting our customers.

Customers. It was the greatest problem of all. The solution could make us rich, but it was a fine line to travel, and one that needed to be trudged with meticulous analysis. Nine out of ten businesses failed every year, and million dollar ideas were driven into million dollar debts every day, and most of it was due to a single factor; ego. The customer didn't always want what one deemed a great idea. The customer's idea *was* the great idea. The successful recognized it and quickly adapted in order to deliver; the failures squandered endless amounts of money in an attempt to force something that simply wasn't wanted, or even needed. The ego was always stronger than reality, but no matter what the business, a starting point needed to be established.

I wondered about it incessantly, endlessly scribbling notes on scraps of paper and the inside sleeves of cigarette packs. How could it, my idea of kidnapping the willing, be presented to the general public in such a way as to captivate the attention and imagination of the masses, thus ensuring steady amounts of profits to come streaming into our hands? How could any of it be acceptable? It couldn't be for ransom or revenge. It also couldn't be for any sort of political, or corporate advancement. It had to be presented and marketed in such a way that would induce fascination. It had to be– entertainment. Yes! Entertainment. The same reason anyone did anything... The rush. Diving head first from a bridge, or a plane, or a building, it was all for the entertainment factor. Why not kidnapping? Sure, it was extreme, but only because of the psychological taboo that surrounded it all. The very word *entertainment* could be enough to transcend such a resistance. Extreme entertainment, that could sell. That could work. I could already feel my eyes getting wider, my palms getting sweaty, my heart rate increasing. If I could manage to sell it as entertainment, surely people would bite. It was the worm at the end of my hook trolling deep in the river bed of bored, desperate, lonely adrenaline junkies the world over. Extreme entertainment. No harm meant. No foul done.

Interested?

I was interested. Regardless of the consequences, I was going for it, balls out, no turning back. It was all far, far too late. *Death or success. This or another job. Prove it to yourself, never mind the others, do it for you. Go for it.* Entertainment. It felt like my ticket to freedom–sanity. I was ready to plant the seed deep inside of people's minds, hoping that it would bloom with interest. Were you bored, depressed, lonely, confused, afraid, or just flat out exhausted with the existence you were leading, but couldn't see a way out? How about getting kidnapped? It would be better, and longer lasting, and more intense than any orgasm or drug could ever provide. It would give you life–I hoped. Regardless, it was time to try; enough with the dizzying thoughts, action was always the best solution. It was time to act.

***

The filthy bar bathrooms packed with slurring, sweating, stinking twenty somethings; the bus stations crawling with petty thugs and peddling dope fiends; the university campuses squirming with young bodies, open to all aspects of life, horny for nothing more than excitement–none of them had any idea. We were looking for hybrid adrenaline junkies. Where would such animals spend their time? The demographic was hard to pin down. Who were we looking for, exactly? Interested parties could potentially be found anywhere. This was a new breed, a new excitement, lacking any history to base our decisions on, but that was hardly enough to stop us. We were trying everything we could think of. We hit the punk blaring skater parks and the shady concert halls tucked away in the bowels of the downtown core. We infiltrated the tattoo shops, and the music festivals, and even the independent book stores. Why not? Who better to lure into a fantastic experience than the open minded book worm?

We were unstoppable, plastering every inch of those epicenters of human squandering with subtle business cards;

fouling the scenery around us like parasites spreading over a healthy host, trying to smoke out the fiends and convince them to give us their money in exchange for an unforgettable experience. We needed nothing else. Guts and marketing had built, and would continue to build, vast dynasties and unshakable empires that would stand the test of time. *Go for it*.

The cards were simple, and consisted of nothing more than red writing against a black background with simple words that confused, but weren't so easy to forget. "Ever been kidnapped? Interested?" And a phone number– my phone number. The mysticism of it all was intriguing, and the name I had given the idea was the fuel that suddenly caused everyone to be asking the same question. Crypto Fear. What did it mean?

What did it mean?

The seed was being planted, nurtured, and nursed into full bloom. The only thing needed now, was time. Time would churn the idea through opened minds. Late at night, bored at work, right after a break up, it would suddenly come to the forefront. Kidnapped? Interested? Maybe that could make a difference? Crypto Fear. Could it change lives?

CHAPTER 18

"It could happen anywhere," I said. "And at any-time, it's all part of the excitement."

She smiled nervously, biting her bottom lip and darting her eyes around the coffee shop without focus. She wrung her clammy hands together, suddenly staring at the black and red business card she'd found in some filthy bar bathroom. She shifted her mass in her seat, thinking. I could tell that she was nervous, but I was hoping that the cause of it wasn't the fact that my own towering anxiety was blatantly obvious. I was riding a sickening roller coaster of unsure emotions, turning my stomach into tensed knots, my breathing shallow. I was doing it! With every word, my dream was becoming reality. This was for real.

She suddenly nodded, snapping herself out of a deep inner debate, apparently coming to a final decision. "So–it's five hundred bucks?" she asked.

"That's right," I said, smiling, but unsure of if I should have been. I wanted her to trust me. I wanted to make her feel comfortable with the decision she was reaching, but comfort was a far cry from the painful and nervous instability rushing through my bowels.

She nodded again and licked her lips, tucking a wisp of hair behind her ear. Her name was Ellen Monroe, thirty two years old, with big almond brown eyes encased in a slab of makeup artificially solving a host of dermatological troubles. But none of that was my concern, mine was with terminating the transaction, standing up with a smile, extending my hand, and congratulating her on being the first real life client of my very own monster–Crypto Fear. In my mind, it was to be the eccentric pushing of personal limits to a point so elating, and perhaps even mystical, that something had to break, and something else replace it. The unknown side effect. The arcane orgasm. But who knew? Anything was possible. This person seated before me, this stranger, only she could confirm or deny my intentions. Theory was only imagination until proven, and proof took action. Ellen Monroe was going to be my action. She would be proof.

I took a sip of my coffee, staring at her intently, trying not to push her, but deep down wanting to stand and scream, *"Well? Yes or no, goddamn it?"* The internal pressure was too much, but only with patience would I prevail.

She stared at the table top in front of her, unflinching, and concentrated. "Okay," she said, and slowly lifted her eyes to meet mine. "I think this is worth it. I mean, well, I don't know what I mean," she giggled nervously. "It feels right, I guess."

I smiled, my eyes growing wider, my face getting warmer. "Excellent," I said. "That's... it's great." I was trying not to seem unprofessional despite the fact that I had absolutely no idea of what I was doing. "I promise you will love it. I mean, seriously, who the hell can say they've done what you're about to do?"

"No one," she smiled, suddenly much more excited about the whole thing; she was mine. "I think I need something like this, you know?" she half smiled, her eyes searching for understanding on my part.

"Absolutely," I replied. "It will be the greatest thing you've ever done, and definitely the best bragging rights you've ever had, unless of course you happen to meet an assassin. You have to admit, that's a pretty cool job."

She laughed, relaxing the tension between us. It was done. She had said yes. I didn't even know the girl, but goddamn it, I wanted to kiss her I was so happy. The laughter died off and the silence returned us to a serious mood once again.

"So, how does it work exactly?" she asked.
"Well," I said, straightening my posture. "You leave here and continue on with your life as normal. Within two weeks, it

will happen, but like I said, you won't be expecting it when it does." She squinted her eyes, waiting for more. "We will take you by force, per se, and give you an experience that you will never forget, I promise."

"Will it be in public?"

"Yes," I replied, and smiled kindly. "It adds to the experience. You are also free to fight back, and resist, whatever you feel will help you gain the most out of it, you have a *carte blanche*."

She nodded, her eyes pensively directed to her coffee cup. "Okay," she said. "But, no offense or anything, how do I know you're not just ripping me off?"

"Fair question," I replied, and reached into the manila envelope resting under my forearm, pulling out a form and placing it in front of her. "In order to protect both of us, I have a waiver for you to sign. It's nothing binding in any way, it just states that you've paid in full for a service that is guaranteed to be fulfilled within two weeks of today." I stopped and stared at her. She nodded. "It also states that you are aware of the potential harm that could happen while partaking in the service, this being high risk and all, and that you will not hold myself or anyone associated with me liable in the event of personal harm. But as I've said, this is for entertainment purposes only, and we take the highest precautions in order to ensure that your experience is safe and fun. The last thing any of us wants is for someone to get hurt."

She stared at the form while I spoke, reading it over, and I then signed a second copy for her safe keeping. She smiled, her face brightening, her breath deeper.

"I can't wait!" she declared. "This sounds like so much fun."

"It will be," I quickly replied, my own excitement probably tenfold above hers. "I promise."

"Well, good," she said. "I could use a little excitement in my life. The universe seems to be unhappy with me. It likes to treat me like a punching bag sometimes–I'm sorry," she smiled shyly. "I don't mean to bore you with my complaints."

"Not at all," I said. "You're exactly the type of person this whole thing is meant for. It's meant to be exciting, and different."

"Well–good," she said, still smiling, and wringing her hands while holding a breath. She reached into her purse, pulled out an envelope, and slid it to me across the smooth table. Inside were five crisp bills. Something ruptured inside of me. Somehow, my insanity was working. I had one on the line. In little time, this would be my life. It had to be.

"Excellent," I said. "And within two weeks, we will see each other again." I returned her smile. "I just have a couple more questions for you and then we're all done. These are just to help us provide you with the element of surprise. It helps if we have a little bit of information to work with beforehand."

"Of course," she smiled. "What do need to know?" I handed her another form with a simple set of questions designed to give us an idea of her habits. *Where do you work? What time? What is your address? Are you married, dating, or single? What kind of car do you drive? What's the license plate number?* It was simple stuff, but necessary in order to deliver on our promise. She filled in the blanks and slid the form back to me, smiling, still excited.

"Excellent," I said. "And lastly, if you don't mind, I will need a picture of you. It's only for visual confirmation, you know–we need to make this as safe as possible for everyone."

"Sure," she said. "Go nuts."
I snapped a photo with my camera, showing her the result, and then smiled.

"Well," I said. "That's about it. You're all done."
"Awesome," she replied, obviously relieved. "I think it's crazy, but that's why I'm doing it. I need something crazy in my life. To hell with the universe."

I smiled, and then stood, extending my hand. She took it and we shook, sealing the deal.

"Thank you for choosing Crypto Fear for your extreme entertainment," I said. "Congratulations, you've taken the first step in changing your life forever, It will be the best time of your life. I'll see you again soon."

She thanked me, fumbling with her purse, and left the coffee shop, her eyes radiating with bewilderment. I watched her through the glass, my thoughts suddenly stunned. I couldn't believe it. It had worked. It had actually worked. I could feel the excitement rising inside of me. The possibilities seemed vibrant, and unending. If we could properly pull it off and give the girl the thrill of her life–what could stop us then? People would line up around the block to get a piece of it. At least, that's how it was working inside of my head. The reality, well, reality remained to be seen. Like all things in life, I could only take one step at a time, but at least I had my first one. Bring on the future.

***

For three days, we stalked Ellen Monroe like sadists after a new victim. From home, to work, and back, we followed, watching her from a distance behind the tinted glass of our van. If she moved, we followed. Her life was our sole interest. Her actions our only focus. Ellen Monroe. We were going to give her the thrill of her life.

Three days of thinking about possibilities, consequences, good and bad, and trying to work up the nerve to just do it was beginning to weigh heavily on my mind. I needed some action, but I didn't want to strike too soon. I incessantly wondered about what she was thinking. Was it still fresh in her mind? Did she expect us sooner, or later in the next two weeks of time?

I couldn't stand it. The three of us were crammed inside of a van, trying to put up with each other's restlessness. We were parked outside of her apartment building, following her there from work, watching over a lot of parked cars, waiting. Always waiting. Our job would have been much easier if we could have bugged her phone and watched her from cameras, but none of that was feasible, or legal. We had to do it the hard way. We had to tough it out, exactly like we had been doing for the last three days. But we were rather lucky, it seemed, because Ellen Monroe was a dedicated creature of habit who never deviated from her routine. Same time, same roads, same places. Simple.

I looked at my watch, it was 7:00 p.m. already. Only one more hour and–

"Wait," I said, capturing the bored attention of Polaris and Steve, trying their best to stay awake while staring at the bland walls of the van. "There she is," I exclaimed.

We watched her come out of her building, striding through the lot completely unaware of our presence, heading for her vehicle parked only a few rows away from ours.

"Where do you think she's going?" Polaris asked, squinting her eyes.

"Who fucking cares?" Steve said, still lying on the floor, bored out of his mind. "Why the fuck are we still here? She goes to work, she goes home. Boring fucking life. We just sit here and do nothing all day, just watching, waiting for something to happen. Jesus fucking Christ."

"Exactly," I said, suddenly smiling, my hands slightly numb. They both stared at me, confused, and frowning. "She does something different, and so do we," I said. "Fuck it, let's do it."

"Right now?" Polaris asked. "Here?"
"Let's follow her," I said. "Wherever she's going, we can do it there. She won't expect it. It's perfect timing."

"You goddamn right it is," Steve replied, sitting up from the floor and staring out of the window in her direction. "I think if I sit here for one more day I'll fucking kill somebody. Let's just get this over with."

The game was on. The prey was on the move. The stalkers were in place. It was time to stop pretending, and start acting. It was the only cure for what ailed us most. A dose of reality for our overactive imaginations.

We watched her get into her car, well dressed, unsuspecting, and seemingly late for wherever she was going. We followed, keeping at least two car lengths behind in the opposite lane, our eyes glued on her vehicle. Traffic was light, but still heavy enough for us to remain inconspicuous.

The trip was short. She pulled into the lot of a classy Italian restaurant and met a tall, well dressed geek outside, hugging, and following him inside of the building. I could feel it bubbling inside of me. The time had come. The location was perfect. Tonight was the night when boredom would finally give way to a heart crushing orgasm of released anxiety. We would take her on her way out.

My hands were suddenly clammy, but cold. Realizing, as it were, that the rush would possibly be far greater for the abductors, than for the abductee. I looked at Polaris, and then to Steve, their eyes were wide and glossy, excited, unsure, ready–maybe. The van was suddenly dead quiet, nervous. Darting eyes covered the lot, but we couldn't see inside of the restaurant, putting us at a disadvantage. We needed to see her, watch her, prepare for the attack before she even made it back out of the doors.

"Polaris, can you bring the van around to the front? We need to see what's happening."

"I'll have to swing around the block, this is a one way street."

"Yeah, all right," I said. "We can't plan anything from here, and the van is too far to try and drag her all the way across the lot, we'll never make it without problems."

She started the engine and pulled back into the small one way street, rounding the block until we found ourselves parked in front of the restaurant. She got out to feed the meter and returned to the driver's seat, the engine running, ready to bolt. Silence. There she was, Ellen, just behind the window, sitting across from the geek, her face glistening in the dim light, smiling.

"Are you guys ready?" I asked, never taking my eyes off of our prey.

"Yeah," they replied in unison, their voices nervous. It was time.

I felt like I couldn't fill my lungs with enough air, I couldn't smoke enough cigarettes, I couldn't calm down. Not yet, not until everything was done. *Success. This or another job. This or another job.* I was so goddamn thirsty.

Forty minutes passed.

"Okay," I said. "Let's go over this. It has to be fast. As soon as she passes by the van, Steve, you open the side door and I'll jump out and grab her, but you may need to help me get her inside." I licked my lips, tasting sweat. "We'll throw her into the van and as soon as I yell go, Polaris, you smash the accelerator to the floorboards and get us the hell out of here, okay?" She nodded in confirmation, her lips pursed, her eyes dilated. "Once she's in, we'll put the bag over her head and tie her arms and legs. Don't let her speak, if she says anything, tell her to shut up. Remember, it has to feel real, okay?"

"Yeah," Steve said, nodding. "We'll get it right. Just as long as we get out of here before anyone calls the cops on us."

I didn't want to think about that. It was a detail better left tucked away behind the veil of irrationality. I ignored the comment and returned my attention to inside the restaurant. "Okay," I said. "I think they're almost done." We watched as the waitress delivered their bill. Ellen and the geek were still smiling, unsuspecting. Time was ticking. We pulled our black ski masks over our heads, just about ready to test our twisted business prospect. We watched them stand, the geek helping her with a sweater, and already the vicious sting of sweat was assaulting my eyes, my hands were slippery, my face was on fire. I was ready. They emerged from the front doors, giggling and snuggled into each others arms, our white van parked nearby the last thing on their minds. They came closer, heading for the parking lot, and I began counting down the seconds. Soon. Soon. Soon. "Now!" I screamed. Steve pulled violently on the door, sliding it out of my way with a bang. I pounced toward them, my arms spread out in front of me, my teeth snarling underneath my mask, and as soon as my feet hit the ground, our plan was savagely ripped to shreds, leaving us trapped in heavy confusion and totally unexpected reactions from every angle. It was pandemonium.

I lunged for her like a werewolf from the darkness and her reaction was instinctive, terrified. She wailed and grabbed on to the geek's arm, tripping over her own feet in avoidance. She managed her balance and swiftly ran away from me in the opposite direction, her voice suddenly trapped in her throat. The geek couldn't believe it, his eyes darted wildly around him, shaking his head in confusion, unsure of what to do next.

"Shit!" I screamed, and dodged the geek, racing for my prey with everything I had. Steve soon found his bearings and was suddenly standing on the sidewalk, facing the geek, but unsure of what to do. Suddenly, a bloodcurdling scream echoed off of the adjacent buildings.

"Help!" she screamed. "Someone help me!" Immediately, as if coming to his senses, the geek suddenly moved in on Steve and attempted to block his way, yelling at us like we were unwanted rodents stealing his garbage. "Hey! Get away from her! Who the fuck are you guys?"

He managed to get a hold of Steve's shirt, yanking him to the ground, unwilling to release him while I somehow managed to get my own good grip on the girl. The tension was high, it was taking too long and the bystanders were already staring at us in horror, very close to either jumping in from all angles to help, or calling the police, or both! Goddamn it. I struggled with all of my might to keep her in my grip while she squirmed, and screamed, and fought back like a rabid animal. We only had seconds left before the whole thing fell apart, the consequences disastrous. I suddenly thought of The Terror, his consequences far worse than anything the law could imply. I used it as my motivation, my determination. The bitch was coming with me at all costs! She twisted violently to the left, pulling powerfully against me, away from me, but I would have none of it. She bit into my arm, clenching my skin hard into her mouth. I screamed in surprise, but took the pain. This was too important. I couldn't fail. I refused to fail!

I could hear Steve screaming behind me, still fighting the geek. I hurled her body up into the air, toppling her balance, and then dragged her as quickly as I could back toward the van while she kicked and screamed. A totally unwilling participant.

"Hey! Hey! Where are you going with her?" a woman tried fending me off, but I was in no mood for interventions. Not now.

"Fuck off, lady!" I snarled. "Or else you're next!" She backed off in surprise and reached into her purse for her phone, rushing to alert the police, but I was too close to care, too close to fail. I turned and saw Steve collapsing to the ground after taking a hard punch to the face. What was happening? Why was she fighting so hard? Why wasn't this working as easily as we had planned? If that geek got to her, we were done. Something had to happen, and fast.

Suddenly, Steve was back to his feet, returning a blow to the geek's face, causing his knees to buckle and his body to crumple like a broken mass on the sidewalk. He was knocked unconscious. Finally!

"Fuck you!" Steve snapped at the limp body below him, and immediately rushed toward me to help with the girl.

"Help me!" she was still screaming, her vocal chords pushed to their limits, her body squirming violently for freedom.

"Get her legs!" I yelled to Steve, but when he got there she landed her foot in his crotch. He hit the sidewalk like he'd been shot in the belly. Wretched pain rushed through his face, rage, and before I could even do anything else, I noticed that Polaris was next to me. Her fist flew through the air with astonishing speed and landed in our victim's face, calming her feverish defense just long enough for me to hurl her into the van. She thumped against the tin wall while I grabbed Steve by the back of the shirt and threw him in behind her. I jumped in and slammed the door shut, screaming, "Go, go, go, go!"

Polaris slammed on the accelerator and sent the lot of us flying into the back doors, each complaining of various minor injuries. I struggled to get back up against the force of acceleration, grabbing wildly for the girl who was still

screaming and kicking madly at the walls. I managed to tie
her arms after an incredible struggle while Steve threw his
weight over her legs, struggling to get the tie wraps around
her ankles. He managed, but barely.

"Fuck you!" she screamed, thrusting her restrained
body in multiple directions. "You won't get away with this!
You're going to fucking regret this, you pricks!"

I bagged her head, wondering what the hell was happening. She had paid us for this type of treatment. She had
consented; why was she still screaming at us?

I fell back, leaning my weight against Steve's. We
were both panting heavily, trying to catch our breaths. He
was still holding his coveted crotch, desperately attempting
to hold back the vomit, wincing in pain. Polaris drove like a
pro, weaving in and out of busy lanes just fast enough to get
far away from the scene, but not enough to warrant a police
chase. There was no denying it; the girl's wild performance
had given us all a bad jolt. Why had she fought so hard, and
with such a stringent determination to get away from us and
find help? Why was she crying? Why–why was she still
screaming? We had agreed, before I had leaped out of the
van and lost control of the scene, that we wouldn't allow her
to speak and tell her to shut up if she did, but none of us did.
We were sunk into an uncomfortable, eerie silence, with the
same thought flowing through each one of our minds. Had
we kidnapped the wrong person?

The thought of it was grueling, unforgiving. If that
was the reality, then what? Would we be able to simply cut
her loose with an honest apology and a friendly wave goodbye? It was highly improbable. The realistic probability was
the one already assaulting our minds with grave menace; we
would all be completely fucked.

No one except the girl, the victim, spoke while
Polaris negotiated the traffic on the way back to the warehouse. She was whimpering, and moaning, and shifting her
weight around on the floor with less and less determination
as time passed, only adding to our savage paranoia. She
was still crying! Goddamn. There was no getting away from

something like that, no fixing the emotional damage caused by kidnapping a truly unsuspecting citizen. The hammer would come down on our heads with unfathomable force. The punishment ungodly brutal, and blunt. We would be made an example of, and Steve's possibly crushed testicles would seem like child's play compared to a judge's wrath. He would undoubtably say ugly things like, "What if it had been my child, or the child of one of the jurors? How much sympathy do you think they should extent to you fools and your unmatched stupidity? You are decrepit members of our modern society. Idiots! I sentence you all to twenty five years of man raping, soul crushing, knock your teeth out incarceration." The thought of it made my skin crawl. I was, we were, suddenly filled with guilt and disgust by our stupid actions. What the hell had we just done? How could any of it even happen? My God–I wanted to puke.

After what seemed like a cross country trek, we finally arrived at the warehouse. The van was incredibly silent, disturbed. She had given up the resistance and fallen into an eerie silence, sniffling, and occasionally shifting her body in discomfort. Polaris pulled the vehicle inside of the warehouse and turned off the engine. Quickly, rushing, we all hopped out of the van, leaving our victim inside while we raced upstairs to speak in private, away from victimized ears.

"Holy shit!" Polaris screamed. "What the fuck just happened?"

"I... I don't know," I replied.

"What the fuck, man!" Steve snarled, angry as all hell. "That fucking bitch beat the shit out of my nuts! And that motherfucker she was with almost knocked me out! What the fuck is going on?"

"I don't know!" I snapped, frustrated, worried. "I don't know."

Polaris held a look of deep concern. "Do you think..." she said softly, swallowing hard. "Could it be that..." she couldn't say it, but she didn't need to either.

"Maybe," I replied. "I can't be sure."

"You can't be sure?" Steve snapped, his eyes wild with rage.

"Goddamn it! We probably kidnapped the wrong fucking girl and you can't be sure? We're going to prison for this shit! Do you know that? They're going to rip us to shreds!"

"I know," I said, unable to think, confused. "I know."

There was nothing else for any of us to say. We felt silence press on us like the walls were closing in. What were we going to do?

"Okay look," I finally said. "Let's just put her in the room and we'll lock her up as per the contract, and in the morning, well, we'll see."

"Are you out of your fucking mind?" Steve screamed.

"We have no other choice!" I retaliated. "We could always claim mistaken identity, or a lapse of sanity, anything, but not right now. If it's true, then it's already too late. What's the difference?"

They both stared at me uneasily, their body language screaming with the horror of it all. We had no choice, it was already done. I led the way back down the stairs, toward the van, trying to keep the anxiety at bay until after we got her out of the vehicle, but when I opened the door, her screaming rage instantly resumed.

"Youfuckingcocksuckersaregoingtogetit! Help me! Help!!"

"Shut up!" I snapped, angry, but mostly with myself. "What do you want from me?" she demanded, her face still cloaked by the black bag over her head. "Please don't rape me! Please, I'll do anything."

"Shut the fuck up!" I screamed and grabbed her arms, yanking her out of the van. Steve grabbed her legs at my insistence and helped me carry her across the warehouse and toward the door I had labelled, The Monkey Den. I had transformed the main floor office into a hardened holding cell, sound proof, secure, and at the moment, yet another stupid fucking idea from my grand imagination. The realization of my own stupidity was staggering, even to me. We dropped her exhausted body onto the mattress on the floor. The room around her was equipped with a toilet, a sink with running water, and was stocked with a little bit of food. Capture and defeat for the victim. My very own stupid idea. With our masks back on, we removed the plastic tie wraps from her wrists and ankles, and swiftly pulled the bag from her head before hurrying out of the door. I locked the door behind us, hearing little resistance on the other side, tucking away the nightmare for the night. I stared at the door before lowering my head against it, taking in a deep breath, gripped by fear.

"All right," I said softly. "Let's go and do something. I can't handle this right now. We–I–we need to figure out what to do."

There were no responses from behind me. I felt defeated, and stupid. Could it be? Was it actually happening? Had we truly been so stupid? A harsh reality was suddenly creeping its way into my mind. I was an idiot. My ideas, my determination to go forward against the grain and buck the system; why was I so hellbent on sabotaging my own life no matter what I tried? This was serious. It couldn't easily be swept aside as a simple mistake. It was too bad, too wrong. I felt like my entire life, my hopes and dreams were nothing but a scam. We couldn't all grow up to be celebrated rock stars surrounded by fame and money, and even less so my-self, because there was simply just too much stupidity hard wired into all of us. Hello to my fifteen minutes of shame. My life, our lives, our futures, were completely fucked.

CHAPTER 19

Guilt. It had woven its way into every molecule of my body, into every thought, heightening my anxiety to un-acceptable levels. I was about to crack. I clenched my teeth and ground them against each other as another solid wave of self-loathing washed through me. How could it be? How could I have been so stupid? Goddamn it. The night had been excruciatingly long, and filled with ghoulish thoughts and inner torture. My bowels were irritated, mean, and twisting in agony in response to the flashbacks in my mind. A severe, menacing worry had us gripped by the throat, and there was nothing, nothing sexually gratifying about it.

I sat on the floor for most of the night with Steve and Polaris on either side of me, staring desperately, pleadingly at the tiny digital photo I had of Ellen Monroe. Punishing hours passed by, each sinking us deeper into an introspective nightmare of doubt and disbelief.

Guilt.

We had endlessly gone over the details, looking for some type of undefined confirmation that could help calm our terror, but all we could come up with was more uncertainty, more frustration, more fear. We had watched her for days, followed her everywhere, and determined a pattern of her habits. She had been in the restaurant–admittedly, we had left for a minute to round the block, but she was still there when we had returned. A minute! It was a terrible fact–one minute was all it ever took to completely fuck your life up. I needed the toilet again. Emergency! I felt dirty, and foul, and filled with fake reassurances so uncertain that doom was the only prominent emotion. I wanted to jump out of the window. We needed confirmation!

I looked at the clock, it was 6:25 a.m. I couldn't take it anymore. Minutes felt like days, hours like months, it was too much. I was exhausted, and stiff, and out of my goddamned mind.

"Fuck it," I said, startling the others from their own personal inner tortures. "It's too much. I'm going down there." They didn't say anything, but their eyes flashed with the horror of it, wanting it so badly, yet not. An unbearable debate. I rubbed my eyes roughly with my knuckles, the fatigue unrelenting, "You can stay here if you want, but I'm going."

I left, not waiting for an answer. I was determined to end it. Whatever the consequences, it had to be done. I made my way down the staircase and toward the door of the Monkey Den, shaking. I fought hard to find the guts to do it, but eventually, methodically, I slid the key into the lock, holding my breath. I heard the mechanism turn, and took a moment before opening it to look behind me at Steve and Polaris watching from a safe distance at the top of the landing. The air was tense. I pushed back on the door, peering inside as though it were a wormhole to an alternate dimension. In the dim light coming in from behind me, I could see her silhouette sitting on the floor, cradling her knees up against her chest, her head resting silently on top. I stepped into the room, and she turned her head slowly, staring at me with blood red eyes. Her face was droopy, and wrinkled with exhaustion. I was out of my mind with worry. How was she about to react? Would she start screaming to all hell? Would she attack in a desperate attempt to escape? I stared in silence, fighting back the ghoulish possibilities that were overtaking my mind. She let go of her legs and straightened her back, stretching her shoulders, but never took her eyes off of me. Terrible.

"Hi," I managed a whisper. She squinted her eyes, frowning a little.

"You hurt me," she said hoarsely, and then stared with nothing else to add. What could I say? The anxiety I felt was belligerent–brutal.

"I know," I said. "I'm sorry, but I think maybe we need to talk about what happened last night. You need to understand what the motivation was behind our actions."

"Money," she replied quickly. "It was the best I've ever spent."

"What?" I gasped, suddenly breathless, and confused. Had I heard her right?

"What do you mean?" she replied, squinting her eyes again to see my face clearly. "What's going on?"

"Are you Ellen?" I stammered.
"Who the hell else am I supposed to be? I paid you–remember?"

"Jesus fucking Christ!" I exclaimed, and something happy ruptured inside of me as my eyes welled up with tears. I was numb, my tongue thick. "I'm sorry," I panted. "There was–you just–you scared the shit out of us. Why the hell were you crying and screaming about rape for? Goddamn," I laughed. "I thought I was going to prison for the rest of my life. You scared the shit out of me."

"You told me to fight back if I wanted it to feel real," she said, shrugging, and grinning slightly. "It felt real all right. It was the most amazing thing I've ever done. Right there in public like that, I really wasn't expecting you guys so soon, especially not last night."

Damn right it felt real; too real. My heart was racing, my breath shallow, my arms shaking. It was her, Ellen, the one who had paid me, the right girl all along. What cruel, ugly minds we all had. The morning suddenly seemed brighter, the warehouse less demeaning, the doom starting to dissipate. It was absolutely ridiculous. I had felt like an idiot before opening the door, but now that I had, there were no available words to describe the championed level of stupidity I felt. I truly was insane–batshit crazy–but as the fear and the doubt gave in to the settling reality of it all, I felt–a rush. *The* rush. It had been the most intense night of our lives. I was suddenly filled with energy, pride even, despite the sinister nightmares still present in the back of my mind. What a fucking rush!

"Get down here," I turned and said to the other two huddled at the top of the stairs, fear still the master of their beings. "It's okay. Come on."

They approached with apprehension, feeling their own particular brand of stupidity on their approach. We had allowed our minds to get the better of us. The irrational fear had victimized us for hours on end with complete disregard for any sort of rational reality. Being conscious was often a terrible thing.

"Nice punch, by the way," Ellen said to Polaris, who shied and blushed immediately.

"Sorry," she said. "But we were out of time."
"It was awesome!" she said again, smiling widely now. "My God, I've never been so scared, and excited, and just–rushed like that before. You guys did a great job."

Exactly! The girl understood what we were after, she had experienced it first hand, face first, and without any reservations. She had fought, screamed, squirmed, and made the rest of us look like complete idiots. The stalking, the take down, the struggle, the fear–it was the greatest feeling in the world. She stood up from the floor, stretching her body with her arms high in the air, yawning, and smiling while tears of fatigue flowed from her eyes. She seemed pleased, despite the various bumps and bruises. We'd had a totally primitive connection with each other. The body to body contact, the submission to domination, the fear of the unknown; we were suddenly behaving as though we were reunited best friends.

Steve was all smiles, but he didn't have much to say about the ordeal. He had been afraid–so much, in fact, that his eyes still hadn't recovered. He was still trapped in some undefinable, innate fear, debating whether it had all been worth it or not. For too many long hours, we had all thought our lives were over; we were as good as dead. What now?

What now?
After some conversation spent on reinforcing our relief, I drove Ellen home, trapped in a weird haze of exhaustion. My vision was blurry, my limbs numb, but inside, something was on fire–and I loved it.

I pulled into the parking lot next to where the kidnapping had occurred, dropping her off at her vehicle, desperate to get back to the warehouse and get some sleep. I could barely make sense of anything anymore. I–we, all needed some rest.

"Thank you, again," she smiled. "What you have going on here is pretty great, Mickey. I mean, it was just amazing. I'll tell as many people as I can. More people need to live a little, I think."

"I appreciate that very much," I said, returning her smile. "You have no idea how great it makes me feel to hear you say that. I thank you, and wish you the best of luck. If you ever need any more excitement, you know where to find us."

She smiled again, her face puffy, and red. "See you later," she said, and closed the door, clutching the keys to her car in her tired hand. I sped off and rolled down the windows, turned up the radio, and rested my heavy skull against the backrest, cruising at a mellow speed. Proud. Peaceful. The brutal anxiety had vanished like a phantom dream, the insane paranoia non-existent, and all bodily functions seemed to have returned to normal functioning. I felt as though some kind of mystical wisdom about the nature of humanity had been gained through the experience; a lesson I couldn't quite discern. The real life mistake had been too close, our actions too sloppy. It was too important, and too dangerous, to not be sure. We needed to be absolutely sure, anything else was pure stupidity. It was our second chance, and we weren't going to screw it up. Never again.

CHAPTER 20

By the end of the first week after our foolish attempt, we felt confident that we had developed fool proof tactics to ensure that our next kidnapping would be flawless; and by the end of the second week, we were chomping at the bit to put them into action, feverishly intent on perfecting our craft; and by the end of the third week, still completely devoid of any further interest by anyone, I was desperately nearing the cusp of a mean depression. What had happened? Why had only one person come forward, suffered through the savage excitement, gone home in a state of nirvana, and then–nothing? Why? What were we doing wrong? We hadn't stopped distributing our cryptic cards, spreading the word about Crypto Fear, planting the seed into people's minds. We added more locations to our list everyday, and still, nothing. Something was wrong. Something needed to change; The Terror's six month deadline felt increasingly menacing with every hour that silently vanished into the past. The man accepted no excuses. The terms were very simple; you either had the money and he was happy, or you didn't, and he made you pay in other, much more horrible ways. What could we do?

I noticed the fear building in Steve's and Polaris's eyes with every passing day. They were also worried about the future, consumed with the thought that maybe we had overestimated the demand for it all. So what if some demented girl got a kick from being kidnapped? One out of a million was a shitty statistic. We were all relying on it, success, freedom. We were putting all of our eggs into one basket and hoping to high hell that something came out of it, otherwise– I didn't want to think about it anymore. I needed to stay positive, comfortable with the fact that our service was one that

seemed rather extreme, as it was, and that a general acceptance of it could take a while, but it would come. Eventually,
if we believed in it for long enough, it would pay off. I had
to believe. Success was there, somewhere through the fog, it
was waiting for us. I could feel it in the pit of my stomach.
Just a little longer.

The warehouse had grown increasingly silent over
the past weeks. With Polaris and Steve now also living in
the warehouse, the general excitement we had originally felt
was steadily deteriorating. The positive mood was giving in
to impatience, the good humor to stern frustration, and the
friendships to annoyed tolerance; something had to happen,
and soon, but in the meantime, at least we had our various
distractions to focus on. Steve kept occupied by focussing
on his usual escapes–hard drink and women–and Polaris
was demanding more brutality by the day, pushing it further
toward the edge and extending the time without oxygen for
just a little longer each time; but those were all superficial
distractions. In reality, we were all lost and turning in circles,
looking for answers, but the universe wouldn't allow us any.
Not yet, and certainly not with any indication of it in the
future. All I could do to remain sane was to ignore the foul
reality of it and continue to focus on Polaris–the only real
excitement capable of keeping my mind from dwelling on
the lack of progress.

**

For the third time in one day, her eyes were bright
red, the veins exploded, her quivering lips blue, and cold. I
rolled off of her, trying to catch my breath while reaching for
my cigarettes, my mind, once again, blown. Why was that?
What made it so spectacular? So right–yet morally wrong.
I lit my cigarette, holding in the first drag while staring at
the ceiling and listening to Polaris come back to life. She
coughed and laughed, simultaneously satisfied and elated.
We were psychotics. I was caught in introspection. Time,
what a son of a bitch. It passed by too quickly when you

wanted things to last, and too slowly when you didn't. It held zero consideration for anyone, in any way. It simply passed, inconsiderate of our perceptions of it. It could either make life amazing, or horrible, but it rarely balanced between the two. Three weeks was too long of a wait, especially after already having tasted the thrill of doing it, the rush of finishing it, the gawking faces on the sidewalk, stunned, and confused, it was all just so intense. Out of frustration, I felt like going out on the street and kidnap anyone who happened to catch my eye just to satisfy the urge; but without the payment, it still wouldn't solve anything. The experience would be incomplete, fake. I needed customers. *We* needed them, for our sanity, for our future, for our happiness. Where were they? What was stopping them? Impossible.

"What else do you think we should do?" I asked Polaris, taking in another drag, still staring at the ceiling. Her breathing was normal again, her movements fluent, consciousness restored. "I mean, what the hell is happening? Why isn't anyone else calling us?"

"I don't know," she said, lighting her own cigarette, exhaling the first drag slowly, pensively. "It's bound to happen again. That girl couldn't have been the only one, there has to be more–somewhere."

Somewhere. It wasn't helpful. It wasn't definite enough.

"We need this," I said. "We've come this far, and done so much, how much longer are we supposed to bang our heads against the wall before we admit that it just won't work?"

"It's only been a few weeks," she said, gently placing her hand on my arm. "Don't give up too soon, Mickey. I just–I don't know why, but I feel like what we're doing has some potential for things we may not even realize yet. I think we just need to stick with it, it will come around."

I sighed. "I hope so. This fucking sucks."

She nodded and sat up in bed, stretching out her back. "By the way," she said. "Where the hell is Steve?"

"I don't know, probably out chasing after girls, get-

ting drunk as shit, the usual. Hell, he might even be trying
to choke some poor girl right now who doesn't quite understand what's going on."

"Yeah," she chuckled. "He sure does like his wom-
en, huh?"

"The man will never change," I said. "He's hopeless.
Even when we were–"

What was that?! The phone! It was ringing! I leapt
from the bed, tripping over the corner of the mattress, rushing for the dresser against the opposite wall where the phone
was playing through its ring tone. My heart raced at impossible speeds. Was this it? A new customer? I swore that if
it was a telemarketer I would find out where they lived and
burn their goddamned house to the ground–I was in no mood
for false hopes. I reached the phone, fumbling with it for a
second, and finally hit the talk button.

"Hello?"
Silence.

"Hello? Anyone there?"
Still nothing.

"Goddamn it! How do I check–"
"Hello?" It was a male voice.

"Hi," I said quickly, sounding frantic. "Who is this?"
"Ah–" the voice stuttered. "Hi... My name is Chuck. Who is
this?"

"This is Mickey," I said, trying to remain calm. "Is
there anything I can help you with, Chuck? Where did you
find this number?"

"It was on a card," he replied apprehensively. "I
found it in a bar. Is this the right number?"

"It is," I said quickly, looking behind me at Polaris
who was sitting on the edge of the bed in full attention, the
excitement brightening her face. "Ah–so, did you want to
meet, Chuck? Perhaps go over the details of what we do?"

"Do you kidnap people?" he asked bluntly.
"Well, sort of," I replied. "The willing, anyway. It's for entertainment."

"Right," he said, and I was suddenly unsure of his

motivation. Had I scared him away? I suddenly felt like begging him, but I knew better. That was no way of conducting
business. "Well, I think I may be interested," he finally said,
relieving the pressure I felt in my chest. "How does it all
work, anyway?"

"Well, it's a little long to explain, but if you'd like to
meet I can explain everything to you and you can make your
decision from there. There's no obligation to go through with
anything. All I can do is present our service to you. You can
do with the information whatever you will."

There was a pause that felt much longer than it actually was. "All right," he agreed. "When can we meet? It's
getting kind of late tonight."

"How about in the morning?" I suggested. "Say
around ten or so?"

"Sure, that works," he said. "Where did you have in
mind? I live downtown."

"Downtown is perfect," I replied. "There's a place
called Judy's Coffee Shop, do you know it?"

"Yeah, I know where it is," he said, his voice sounding much more confident about it all. "Ten o'clock."

"You got it," I said. "See you there. Take care."
I hung up, my hands were trembling horribly, my mouth dry.
Finally. There were more out there after all. The confirmation that Ellen Monroe wasn't a one hit wonder was elating,
exciting. I couldn't wait. I would sell this Chuck person on
Crypto Fear like a cult leader desperate for new members.
We needed him, and then we needed more to follow. I looked
at Polaris, her hands were clasped together in anticipation of
what I had to say.

"We got another one," I smiled excitedly, moving
quickly to sit next to her, the past three weeks of worry suddenly erased, and non-existent. It no longer mattered.

"That's so awesome!" she exclaimed, visibly excited, hopeful. "And he sounds interested?"

"He does," I said. "He knows the basic deal and
he's still interested. All that's left is for me to sell him on it.
Hopefully this is the beginning of a trend. Maybe one per

day, or more. That would be fucking awesome. This just might work after all."

She smiled, squinting her eyes, her face suddenly glowing. She cupped my face in her hands, "Have you had enough time to recover yet?"

I pushed her back onto the bed, smiling and giggling. "Get ready for the rush of your life," I said.

"Hurry, Strangler. I'm already bored."

***

I had barely slept a wink. My head was swimming with fatigue, my limbs heavy and sluggish, but the excitement inside of me was undisturbed. It was pushing my imagination to churn through endless possibilities, endless hope. I waited for him in the coffee shop, sipping on a fresh cup, trying to contain my anxiety. I was nervous, but confident. I could make this happen. *This or another job. This or another job*. It had to happen.

I watched herds of people come into the shop and go about their daily routines with some kind of motivation behind their actions. Their tired eyes wandered around the shop, impatiently waiting for orders of hot drinks and toasted bagels, hurrying, scurrying to get into work and begin another day of making another man rich at their expense. No more of that for me. No more of that for us. It was no way to live, not in a land of opportunity. There were always options as long as you wanted them badly enough. The rest were all excuses. We could do it. This Chuck kid would be the beginning of something big, something new. We were going to make our own damn selves rich. If other people could do it, so could we.

At around a quarter to ten, a college kid came walking in with an obvious search in his eyes.

"Chuck?" I asked, standing from my chair and extending my hand. He smiled and shook my hand, pulling out the chair to sit across from me.

"Mickey," he said. "It's nice to meet you."

"Nice to meet you too," I replied. "Busy place, huh?"

"Yeah," he nodded. "I've only been here once before, but I imagine it's always about the same."

I was already sizing him up. This kid, he was a college geek who oozed nervousness from his acne infected pores. He was already drenched in sweat, licking his lips uncertainly. His eyes darted wildly, not comfortable with direct eye contact. I smiled. This was what Crypto Fear was all about. It was a suffering of grueling, uncertain, and even dangerous emotions, only to come out a much better, and much more confident person on the other side. It was to exercise our human ability to do something deemed insane and be rendered into a filthy mess of ecstasy solely by the experience. What greater thing could anyone expect out of life? The ultimate kick. The biggest, fastest, craziest rush. Life.

"So," I said. "What do you know about what I do?"
"Only what you told me over the phone. You–" he leaned in closer, lowering his voice. "You kidnap people–I'm guessing for a fee."

"Exactly right," I said. "You pay me, and I give you the thrill of your life in return."

"Okay," he said, licking his lips. "So how does it all go down?"

"Well, I'll need you fill out a form with basic information about yourself so we can properly time our moves, and then you go about your life as though we have never met. Within two weeks of today, should you chose to go ahead with this, we will fulfill our promise to you and perform the kidnapping. You won't see it coming, and you won't be expecting it when it happens. It will also happen in public, it adds to the whole experience, during which time you are also encouraged to fight back and resist our attempts at capturing you. It just makes it that much more realistic for all of us; pretend it's a movie."

He smiled, nodding, seemingly liking what I was telling him. "Does it hurt at all?"

"Does your life hurt, Chuck?" I asked, not really sure of why, but it had the effect I was looking for.

He shrugged quickly. "I guess so," he chuckled. "I just–you know, my whole life, I've just felt like a wimp. I'm always too scared to do anything wild or crazy. I'm always playing everything safe and just dreaming of doing exciting things, but I never actually do anything. I'm tired of dreaming, it's time to do something before it's too late."

"No need to justify," I said, holding my hand up in objection. "I kidnap people for Christ sake, I'm not judging you. I'm here to help people like you. This is strictly entertainment, but it is entertainment that is meant to have a lasting effect. If I can help you become a better person by your standards, then my job is done. That's why we're here. Entertainment to change your life."

He smiled again, his eyes holding contact with mine more and more as we spoke. He was beginning to trust me, and I him. He was already sold. I passed him the forms which he filled out quickly, excited to commit to something different in his life and perhaps make a lasting change. We completed the agreement and signed the waiver before I followed him to an ATM for payment; and as quickly as we had met, he left, returning to his life, and leaving me teeming with confidence. This would work. I could feel it deep down inside of myself. It would work. I was hoping that he would put an end to our dry spell and somehow cause more calls than we could handle to come in. I wanted a new problem in my life, one where I had too much money instead of not enough. I wanted to feel freedom, real freedom. I wanted to be disassociated from the mundanity of the world. I wanted to be, and do, whatever I damn well chose to be or do, without constant outside influences holding me back in ways I couldn't control. It was enough already. Enough. Chuck had no idea what he was getting into, but he would quickly learn. We were about to blow his mind.

***

"How did it go?" Polaris asked.

"Perfect," I said. "He's on board."

"We have another one on the line?" it was Steve, suddenly home, but he wasn't alone. Standing next to him was a woman, a familiar face I couldn't quite put my finger on. I knew her from somewhere–but where?

"Yeah," I replied. "Some college kid. The demographic we were looking for."

He nodded and smiled. "This is Dominique," he said. She smiled and extended her hand, which I shook, trapped in wonder. Where did I know her from?

"How's the van treating you?" she asked.
"The van?" I questioned, confused. "What van?"

"You know..." she cocked her head to the side. "The van."

I fought to keep from bursting in laughter. I did know her, she was the girl from the dealership, the one Steve had shamelessly hit on in front of her boyfriend, at work. I could tell that Steve hadn't had his way with her yet, mostly because of his gentleman-like behavior around her. It was pure entertainment to watch.

"It's good," I said and smiled, still not believing that she was standing in front of me. "Nice and solid."

"Well, good," she smiled, but didn't seem to have anything else to add. I looked over to Polaris, she was smiling, her eyes bright, excited with the prospect of a new customer.

"When are we doing this one?" she asked.
"Well," I said. "I was hoping to get this one done quickly. I don't think I can wait three days again. I'm getting impatient already."

They all nodded, the blonde not even knowing why, but following suit anyway. The room buzzed with high hopes. This had to be it. After we were done with this kid, he had to go back to school and proclaim just how mind bending of an experience he'd had, hopefully enticing many others to follow suit. He was our ticket to a very lucrative demographic. In no more than two days, Chuck would be mulched and reborn before he could even understand what had happened. It felt like it was finally all coming together.

CHAPTER 21

Sheets of rain assaulted the van, diminishing our visibility, but it was too late to turn back. Rain or shine, we were taking the kid by force. Polaris and Steve were on edge, sitting next to me in the back of the vehicle, staring at a bus stop across the street. We had only stalked the kid for one rather uneventful day. To school and back, a quick run to the convenience store, and that was it. The bus stop we stared at was where he waited to catch his ride to school, and at any moment now, we would see his scrawny body hurrying through the rain to join the rest of the huddled bus riders trying to stay dry inside of the booth. Any minute now, my heart rate would begin to rise, the urge to attack unbearable. We'd already had quite enough of the waiting; action was necessary.

"It's pretty quiet out there," Polaris said.
"Yeah," I said. "Hopefully it works to our advantage."

"Less people to interfere," Steve added. "Although, I have no problems punching motherfuckers out."

We chuckled, still searching the streets on either side for a view of our prey. Chuck, he was a tall and lanky kid, infected with acne, and blessed with the muscle mass of an ant in the corner of your kitchen. I wondered how much difficulty he could give us if he did in fact plan on fighting us. Our last victim, Ellen, was light in mass, short, and could be manhandled despite her resistance. Chuck on the other hand could probably be manhandled by Ellen herself, but could he run? His long skinny legs had him standing at over six feet tall; if he did run, could we catch him? What if he got away? Could we simply shake it off and try again? I didn't know. We had never thought about it. We had focussed on success so much that we'd forgotten about establishing a contingency plan. I suddenly felt quite stupid once again. Why couldn't I get it right in my mind? It couldn't be that difficult, could it? It wasn't too late.

"What do we do if he runs?" I asked the others. "I mean, say he's some mutant track and field star who can hop fences like they're hurdles and gets away–do we just wait and try again? I've never thought about it until right now. Seems kind of stupid now."

"Why not?" Steve replied. "The contract says two weeks. Shit, it would probably work to our advantage. The kid would be on high guard for the rest of the time, always expecting us around the next corner. If we miss him, I think it would heighten the thrill for him."

I nodded. "Yeah, maybe," but I was feeling little comfort with the idea.

"As long as we get him within two weeks, we're still within the contract. It doesn't state how many attempts we have," Polaris added.

"True," I said. "But still, I don't want to miss any-one. Call it pride. I want to get it right the first time, because if this thing ever does take off and people start calling us, we won't have the time to try again–I hope." I smiled, imagining the unreal possibilities in my mind while scanning the side-walks, still seeing nothing. "Where the fuck is he, anyway?"

We scanned the distance on either side of us in uni-son. Nothing.

"There's the bus," I said, watching the boisterous machine pull up to the stop, my eyes scanning frantically around it, looking for a sign of Chuck. "Where are you, you son of a bitch?" I whispered, biting my bottom lip. The bodies rushed toward the bus from the booth, ducking under umbrellas and newspapers to keep dry, but still no sign of– "There!" I exclaimed. He was late, and running with impressive speed toward the bus. "Shit. What do we do?" He rounded the corner of the street, only a few feet away from the bus, and joined the line of boarding riders. We watched him hop on in a hurry, shaking the water from his hair, looking for a place to sit. It was too late; we had missed him.

"Damn it," I said. "Why do you kids always have to be late, Chuck?" I was trying to come up with a new plan, we weren't about to stop the bus and drag him off, it would never work.

"We'll get him at the school," Steve said quickly. "Yeah," I agreed. "We can beat the bus and wait for him there. Get him as soon as he gets off."

Polaris nodded and hurried to the driver's seat, turning the engine on and pulling away from the curb as we watched the bus gain speed down the street. We drove right past it, hurrying to its scheduled destination before it could get there, my eyes riveted on the kid. Chuck. He had no idea what was coming. The traffic was fairly heavy, but fully manageable. In ten minutes, we were already parked across the street from the same stop Chuck had gotten off at the day before. I wrung my hands and licked my lips, filled with anxiety, ready to attack.

"Are you guys ready?" I asked.
"Yeah," they both replied, their eyes wide, staring through the rain for first sight of the bus.

"All right," I said. "Let's get ready, it shouldn't be much longer. When it gets here, we'll let him get off, and as soon as the bus leaves, I'm going to tackle him to the ground. You'll have to help me drag him back across the street." Steve nodded. "And then it's the same as last time. We get him in and we get the hell out of here."

With everyone in agreement, all that was left was the arrival of our victim. The school itself was half a block away from our position, thick with enough witnesses to make the kidnapping exciting, but not dangerous. The school had security patrols driving around the parking lots, and the police were never far away. Those we could not afford. Our location was perfect for the attack. *Focus. Don't think, just act.*

Five minutes later, we caught sight of the bus pulling up to a final stop before reaching us. We did a final check with each other, all ready to perform, all ready to attack. Steve and I pulled our masks on, the heat on my face instantly sucked sweat from my pores. I was ready.

The bus slowed and pulled up to the stop opposite us. The kid stood amid a heavy line of young bodies, all tired and distracted before getting to school, waiting patiently to disembark. Steve cracked the side door open, ready to swing it out of my way when I gave the command. Chuck followed his queue in line, exiting the bus with his attention on his phone, the sight of him momentarily blocked by the bus. We heard the air brakes release and the transmission shift into gear. The bus pulled away slowly, and left behind a sidewalk full of college kids marching toward school like a contingent of lemmings in the rain. It was time.

"Okay, go!" I yelled, and Steve pulled on the door, sliding it back and out of my way. I leaped out of the van and hit the ground with aggression, running in a direct line for the kid. The sight of two men in ski masks merited confused gasps from bystanders, but they were none of our concern. The kid still hadn't seen me, his eyes were still glued to his phone. I was ten feet away, five, three; I lunged for him at full speed, tackling him in the mid section like a football player, wrapping my arms around his torso tightly as we both crashed violently to the ground. I heard him grunt in surprise and confusion, the air knocked out of his lungs. I struggled to get back up and take control, but he was beginning to understand, and responded with flailing legs and arms, trying to get me off of him. He was stronger than I had anticipated, but not quite strong enough. He squirmed and twisted his body violently, screaming, and trying to break my hold from him, but I wouldn't allow it. He managed to get to his knees, but I hurled his mass in the opposite direction, body slamming him onto his back, once again knocking the air from his lungs. Bystanders were spreading away from us in a circle, keeping their full attention on what was going on. This kid was getting his ass kicked right there on the side-walk, but he wasn't taking it lying down. He was still fighting, kicking and angry, desperate for me to let him go. Steve suddenly lunged out of nowhere, and landed on top of the kid with his full weight, grasping for his legs. I let go of his

torso and quickly stood up, grabbing him in a headlock from
the back and began dragging him toward the van while he
tried kicking Steve. I flexed my arm around his throat, cutting off his air supply while Steve managed his legs. He got
a hold of them and lifted his lower body into the air. I took
my arm away from his neck and grabbed him underneath the
arms, carrying his twisting body across the street, desperate
to keep my grip. People were calling the police, we had to
get away, fast.

We got back to the van, forcing a car to stop in the
street, when he finally got his right leg free and kicked it
violently at Steve. Instantly, Steve responded with a blow
to the face, calming the kid down, stunning him enough to
be hurled through the opened door. Steve jumped in behind
him, and I behind him, slamming the door shut.

"Go! Go!" I yelled, and Polaris responded with a
revving engine and a surge in acceleration, leaving a crowd
of confused, ill feeling bystanders staring at us from an as-
cending distance.

"Fuck you!" The kid snarled, his face caught in
rage, he hadn't expected to be handled with such violence.
He fought back from the floor, his body thrashing, his limbs
swinging in defense.

"Too late, kid!" I yelled, and jumped on top of him
once again, wrestling to restrain his limbs. I managed to bind
his wrists, then pulled the bag over his head and sat on his
legs while Steve secured his ankles. It was done. We had
done it. He was kidnapped.

"Are you Mickey?!" he snarled from under the
mask.

"Shut up!" I snapped, taking the mask off my head,
and then it occurred to me. The real rush of Crypto Fear was
mostly found in the fact that men cloaked in masks were
attacking you in a public place with violence and determination. Our clients expected an attack, and they mostly knew
that we were the same people they had paid, but the masks
provided a special shred of doubt in their minds, pushing
their anxiety level further with a sudden rush of ugly ques-

tions. What if it was all for real? What if it was just some incredible coincidence that someone else was doing the kidnapping–someone yet to be paid, what then?

The rush.

We sailed through the morning traffic with minimal difficulty, and without the sound of sirens approaching us. The kid was trying to speak, trying to confirm our identity, but we wouldn't give him anything aside from a stern command to shut up and a slap in the head, nothing more. Welcome to the most exciting time of your life.

We pulled into the warehouse and dragged the kid out kicking, the forced blindness enraging him. We dropped him in the Monkey Den and quickly cut his restraints, left the bag over his head, and made our escape. He was furious, scared, and beaten, but he would thank us for it in the end. It was what he had paid for, and he would realize it in a few hours.

I took the key out of the lock and faced Steve and Polaris, proud of having pulled it off without a hitch. It could be done. It could work. If this kid's mind had been blown, he would tell everyone at school about it. This idea wasn't as stupid as I sometimes thought it was, after all. I felt great. There was no need to spend another grueling night staring at a digital photo in disdain; to the contrary, it was time to get drunk in celebration.

CHAPTER 22

In the six weeks following Chuck's kidnapping, we had become professionals capable of nabbing nearly anyone off the street with the skill and agility of a finely honed swat team. We made no mistakes in our planning or execution of a brutal attack, no second guesses, and most importantly, no confrontations with the police.

After we'd ground the kid's ass into mulch, pushed his limits far beyond anything he had ever expected, and scared the festering anxiety straight out of him–things began to change. Chuck's mind had been blown, and to our great benefit, a gag wouldn't have been enough to keep him from bragging about it. Suddenly, calls were coming in, curiosities were pushed to the point of discovery, and money was stacking up in our hands. With every successful job, every mind blown, and every person who stumbled weakly out of the Monkey Den in the morning, three others stood in line behind them for a piece of it.

Crypto Fear was something you had never done, had never thought of doing, but if you dared to take the plunge, it changed something inside of you. Whatever problems you thought you had, whatever things made you feel bad about yourself and your life, none of it mattered after Crypto Fear. Everything else paled in comparison. You've just been kidnapped, what else could possibly be so troublesome?

Around the warehouse, between Polaris and Steve and I, things were going smoothly. We knew what we were doing, and we were able to anticipate each other's moves. We attacked as a team, a unit, all on the same wavelength, and at five hundred bucks a head, the extra pressure I felt about having to pay The Terror back on time was gone. It could be done, all it took was more action.

We hit the streets hard, snatching up one interested victim after another, showing them a part of themselves they had never consciously considered. Drugs were great for a kick, but fear was the greatest drug of all, and a vast multitude of people from all corners of society were flocking to us, looking for a fix. It was the greatest thing any of us had ever done. I had a black eye from being kicked in the face by a frantic nurse, Steve had lost a tooth in the ensuing scrap with a man that was far too big for us to handle, and even Polaris had broken two knuckles on her right hand after nailing some girl who had almost gotten away from us.

Six straight weeks of success was elating, the biggest thrill of all, but on the horizon, a change I hadn't anticipated was coming. It was unexpected when it came, revolting even, in the beginning, but somehow, it was only a natural progression from what we were already doing. It was another part of the dark and convoluted human psyche coming to the surface, a fetish, and it was hardly easy to understand, but it was real, and the demand for it was coming. It had all started with a single client, a person named, Cory Edwards.

Cory Edwards was only 22 years old, but age hardly had anything to do with maturity. At that age, he already exuded a better understanding of what it meant to push things to the limit than anyone I had ever met. He was full of life, and inflated with a brutal sense of adventure that would make most people quiver and cry in fear. A pure adrenaline junkie who had already jumped from the planes and the bridges, and already done the incredibly potent drugs, and already pushed the laws of physics to their absolute limits of speed without the slightest concern for his safety. And already, the kid had uncountable years of boredom staring him in the face as a future. He couldn't stand it–and then he'd heard about Crypto Fear.

He got our number from our second victim, Chuck, whom he attended biology class with. The frail geek had told him all about the experience, the rush of it, the amazement of bystanders watching from a distance, the violence–the kid couldn't resist. It was right up his alley and he wanted a part of it, immediately, but he had a slightly altered expectation in mind. As far as I was concerned, everything was perfect, but for him, Crypto Fear needed more, and he was calling on me to infuse my idea with a bigger rush.

I met him in the same coffee shop I had met with Chuck. I watched him pull into the lot with a car that could cause many grown men to orgasm just from the sight of it. He drove a 1969 Dodge Charger, black on black, and made no apologies for the rumbling noise that blasted from the mufflers. A gorgeous machine, and admittedly, an exciting personality to be around. He came into the shop, searching and finding me immediately. He never shook my hand before sitting down and staring at me without blinking, frowning slightly.

"So you kidnap people, huh?" he questioned. "Only the willing," I replied, matching his tone. "Why? Are you interested?"

He broke eye contact and glanced around the room before leaning in a little closer to me, staring deep into my eyes. "I'm not interested in any pussy shit," he said.

"Well good," I said. "Cause I'm not offering any pussy shit. If you want to be kidnapped, you pay me and I snatch you–"

"Yeah, yeah," he interrupted, nodding his head. "I get how it works. But I want more."

I frowned. "More? How do you mean?"
He licked his lips, never taking his eyes off of me, his confidence was total.

"I want you to beat me," he said rather plainly. "What?" I was stunned. "Like, beat you how? We're pretty rough, you know."

"Not rough enough," he said. "Here," he pulled a thick envelope from his pocket and slid it across the table. I took it and opened the flap, looking inside. It was filled with crisp hundred dollar bills, but there was far more than $500 inside.

"What's this?" I asked.

"It's two thousand dollars," he replied, still not batting an eye. I stared at him in astonishment, it was four kidnappings worth in one sitting.

"It's only five hundred," I said.
"I know, but that's for your pussy shit," he grinned. "Not for what I want."

"Okay–" I was confused. "So what is it, exactly, that you want? Shit, for two grand I'll whip you with thick chains if that's what you want."

For the first time, he smiled. "Close," he said. "But not exactly." He squinted his eyes, sizing me up. "Do you own a gun?"

"A gun?" I snorted. "What the fuck for?"
"I want you to kidnap me with it," he said. "Right out of the bar, and then I want you to beat the shit out of me, and no pussy slaps either, I want fists."

I shook my head, trying to understand. "Why?"
"Because I just paid you two grand for it, that's why," he grinned again. "I'm having trouble finding excitement in my life, so it's time to try something new, isn't it?"

"Sure," I shrugged, still stunned. "But I'm gonna hurt you, kid."

"You better," he said. "That's a lot of fucking money."

I snorted again, baffled. Was this for real? Who was this kid? And why the hell was he so hell-bent on this? He suddenly stood up from his chair and slapped the table with his hand, commanding my attention.

"I know the score," he said. "Within two weeks you'll take me and all that crap. I'll be waiting for you. I hope you're ready to push yourself, man. Cause I won't be going without a fight."

I liked him. The kid was exciting, fearless, and de-termined. He reminded me of myself in many ways. He was ready to take the plunge, and since I had already made it this far, so was I. This was what Crypto Fear was about. Pushing it. Fuck the norm, and the limits, and people's pretentious little morals. There was no room for any of it in our so-called "free" society.

"I'm looking forward to beating the shit out of you," I said and pulled out my form of questions. "Fill this out, and you'll get what you're looking for."

He quickly filled in the blanks and handed the page back to me before speaking again, "Two weeks. I look forward to it."

"Me too," I replied, and watched him leave the shop, heading for his beautiful car. His personality was electrifying, and–uncommon. This guy was for real, through and through. I shook my head while staring at the form, trying to believe it. At the bottom of the page he had scribbled, 'Don't be a bitch about it'. $2000 was a lot of money for one client. Were there others like him? I thought about it while watching him peel out of the lot in a cloud of rubber smoke. Was I really about to beat the hell out of this strange kid I had just met? Would I really smash his pretty little face in like a melon? Of course I would, but the one detail I sat nervously on was the gun. Not with actually owning a gun, but in taking this fool right out of a crowded night club surrounded by looming bouncers and hordes of people watching from every angle. Things could go horribly bad in a flash, and although I felt somewhat comfortable with the fact that I could argue consensual kidnapping in court, waving a high powered pistol through the air was a whole other animal. There was nothing consensual about it. I stared at the form again. *Don't be a bitch about it*. It was time to push my own limits. Success was now demanding more guts than I had ever needed before. Things were suddenly getting serious.

***

Guns, they were considered by some as the pinnacle achievement of the human mind. I had fired weapons in the past, but never a handgun, only rifles in the backwoods of the Rocky Mountains. Rifles were for the bush, handguns were for the city. I never figured I would need one, not illegally anyway, but exciting things necessitated the need for risks. The bigger the risk, the bigger the payoff; at least, that was the cliché. I was decided–I was buying a gun. Luckily for me, I already had a line on such things. When you needed a gun without attracting unwanted attention or having your name added to some obscure government file in the name of national defense, there were no problems when you knew an avid smuggler of everything illegal. Once again, I was going to see The Terror.

I had intended for a quick visit–get in, get it, and get out–but The Terror was like a child in a candy shop. His smiles were big and his eyes wild as he began our meeting with the line, "Here's every possible gun known to man, which one would you like?"

I knew nothing about them. The smell of them, the weight, and the individual power each happened to offer was as alien to me as discerning how a woman's emotions worked–but that was hardly the case with The Terror. He knew all about them, talking gibberish about grains and kick-backs, escaping gases and the potential damage each was ca-pable of causing. I had no idea. I let my eyes glance over his massive collection laid out over five foldable tables, and then the ones hung neatly on the walls. I was in over my head, but lately, I was growing rather fond of that. It was revealing a whole new level of existence that I had never been aware of. I felt lucky, especially since I knew that most people didn't find themselves in a room with the legendary gangster, and then able to walk out unharmed. I was lucky.

I picked up a few weapons and examined them closely under the dim light. I was absolutely clueless, but fascinated nonetheless. Weapons–a newly added facet in my life. After a quarter hour of hustling about, staring blindly at guns I couldn't discern one from another, I found one I liked, but only because of the way it looked. A beautiful piece of modern engineering which The Terror kindly explained was a .45 caliber Glock. It was compact enough to conceal, but powerful enough to blow a healthy hole through any part of the human anatomy. The six shot magazine was plenty– I wasn't joining a gang of hardcore thugs, nor was I even planning on actually using it on anyone, it was mostly for the show. To me, a gun was a gun, and at the sight of one, people moved, end of story; but to a man like The Terror, guns were a thing of absolute beauty and perfection. "An extension of your cock!" he had proudly declared. "And that right there is a tiny one, boy." I chuckled and asked him how much he wanted for the piece, citing that the .45 was power enough, but he ignored my question and fell into an incessant rant about how much more use I could get from choosing the .50 caliber he knew and loved so much.

"How about this one?" he held the monstrous thing up for me to see, sliding his hand over the top of it, showcasing it. "The monster himself. The .50 caliber Desert Eagle. This son of a bitch will blow a hole six inches wide from the top of the head, and right through the asshole."

I was at a loss for words. My little gun would do fine for my application. "Ah, no thank you, Mr. Labelle," I said, smiling, my eyes wide. "It's a little much for what I need."

He cocked his head to the side, winking his eye, and smiling. "It's true," he said. "I've seen it done. A beautiful application of power."

I smiled uneasily. I had no need for such a thing. I needed something flashy and easy to carry around, not something to blow a body in half with a single shot. I thanked him for the attempted persuasion, but I would take the Glock. I insisted on payment, but he assured me that it would be covered in our future business transactions. Whether I liked it or not, it was far too late for me to pull away from him. I owed him a lot of money, and favors, and who knew what else? It was too late; I reluctantly accepted the weapon.

"Thank you, Mr. Labelle. But seriously, I can pay you for this."

"Nonsense," he boasted. "A man can do favors for those he likes, can he not?"

I nodded, not liking his words, but not having much of a choice either. I still had a few months left before my first payment was due, but he seemed completely unconcerned, and never even asked a single question pertaining to what I was up to with his money, or what was happening at the warehouse. He gave no indication of interest, and I, therefore, offered nothing willingly in return. The gun was enough. I needed to make my plan to kidnap Cory Edwards. The time had come to push myself further than I had ever attempted. My stomach was already in knots. My earlier assessment, it seemed, had been correct. I was truly, and completely, insane. Here we go. I left with the gun and my complimentary box of shells. Best damn customer service on the planet.

CHAPTER 23

I stalked Cory Edwards for a week and a half, and for a guy who insisted on constant thrills, he was an odd creature of habit. He went to school, then went to work, and then went to the bar, usually leaving with a giggling short skirt in tow gawking at his boyish face. I was pumped to make this one happen, classifying the kid as a personal challenge in my mind, but I was still highly nervous about the possible implications. In a place packed to the brim with drunken fools, heavy security, and pounding music, the potential for panic was rampant, and could easily mean heavy disaster. We had to be smart about it, swift, and devoid of any mistakes. It was a serious prospect that carried heavy punishments for failure. Nevertheless, I was convinced; I was going to conquer the little fucker and give him every penny's worth.

The time had arrived. We were parked outside of the club, nervous, but feeling that this attempt would undoubtably be the greatest rush any of us had ever experienced. A gun. What a fucking tool!

Cory Edwards was already inside, getting drunk, or whatever the hell he did in there night after night, while we prepared our attack in the parking lot. I was going to do the dirty work, having personally accepted the kid's challenge to push myself. Fuck him, he would not make a fool of me. Steve and Polaris were there to help, but only once we were outside of the club. In the meantime, I would need them to hang around the doors and monitor the perimeter for signs of trouble. Given the setting, masks were out of the question. We had parts to play, complete with cologne, and gelled hair, and clothes to match the rest of the fools inside. Still inside of the van, I was trying to reject the fact that there were too many variables for anything concrete to have been laid out in advance. I hated not being in control. It was too risky, but it had to be done. The appeal was far too great for me to ignore. Polaris and Steve, on the other hand, had feverishly protested even doing it in the first place. They were highly uncomfortable with the implications, and wanted nothing to do with guns, but I was decided. With or without them, I was getting this kid, and it wasn't for the money, or even the satisfaction. It was for reasons I couldn't explain–it was a new level of thrills.

"Everybody know their positions?" I asked.
"Yeah," Polaris answered, her eyes filled with worry. "We'll stand by the door and watch for trouble–but be careful–okay Mickey?"

I nodded, looking from her to Steve, who was also evidently on edge.

"You really think we can do this?" he asked.
I pursed by lips, shrugging my shoulders. "Only one way to find out. Are you ready? I'm going in, you guys come behind me in a few minutes."

"Yeah," he said. "We got it."
"Okay," I said. "See you guys later."

I left them in the van and approached the doors, feeling the weight of the gun tucked into the waist of my pants. I handed my I.D. to the bouncers at the door, who let me in without problems, and once inside, the reality of it all hit me. I hated goddamn night clubs with their drunken kids and slutty little girls excitedly slurring their words to mistakes they would regret in the morning. The place was packed with people, but I couldn't immediately see my prey. I pushed my way through thick crowds of bodies, heading for the bar, and ordered a beer from the bartender. I needed to assess my options for escape before doing anything else. From my vantage point, I only had two choices; the front door, or the back door. It would not be easy.

The lights flashed wildly over the crowd from the ceiling in sync with the music. The heat was overwhelming, causing me to sweat profusely and worry about the gun slipping out of my belt. I checked on it by leaning against the bar behind me. It felt fine. I glanced around the place in search of the kid. There was no sight of him. There were no places to sit, no tables to–wait!

There he was, dancing with some kind of trance-like motivation behind his trusting moves. For a moment, I watched him smooth over the girls around him with ease. His innate charisma was clearly obvious, even from across the room. I was excited to bash his face in.

I finished my beer, keeping my eyes on him, almost ready to make my move. I searched near the doors for Polaris and Steve. They were in position and had a clear line of sight to me, nodding that everything was still good to go. I nodded back to them. It was time.

A new annoying mess of electronic music blasted through the crowd, keeping the bodies jumping, and my prey oblivious of my presence. I crept swiftly through the buzzing crowd like a leopard, the kid in sight, my arms tingling numbly. I approached from the back and stood behind him for a few seconds, watching him hurl his mass around, his sweat flying through the air. He threw his head back, twisting his body to the music, and suddenly slammed right into me before he realized what was happening. He was genuinely stunned.

"Oh shit!" he snapped, and immediately attempted to pull away from me, but I gripped his arm and quickly pulled the gun from my belt, jamming it under his jaw bone.

"Don't even think about it. I'll blow your fucking head off," I said sternly, my eyes darting wildly, looking for signs of danger. He said nothing in response, his eyes were wide and glossy, and his face covered in hot sweat. I turned him around and shoved the muzzle of the gun into his back, still trying to process the situation around us. I hadn't heard any screams, or seen any other guns. So far, so good.

"Go!" I pushed the muzzle deeper into his back, forcing him to wince, to walk. We slowly made our way through the inattentive crowd, my hand shaking slightly on his shoulder, the anxiety in my body mounting to unsustainable levels. I constantly shifted my eyes from Polaris and Steve, to the bouncers, to the huddled crowds, to the doors. We had to make it to those doors. Keep moving, slowly. The kid was behaving, but I had a feeling that he was already aware of his advantage. All he needed to do was scream, or even just pull away from me quickly, and all hell would break loose. I was terrified of the possibility and gripped my hand even tighter on his shoulder. We made it off the dance floor and passed the bar where a bouncer suddenly took interest in us. Immediately, I altered my stance, appearing heavily intoxicated and leaning on my friend for stability. He lost interest as quickly as he had taken it. We had to get out, fast.

"Go!" I pressed into his back again, forcing him to walk. We were getting close, so close that I could clearly see Polaris's face relax a little. Steve nodded and made his way outside, prepared to help with the kid, and Polaris followed behind him, going to start the engine, ready to get us out of the mess in a hurry. We approached the doors and without any indication to the kid, I returned the gun to my belt, keeping it away from the bouncers' eyes at the entrance. The doors opened to a cool wave of fresh night air, the entrance semi blocked by a crowd of smokers. We walked through them, and just ahead of us, I could see Steve standing next to the opened door of the van, keeping tabs on the situation from a distance while Polaris was already in the front seat with the engine purring.

"There, you fucking psycho," I said to the kid. "I got you right out of the bar." But at my words he suddenly stopped, confusing me, forcing me to push him forward, but he wouldn't budge.

"Not quite," he said, and I suddenly noticed his shit eating grin from the side.

"What do you mean?" and then, my worst nightmare came true.

"Gun!" he screamed and pulled away from me, breaking my tense grip on him. Instantly, panic ensued, and we suddenly found ourselves in the middle of a drunken buffalo stampede. There was madness running in every direction, high-pitched screams, and people diving for the asphalt in frantic avoidance of phantom threats. I turned in circles, badly confused, and angry. That little prick was going to get it. I ran after him, chasing him in between rows of cars as bouncers flooded the lot trying to find the source of the panic.

"You demented little fucker!" I screamed at him. "This is your idea of fun, isn't it, you little bastard."

"Woo hoo hoo!" I heard him yell. He was enjoying himself. He rushed into a gathering crowd of panic and I momentarily lost sight of him, but I wasn't about to lose him for good. For two thousand dollars, he wasn't going anywhere except into our van, even if I had to shoot him. I suddenly caught sight of the back of his head bobbing through a crowd of panicked people.

"Got you!" I snarled, and ran after him like an Olympic champion. "Get the van!" I yelled back to Steve. "Bring the van!" He was heading for the back of the lot, toward the intersecting street. If I couldn't catch him quickly, we would lose him for the night. Unacceptable! I thought of what I could do, how I could catch him, and then it dawned on me. He was enjoying himself after all, making us look like fools. If excitement was really what he wanted, then I was going to give him more than he expected. I managed to gain ground on him thanks to a few bodies blocking his way, but I wasn't close enough, I needed to distract him even further. I snapped the gun from my belt, raised it, and fired two quick shots into the sky. The panic was rampant. There really was a gun, and the stampede was now dangerously real. It had worked. The kid took a moment to look behind him, his face trapped in disbelief, trying to see if I was actually shooting at him, and it was enough for me to finally get the upper hand. I lunged for him, tackling him in the mid section. We crashed to the ground with my full weight on top of him.

I heard tires screech dangerously close to our heads, and Steve's voice was suddenly screaming, "You crazy fucking assholes! Are you insane?!" He jumped out and punched the kid in the head, grabbing him by the shirt and hurling his body into the van. I was exhausted, but the kid was already back to his feet, his face wild, and looking for a mean fight. It was hardly over.

"Go!" Steve screamed. "Quick before the fucking cops get here."

Polaris slammed on the accelerator, panicked, nervous. Cory Edwards was acting like a cornered animal, foaming at the mouth, rigid with a desperate fight, vicious. He was laughing at us, taunting us, wildly swinging his fists, calling us on. Polaris took a sharp corner and gave me an opportunity to tackle him to the floor where Steve and I unleashed a savage beating on the poor bastard. He fought back, but with little hope. My lip was bleeding, and swollen, but our fight was far too intense to stop and think about it, we had to get him restrained. We smashed his face in, and although I could hear every hit echoing through the van's frame, he wouldn't let up. The bastard was rabid.

"Two grand!" he was yelling at us. "Come on, you fucking pussies! Is that all you've got? You hit like my grandma, and she's dead!"

Finally, Steve landed a stiff blow that left the kid obviously seeing stars. He laid there in an uncomfortable haze, trying to make sense of what was flashing in his vision. Steve and I desperately attempted to catch our breaths while tying the son of a bitch down with plastic ties, but not putting the bag over his head. We were exhausted, and weak, but the kid was still laughing at us, blood spitting from his mouth. "Ha, ha, ha, you pussies. That was a lucky shot."

When we pulled into the warehouse, the van was far from quiet. He was still taunting us, laughing at us, squirming, and trying to get loose. We hopped out of the vehicle and dragged him out, but we weren't heading for the Monkey Den. I hadn't told Polaris and Steve what I intended to do beyond kidnapping him with a weapon, mostly because I was unsure of doing it, but with the performance he had just given us, the kid had sold me on it. I was hardly done

beating the shit out of him. In fact, everything leading up
to now had been foreplay. I told Steve to hold him by the
van while I fetched a chair and placed it in the middle of the
empty space, to which I tied the kid. The lighting was dim,
all sounds echoed, and the kid was panting, getting tired, but
he was enjoying himself. He sat and garbled gibberish from
his swollen mouth, his eye sockets already black and blue,
but a big smile still graced his pretty little face. I looked at
Polaris and Steve who stood behind me, their eyes question-
ing what I was doing. It was away from our regular plans.
I turned back to the kid, staring at him like a beast while I
cracked my knuckles. He lifted his head and stared at me
with a bloody smile. "I'm still bored," he said.

CRACK! I punched him hard in the face. The two
bodies behind me shuddered in surprise, and disbelief.

"How about now?" I asked.
He sighed loudly, "Yup. You're still a pussy."

I hit him again, forcing a painful yelp from him
when the bones of his nose crushed under the thin skin.

"Mickey!" Polaris cried from behind me, but I ignored her, feeling that I understood what the kid wanted for
his money. He lifted his head once more, nodding, wanting
more. I felt a tooth break simultaneously with the middle
knuckle of my right hand.

"More?" I screamed.
I fell into a dark zone, on a level of subconscious liber-
ties only the two of us could possibly understand. We were
strangely connected in it. It wasn't about hate, or violence,
or even about proving anything. It was all about the savage world around us, ever pushing us deeper into the depths
of a debilitating, universal depression. It was a rebellion,
a retaliation against the stupid beliefs people liked to foul
their minds with in order to blind themselves from reality. Our lives meant nothing to anyone; nothing at all, and
there was nothing wrong with that. People needed to per-
ceive themselves far less important. He, I, and every one
else, were really nothing other than sub-microscopic germs
living on a rock that was floating through space; part of a

universe so ridiculously vast, so huge, that delusions were almost necessary to deal with it. But we'd had enough of the superstitions, enough of the small, tiny, germ like thinking. Every religious leader who told us we were going to hell could kiss our asses. Every teacher who told us we were stupid were only projecting their own inadequacies in life. And every politician who passed laws for their own benefit could all be brought down to their knees and executed. Fuck every single one of them. This was about freedom from the willing ignorance people embraced, and the stupidity of their illusions, and of the grandeur they placed upon themselves. It was about finding a place in a world that was so vaguely defined, and contradictory, it no longer even made sense to search anymore. That was what every punch was about, every scream, and every broken bone. It was about freedom from the stupidity. It was about identifying with the primitive humanity, the instinct that made us what we were, not what we pretended to be.

The final strike knocked him onto the ground with a chilling thump, completely unconscious. I stared at his limp body, completely out of breath, clutching my hand in agony.

"I broke my fucking hand," I complained, but from behind me, the bodies were silent. Shocked. Their eyes shuddered in disbelief–what had I just done? Where had I just gone? Why?

I panted heavily. "Put him the den," I said.
"He needs a fucking doctor, man," Steve protested.

"Put him in the den," I said again. "If we call an ambulance, this kid is going to be pissed. Trust me, this is what he wanted. It's what he paid for. Just give him lots of water, make him comfortable, it's going to be okay."

They both stared at me uncertainly, unwilling to follow through with it, but reluctantly doing so anyway. "What ever you say, man," Steve said, untying the limp and bloodied body on the floor and dragging him to the Monkey Den. It was a fabulous affirmation of our modern lives. Screw every single moron who subscribed to anguished forms of make believe existence. We'd had enough of the stupidity.

We were the new generation, the enlightened one that could see the writing on the wall for what it was, free of illusions. We were here, alive, end of story. Nothing else needed to be explained because the answers didn't matter. We were here, and we had a choice in our experience. We were the new generation, and this was our world.

CHAPTER 24

    I hung up the phone, shaking my head in disbelief. This thing, this Crypto Fear idea of mine, it had caught on. It was real, and it was becoming almost unmanageable for just the three of us. There were too many calls coming in, too many interested people willing to take the plunge and see what happened. I had a waiting list, a thing I couldn't believe even as I held it in my hands. It was inevitable, in the next few weeks, we would need help, and when that happened, this thing would truly be kicked into high gear.

    A full month had passed since Cory Edwards had been taken at gun point, beaten, and left to rot in the Monkey Den. A full month since Steve and Polaris had stared at me in disgust, and worry, wondering if I had finally cracked and lost my mind. A full month, and my broken hand was still sore from smashing it against the kid's skull. I still hadn't been able to repeat the experience since then, but it was hardly a shame. With the number of people clogging up the phone lines, demanding decadent thrills, I really couldn't complain. The money was pouring in faster than we could figure out what to do with it. It was all cash, crisp, and handed over in a hurry for a chance at living.

    The kid, Cory, had spent the night in the Monkey Den, unconscious, and severely beaten. His blood had pooled, his face had swollen, his mind was set free. He had gone back to school afterward, his face still as ugly as all sin, and demanded that his peers call the number and live a little. He was quite the influence in the college circuit. He was popular, and liked, and listened to. It had all started with Chuck, but Cory was the one who had truly broken ground with the demographic, sending thousands of dollars my way.

I would need to send him a thank you note attached to a pound of weed in appreciation. Silly kids.

It felt fantastic, but that pride in turn created fear. As with anyone who had a good thing going, I didn't ever want it to end. The very thought of it was devastating, and I was determined to keep fighting, tooth and nail, to keep it going. At all costs, as far as I could control things, I was going all the way. I was on top of the world, the master of my universe. Polaris and I were getting along better than ever, and Steve and I too, especially since he was free, money wise, to party all he wanted. Every night meant a new girl on his arm, drunk, and horny. We were all champions in our minds, ready to take on the world and conquer whatever came our way. It improved everything around us; confidence was a powerful drug. We lusted after more challenges, bigger triumphs, and despite our growing lack of manageability–more customers. We would find a way to deal with it. I still had time left before my first installment to The Terror was due, and with the way things were going, I could probably pay the man two thirds of what I owed him on the first visit. In little time, I would be free, and my face unharmed. It was a beautiful feeling, and we had come up with an ingenious plan to attain such wealth.

The warehouse was a big, empty space, and in that space, we needed bodies. Paying bodies that would help us attain goals we hadn't even dreamed of yet. The solution was a party. A huge assembly of psycho degenerates and fake citizens of society–from rich to poor, important to not, and from all walks of life–they were all invited. Bank managers and car salesmen, nurses and drug peddlers, gangsters and store clerks, every one of them interested, demented enough to want a part of it. The idea had been Steve's, the party animal himself. Get a bunch of halfwits with pockets full of cash crammed into the same room, all of them depressed with their lives regardless of their respective occupations, and let them feed off of each other's excitement like hyenas on a fresh kill. But quite unlike the greedy hyena, these animals were damn near philanthropists for a foul cause, willing to give up their hard earned cash in exchange for answers to the rumors they'd heard. All I could hope for was more participants willing to fork over two thousand dollars and test my still sore hand.

***

The warehouse was equipped with a powerful stereo system, stocked with tables and chairs, and a bar that served vast amounts of illegal drinks, mounting the sense courage in the room. It was packed, and the excitement was high. People were lusting after the stories of the kidnappings we had already accomplished, playing the scenarios through in their minds, imagining themselves in the situation, and then cheering each other on to shove palms full of cash into my face, ready to take the plunge. I couldn't stop smiling. The idea had been genius. What better way to convince people to try something than to have them convince each other? We no longer needed to crawl through shady bars and plaster them with our simple but mysterious business cards–no–all we needed now was to have fun, get drunk, and host a party. It was beautiful.

"To Crypto Fear!" I toasted my drink in the air, and the response was overwhelming. It felt like a yearly stock meeting for a truly demented company.

"Crypto Fear!" people yelled in response.
I felt amazing. I was the king of my life. The warehouse was filled with beautiful women, young and old, dancing to the music, flirting with the men while money was being handed over in all directions. Everyone was having fun, but no one, not one, was having a greater time than my old pal Steve. He was in his glory. The women, the booze, the strangers–there was no stopping the man. He seemed on the verge of some kind of animalistic orgasm, becoming the loud, frantic, sweating life of the party. He had girls hanging off his arms, potent powders fouling their noses, their eyes wrecked beyond recognition, and loving every second of it. The man was unleashed, tuning into some supernatural

frequency that allowed him to push the experience much further than a simple way to reach more clients. He was going for the glorious stars of complete decadence, but there was something else changing in him too–there was the blonde, Dominique, the girl he had approached at the dealership. She was still around, and it was an odd thing for Steve to be doing. He wasn't one for relationships, and usually destroyed emotions whenever they even hinted at anything that meant being involved. I could tell that he liked her, but there was a problem–she was still attached to her overly nervous, ridiculously professional salesman boyfriend, and Steve hated it with every ounce of his being. As a result, he retaliated in the same fashion he always had–with drugs, booze, and women. He fouled himself with them, proclaiming his hate for the girl, Dominique, all the while accomplishing nothing more than a further breaking of his heart. He liked her, and was perhaps even starting to love her, but her refusal to leave her boyfriend was devastating. He would binge for days on end, pushing himself, only to wake up filled with guilt, and shame, his mind back on the straight and narrow, and barely even smoking a cigarette for days. All in all, with the constant repetition of this same old vicious cycle, my best friend was turning into an addict. I had tried talking to him about it, but he wanted none of it. Who was I to judge? Live your life according to what you believe is right for you. To hell with everyone else.

Beyond that, Polaris was also happy, and our relationship had somehow even progressed beyond a simple primitive fetish. It was more than just me chocking the air out of her throat until she flapped about like a struggling fish and her lips turned blue–it was–damn it, it felt like love. And although I wasn't sure of how she felt about it, or even how I felt about it, really, there was no denying it. Like everything else in my life, it was happening, and there didn't seem to be much that could stop it. At least, I was fully unwilling to accept that anything could. I was in control. I was in power. I was calling the shots. And it was the most beautiful illusion I had ever emersed myself in. I was the king, and nothing could knock my ego off balance.

In the end, the party had been a monstrous success. We signed up twenty six new customers, fully paid up front for the experience. They had shoved the cash into my hands with baited breath. Of course, most of these excited clients wanted the kidnapping, but two of them had heard about Cory Edwards, and they too wanted a piece of it. I smiled at the thought of it. It seemed as exciting as my first night with Polaris. A new fetish. A new thrill. A new reason to launch our lives blindly into the dark and simply wait to see what would come out of it as a result. It was the greatest rush in the world. With possibilities reached, more possibilities presented themselves. It seemed to me as though the whole thing was forming into a culture on its own terms. A myth that people only sort of knew about, but they were somehow empowered by. It felt like freedom. It was throwing every-thing loose, all of the depression of our lives, the frustration, and the fear of judgement, and just going for it, uncaring of what would happen. It was taking a risk, and the payoffs, as varied as they were, were taken with pride.

After the success of our first party, it was decided that we were going to host more on a regular basis and bring in far more people than we could actually handle. We would need employees to help us grow our twisted business. Sud-denly, my wild, crazy, completely insane idea had surpassed anything I could ever have imagined. Success. We didn't need another job. Fuck jobs. We had made it, and the end was nowhere in sight.

The only thing I cared about now was how many other people were willing to fork over two thousand dollars worth of hard earned cash in order to get what the kid had gotten. It was inevitable–there had to be more, and I was de-termined to find every single one of them. The twisted circus had begun.

CHAPTER 25

The blunt packing sounds of knuckles hitting bones echoed off the walls, sickly accentuating the sour smell of sweat and blood coursing through the air. Bang, bang, bang, a quick procession of blows, followed by garbled moans of unintelligible gibberish and eyes rolling to the back of the head.

"Put her in the den!" Polaris hissed, gasping for air, painfully wringing her fist in her other palm. Freedom. In light of the fact that the victim was female, and that my hand was once again shattered from beating some tie wearing executive wimp, Polaris had stepped up to the plate, curious to find out what two thousand dollars bought not for the victim, but for the assailant. It was magical.

"My god," Polaris said. "That was better than sex."
"I know," I said, smiling. "Nothing can touch you after that."

Steve had tried it too. He had come in hopelessly drunk, his eyes unfocussed and red, his breathing shallow and erratic. He had hobbled around the room in a drunken rage, hissing about Dominique and how much he hated her guts. It was a love filled rage, and he let it all go on some poor sap who kept yelling about how much he hated his wife; there was common ground between them, heightening Steve's fury until the guy was flopping around on the ground in unconscious convulsions and Steve broke down in a fit of tears. It was simultaneously beautiful and foul. But these victims were hardly the only ones–no–suddenly, there were more. In the two months since our first party, the line of willing participants had quickly shifted over from simple kidnappings, to going all the way. Only a week after the first party, we had hosted another, and then another, until we found ourselves with the warehouse packed to the seams with gluttons of depravity every night. Business was pouring in faster than we could handle it, and still, there was no end in sight. Before I even understood how, the warehouse underwent a drastic change. The vast, echoing space was replaced with newly built walls, framed into cubicle-like rooms that allowed us to cram more paying bodies into a single day than ever before. Within each room, a single exposed light bulb hung from an electrical cable, crudely highlighting a wooden chair sitting in the center, uplifting the sense of terror the victims came in with. Beyond that, each room was also equipped with its own Monkey Den, ominously muffling out the sounds of the dying souls trapped inside, clawing at the edges, looking for the control of their lives back. A beautiful dream was now reality. We hired employees, all of them past victims, and all of them looking for a rush that paid exceptionally well in more ways than just money. Our business, Crypto Fear, now had four vans incessantly stalking and kidnapping people from all over the city. We were the new popular drug on the Californian coast, a dirty little secret tucked away in some obscure industrial park in the middle of nowhere, giving people what they seemed to be craving most out of their lives. Chaos. Every human mind craved it in one form or another. On some primitive, instinctive level, it meant freedom from the strict mundanity of our lives. Freedom from the illusion soaked, morally biased, plutocratic society that pushed us all to fall into place like mindless little sheep. These people had had enough. It was time for a change of pace, and we were suddenly the best damn answer they had ever heard of. We kidnapped them with brute violence and professional speed, wielding guns and racing wildly through residential communities only to tie them to a chair and give them the beating of their lives. It was exciting, and it was absolutely ridiculous in every way, but goddamn it–it had worked.

Inevitably, in light of our explosive success, we soon became the facilitators of all kinds of strange requests from the bowels of tortured minds. "I want music in the background," "I want to be whipped," "I want to be naked."

"Okay, sure. We can arrange that."
Why not? Give the people what they want. For two thousand
dollars a head, I would fulfill nearly any sick and degraded
request that came our way, what the hell did I care? My
dreams' dreams had come true. I had money, I had fans, and
I had taken something from the tired, dark, frustrated pits
of the common mind and forced it into reality. Despite the
strange requests, the overwhelming demand from nearly
every mouth was, "I want to be beaten." Not a delicate, slap-
ping type of assault, but a hard packing, eye socket shattering, knock your fucking teeth out beating. The actual kidnapping had become less of the object of interest, it was now the
catharsis to the chaos. The foreplay leading to the towering,
life changing explosion of emotions.

        Having a gun shoved into your face gets your heart
pumping whether you've paid for it or not. With a bag over
your head, subdued in the back of a van with strangers wearing masks, it's interesting to see the kind of reactions you'll
give out. Being tied to a chair, repeatedly punched in the face
while you cry and moan and suddenly fall into some cryptic
happy place that hides deep inside of your mind, well, that's
orgasmic. That's the feeling you've paid for; the answers
you've been searching for over the course of your depressing
little life.

        But there was more to it than that. There was a
new aspect to it all that seemed to be a natural progression
of what we were already doing, and it was the thing these
people were truly after. They wanted–*needed*–something
more than just a beating; what they truly lusted was for their
entire existence to be shattered into meaningless little shards.
They wanted it all teared down, their minds along with their
bodies. They wanted to be stripped of all the bullshit they
couldn't escape, all of the defense mechanisms they instinctively hid behind, all of the biased belief systems that had
been drilled into their minds since day one–they wanted
all of it to be broken. A brute, violent cleansing of the soul.
While beating someone, I focussed on everything I hated
about society, about my life, my troubles, my pain, and my

rabid frustration with the plastic wrapped pre-packaged reality I, we, had all been slaves to. Night after night, it became the fuel that transformed me into a twisted, rampaging militant force.

"Who are you?" I would snap and quickly follow it up with a harsh blow.

"What?"

Crack!

"Who are you?"

"I'm... I'm Bradley."

"No!"

Crack!

"Who are you?"

"I'm–I'm no one."

"You are a sad, insignificant digital manifestation in this world! You do not live! You only exist! You are fake!"

Crack!

It was all quite natural for me, using rage for motivation. The last thing anyone wanted was for the beating, the thing they'd paid so much money for, to be faked too. It needed to be real against the artificial backdrop their lives ground against. After a while, all of the faces began to look the same. Male, female, it no longer mattered. They were all tuned into the same deprived vein of existence, begging for a slice of realism.

"How do you place value on your life?"

"I... I"

Crack!

"Is that how? By babbling like a scared little girl?"

Crack!

"You are addicted to the moral propaganda! You are a perpetual illusion, meaningless, and foul! Where is your humanity? Prove to me that you're alive, you worthless little shit!"

Crack!

"You are a wimp!"

Crack!

"The sum of your existence is out there on the internet! You are not a real person, you are a Facebook page! Have you been tagged lately, you fucking loser!"

    Crack!

 "You are nothing but a random IP address! Your life is digital! How do you live with yourself? How do you hold on to reality? Fucking wake up!"

    Crack!

"What happened on reality TV last night? Were you thoroughly entertained?"

    Crack!

"Why don't you take another pill to deal with it? Don't you need another distraction right about now? Hurry, reality is starting to settle in, you fucking useless tool!"

    Crack!

"Everything you know about the world has been filtered through your news media addiction! What do you know? What do you know?!"

    "Nothing!!!"

Crack!

    "Do you like video games? How real is this hit?"

Crack!"

    "Do you enjoy long walks on the beach?"

"What?"

    "How about a punch to the face?"

Crack!

    This went on. A participatory cleansing. A necessary evil needed to put everything out on the table. Everything was exposed for its intrinsic ridiculousness, and it was nothing short of amazing to see what people suddenly discovered about themselves when under the pressure of a mighty beating for babbling out the wrong answer. The truth, of course, was that there were no answers. The words came from my own frustration with the world, they were my expressions of discontentment with society and its ridiculous ways of "living". Why not? It was working, and it was causing the money to flow in like a raging waterfall; and even beyond that, it helped people to reflect on why they were alive, and what they should be doing with their lives. It was free of irrational expectations. It was returning them to themselves, devoid of influence from other people who just couldn't stand to mind their own business. It was the biggest fuck you they had ever given the world, and it was liberating. I would pound them until they either lost consciousness or I made it to the final terrifying question.

"What is the meaning to your life?"

Crack!

"What is it?!"

"I–I don't know!"

Crack!

"Tell me! What do you mean in this world? Why are you here, squandering time, randomly walking around the planet with no goal in mind? Why? Why?!"

"I–I can't..."

Crack!

"What is your purpose when no one hears you, no one sees you, and no one, no one gives a flying fuck about you? What do you mean?"

"I don't know! I don't know!" They would plead with bloodied mouths. "I have no purpose! I don't even exist! Fuck! I don't even exist! I have no meaning! I'm sorry."

"Don't ever apologize for who you are. You are you, now quit crying about it, goddamn it. You are entitled to nothing! Accept it and work something out from it. You are responsible for yourself, no one else. Now, goodnight!"

Crack!

No drug could provide that. No religion could rival it. The absolute breaking down of people's bodies and minds was something raw, ugly, chaotic, and enlightening. It was the realization, in blunt force fashion, that no one is sure of any real purpose, they only *felt* something–sometimes, and there were no set in stone answers for anything. There was nothing static about anyone's life, and the initial realization of it was so heart-wrenching, so unbelievably devastating, that fear of anything else in life soon became irrelevant. There was beauty in that somewhere. Suddenly, Crypto Fear felt like coming back from the dead and realizing that your credit card debt was gone, and replaced with a complimentary orgy waiting for you at home. It affected people like a near death experience, awakening something deep inside of their minds. Themselves. The result–I suppose some found life, and I got paid.

CHAPTER 26

"Here's the first payment," I said, sliding a thick envelope across the table. I swallowed nervously and tried maintaining eye contact. "On time, and no worries about the future," I smiled awkwardly while shifting my weight in my chair. He stared me down suspiciously, not blinking for a moment, and not returning my smile either. He took the envelope into his left hand and held it above his shoulder, still staring at me like a beast. I was sweating bullets, trembling, and somehow even cold. Mr. Gordon came up behind him, took the envelope from his hand and walked to the far corner of the room with it, inspecting the contents. We were sitting in the same room I had managed to nervously babble out enough words to score myself a loan; on the second floor of his classy amusement park for rich perverts.

"Is there a problem?" I asked, my throat horribly dry, my lungs impossible to fill with fresh air.

"I'm not sure," he smiled crookedly. "Mr. Gordon?" "Ten grand," Mr. Gordon reassured, causing The Terror to arch his eyebrows, and nod his head in contentment. It was five times the expected amount.

"Then there is no problem," he smiled before swigging the rest of his whiskey and then holding the glass up in the air between us. "Would you like a drink?"

"Sure," I said, licking my lips in a feeble attempt to calm the anxiety, but not really succeeding with it. "Whiskey, please." The man's presence was overwhelming, and unmatchable. He was terrifying even as he relaxed. He held his glass toward one of his overgrown goons, who immediately understood the order. Fill'er up. The bodyguard returned in under a minute with fresh glasses for us. I smiled and thanked him.

"So," The Terror spoke again. "Tell me, how did that gun work out for you?"

"The gun?" I straightened my body in my seat. "Ah, well, it's a good gun, no doubt about that. Scares the shit out of people, which is good, because that's what I needed it for."

"Good," he replied with a nod of his head. "But it is so small, and weak. Not the greatest extension of your cock, is it?" I believed that this was his attempt at a joke, so I chuckled, nervously at best. "You should really try the Desert Eagle, you know?"

I cocked my head to the side, grinning shyly. "Ah, no thank you, Mr. Labelle," I replied. "The Glock is perfect."

"Well," he said before sipping from his glass. "You know where to come and find it once your balls drop."

"I do," I said, certainly taking no offense. "Thank you, sir. Um, so aside from that, you're okay with the payment? I mean, I can come back in a month with more for you."

"Kid, any time you have money for me, I will gladly welcome you into my perverted amusement park. I haven't forgotten that wonderful description. It's made my business better, you know."

"Well–good, I'm happy I could help," I shifted in my seat again, prepared to leave, but not wanting to be rude in any way. He could sense my apprehension.

"Relax, kid, have your drink, there is no need for you to leave so soon. This is an amusement park, remember?" He smiled widely. "You should stick around, maybe try a few rides on for size."

"I appreciate the offer, Mr. Labelle, but my life has become disturbingly busy over these past few months."

He shrugged. "A busy mind is a healthy mind," he replied. "But you should always take the time to relax, at least once or twice a week. You know what, I have a gift for you."

"A gift?" I was stunned, and–terrified. "That's all

right, Mr. Labelle," I protested. "Your generosity has already far surpassed my expectations. I've never been one to–"

"Bullshit," he cut me off, taking a healthy drink from his already half empty glass. "I'm not one to ask questions of my customers, because I don't care how you get the money, I only care that you get it. And you have. In fact, you've already paid me more than you owe on your first payment, which leads me to believe that you and I might even have a long, friendly future ahead of us. I like you kid, you remind me of myself at your age. You're hungry, and willing to fight. Please, accept my gift."

I chuckled nervously, unwilling to either accept or deny. I couldn't decide on what to do. What did he even have in mind? A lap dance? A Desert Eagle? A fork through the skull?

"*Claude,*" he called to his assistant, Mr. Gordon, who quickly came over for his employer's instructions. "*La nouvelle fille, Angèle, avec les cheveux multicolore. Montez la dons içi pour notre nouvel ami.*"

"*Certainement,*" Mr. Gordon nodded politely, pursing his lips respectively in my direction. The Terror returned his attention to me, smiling.

"Mr. Gordon will get it for you," he said, and then finished the rest of his drink, directing his eyes to my glass. "Would you like any more whiskey?"

I didn't know what to say. What was happening? For all I knew, Mr. Gordon was gone to get a firing squad. I brought the shaking glass up to my lips, feeling a surge of anxiety wash through my chest, and then downed the remainder of my whiskey, wincing as it went down.

"Sure," I said, clearing my throat. I passed my glass to the same guard who had served us the first time, and I expressed my appreciation once again.

"Are you from Los Angeles?" he asked, lighting a cigarette and offering me one, which I accepted.

"Not originally," I said. "I'm from Colorado."
"Ah, yes," he nodded. "I've been to Colorado, very nice. The same mountains we have in Canada."

"Yes," I smiled. "But I like it here. It's a nice place." He nodded quickly. "*La ville des rêves*," he said, and then realized that I didn't speak french, and smiled. "The city of dreams," he repeated. "I like it here, too. Plenty of opportunity for any interest anyone could ever have."

I nodded in full agreement. Literally–anything. Even something as foul as kidnapping. The door opened again and through it came Mr. Gordon, followed by a beautiful woman.

"*Ah, oui,*" The Terror said and stood up, greeting the girl with full respect, and smiling widely. "How are you, my dear?"

She smiled, her eyes radiant. "I'm very well, sir," she said. "Thank you." He thanked Mr. Gordon and placed his hand on her shoulder, leading her toward me while I wondered what exactly he had in mind. I wanted nothing more from him. I had my debt, and it was already about as heavy as I could handle. I had no need for additional "gifts".

"Mickey," he said. "Meet Angèle. Angèle, Mickey." She smiled widely, genuinely pleased to meet me. I stood from my chair, following The Terror's excellent people skills, and shook her hand.

"Hi," I said shyly, feeling my heart rate rise, still unsure of what was going on, suddenly afraid.

"Angèle here is one of my newest additions to the amusement park," he smiled. "A beautiful girl, by all means, please have a seat." He gestured for her to sit with me. My mind was reeling. What was this–a lap dance, or something more? I wanted nothing more. I wanted to leave and get back to work, rake in more cash, punch in more faces, anything but spend any more time hanging out with the famous gangster and his expensive whores. She sat next to me, and The Terror sat facing us, smiling. I had no idea what to say. It was fascinating to note that even though I had no problems with beating the life out of people, sitting next to this girl, in this room, made me uncomfortable. It was a lack of control. The control was his, and I, like everyone else in the room, was nothing more than a pond in whatever game he had chosen to play. He was the boss, and there was no mistaking it. He cocked his head, looking in the direction of the bar. "Behind that door is everything you'll need," he smiled. "I hope you enjoy her."

I shook my head apprehensively, trying to get my protest across.

"Is there a problem, Mr. Tyler?" he asked.
"Ah–" I stuttered. "Well, Mr. Labelle, I truly do appreciate everything you've done for me–but, I–I already have a girlfriend."

"A girlfriend?" he seemed genuinely amused. "Christ, kid. I have been married for fifteen years, I don't cry about it. Women are the most beautiful creatures on the face of the earth. Is this because of the small extension of your gun?"

I didn't know what to say. I didn't want to do this. She was beautiful, she was incredibly beautiful, stunning, but, I had Polaris. I had Crypto Fear. I had–I had–something heavy landed in my lap, and at the realization of what it was, my heart sunk in horror. It was the object of The Terror's recent obsession–the .50 caliber Desert Eagle. What the fuck was going on? The girl sitting next to me suddenly cupped my face into her hands and whispered softly into my ear, "I want you with a gun to my head." It was unbelievable! What was I supposed to do? Say no? What then? Would I need this monster of a weapon to get out of it? Was there a way out? Jesus Christ, the man truly was the goddamned devil. I stared at him, my eyes blank, my breathing coming in spurts, my head spinning, my hands sweating as I held the heavy weapon.

"Be careful," he smiled. "One shot would send her head flying straight through the wall, and then, well, I'd have to knock your teeth out with a ball pin hammer and fry your liver for dinner."

I was lost. What if I didn't follow through? Would he consider it a personal attack on his generosity? And what about this girl–a gun to her head? Really? I was suddenly wondering which was worse, choking a girl in wild primitive lust, or holding an ungodly powerful weapon firmly against her temple? No matter which way I looked at it, they were both equally twisted. And why was The Terror making me do this? What was the purpose of forcing me despite my protest? Was it simply to satisfy his skewed sense of absolute power and ownership, or was it his genuine way of offering a gift to someone he liked? It had to be a little of both, but I didn't like it. I felt threatened, and forced, and goddamned terrified of the man. He was pushing me, testing me, but for what purpose? I owed him money, I had paid him money, what else could he want from me? *Son of bitch!* The girl stood up and clasped my hand into hers, gently pulling on it for me to get up with her. I remained seated, ignoring her, staring at The Terror with eyes that beamed with defiance. *Seriously? You're going to make me do this? I hate you with all of my being.* I felt the full weight of the gun in my hand, wondering how long I would live if I had the audacity to fire a shot into his face. It wasn't worth it. I might as well blow my own head off. I was trapped, under his control, under his ever present threat, and I hated every second of it.

"Be careful with her," he warned again. "She is one of my favorites."

I had no expression, my limbs were numb, and I was praying for a divine intervention of erectile dysfunction. Just this once. Please! She pulled on my arm again, shifting my weight until I gave in to the pressure and stood of my own accord, nervous as all hell. She led me behind the bar while I stared at the oversized handgun in my hand, still wondering if it was all for real. What kind of twisted beings were we? A gun to her head? My hands around her throat? There was something innately wrong with all of us. We were all foul in our own little ways. She opened the door, and all I could think of was; *what the hell am I doing? I'm letting the debt mount even higher. I am a pure, genuine, never going to doubt it again, fucking idiot.*

CHAPTER 27

"Get the fuck out of here!"
Shattering glass and violent screams were what shocked me straight out of bed with my heart racing wildly, and my mind in a panic. "What?!" I screamed in surprise, but there was no one else around to hear me. "What the fuck is going on?" I was already on my feet, dancing in place, searching for the source of the incredible noise. Where was it coming from? I violently slammed the door of my room into the wall behind it and rushed out into the hallway, still completely nude. There was a girl curled up on the floor just outside of Steve's room with a crazed look of terror in her eyes. I ran toward her, pushing her aside so I could poke my head inside of the room, expecting to see a rabid animal being held against its will. I did. Inside was Steve, surrounded by a horrible mess of broken glass and splintered wood, screaming at the top of his lungs, his eyes blinded with rage.

"What the fuck are you doing?" I screamed, trying to grab his attention, but he didn't seem to notice me. He grabbed a television and threw it into the wall with immense force, filling the room with rancid smoke and wild spurts of electrical sparks. He grabbed at his hair and ripped out a healthy chunk from his scalp, the veins in his neck and forehead were horribly swollen under his skin. He had lost it, the reasons unexplained.

"Hey!" I screamed again. "Hey, man. Get a fucking grip! Whoa!"

He suddenly stopped raging through the room like a bull, seemingly hearing my voice for the first time, his rabid eyes riveted on my figure in the doorway. His face was unrecognizable, drooped and shifted under the kick of whatever mighty drug was tearing through his demented brain.

"Where did you put it?" he suddenly snapped, his eyes darting around the room frantically, searching for... It– whatever it was.

"Put it?" I replied. "What the fuck do you mean?" "The lizard!" he snapped, his teeth unsheathed like an angry werewolf. "Where did you put it? It's here somewhere! I need to eat it! For safety!" I felt my face contort in confusion. Dear God, I thought. His mind had finally snapped–this was it–he had finally descended into blatant madness. "Did you fuck it?" he snapped, gnashing his teeth.

"Goddamn it, man! Get a fucking grip! What are you talking about? What did you take?" I screamed, my own rage overtaking me now, panic. I turned to the girl in the hallway, still hugging her knees close to her body, crying with her eyes closed tightly. She wasn't Dominique, this was a replacement Steve had found somewhere in the gutters–an object to unleash his unsteady hate/love relationship onto. "What did he take?" I snapped, my patience at zero tolerance.

She jumped at the sound of my voice. Her body trembled as she swallowed hard before speaking. "Meth!" she screamed. "Just meth."

"Meth?" I snapped. "You goddamned junkies!" I turned back into the room and watched Steve blast his foot through the wall, still screaming gibberish at the top of his lungs. "You demented fucker!" I snapped. "Look at you! Calm down!" But there was no getting through to him, he was a convoluted mess of misfiring neurons and undirected brain waves.

"I need the goddamn lizard!" he declared, his face bright red, his body drenched in sweat. I stepped back and guarded myself against him as he rushed through the room, screaming like a demon. "Argh! Argh! Argh!" He was at the extreme peak of the experience, tearing the place apart with his bare hands. I had to stop him.

"Hey!" I screamed at him again, but this time he stopped, and was suddenly sizing me up like an enraged beast, his eyes horribly filled with insanity. I felt threatened by the pose.

"Stay away, you fucker," I pointed sternly at him, taking another step away from him. "I'll cave your fucking skull in!" But his brain couldn't make sense of the situation; I was a threat that needed to be obliterated. He took a slow, shaky step toward me, gnashing his teeth again, as angry as a lion who'd just been robbed of its carcass. "Get back, you freak," I yelled again, feverishly looking around the destroyed room for something to beat him with. At any moment now, he was going to lunge at me, and I could easily find myself in an ungodly amount of trouble as a result. He was no longer a man, he had been transformed into a drug fueled monster, grinding his teeth horribly against each other, his actions misunderstood. I couldn't wait any longer, I needed to take control of the situation. I lunged at him with my shoulder tucked in low, hitting him hard in the hip and sending him flying on top of the shattered television. His brain was unable to comprehend what was happening; his eyes rolled wildly into the back of his head. I jumped on top of him, still butt naked, and pounded my fists into his face. Like clockwork, I fell into my new role.

"You're a goddamn junkie!"
Crack!
"You are an empty, rotting carcass with a head full of shit!"
Crack!
"You are no one! Nothing! You're a fucking cockroach!"
Crack! Crack! Crack!
His body limped and left his tongue hanging from the corner of his mouth, the white of his eyes filling his half opened eyelids. My lungs were burning with every breath. I was desperate to make sense of what in the hell was going on with my friend. Why was he doing this? Why was he letting a girl destroy his entire life? What a fucking idiot! I was trapped in rage, covered in blood, and feeling as rabid as he had been only moments before. I had unleashed an inner hatred that could only come from caring, it came from the love of two

best friends. I caught my breath and stood up, turning to face the crying girl in the hallway, her eyes still frantic, obviously fearing that I would beat her next–but she hadn't paid me for it.

"Get the fuck out of here, you goddamn junkie!" I screamed in rage. "Get out, now!"

She jumped like a startled cat, landing on numb legs, terrified, and rushing to get out and escape the madness. I heard her exaggerated footsteps rush down the stairs while I stared back at Steve. He was covered in blood, his chest heaving up and down in labored breaths, completely unconscious.

"You fucking idiot!" I snapped at his limp carcass. "What the hell are you doing, man?"

The room around him had been completely annihilated; the victim of a drug induced rage brought on by jealousy. I knew it was because of her–Dominique–she was tearing the man's heart out, causing him to tear his own heart out. Escape, it was the only interest he had when he was angry with her, and lately, anger was all he felt about her. Goddamn lunatics. It wasn't love, it was complete insanity, and something had to be done before he threw everything away for the sake of a girl. Stupid. Childish. Common. But what could I do? I was his friend, not a psychiatrist. I was frustrated, and angry, and still feeling like I should continue stomping his unconscious body until I either killed him, or broke down crying–whichever came first.

I grabbed his legs and dragged him down the hallway, leaving a long trail of fresh blood behind him. I was going to lock him in a Monkey Den and let the fucker rot. With difficulty, I carried his useless weight down the stairs, debating, in light of my rage, if I should simply let him crash downward and pick him up at the bottom. I didn't, despite my anger, and managed to get him all the way into the den safely and lock the early morning nightmare away on the other side of the door. I was already exhausted, naked, and filthy with blood. I didn't know who else was in the warehouse, if anyone. Where was Polaris? And the employees?

What the hell kind of morning was this anyway?

I was still catching my breath, thinking about what had just happened, when I heard voices approaching my direction from the front office. Fantastic! I thought. Exactly what a naked man covered in blood needs after having been so rudely awakened by a panicked meth fiend trapped in a nightmare. It was too late to hide, the doors were already opening to the horrible scene of me standing there like some sex obsessed vampire. The conversation was abruptly halted by surprise.

"Holy shit!" Polaris yelped. "What the hell are you doing?"

"Ah–nothing," I said, trying to act as normal as the situation could allow.

"Is that blood?"

"This?" I said, looking down at my blood stained skin. "Yeah. Um–it's a long story. There was–" But I couldn't continue making up an explanation, because from behind her, a man was stepping into the warehouse, wearing a hoodie, and slowly peeling the hood away from his head. The sight of his face caused a sudden electrified jolt to tear through my chest. Was this a joke? Was I hallucinating? What was happening?

"Hello, Mickey," his calm, steady voice said, sounding pleased to see me, but my brain was refusing the situation on a bases. It couldn't be. I shook my head, staring in astonishment, letting the disbelief fight openly against the obvious reality. I couldn't breathe.

"Grant?" I said. "What the fuck are you doing here?" He smiled widely, seemingly unaffected by the sight of a naked, blood covered man openly standing before him.

"I need to speak with you," he said. "We have many things to discuss."

Discuss? How could it be? This was the embodiment of my past coming back to haunt me. This was–it was fucking karma in all of its glory. It was impossible! The graceful winds of fate that had carried me to where I was, were now looking for payment. The winds weren't calming to stable breeze of unending wealth, they were whipping up a raging

tornado about to tear its way through my life. I felt something dangerous beginning to stir inside of me, and I didn't
like it for a second.

CHAPTER 28

I felt a cold chill rush through me. I still couldn't believe it. It was Grant, the bumbling, babbling, scared shitless pack of nerves I used to call my boss. The one I had blackmailed with the accidental discovery of a fetish, and then defended in the face of some egotistical tyrant trying to make up for his impotence. He was in the past, forgotten and gone, only to be standing in front of me many months later in my new world—my new form of existence that made everything before it seem like it had been from another dimension. Grant. He was looking calm, and healthy, and noticeably lacking the stutter in his speech, and the nervous crackling in his voice. It was all far too much for just one morning. Too much. I suddenly felt like I was losing control over everything, and even worse, I couldn't quite put my finger on the threat I was feeling. It was like the very air around me suddenly felt wrong. Grant felt wrong. I was living a new life and I wanted nothing to do with my past, not ever again.

I washed Steve's blood from my body while Polaris took Grant upstairs to wait for me. I checked on Steve, he was still zoned into some weird nightmare from an alternate dimension, his limbs and face twitched sporadically in sync with the garbled moans coming from his mouth. He was out for the count, and I was suddenly feeling the world around me crumbling to pieces. How did these things happen so quickly? The business was churning ahead at full speed, but Steve was falling apart. And The Terror, he had made me do something for reasons I still couldn't fully understand. What the fuck was going on? I hadn't told anyone about it, and especially not Polaris, but somehow, it was almost as though I didn't need to. It felt as if she already knew all about it. Was it just my imagination? I was convinced that even without her knowledge of my actions, it was placing an unsettling division between us, a wall that was steadily growing thicker, but without either of us able to fully understand how, or why. Goddamn relationships. How could they inevitably become so complicated when even those involved seemed incapable of understanding the reasons? The gnarly undertones simply continued to blaze their own paths into the future, uncaring of anyone's emotions. Were there any other options? I didn't know. All I did know, was that I suddenly didn't like the way the world felt around me. Something was wrong, and it was getting worse.

I locked the door and made my way upstairs, feeling heavy, and confused. Haunted, even. Grant was here. What a fucking asshole.

I was in no mood for chit chat, and was truthfully planning on just discounting his visit and sending him packing on his way. It was too real, too weird. When I entered the room, Grant was sipping on a fresh cup of coffee, speaking with Polaris about the weather. I stood in the doorway for a moment, squinting my eyes, trying to judge what was happening. What did his presence mean? I wanted nothing to do with him.

"So," I said, approaching quickly, frowning. "What are you doing here, Grant?"

He smiled gaily. "Mickey," he said, his voice sounding confident, a trait he had severely lacked in the past. It was throwing me off balance. "I see you're doing very well since–"

"I'm doing fine, Grant," I interrupted. "Look, I don't mean to be rude, but this morning has been a little too much to handle. Is there anything I can do for you? I'm very busy."

He squinted his eyes, sizing me up, the nervousness in him completely obliterated. How could it be? "Do you remember that day?" he asked, grinning with his eyes riveted onto mine. Impossible.

"When?" I replied. "When I quit?"

He nodded quickly, arching his eyebrows. "Yes, the day you

quit. It was a very exciting day, wasn't it?"

"I guess," I shrugged. "What does this have to do with anything, Grant? I'm not sure what you want from me."

"You changed my life on that day," he replied quickly. "Believe it or not, you're responsible for who I am today."

I chuckled. "You're right, I don't believe it. Everyone is responsible for themselves, Grant. If I inspired you, then good, but I didn't do anything for you. That guy was a prick. I should have burnt his fucking house down, if anything."

"Maybe," he said, looking over to Polaris who was sitting quietly, listening to the conversation. "But regardless of what was, or wasn't done, there are two drastic things that happened to me that day, and I can never thank you enough for them. Not ever."

I shook my head. "Okay," What the hell was he talking about? I wasn't going to be in any of his amateur internet movies, no matter how desperately he was prepared to beg.

"First," he continued. "I realized in that moment, because of your sheer fearlessness of him, that everything I was afraid of in my life, everything I had allowed to sink me deeper into a foul depression for too many years, was quite realistically irrational. Up until that moment, every phobia I'd ever had wasn't real. In fact, some of them were so far fetched and ridiculously blown out of proportion that it makes me laugh now, but back then, they truly scared the hell out of me."

Right. You had mental problems. Whatever. What do you want from me? Goddamn it! None of this felt right, and every word was making it worse.

I said nothing in response and elected to stare back suspiciously, waiting for him to continue.

"Well," he said. "That was the first thing. I realized that I was a wimp. I was scared, and mostly for reasons that made absolutely no sense to anyone, let alone myself, but what truly changed it for me, what actually helped–were your words."

I arched my eyebrows, on the verge of smiling, but still not daring to show any friendliness; not quite yet. "My words?" I questioned. I had never said anything meaningful to anyone, ever. I was a fool, exactly like the rest of the population. There was nothing special about me, it was just me–little old me, starting to feel the world spinning out of control.

He nodded quickly, "You told me to grow some balls and tell the guy to go screw himself."

"Uh huh," I nodded, still not making the connection with the rest of his drivel.

"Well–I did," he said, causing me to frown and cock my head to the side. He did? He did what? Found his balls? They were already all over the internet, moron. "That night," he continued. "I didn't sleep a wink, I was trapped in deep reflections on my life, the meaning of it, the reasons for why I hated myself so deeply, and so profoundly. The very next day, he came in yelling about improper reports filed, and the importance of rules, and as his lips were flapping, the words suddenly began to lose meaning, and something major happened to me. I was–enlightened. I took your advice, I told him to stick it up his ass, and I left. I just left. It was hard, because my job was all I had, and all I had ever cared about, how pathetic is that? I mean, look at me now, Mickey. I can have conversations with people without stuttering, or feeling my head swooning, do you understand the kind of freedom that makes me feel?"

I rubbed my forehead, breaking the eye contact he was holding with full confidence. I was confused, lost. Why should I care?

"Well," I said. "I'm very happy for you, Grant. You look good, and confident, and–changed, but you did it all on your own. I'm glad I could be of inspiration to you, but you didn't need to come and thank–"

"I want to be kidnapped," he interrupted, his eyes suddenly wider, his breath baited. I shook my head, looking over to Polaris, then back to Grant.

"Of course you do," I said sullenly. "Who doesn't

these days?" I couldn't understand the source of my apprehension, but what I did know was that I wanted nothing to do with Grant. He represented a piece of my life I simply wanted to forget. I was looking forward with blinders on, to hell with the past, it was the past, all I could see was the future, and Grant had no place in it.

"The thing is," he said, refusing to acknowledge my obvious resistance to his request. "I'm just beginning to feel the freedom of life, real life. I feel confident, and strong, and healthier than I ever believed possible, but I'm not all the way yet. Years of thinking like an idiot, reacting to my life like a wimp, doesn't just disappear over night. I'm on my way, but there is still plenty of mental walls I need to break through. I mean–"

"All right," I interrupted, raising my hand in the space between us. "Take it easy, Grant. This isn't some kind of seminar for the psychologically oppressed. I'm not giving anyone a psycho analysis and adjusting their experience accordingly. It's not a fucking self-help group."

"Yes it is!" he said quickly, intensely. "Yes it is, Mickey. Maybe you don't fully realize it now, but I've met with people who have already been through Crypto Fear. You've completely altered their lives for the better, seemingly forever."

I didn't believe it. I stared back in silence, frowning, trying to gauge where he was going with it. Altered people's lives–maybe. Forever? I was doubtful. And even if I had, and was, it still meant nothing to me. I was in it for the money, for the thrill, for the stability of my own future, what did I care what people did after they left the warehouse? I didn't, and I wouldn't. Crypto Fear was a form of entertainment, nothing else. If people got more out of it than that, great, but I had no interest in taking responsibility. Everyone was responsible for themselves, and blaming others for the good and bad aspects of their lives was nothing more than a cop out; it was a comfortable illusion designed to spare themselves of all responsibility. It was a pathetic way of thinking, and I certainly wanted no part of it.

"I don't know, Grant," I said, hesitant to even speak about it any further. I had no problems with beating the life out of a stranger, but Grant was no stranger. In fact, I had never truly liked the man to begin with. I simply wanted him to leave. "I don't want this to turn into something it's not. You need to understand, just like everyone else, that what we do in this warehouse is nothing more than entertainment. It's a kick, nothing more. Granted, it does get pretty intense, and at times even brutal, but I won't make any guarantees past that. If you don't get what you were looking for, well, it's not my fault. All I do is provide an experience, a non-refundable experience, the rest, I honestly couldn't care less about."

"Yes," he replied, nodding his head quickly, shifting his weight in his seat. "I understand. You only provide the vehicle for the catharsis."

What the hell did that even mean? The man was obviously unstable.

"I don't even know what that means," I replied. "And I don't want to–listen–what do you want, exactly?"

"The works," he smiled, his eyes unstable. "I want to be set free. I want to be kidnapped, and then I want to be beaten, and I would like to request a beating far worse than any you've delivered so far. I want to be an inch away from my death, broken from my mental cell."

I thought about the day I had blackmailed him with an internet porn video I had never even seen. He had been, and obviously still was, a strange little man who looked for kicks from things he didn't seem to fully understand. I didn't know how to proceed, or even what to tell him aside from the fact that he was making me incredibly uncomfortable. But on the flip side, I had done the exact same to him once upon a time. I was torn. I didn't want to accommodate his request, yet I felt bad for our past together. Karma was a fucking bitch.

"Here's twenty five hundred bucks," he said, sliding a thick envelope toward me, licking his lips in anticipation.

I sighed heavily, unwilling to proceed, but still, inexplicably, unable to deny the man the service. Who was I to judge him? This was for kicks, and the man wanted a kick. Why the hell did I even care? Crypto Fear was for making money, not for the benefit of my emotions. The man had cash and the willingness to go through with it; I had no real reason to deny anyone, regardless of my personal feelings.

"It's only two thousand, Grant," I sighed. "I know," he nodded. "Take the extra as a bonus, for the work you've already done."

I shook my head, feeling as though he wasn't fully understanding the terms. They needed to be made crystal clear to him. "Okay," I said. "But again, Grant, you really need to understand this. This is not some magical psychological examination of yourself. If it becomes that, then, it's on your own terms. This is for entertainment purposes only. Okay? Strictly, and solely, entertainment. Do you understand what I am saying?"

"Yes," he nodded excitedly, causing a wave of chagrin to wash through me. I explained the details of Crypto Fear to him, and even though he acted like he knew them already, I acted as though he didn't. He needed to fully understand. Once I was done, he signed the waiver with a shaky hand and beads of sweat streaming from the crown of his perfectly smooth head.

"All right," I said, staring at his signature. It was done. "That's it. You leave here and go back to whatever it is that you do, and when the time is right, we will take you." He was in full attention, his eyes wide and bright. "And here's a tip, Grant. I know you're looking for the most out of this experience, so when we come for you, the best thing you can do is to fight back, pretend that you're unwilling. If you act the part, it will provide you with the rush you're looking for."

"Perfect!" he exclaimed. "Absolutely. I can't wait. Thank you, Mickey. Thank you. This is going to be so great."

I nodded uncertainly, wanting him to leave. It was only ten in the morning, and I'd already had enough excitement for a week. I wanted solace, peace, far away from disturbed people like Grant. He was too much, too weird and unstable. I shouldn't have agreed to any of it, but the man had the money, plus a bonus; it was all I should have cared about. I was not involved with my customers. I didn't care who they were or what they did. Hand over the cash, I deliver on my promises, end of relationship. It felt wrong to do it to someone I knew, but he was convinced of his interest, and he would discover, just like the others, that I had no real advice for anyone. Your life sucks! You're a meaningless little shit! A punch to the face, and call it a day. That was the extent of my advice. Two thousand dollars for a repeat thrill, otherwise, leave me alone. This was my business. It was my life. Nothing else.

He thanked me repetitively, and was then escorted out of the building by Polaris. I watched him leave from the top window of the warehouse, sighing loudly as he did, still unsure of my decision to accept him as a client. Shortly after, Polaris returned, unconcerned with what had just happened.

"Where was he?" I asked.
"What?"

"Grant, where was he? How did he show up here?"
"I don't know," she said, shrugging. "I went out for coffee and he was in the parking lot when I got back."

"Really?" I frowned, shaking my head. "Then how the hell did he know where this place was?"

She arched her eyebrows and pursed her lips, "I don't know. Maybe someone told him."

"Maybe," I nodded. "It just–I just don't like this. I'm getting some bad vibes from him. I'm not sure I should have agreed to kidnap him."

"I'm sure it'll be fine," she said, and turned her attention to the hallway, to the blood on the floor. "So–what the hell happened, anyway?"

"With Steve? He ah–I don't really know. I woke up and he was freaking out, smashing everything. I had to stop him," I sighed loudly. "I don't know what the hell is going on with him lately."

"He's turning into an addict," she said plainly.

"Christ, he drinks everyday now, not to mention–"

"I know," I interrupted rather sternly. I already knew all about it. The man was my best friend. She didn't need to spell it out for me. "But what are we supposed to do? He's a grown man and he can do whatever he wants. As long as he's doing the job, which he is, what are any of us supposed to do about it?"

She looked at me strangely, her eyes conveying annoyance.

"I'll talk to him, all right? Just don't worry about it, okay?"

"Whatever," she said, the tone of her voice matching her rolling eyes. She was getting annoyed, and irritated with me, and truthfully, I with her. I couldn't understand why, but it was happening. Like everything else in my life, it suddenly felt like our relationship was also reaching a breaking point, like it was about to collapse into a fiery heap. Goddamn it. The truth was, I was also concerned about Steve, he was my best friend, after all, but I wanted Polaris to stay out of it. As involved as we all were in each others lives, it was none of her concern, or mine, really. Steve was capable of making his own decisions, I could talk to him about it, but I couldn't make him do anything he didn't want to do. Like everyone else, it was all up to him.

In the afternoon, I decided to drag his wasted body out of the den and shove him into the shower. I propped up his limp body against the shower wall, turned on the water, and waited for the sporadic moans and twitches to turn into awareness. Eventually, he began staring around himself, his eyes highly confused, and his mouth garbling nonsense for a while before going completely quiet, breathing laboriously, trapped in dark thoughts and evil memories. The guilt was feverish in his eyes.

"I'm really sorry, man," he whimpered, trying to hold back the tears, rubbing his swollen face with his hand. "I'm just, I don't know, man, I'm depressed lately. I'm just trying to get shit straight, but it seems like whenever I do, it just all gets thrown right back into my face."

I shook my head. "Nah, man. Look, we're making a fortune, things are good. I think we just need to concentrate on work. It's fine to let loose once in a while, but you know, I just want you to be careful, man. You're my best friend, and I love you, I don't want to see bad shit happen to you, you know? And I know it's none of my business, and you don't have to listen to me, but this Dominique girl, she's ruining your life, man. You need to deal with her, I don't want to have to beat the shit out of you again."

He smiled and snorted. "You got a lucky shot in," he said. "But I think you broke my fucking nose."

"Yeah, well–you should have seen your eyes, man. I thought you were going to eat my face."

We chuckled about it, but the guilt in his eyes was highly evident. He had screwed up, and he knew it, but I was unsure of if it would make a difference. In the heat of the moment, things were easy to say, but time always had a way of diminishing the apparent importance of things.

Eventually, enough stability returned to his legs, allowing him to stand in the shower, his clothes heavily drenched, but the fatigue was still overwhelming.

"I need some sleep, man," he said, despite having slept the better part of the day away. "I need to get my head together."

I nodded in understanding. "Yeah," I said. "Shit man, you scared the shit out of that girl too."

He stared at me, frowning, his eyes searching mine. "What girl?"

I smiled awkwardly, worried about my friend. "Never mind," I said. "You should sleep, man. We have a lot of work to do this week."

"Yeah," he nodded, forgetting about the girl, rubbing his eyes with his knuckles. I helped him up the stairs and into his room where a well deserved, "What the fuck?" was muttered from his mouth. I said nothing and simply helped him through the devastation inside to his bed. He was once again unconscious in minutes.

I spent the rest of the afternoon relaxing, smoking

joints and having a few drinks, reflecting on what was happening in my life. Crypto Fear, Polaris, Steve, The Terror, Grant–where was it all going? Why did I suddenly feel so threatened? Where were the undertones coming from? It felt strange to realize that I had reached my dreams, that my ideas were now reality, and yet, nothing felt quite like I had expected them to. It felt like meeting your favorite rock star, only to realize that he was just as human as you were. It was devastating, because no one wanted the same things, everyone wanted super heroes. They wanted people that were absolutely nothing like themselves, and everything they would never be. It was a powerful human fallacy, the desperate need to connect with some type of importance, no matter how artificial. That was the magic behind the success of Crypto Fear. What we were doing, what was truly happening in the warehouse, was destroying the comforts of living vicariously through larger than life ideals. When you walked out of Crypto Fear, you were the fucking rock star. How long could such a thing really last?

CHAPTER 29

Steve was rolling on the sidewalk cupping his already broken nose, moaning in agony. "Son of a bitch!" he snapped, his ski mask half up the length of his face, the blood flowing from in between his fingers. Grant, it turned out, was one vicious bastard. He had obviously taken my advice of fighting back to heart and unleashed a hell storm of trouble for us. When Steve had lunged for him from the van, he was instantly met with a hard punch to the face before his feet had even hit the sidewalk. It was almost as if he had known that we were there, stalking, waiting for him, but how? Once Steve had hit the ground, his nose gushing excessive amounts of blood, Grant had taken the opportunity to kick him hard in the ribs before sprinting down the street in an attempt to avoid capture.

"Shit!" I yelled. "Polaris, get Steve back in here, I'm going after Grant. Come and find us with the van, quick!"

"Get up, man!" I yelled at Steve. "This cocksucker isn't getting away from us!"

Grant, a skinny, feebly framed man, was surprisingly fast. He was already far ahead of me when I started chasing after him. He found an alley and cut in between two buildings trying to escape my view. I made it to the alley just in time to catch sight of him rounding the corner, following another alley that ran the width of a building, but I was catching up, surprised by how quick a man at least fifteen years my senior could be. I was determined to catch him! I rounded the corner, catching sight of him throwing garbage in my way, which I dodged, and soon found myself close behind him. He turned to look back, seeing that I was closing in, but he wasn't giving in. I was losing my breath, my stamina being pushed, but I wasn't giving up.

"Come and get me, Mickey!" he yelled, and pulled his head down, trying to find every ounce of energy he could muster. I was getting close, only feet away, closer, closing the gap, I pulled the gun from my belt and brought it crashing down on top of his right shoulder. Like a lifeless puppet, he collapsed to the ground, dizzy, and moaning in pain. Before he could move again, I kneeled on the back of his neck and desperately searched for the van.

"Come on!" I yelled, my voice echoing off the building walls. "Where the hell are you?" The van needed to show up soon, or else it would all go horribly wrong. The street we had attempted to grab Grant on had been packed with witnesses. Surely the police were on their way, and it was that fear that was causing my heart to pump hard with anxiety. What if they'd already been confronted by the police? What then? I would have to escape from the bowels of the city like a fugitive. And then what? I still had to pay The Terror. The police were an unwelcomed possibility.

My phone suddenly rang, it was a frantic Polaris. "Where are you?" she screamed. "The cops are coming, I can hear them. Where are you?"

"An alley, to your right," I said. "You can't miss us." I suddenly saw the van zoom by, passing us in a hurry before coming to a violent halt. She reversed while I picked up Grant's moaning mass from the pavement, pushing him with vehemence toward the street. I could hear the sirens, this was the closest we had ever been to getting caught. Steve slid the door open in rage. "Get in here, you cocksucker!" he snapped, and pulled Grant inside by the ear lobe, screaming obscenities into his face. His body thumped inside of the van, but he was still fighting us off, his limbs flailing wildly in every direction. I managed to punch him in the face, causing him to wince and present us with an opportunity to jump on top of him, struggling to get his arms and legs tied. Polaris was already speeding down the street, desperate to avoid capture by the police, but Grant was still screaming at the top of his lungs.

"Shut him up!" Polaris screamed. "He's making me nervous. Shut up!"

Steve landed another hard blow to Grant's head, trying to shut him up, but to no avail. I took off my shirt and fashioned a gag with it, then tied it over his bagged head, not stopping the screams, but muffling them to a more comfortable level. The blaring sirens suddenly seemed distant, promising us an imminent escape, satisfying us with a fantastic thrill. It had been close, but close was still not a definite of any kind.

At the warehouse, the van came to an abrupt stop. Steve and I grabbed Grant with violence, angry with him, and about to let him know all about it. We tied him to the chair and took the bag off of his head, but we found ourselves staring at a disheartening sight. The man was smiling, bloodied, and waiting for the apex of the experience.

"Get that fucking smile off your face!" I snarled, and back handed him as hard as I could. His head snapped back, his eyes closed, but the smile never left. He looked at me again, his breathing heavy, intense, his face desperate for more. I would give it to him. I could feel it bubbling inside of me. He was about to get it for all of the times I had bitten my tongue and said nothing, all of the times I had watched him fail to gain authority on a situation, and for all of the times the entire ensemble of staff, supervisors, and managers had gathered together, pointing at him in ridicule, laughing at him behind his back, and directly to his face, and not once, not a single time had he taken a stance for himself. He was a pathetic little dweeb!

"Give it to me," he whispered.
Crack!

I smashed my fist into his face, feeling his cheek bone crack with the blow.

"Give it to me!" he snarled.
Crack!

His head twisted like a rubber doll's. His breathing was heavy, his eyes disturbed, unfocussed, yet intent on punishment.

"Give it!" he screamed.

I knew what he wanted. He, like the others, wanted the lecture. He wanted the words more than the actual beating. The blows were the bonus, the way of getting the point across; the words were the weapons used to decimate. Luckily for him, I was feeling especially frustrated with the world lately, and he was about to be the useless sack of shit I took it out on at somewhere near one hundred bucks per blow. It came flowing out of me like a beautiful tune.

"You're a sorry excuse for a man!"

Crack!

"Your life is as important to the world as a goddamn hole to the head!"

Crack!

I felt a tooth break, his jaw shifted unnaturally.

"How sad is it that your entire sex life takes place in front of a goddamn computer? You're a fucking loser! Useless, and unimportant to anyone, anywhere. You're less than dog shit!"

Crack!

"Jerking off to strangers!"

Crack!

"Void of any meaningful human connections!"

Crack!

I felt an eye socket split, the swelling instant.

"No fucking reason to live!"

Crack!

His face was horribly smashed, but he was still panting, begging for more of the nonsense, and suddenly, I found myself beyond nonsense–I simply lost it. I fell out of character, snapped, and gave the whole thing a horrible personal edge. I lunged at him, chocking him with one hand and jamming my knee into his chest, blasting fist after fist into his horribly beaten face.

"I fucking hate you!" I snapped. "You're a goddamn pussy! A fifty year old fucking loser! A little boy loving cocksucker that should be hung by his balls and dragged behind a fucking truck!"

Crack! Crack! Crack!

"You pussy! You scared little shit faced cockroach!" my throat was horribly dry, my voice hoarse, and pushed to its limits. I was lost in my own personal rage. "I should do the world a favor and put a fucking bullet in your head!" I grabbed the Glock and pressed it hard against his forehead. "Is that what you want? Huh? You want me to end it all for you? You want me to blow your sadistic little brains out all over the walls? Tell me!" I screamed into his face, my eyes blinded, my body shaking violently. "Tell me why I shouldn't do it? Tell me why I should let you live? Tell me why, goddamn it! Tell me!"

I stepped back and noticed that his eyes were suddenly filled with muted fear, terror—what the hell was I doing? He was obviously petrified, fully believing that his life was over. I raised the gun into the air and slammed the butt of it into the side of his head, instantly causing the animated life to leave him. He fell to the concrete floor, still strapped to the chair, flopping and twitching like a damaged fish.

"Jesus Christ!" I heard Steve's terrified voice from behind me. "What the fuck, man? I think you fucking killed him!"

I had no idea. I had been so caught up in the moment, so enraged by his stupid little face and his scared little eyes lusting after some kind of arcane truth that never existed, I hadn't noticed where he was at before I tried to kill him. I was still fighting the urge to empty the Glock's clip into him.

"Oh, my God!" Polaris whispered, passing by me to join Steve and check if the broken body still had a beating heart. I was exhausted. Lost, and angry. I was thrilled. I looked at Grant's body, and then to Steve's and Polaris's concerned eyes, frightened. He was horribly beaten, mulched into a mangled carcass on the floor. I couldn't see him breathing, but there were still no excited screams coming from the other two. He was still alive.

"Put him in the den," I said, just barely catching my breath.

"You almost fucking killed him, man!" Steve snapped, truly enraged. "What the fuck are you doing? He needs to get to a hospital, he won't last the night."

"This is what he wanted," I said, unperturbed by their concerns. "Just do it."

"Fuck sakes!" Steve snapped, shaking his head in disbelief. The blood was already collecting into a pool under Grant's head. I coughed horribly, totally wasted, shaking violently.

"Just put him in the fucking room!" I snapped. "I don't fucking care anymore!"

CHAPTER 30

For weeks, I had no idea of what had happened to Grant. Neither Polaris, nor Steve would tell me anything about it. I suspected that they had taken the broken fool out of the Monkey Den in the middle of the night and raced his failing health to the hospital, but I had never received a firm response about it. They had been angry with me, were still angry with me. Kidnapping people and beating them senseless was one thing, but losing your mind and nearly killing one of them, well, that was a trip neither one of them was prepared to take. It was too risky, knowing full well that no matter who had done the beating, all three of us would be held accountable for the end result. Too much.

Polaris, for one, was especially angry with me because of the fact that I would not admit that the true source of my outburst lay in the fact that I had seen myself in Grant's eyes, and attacked. It was pure foolishness. I had nothing in common with Grant. He was the embodiment of everything I hated about modern society. He represented all of the squabbling little wimps I saw every day crying about self-indulgent trivialities. He was the face of those who were too stupid to see the hypocrisy of their convictions or their affinity to complete ignorance; those who preferred illusion above all sense of logic, reality, or rationality.

The fake, the insane, the wannabee degenerates preaching their self-serving ideas as unfounded truths, and then claiming offense from any challenge–refusing to acknowledge that they were by far the most offensive, foul, and moronic pieces of shit fucking idiots to have ever roamed the earth.

He was the symbol of those too weak to take control

of their lives, too scared to be themselves, and too damn gullible to take a stand against the status quo in any way. The fact that the willful choosing of superstitious ignorance was still so prevalent after thousands of years was quite simply flabbergasting. That was offensive, and that was what Grant had awoken in me. A seething hate for those who acted as though anyone was supposed to care about their skewed opinions or beliefs. They could all kiss my ass, and so could Grant, and Polaris, and even Steve for that matter. I'd had enough of it, and the next motherfucker who cried to me about how crappy their pampered little life was, was going to get a goddamn bullet in the head. I wondered what had happened? When had the planet become a breeding ground for bleeding heart weaklings? Where were the strong minded beings who gave hope to the future of the human race? I felt like I was about to collapse from the pressure, from the rage. My entire life suddenly felt dark, putrid, and filled with hatred. Loathing. I could no longer even trust myself to beat anyone, I was afraid of myself, knowing deep down that it was only a matter of time before I truly did crush someone's skull open like a watermelon against the cement. I had to do something, and Polaris wasn't helping anything, because beyond my seething hate of society settling in, she was also upset with me because I refused to choke her anymore. I simply didn't want to. There was just too much depravity in my life, and I suddenly found myself wanting to have a normal, human relationship, not some form of psychological disfunction. Of course, being highly depraved of her coveted suicide orgasms, she was nowhere near happy about it. I would hear about it endlessly; how she couldn't feel the excitement of pushing it further and further, she couldn't feel alive, she couldn't blah, blah, blah, blah, blah, blah. It irritated the hell out of me, and as of late, in true adult fashion, our conversations usually ended with wild screaming, and big displays of intimidation. I was losing myself. Where was I going? What was I supposed to do? What was Crypto Fear even about? I was suffering through some type of mass identity crisis, and every second of it was brutal. There was no taming it. I needed to relax, but there seemed to be no escape.

In reality, I occasionally did find myself wondering about Grant, and how badly I had actually hurt him. Had he gone to the hospital for obscene amounts of stitches and medical grade staples to close the gaping gashes? Had his jaw been wired shut in a nasty seam, forcing him to eat liquids through a straw? Had he been reduced to a dumb beast, wearing helmets and slobbering his laughs all over the front of his chest? Nobody knew, but what I did know, was that something odd was happening out there, and it wasn't doing anything except heightening my rabid sense of hate for the world I lived in. Crypto Fear had been my baby, my love, but with every passing day, that love was beginning to erode. Out there, in the sea of destitute failures and lost wanderers, something was stirring the very cores of their souls like a sinister tornado. Suddenly, more people than I had ever seen were converging toward me, lusting for the dream, hungry for the illusion, horny for the unrivaled adrenaline pumped experience no one else could offer them. Crypto Fear–the answer to everyone's life–except my own.

The uncanny, the professional, the respected, the wasted, all of them were suddenly discarding their social statuses and coming in with paws full of cash, and desperate looks in their eyes. They all wanted the works. It was overwhelming, and we could no longer handle the amount of bodies flooding through our doors, or the nervous voices clogging up the phone lines. It had all become quite absurd, and especially since the change was doing nothing except confirming what Grant had told me. I was changing people's lives, forever. But who the hell was I? I was no one. I was barely a businessman. I was a fool, filled with foolish ideas that had caught on with other fools who identified with my idiocy. I didn't know what to do about it; aside from recognizing the need for more employees, more vans, and more violence than I could ever have thought possible, there didn't seem to be a way to slow it down. Sure, I was paying The Terror back with ease, but the pride I had originally felt seemed absent. My heart was resisting the success, my soul firmly against it, because I was suddenly feeling trapped by it all, and the hard truth of the matter was that it no longer mattered whether I was beginning to hate what I was doing or not–none of it was over until The Terror was paid in full. Until then, my only choice was to fight through the flaring chagrin inside of me, bite my tongue, put my head down, and just keep going.

I had to expand. The business was growing on its own, and I suddenly found myself trying to keep up with it, instead of the other way around. Organization–I needed to establish better systems, more efficient ways of delivering the Crypto Fear experience to the people shoving insane amounts of cash into my face.

Over the course of a few weeks, I spent most of my time training new employees in what was undoubtably the strangest orientation day any of them had ever encountered. Strictly hands on; thrown to the wolves. One of them broke his foot on his very first kidnapping. Another broke her hand after beating the life out of some Suzy homemaker type with 15 kids and a husband who cared about nothing more than to drink, beat, and stick his fertile organ into her. Those had been naturally adept to it, but it wasn't all smooth sailing. When grooming new employees, it was instantly apparent which ones had the heart for it, and which didn't. A prospect named Derek simply couldn't handle the pressure when push came to shove. He tried beating a man, a car salesman, but was unable to reach that special zone of depravity necessary to deliver on the promise. He broke down and sobbed like a little girl, complaining that his conscious wouldn't allow him to cause such harm to another human being. It was pathetic, but I suppose the whole world couldn't be completely insane like the rest of us. There was no place for wimps in Crypto Fear; he would have to settle for working in his favorite pleasant coffee shop instead.

In no time at all, the gears were once again spinning at top speed, churning through the demand, ensuring that The Terror would be paid in full, and then–well–then I would decide on what to do. In the meantime, McDonald's could sell millions of burgers per year, Starbucks could serve millions of coffees, but I could organize and execute thirty kidnappings per week. It was stunning, but I couldn't ignore my feelings forever. With the relentless waves of people coming out of the woodwork with wide eyes and excited smiles, I found myself wondering about their motivations. Was it really just due to the numbers? Do it to enough people and they will tell others, in turn multiplying the level of customers? It could have been, but judging from the intensity by which people were demanding to be beaten, I was highly suspicious of it. There seemed to be a strong and sudden increase in the amount of word of mouth spreading on the streets, but from where? How? I doubted that it was due to past customers, mostly because the majority of them wouldn't tell friends and family the truth about what had happened to their horrible faces. They would lie, and make things up; not everyone was prepared to hear about the wild depravity that was happening in the warehouse. So where was it all coming from? I couldn't figure it out, but I felt that soon enough, the source of it would come out, and I could only hope that it was something that we could deal with.

      I had the whole thing stringently organized, my employees focussed, every thought concentrated on the goal, every action carefully planned for optimum performance. For weeks, everything was being controlled, until something new started to emerge which seemed to me far worse than the simple number of people coming through our doors and looking for the ultimate kick. It was something so subtle, and obscure, that I wasn't quite sure of how long it had gone unnoticed. But after a few weeks, there was no longer an option of ignoring it in any way. This new trend was nothing more than a context for a bunch of words to be strung together and deliver a message, but it was the lurking message coming at me from the shadows that I wished I had never been made aware of. Suddenly, through the telephones, the doors, and from all corners of the city, the words varied, but the message remained the same. It sounded a little bit like this; "Hi there, I was wondering if I could request the healing of

Master Mickey?"
      What the hell did that mean?

CHAPTER 31

For Polaris, Steve, and I, the success of Crypto Fear had given us all better lives. We had more money than ever, and open options to do what we wanted with it. We were feeling rather secure in our future–but success had hardly come without a cost. Our relationship, both individually and as a group, was severely beginning to suffer. We worked together, taught new employees together, but outside of work, after hours, we barely spoke to each other unless it was absolutely necessary. It was horrible, and I hated every second of it, but what was I supposed to do? It felt like it was already too late, the damage was done, settled, and decided. We would work together, and get along, but superficially at best. There was no one defining incident that had caused this rift between us, which often made thinking about worse, but it had all definitely started with the savage beating I had unleashed on Grant. That bastard, I knew I should never have taken him on. He had shifted something inside of me, changed me in a way I couldn't really define, but I definitely felt it lurking behind my every thought. It was haunting, and disturbing, and making me doubt the full stability of my own mind. What could I do? What was done, was done. The past could never be changed, we could only adjust for the future. Welcome to life.

We had decided, now that the business was fully self-sustaining, that we would at the very least remain as the original team of kidnappers. The team that would take on clients we felt couldn't be handled as efficiently by others. It was working fine, we were standing each other, and truthfully, it was forcing us to speak to each other. It was something I suddenly felt like I needed, because while I was trying to deal with the new trend of weird minds speaking my name like I was some kind of defective deity, there was another aspect of it that came to light, and it scared the life out of all three of us, not just me. The sudden paranoia started with a van, a black van that was suddenly making an appearance wherever we happened to be. The first time we had noticed it, we were speeding wildly down a street, fresh from nabbing a fool, when the van had come at us out of nowhere. Polaris had inevitably clipped the front bumper, but we hadn't dared stop with so many unknowns. And lately, it seemed like every time we were stalking someone, readying our attack from the back of the van, the same words would come out of our mouths. "Jesus, look! Is that the van? Christ, it is! Who the fuck is that? What do think they want?" There were no answers, and the possibilities were making it unbearable. It could be anyone. The police. Reporters. Or maybe even some obsessed psycho, a stalker for the stalkers. It was beginning to affect our performance, and it was clouding our minds with worry. We often wondered if we should we keep going, but what other options did we have?

***

We pulled up to the curb, our victim in sight, the sidewalk crowded with pedestrians, the conditions perfect for a quick kidnapping, and yet–

"Goddamn it!" I snapped, truly frustrated. "Look, there it is again. Who the fuck is that?"

Polaris and Steve stared intently, silently, at the black van parked half a block on the other side of the street, watching. The anxiety this stupid vehicle was causing was unacceptable. Something needed to be done about it, and soon, but what? It was too much.

"I don't know, man," Steve said, shaking his head, and following his statement with a swig from his flask.

"Jesus Christ," I said, shaking my head. "It's nine in the morning, man. Put that shit away, we have to get this job done, and then you can do whatever you want."

He shrugged, but said nothing in response and put the flask into his pocket, riveting his eyes on the van down the street.

"Do you think it's the cops?" asked Polaris. "Could be, I guess," I shrugged, no longer certain of anything. "The Police, or–I don't know. Who the hell would want to follow us like this? And–how? How can they know where we are, what we're doing? It doesn't make any fucking sense."

"Could be a reporter," Steve added. "Maybe," I said, lighting a cigarette, trying to stow away the anxiety building in my chest. "But I don't know. It just–it doesn't feel right. It's pretty fucking scary, actually."

They nodded in agreement, their eyes on the van, ignoring the customer we were about to take. This particular sighting was the fifth of the week. All over the city, wherever we were stationed, from a distance, looming, there it was. Its hopelessly tinted windows gave us nothing from the inside. Something was going on, something bad was happening, and having only the faintest hint of it was driving me insane. What was responsible for these idiots suddenly changing my name to 'Master Mickey'? Who was in that goddamned van? It was unbearable.

My phone rang, snapping my attention from the van. I answered quickly, but the voice on the other side served only to make me angrier than I already was. "Is this Master Mickey?" the voice asked, and something surged inside of me. Wrath! "No, goddamn it!" I screamed. "Wrong number! This is Master Molester! Now, fuck off!" I hung up, staring with wide eyes to Polaris and Steve. "What the hell is going on with this–this Master bullshit?"

"I don't know," Steve shrugged, having another swing of his flask. "But it sure is profitable." Almost immediately, our attention was returned to the van. "I'm going to go see who it is," Steve said.

"What?"

"The van," he pointed to it. "I'm going to try just walking up to it. What's the worse that could happen?"

I could have riffled off a list, but the truth was that I wanted to know as badly as they did, maybe even more. I was desperate.

"I'll be right back," he said, pulling open the door and wobbling outside, being sure to keep out of sight of our prey who was still oblivious to our presence. He stumbled off balance, and just as he came around our vehicle and faced the van, the headlights suddenly lit up with the roar of the engine, and the vehicle peeled straight past us down the street.

"Jesus!" he said, jumping back into the van. "Somebody's anti-social."

"Yeah," I said suspiciously. "What the fuck is going on?"

We hadn't seen it again after that, and we were able to pull off the kidnapping without a hitch, waiting for our prey to make it further down the street before unleashing our attack. That side of the business was good and well, but the rest of it felt like it was falling apart. Spinning far out of my control. Every phone call seemed to include the words, *"Master Mickey? Is this he, himself? Do you really answer phone calls?"* The words were infected with tones of idolization, but how the hell did these people even know who I was? It didn't make any sense. "I want the Master to heal me." "I want the Master to beat me." "I want to have the Master's babies." Goddamn it. Something needed to be done.

***

"Look!" I pointed far down the street. "See it?"
"Yeah," they both nodded, their eyes frightened, suspicious.

"Oh, my God," Polaris mumbled. "This is creepy. What are we going to do?"

"I don't know," I said. "This is the fourth time this weekend."

"We should kidnap the fucker," Steve said.
"Yeah," I replied. "Kidnap him and beat the shit out of him– or them."

"Yeah–what if there's more than one?"

"I–I don't know anymore, guys, but whoever it is, they seem to be a step ahead of us all the time. How could they know where we are when even the employees have no idea of where we are? Have you guys seen it around the warehouse at all?"

They both shook their head. Neither had I. "Well we can't keep going like this forever," I said. "God-damn it, this is getting ridiculous."

"I don't know," Steve said. "Maybe we should shoot at them, that would get the point across."

"Unless they're cops," I said. "Fuck sakes." I was at a loss, but there was no longer any time for debate, our prey was in sight, unsuspecting. It was time to kidnap him, and then move on to the rest of our busy day. In a flash, we attacked our victim, but not without constantly looking over our shoulders, forever paranoid. We took the geek off the street and shoved him violently into the van, speeding toward the warehouse, haunted by a brutal silence on the way. We were too enthralled with staring out of the windows, keeping a keen eye on the black van. It followed us faithfully for a few blocks, even taking our deliberate detours, keeping us in sight before suddenly, inexplicably, turning off and disappearing into traffic. Impossible. I stared at Steve and Polaris, my eyes reflecting their thoughts. Why didn't it ever follow us all the way back to the warehouse?

The geek stranded on the floor of the van was giggling excitedly, pumping himself up with "How awesome" it was all going to be. We should have been telling him to shut up, punching him in the head in retaliation for every sound he made, but we were stunned with uneasiness. When we finally arrived at the warehouse, I was focussed on a single idea. This idiot we had just taken had specifically asked for the '*Master*', and I was going to find out why. Enough was enough, I needed to understand what was happening. I needed to fend off the threat I could feel, but not define with any certainty. After parking the van, I told Steve and Polaris to set him up, I was going to do this kid myself. I ran upstairs, automatically checking the messages. There were fifty eight of them, each saying filthy things like, "Yes, hello, this message is for Master Mickey," and, "I just wanted to thank you, Master, for the fantastic confidence you've instilled in me," and, "Master. I need your help. My life is horribly shattered. Can you call me back? I desperately need this." Master. Master. Master. Master.

"Fuck!" I snapped. "Is this some kind of joke? What the fuck is happening?"

I frantically searched through my junk drawer for a digital voice recorder. I violently snatched the thing and made my way back downstairs, fuming with rage. I opened the door to the room, and there he was, the geek, sitting there with a smile on his face, not believing that the Master himself was about to beat him into submission. He was staring at me like I was some kind of hero, some kind of guru with answers, some kind of fucking rock star, larger than life and above everyone else. Enough! I pressed the record button and put the machine on the floor. Cracking my knuckles, I approached him with murderous intent. He was just about to open his mouth and say something stupid, when I punched him hard in the face, screaming crazily, unhinged.

"Who am I?" I demanded.

"Wh–what?" he mumbled, the fear in his eyes obvious, this wasn't what he had expected.

Crack!

"Who the fuck am I?" I screamed again. "Who am I? How did you get my number?"

The confusion was heavy in his eyes, wondering what was happening, why was I so angry? This wasn't what he had heard about, nor was it necessarily what he had paid for, but that was hardly my concern. I needed some answers, immediately.

Crack! His nose gushed with blood.

"Do you work for the police? Who are you?" I was losing control, my arms shaking unsteadily, my eyes horribly focussed on the fool before me.

"I– I..." he stuttered. Unacceptable!

Crack!

"How do you know me?" I screamed again. "Why do you call me Master? Tell me, goddamn it! Now!"

Crack!

"It's all over the streets, man!" he finally garbled through his swollen lips.

"What is? Tell me, you motherfucker!" I lost my composure and paced around the room pulling on my hair, trying to catch my breath. "Answer me!" I screamed, and landed another hard punch in his face.

"Argh!" he winced. "On the streets, man!" he was begging now. "It's all over the place."

"What is? Tell me, now!" I paced the room feverishly, rabidly, trying to make sense of what he was saying. Who the hell was out there trying to get me?

"You're the savior, man. You're like a god."

I stopped dead in my tracks, riveting my insane eyes on the fool, something sinister exploding inside of my brain.

"I'm what?" I whispered, unwilling to admit that I had heard him the first time around.

"You're a–you're a god, man. You save people."

Rage filled my veins, and without even realizing it, I kicked him so hard in the head that his body crashed onto the floor, totally unconscious.

"Fuck!" I screamed in frustration, rubbing my face with trembling hands, sweating profusely, ready to break down in tears. "What does that mean? This isn't good, man. This is no good!" I continued pacing the room, unfocussed, a thousand thoughts per second racing through my mind. I couldn't make sense of anything. I felt threatened. What did anyone want from me? What had happened to the entertainment? This had nothing to do with it. It felt like everything was failing now, crumbling right in front of my eyes, and there was nothing I could do about it. The end suddenly felt very near. Something was about to break, and the consequences were unknown, the future–dark. What were we going to do?

CHAPTER 32

Sheets of rain assaulted the frail exterior of the warehouse, accurately reflecting my overall mood. Soggy, foul, and vengeful. I held the recorder close to my face, endlessly rewinding and replaying the same chilling sentence.

"You're the savior, man! You're like a god!" Every time I heard it, I couldn't help but shake my head in disdain as a fresh wave of self-loathing washed through me. How could it have happened? More importantly, what was I supposed to do about it? I didn't know. I was frustrated, and angry, and unwilling to keep going with Crypto Fear–I was losing my grip on it. The whole thing had slid sideways, spun out of control, and was suddenly far beyond my understanding. A master. A god. A savior. Fucking ridiculous. I was filled with confusion, desperate to find answers, determined to solve the mystery of the black van. Where could I turn? Who could I speak to? It felt hopeless.

I stared out of the window, uncomfortable in my own skin, incapable of focussing my thoughts to find any kind of realistic answer. Everything seemed unrealistic, fake, threatening. The silence of the room felt oppressive, heightening my worries, deepening my depression. I was alone, upstairs in the warehouse, trapped in my very own nightmare. Steve was out partying again with a slew of filth ridden women, still allowing Dominique to destroy his emotions, still compensating with wild binges and kinky fornications. I probably wouldn't see him for a while, maybe days.

The pressure inside of me was crushing, and it was certainly made no better by a new parasite gnawing at the back of mind, and that parasite's name, was Polaris. Only a few days ago, she had beaten the pretty boy look right off of some muscle inflated meathead. His name was Brett. Brett had cried and whimpered like a little girl under the violent beating Polaris had delivered onto him. Brett had called her afterward, "just as a friend", and then picked her up for dinner. By now they were probably talking about how sweet it was that he was sensitive enough to cry. What a demeaning little prick! Sure, our relationship had never been a staple of stability, the whole thing was based on weird fetishes no one truly understood. Furthermore, on most days, I hated her depressing little guts anyway. I couldn't stand her, and vice versa, but we had continued with the illusion of primal love through pain. I shouldn't have cared, I thought about dumping her on a regular basis, but for some reason, this Brett motherfucker, I wanted to beat him to death, free of charge. I wanted him to feel my fists cracking his ribs. I wanted to listen to him plead and cry for me to stop. He was threatening my only escape hatch. I wanted her degraded, diseased, demented little needs all to myself. I needed her to need me. Fuck my life, I couldn't take it anymore.

I rewound the recording and listened to it again. "You're the savior, man! You're like a god!"

I suppose some would argue that I should have been quite satisfied with the recent turn of events. My little dream had worked far beyond my expectations, The Terror was nearly paid off, with interest, and I had even managed to become some kind of demented idol to throngs of people who wanted nothing more than to shove more money into my face, indefinitely–but I wasn't. What I was, was disgusted, and annoyed beyond acceptance. I was repulsed by it, unable to understand how I had lost control over every aspect of my life, simultaneously. Crypto Fear had started as an amateurish plan to take over the world, placing us in total control of our lives. It had started as an exciting challenge between Polaris, and Steve, and I, but now, it was turning very ugly, very fast. So ugly, between Steve and his drug induced comas, and Polaris with her unending unhappiness, and with all the money, and all the bullshit that came with it, it was now fully obvious–Crypto Fear had ruined our lives, not made anything better. We hated each other, barely even spoke to each other, and everyone was off chasing after their own pursuits. Steve was gone, Polaris was gone, and all that was left was me, trying to push back the weight before it crushed me to death.

I sighed heavily, throwing the voice recorder to my side, lighting a cigarette while staring out into the drenched parking lot when a voice from downstairs suddenly snapped me out of my horrible thoughts.

"Mickey? Are you home?"

"Goddamn it!" I snapped. My face instantly flooded with heat, anger blasted through my veins. "Who the hell is this now? Some other rat faced freak looking for me to deliver him from evil? Fucking lunatics!" I stomped down the stairs, ready to kick someone in the face, but when I got there, I was stunned.

"Mr. Labelle?" I said, the air caught in my lungs. "Oh, hi, kid," he smiled, his eyes darting around the place, his three bodyguards looming behind him. "Wow," he said. "Things have been good for you over here, haven't they?"

"Well, they're okay," I replied, suddenly feeling sheepish. "Please, come in. Would you like a drink?"

"I sure would," he smiled. "I sure would." They followed me upstairs where I poured a whisky for The Terror.

"None for them," he pointed to his goons. "They're on duty."

"Right," I said, and sat down on the sofa opposite him, handing him his drink. "So, what can I do for you, sir?"

His eyes wandered aimlessly about the place, sizing it up, taking it in.

"You've been having some success, haven't you?" he asked.

"Well, it's starting, I guess," I replied. "Thanks to you, by the way. And I will also have the rest of your money by next week."

"Yes. Yes," he said, waving it off with his hand in the air. "I am not worried. I trust you."

I smiled uneasily, wondering what he was doing; why had he come to the warehouse unannounced? The man had never once stepped foot inside since I had moved in. Why now?

"You know, Mickey," he said. "The word on the street is that you've been able to elevate yourself as some kind of hero, or something like that. A god? Is that right?'

"Yeah," I said hesitantly, uncomfortably. "It's ah–it's all a big misunderstanding. I'm trying to deal with it as we speak. These people are very confused."

"Deal with it?" he questioned. "I am failing to follow your logic. What are you trying to deal with, exactly?"

"Well," I stuttered. "I don't know. I–I have to stop this somehow. It's pretty unnerving."

"Unnerving?" he arched his eyebrows high and had a drink from his whiskey. "Looks to me as though it is working quite well in your favor, no?"

"Um–well–I suppose. I mean..."

"You mean what?" he questioned. "Mickey," he shifted his weight in his seat. "A true businessman plays into the hand of profit. He does not fold the hand because of unfavorable personal feelings. Money is more than you, and so is your business. You don't try to stop things when they play directly into your profit, that is completely unreasonable. Your feelings have nothing to do with it."

I stared strangely, wondering why he was lecturing me, suspicious of his every word. What was he doing? What did he want?

"Mr. Labelle," I said, frowning in confusion. "Is there anything in particular that I can help you with?"

"Well, Mickey," he smiled, straightening his posture as he did. "Now that you mention it, there is."

Please no!

"I want to be kidnapped," he said, and caused my heart to sink. I couldn't do this.

"Really?" I replied sullenly, beaten.

"No, not really," he smiled widely. "What do you think I am, some weak little pole choker with no sense of excitement in life? Come on, Mickey. I can't believe you would think that."

I chuckled uncomfortably, "I'm sorry, Mr. Labelle. "It's just that–"

"I want a piece of it," he interrupted, squinting his eyes, demanding that I keep eye contact with him. My heart sank, the bastard was planning to extort me!

"A piece of it?" I asked. "How do you mean, sir?" "I mean cold hard cash," he said. "Really, Mickey, I know you're not this stupid. Don't insult me by pretending."

I had nothing to say. I simply stared, until words spontaneously began forming in my head, "Ah–I mean–how... How much?"

He didn't hesitate for a second, "Twenty thousand per week." He sipped on his drink, unbothered by any of my emotions.

"Twenty thousand per week?" I exclaimed, completely astonished.

"Did I stutter?" he replied. "You charge two thousand dollar a head in this place, and you pull this little stunt of yours what, an average of thirty times a week? I did fail sixth grade mathematics, but by my calculations, that sixty thousand dollars a week, in cash, amounting to over three million dollars a year, also in cash. Now, I lent you the money to start this little thing here, I gave you a safe place to operate from, and now, I want you to be grateful for it and give me my dues."

"But–"

"Don't argue with me, Mickey," he warned, sternly pointing a finger at me. "You know what happens to people who argue with me. If you give me any trouble, I'll have your tongue cut out and rammed up your ass, but I don't want to have to do that, kid. I like you, and you're some kind of important monk or whatever now, you're what people are paying for. You're the big star here, and my request is nowhere near unreasonable. Capitalize on what's going on, and put the fucking money in my hand. No problems."

This couldn't be happening. Not now, not this! I was

having enough trouble without this, I was almost done, this was bad. It was far worse than anything else that was going on.

"Mr. Labelle, please," I said, trying to reason with the man, but he wasn't a particular fan of it.

"Mickey," he pointed his finger again, his face forever stern. "You came to me, not the other way around. If you don't comply, perhaps I should tell you about this very special lady I know. She is vey rich, and for unexplained reasons, she loves nothing more than to pay top dollar for what she lovingly refers to as, testicular jewelry. She's into that sort of thing, one of those dedicated feminists, or whatever." His goons chuckled with him, but I was far from amused. "Either way, it doesn't matter. What does, is that if you don't pay me, it'll be your balls she hangs off her earlobes at cocktail parties, do you understand me?"

I swallowed hard. No one could possibly mistake the message. It was the exact same message as before Crypto Fear even existed, back when I was working like a good little slave for uncle Sam–pay or die, bitch. Pay or die.

"Do you understand me?" he asked again.
I nodded yes, and suddenly felt my phone vibrating in my pocket, but I was too stunned to look at it. I was debating on what to say next. Was there an escape from this? A compromise? Shit, I was fucked.

"How do you know so much about what I'm doing here?" I asked. "I mean, you've never asked me a single question about it. You've never even been in here once since I started."

"Mickey," he said as though I was a naive little boy. "I've been watching. Do you think anything happens on those streets that I don't know about? I wouldn't be very good at what I did if I didn't know, would I?"

Instantly, I thought about the van. The black van, always nearby, watching from the shadows, following us everywhere. How could I have been so stupid? How could I honestly have believed that he wouldn't know exactly what I was doing? It was becoming wholly evident to me that I was incredibly stupid, and far too inexperienced to honestly have believed that I could have tackled something with such big risks and come out unscathed. I was in way over my head; I hadn't even seen him coming. I was completely screwed.

"Right," I said. "I know. I'm sorry."
He smiled, seemingly quite pleased with himself. He downed the rest of his drink and placed the empty glass on the coffee table between us.

"Well," he said. "That's it. I am sure you will not disappoint me."

I nodded no, unable to get the words out of my mouth.

"Good then," he replied. "Keep it coming, or keep away from those constricting brief underwear, they tend to devaluate the product." I swallowed hard, not believing what had just happened. "Have a good night, kid. I'll see you next week with the last of your initial payment."

"Yes, sir," I nodded. I had been defeated. He left with his goons in tow, leaving me in the silence of my loneliness, the nightmare magnified to a level I could not have imagined. I was being extorted, forced to continue to grow the very business that was driving me completely insane. A god? I wanted nothing to do with those people anymore. These idiots, paying me obscene amounts of money for something so unbelievable stupid, the very notion of my current success seemed mind boggling. But what else could I do? I no longer had a choice, I had to keep going, and the realization of it was nothing short of breathtakingly brutal. I lit another cigarette, wringing my tight hands together, trying to find some type of comfort inside of my head, but there was nothing there for me. Nothing left. I had been stripped to the bone.

"Goddamn it!" I snapped. "I'm so fucking stupid! They've been watching us for weeks! They know every-thing! How could I not have expected this? Fuck me!" I put my tired face into my hands, trying to control my breathing, trying to get a grip. My phone buzzed again in my pocket. I had forgotten about it in light of the tense shake down I was trying to irk my way out of. I snapped it out of my pocket and stared at a text message.

"Restricted: No Inhibitions night club. 10:00 pm?"
I was in no mood for games. I was balancing dangerously on the edge of a frenzied freak out. I texted back.

"No time for games. Who are you? What do you want?"

I sent it and fell back against the sofa, waiting for a response, unable to keep my body still. Too much anxiety. The phone buzzed again.

"Restricted: Explain everything there."
"Fuck!" I snapped, looking at my watch. It was quarter after nine. I sighed loudly, feeling the unwillingness to go anywhere bubbling inside of me. I needed nothing else for the day. I was done! I stared at the tiny screen, unwilling to reply, but what else was I really going to do? I texted back.

"10:00 pm. If ur not there, 2 bad!"
I waited for half a minute before it vibrated again.

"See u there."
I shook my head and sighed heavily, running my hand through my hair. After a minute, I stood and got dressed to meet my mysterious new pen pal. I loaded the gun and shoved it into my belt, ready to use it, trying to protect myself against an army of idiots who thought I could save them from themselves. Beliefs were dangerous, therefore, I too needed to be.

The traffic was hellish for the time of night, irritating me further. My palms were incredibly sweaty and my body felt the hard rush of incoming anxiety. I finally pulled into the sprawling parking lot and parked by a long line of concrete curbs near the back of the lot. I turned the engine off and waited silently in the dark, scanning the long row of vehicles like some enemy attacker testing the waters before the approach. There was nothing suspicious. Nothing catching my curiosity. A fairly quiet scene aside from a small crowd of smokers gathered by the entrance.

I grabbed my phone.
"Where r u?" I hit send and lit a cigarette. Looking in all

directions for something unknown. It vibrated.

"Restricted: Prk by back door."

I started the engine and drove around the building and...
I jammed the van into park without so much as slowing
down, grabbing frantically for the gun. My fingers felt numb
and beyond my control while I fumbled foolishly with the
weapon. I finally managed my grip, swung open the door,
and stepped out into the assaulting high beams of what I immediately recognized as the black van. Shaking violently, I
pointed the Glock toward the van and screamed.

"Out!" I yelled. "Get the fuck out! Who are you? Get
out and show me your face!"

For a few suspended seconds, nothing happened, and
I wondered if perhaps I had made a mistake and stumbled
onto some pervert who had simply lured a stripper into the
back of his vehicle, now staring back with great concern at
some strange fanatic pointing a gun at them out of nowhere,
demanding to see who was inside. A simple mistaken identity, but something instinctive told me that I was correct. It
was the same obscure vehicle I had been seeing whenever I
cared to look around me.

After The Terror had left with his pack of beasts, I
was content with the assumption that he had been responsible for the black vehicle. Obviously, assuming serves nothing. Here it was! Blinding me with its headlights. Taunting
me with its very presence.

"Get out of the van!" I snarled again. I had the sense
that this could go very wrong at any moment. Suddenly, the
lights turned off and left my irises feverish to keep up with
the drastic change in stimulus. I could vaguely see a form
inside, not moving, and still not heeding my orders.

"Out!" I yelled. "Get the fuck out or I'm going to
shoot you blind!"

I felt the nervous trigger under my finger. Two hundred grains of pure power, ready to ignite at any moment and
blow a good sized hole through anything really. Drill em'
hard.

The door slowly swung open, and I could see the

obscure form moving as the vehicle's suspension compen-
sated for the shifting weight. My eyes stung with hot sweat.
I squinted, trying to concentrate, but it seemed too much for
my mind to handle. What was happening? This could not be!

"Hello Mickey," he said happily. "Put the gun down
please. You, are a god now, remember?"

I could feel my lips quivering. I finally began to understand exactly what had been happening behind the scenes.
I knew where these fools were coming from. The madness
that had been taking my life hostage, I knew, was all because
of this goddamned fool!

"I should blow your fucking head off right here on
principle alone, you fucking asshole!"

He smiled happily. He was completely insane!
"Mickey," he spoke softly. "Master. You have saved my life
twice now. Mine, and countless others. You are a savior, and
you deserve to be honored for your courage and dedication."

I was mad with rage. Unable conjure the words to
properly convey how I was feeling. Psychotic. I spoke as
slowly and methodically as I could, but the rage was impossible to subdue.

"Tell me what you want, Grant, or else in 3 seconds,
I will make your head explode all over your van. What the
fuck do you want from me?"

"I want you to listen. That's all I want. Just listen."
I forced every rage filled bolt of energy rushing through my
body not to pull the trigger and blow his head across the
back yard behind him.

"One day, Grant," I said. "One day, I'm going to kill
you."

Grant smiled silently, seemingly unafraid.
Grant said, "It will be an honor to die by your hand, Master."

CHAPTER 33

A little over two thousand years ago, a man by the name of Yeshua Ben Yosef was allegedly born in the middle east. Ultimately, he grew up to teach a legion of corrupt humans a new way of thinking about life, and became known as Jesus of Nazareth. Fast forward a little more than two thousand years, and here we are, the descendants, still as confused as ever. Still desperate for answers, and still searching for a different way, or at the very least, a comfortable sense of hope.

I was not Jesus Christ. I was not here to save people from themselves or to offer them a new way of approaching their lives. What I had created was a vehicle for making money. The bottom line had always been my stupid, soul corrupting, superficial quest for money, and what was happening with these people, with Grant, was absolutely unacceptable.

A savior? Christ! I was just as scared and lost as the rest of them. The only proper way to save those fuckers was with the help of a finely tuned assault rifle. The lunacy of it was overbearing. Everywhere I went, it seemed like I could feel the vagrant minds lurking around in the shadows, watching me. Before I even knew it, bystanders were trying to snap my picture in the middle of a kidnapping instead of calling for the police. Not to turn me in to the authorities, oh no, it was to have the honor of knowing what my face actually looked like.

I wondered if I had ever said anything that actually sounded like the words of a god. Were mine the words of a strong and confident leader, here to lead the failures toward a path of salvation? What would Jesus think of it? What had

Jesus thought? How had he felt, being publicly overrun by
the very fools he was trying to help? I felt like I was walking around with a bludgeoned sense of self-worth. What was
I even doing, after all? What was my purpose, or even, my
reasoning behind exploiting human desperation? Why was
I the one who had reached his dreams, only to want to jump
off the tallest building in the city? Fuck it all. I could have
run away, desperate to hide from the threats like a cockroach
in a filthy crevice, but I felt like I had a slightly higher level
of self-respect than a dirty roach, and should probably stand
up against the oncoming threats. Push back the wolves until
they retreated, hoping to be allowed to go back to being just
a simple, unknown, boring little person.

Grant had said, "You need to teach these people." He
said, "You need to save them and do to them what you have
done to me." He said, "These people love you and believe in
you. You have saved their lives already. Why not keep teach-
ing them?"

What a demented fool!
I knew nothing of people! Nothing! I knew nothing of my
own life! How could I possibly save anyone else if I couldn't
even save myself? How could any of it have happened? It
was too far. Too foul.

Our meeting had been cut short when the back doors
of the night club had blasted open and puked out 4 or 5 men,
wrestling with each other in a drunken fight. I had taken the
opportunity to run, wanting absolutely nothing to do with
Grant aside from putting a well deserved bullet in between
his eyes.

Grant had said, "I've been spreading your message
to the people." He said, "I've been proclaiming your name,
and telling my incredible story of self-fulfillment through
your process." He said, "We could make books, and bobble
head dolls."

I had quickly jumped into my van and hammered on
the accelerator, aiming the chrome grill directly for Grant's
stupid body. I couldn't get to him, but I did take the opportunity to scream a warning while passing by; "If I ever see you

again, I will put a bullet in your head!"

I had thought about turning him over to The Terror to be taken care of, but then decided against it, mostly because he would probably view Grant as a fantastic marketing machine for this money maker of mine and probably put him on the payroll. I was screwed, simultaneously unable to keep going, or to stop in any way.

Grant had said, "I love you, Master." He said, "We are your disciples." He said, "We have found our purpose. It is you. You are the new hope."

I should have killed him when I had the chance. By the time I arrived at the warehouse and parked the van, my body shook uncontrollably, and my stomach was mangled, heaving in desperation. I wanted to put a bullet in my own head. End it all on my own terms. I was scum!

Polaris was back, and alone, upstairs with unhappiness flowing permanently through her eyes. I could see how much she despised me.

"Hi," I said weakly.
She lifted her head just long enough to have a quick look at me.

"Jesus! You look like shit," she said.
"Please," I lifted my hand in the air. "Please, don't say that name."

"Why?" she questioned sarcastically. "Have you found God? Are you offended by it all of sudden?"

"You have no idea," I replied, holding my hand in the air. "No... Never mind."

The air felt tense, filled with anxiety, and my body was still shaking uncontrollably. I put the Glock on the table and collapsed into a chair.

"Where did you go with a gun?" she asked.
I forced a smile in the face of overwhelming sadness. My eyes were about to pop out of their sockets.

"Do you ah... Do you want me to choke you?" I asked.

"Choke me?" she questioned. "Why? Are you having trouble getting it up?"

"Please," I said. "No more fighting. No more...
Nothing! Nothing."

She looked at me strangely. Confused. The kind of
stare that comes with suddenly feeling bad for someone you
truly hated. I rubbed my face with my shaking, cold, sweaty
palms.

"Okay," she said in a whisper. "Okay, let's go."
I forced myself to move in a very calculated fashion. Rising
from the chair like a dying vampire. So hungry for something unknown. So desperate for freedom. So unbelievably
crushed.

The headboard smashed into the wall like the sound
track to our insipid relationship. She, the singer, screamed
like a sex deprived nymphomaniac finally getting her fix.
I was sweating profusely, and yet, I was so cold. Inside, I
was freezing cold. I tried focussing everything I had into
my trembling hands. I wanted to kill her. I wanted to kill
me. My mind was ignoring all attempts at being controlled,
and instead settled into a horrible awareness, sending incessant flashbacks rushing through me. "You're a god. We
love you," followed by, "If you don't pay up, I'll have your
tongue cut out," then, "Why won't you choke me? You're
such a pussy," moulding into, "Screw you, man. I can do the
drugs I want," and then a quick succession of flashes, "God.
Master. Murder. Drugs. Choke. God! God! God!"

I was lost in it and never even noticed Polaris's
squirming body taking the brunt of my mighty wrath. The
pain in my forehead felt like an inevitable aneurysm was
looming only seconds away. My hands felt so tight, and
so strong; thanks mostly to the white knuckled grip I had
around her slender throat. By my climax, her body was re-
sponding on some basic survival level–jumping and squirming with her arms flailing wildly through the air, her eyes
rolling to the back of her head. Her tongue turned blue and
her arms suddenly fell from the air, thumping on the bed.
A lifeless carcass, limp, and broken, and blue. I collapsed under the rush of dopamine; like shotguns inside of my brain.

Grant had said, "You give life through threatening

death. We love you, Savior!"

I panted like an overheating lion. My limbs numb, my face on fire. I looked at Polaris. Her lips were blue. Her eyes were glazed over with a thin layer of... Of...

"Shit!" I yelled. "Shit! She's dead!"
Suddenly, I was snapped out of my dark depression and shoved into a mighty panic.

"Shit! What did I do?"
I cradled her head in one hand and slapped her face with the other.

"Hey!... Hey!" I said. "Wake up! Come on now! Wake up, goddamn it! Wake up! Please! Please! Wake up!"

She was limp and heavy. A dead weight. An absent soul.

"Come on! Please!" I pleaded. "Come on!"
I slapped her harder now, relentlessly, and suddenly, her body sprung back to life, convulsing wildly on the floor like an electrocuted demon. She was freaking out, her arms and legs flying wildly through the air.

"Argh! Argh! Argh!!!" she screamed. Her face was beginning to color again, but her flailing finger nails remained cold, and white. Her gasping breath was sickening. I felt her fist smash against the side of my skull, followed by a swift kick to the chest. She had officially lost all control. Wasn't that our stupid goal at the beginning of this?

"Hey! Hey!" I yelled. "It's okay! Calm down! It's okay!"

But her mind was too heavily crowded with all kinds of nightmares to make any real sense of the situation. She was lost. I tried stepping back to let the beast have her space, but then felt her foot smash into my gut. I winced in pain.

"Goddamn it!" I yelled. "Calm down! You're fine!"
She stopped just long enough to stare me down in that special way only women can properly pull off. Her face was red. Her eyes mad. Her hair horribly matted in sweat.

"Fuck you!" she hissed, and tears swelled in her eyes. "How dare you? How dare you?"

"What?" I asked. "I'm sorry. So you stopped breath-

ing for a few seconds. You're yelling just fine now." I was
only trying to lighten the situation.

"You prick!" she snapped through her tears. "You
demented shit! You killed me! You fucking killed me!"

"Come on!" I replied. "It was an accident. I'm sorry.
I didn't fucking mean to kill you."

"Shut up! I've had enough of this! Enough! I can't
take it anymore! Not you, not this place, and not this fucking
bullshit scam you've got going on."

"You can't take it?" I snapped back. "Fuck you! You
have no idea what pressure is! You have no IDEA!!!"

She was breathing heavily, still in a panic.
"Yes, I do!" she said. "You think I like this? Huh? Living
like squatters in a goddamn warehouse with a complete
addict in one room, and a twisted freak who suddenly has a
problem with sexual fetishes, but has zero problems beating
the shit out of complete strangers for money? I hate you!"
she snapped. "I fucking hate you!"

"Good!" I said. "Finally! At least someone fucking
hates me!"

She looked at me strangely.
"I haven't told you anything!" I said. "Do you know how I
feel? I've got a best friend hellbent on constant drug binges,
I've got one of the most dangerous gangsters alive breathing down my neck for more money, I've got a whole slew of
scum faced cockroaches who think that I can save them from
themselves, and I've got a girlfriend who can't get off without being choked and then acts like a fucking 5 year old if I
happen to not feel like it once in a while because everything
else is fucking with me! So I'm sorry if I can't always be
in the mood to play your little emo games, but please, can't
you, in any way, at least try to understand what's going on
with me before you lose your shit? My whole life is breaking
away from me by the second here!"

I felt the heavy pressure set in once again. My throat
incredibly dry, and tight. Every muscle in my body felt con-
tracted. Every attempt at being rational, sharply highlighted
with doom. She had nothing to say in response and buried

her crying face into her hands. I stared at the ceiling, listening to her spastic sniffles. I tried to control my breathing. I tried to get a grip. I'd had enough.

"Get out," I said softly.

Her head suddenly popped up and she glared at me with wrecked eyes, blazing with outrage.

"What?" she asked, dry, and hoarse.

"Get out," I said, quite gently once again. It was simple. I was done. I was calm. "I want you to leave. I want you to go, and I don't want you to come back here, ever again."

"This belongs to all of us!" she protested, all of sudden now! Unbelievable!

"This... This is for your own good. Trust me in this, it's for your own safety. Maybe I did love you all along. Maybe, in some twisted way, there is love between us. But it's too late, and I am too tired to do this anymore. Please, just go, and leave me alone. If you want money, I'll give all the money you want. I don't give a shit about money! It has ruined my life! Say hello to my beautiful fucking nightmare! This is not going to end well, all right? Just please, just go."

She stared at me, not sure of whether to respond with another freak out or simply accept what was happening with an ugly mix of sorrow and rage.

"We're all going to get burned," I said. "I can feel it. In one way or another, we are fucked. I have managed to drive all of us into an impossible situation. Listen to what I'm saying to you, Polaris. I have ruined your life far worse than you would even believe right now, but I am offering you the chance to leave before it goes any further for you. You can go now and spare yourself the damage I have already caused. Just take some money, whatever you want, take it all, and go. Please."

I stood up, not even waiting for a response. I wanted her out. I hated her guts. I hated her beautiful body, and her bruised throat, and I hated her ugly, dark, diminished soul so goddamn much, I... I fucking loved her. Fuck.

I grabbed my clothes and left the room. I had nothing to do. I wanted nothing to do. I wanted to wither up and die. I sat with a cigarette in the middle of what we often found ourselves referring to as, "The living room". A hilarious space of pure fucking filth. What the hell were we doing? Who the hell did we think we were kidding? As much as it hurt, Polaris had to get out.

I felt jealous while I watched her disappear into the dark, stormy night. I wanted to disappear into the rain. I felt like that rain. I felt like a piece of shit, but what else could I do? There was nothing good about our future. No hope. Who was I to bring everyone else down with me? I was the idiot. I was the fool. I was the stubborn moron with a boner for fame and big dollar signs in my eyes. I was the one who should have to pay. I... I had to pay–or else.

Grant had said, "You are the myth, turning into legend."

CHAPTER 34

The phone rang endlessly. No answer.

I was trying to reach Steve. He had vanished without a clue, leaving me all alone in the rabid, introspective nightmare. I sighed, imagining this very situation being depicted in the dramatic re-enactments of some shady crime show in the future. The kind that plays at two in the morning with obscure, hopeful actors playing me and all of the other twisted freaks in this savage cast of characters while the Shatner-toned narrator spoke of horrid things like, "11:00 a.m. The weather outside was grim with a Western storm front moving in, and Mickey Tyler could think of nothing more than to smash somebody's skull in." Or, "Mickey Tyler's girlfriend, Polaris, left after he beat her savagely for wanting a piece of the business, failing in his attempt at strangling her for good."

"Goddamn it!" I said, and ran a shaky hand through my hair. "What the hell am I supposed to do? What am I going to do?"

I was sitting alone, upstairs, in the miserably deranged space of my life. Everything around me was either smashed, or at the very least toppled over. I could feel it approaching. The breaking point. The point where I would have no other option but to make an irresponsible, hate filled decision to throw in the towel, and just start digging my own grave. Screw it. I didn't care anymore.

With Grant and his bullshit propaganda, I could see no other course of action but to lash back viciously against all those who stared at me with idealistic eyes. I couldn't be forced to do it; not without The Terror. Till then, I would be the wrathful god they had never expected. I would be the demon unleashed in the very flesh they expected to save them.

I would be the violent, repulsive monster who had suddenly decided for reasons unexplained that his followers were no longer worth saving, and burn the fuckers on a spit. A comforting thought, except it only partly solved my enigma. The Terror did not believe in me. At least, not with Grant's morbid perception. In his eyes, I was a gold mine. I was a giant, overgrown, sparkling diamond that had just been unearthed, and he was looking to cash in. There's no real way of escaping that kind of derelict motivation. I had decided, after my little incident with Grant, that it would probably do me some good to simply hunker down for a little while and hide from the madness. I locked myself in; a willing exile trying to escape the reality I was now completely trapped in. Below me, I could hear the screams. I could hear my employees spewing out the same meaningless crap I had told them to say over, and over, and over again. The muffled, "What is the meaning to your life?" And, "How do you live with yourself when you mean nothing to no one?" Followed by the whimpered screams, the pleas, the desperate cries for help. Broken spirits, smashed to nothing. What a fucking idiot I was!

***

For two weeks, Steve was gone. For two weeks, Polaris was gone. I was all alone with my very own Frankenstein's monster. No one had control anymore over the explosively successful thing I had named Crypto Fear. I tried staying locked up in my dark cave, wearing nothing but a ratty bathrobe, wallowing through filth, trying frantically to get a hold of Steve. I needed his help. I needed someone to tell me what to do. I needed my own god to drop by and save me from myself. I needed... Somebody. I couldn't stand the feeling of being the wounded soldier who'd been left behind in the retreat.

I was hoping, feebly at best, that Grant's little idea of who I was wasn't going to catch on with the masses. That somehow, the whole thing would simply blow over and allow me to quietly bow to the crowd and make an exit out of the back door. *"I'm sorry, Mr. Labelle. People just don't want to be broken anymore. Here's some money. Thanks for everything. I'll send you a Christmas card. Yes. Thank you for letting me keep my scrotum. Greatly appreciated, by the way. Goodbye."* Then make a flat out run for somewhere like New York, or Boston, and simply hunker down, gladly scraping the rest of my way through life. I had learned my lesson. Thank you universe. I was fully rehabilitated from my stupidity.

Stupid little thoughts.

After two weeks of sad, depressive loneliness, all I had left were my employees, kidnapping fool after fool, and laying beating after beating. All of it, quite heart-wrenching enough without the need for a new problem in my life–but what the hell–why not? There was something new happening out there, raising the stakes once again, and I knew without a doubt that it was being pushed by Grant's hand. Out of nowhere, and completely blind sided by it, I suddenly found myself harassed by what was apparently known as, "Testament visits." Yes, it was quite obvious that the whole god thing had not blown over at all. In fact, it was holding on like a tick on my asshole!

"I used to be a hypochondriac," a lady said to me, smiling idly. "I was terrified of every little pimple I got. But you, you change it all for me. I am free now. You saved me." It was followed by an eerie hug. A choking feeling. An urge to put a bullet into someone's thick skull.

"I used to beat my wife. I used to beat her, and then, well, make love to her," a burly fool with shifty eyes told me. "But now, she's never been happier. Now I can make love to her, the right way. You saved more than just my marriage, you know that?"

"Really? Wow! I'm really happy for you. Now get the fuck away from me!"

I was nearly unable to stop some model looking girl from reaching the back warehouse. She had stopped and listened intently to the screams, the packing sounds, the madness in the air.

She smiled, "Setting more inmates free, I see. Is it going well?"

"Oh, yes," I said, smiling sarcastically. "Just fucking fantastic around these parts."

She did nothing but stare back at me.

"What?" I said, sternly. "What is it? What can I do for you, Miss..."

"Legault," she said, and smiled again.

"Right, well, Miss Legault, I'm a very busy man these days, please, tell me what you want!" I was irritated with her shuffling through the place like a rodent.

"Did you know that I used to cry during sex?" she said.

"Ugh, really?" I said. "I can make you do that too if you'd like."

She smiled.

"No. I mean, I had some serious emotional problems," she paused for a moment, listening to a muffled, "You're a goddamn parasite in the world," coming from the back, and she smiled, obviously recalling her own savage experience. "I had real emotional problems. I had panic attacks, and insomnia, and, an inability to really, I don't know, connect with others."

"Jesus fucking Christ!" I said.

"And then I met you, and your little company here, and, well, you saved my life. For almost a year beforehand, I constantly thought of suicide, and then I came here, and it hurt like hell for a week or two, but still, underneath, I could feel the heavy weights being lifted high off of my shoulders. I felt freedom from my inner cell. I felt..."

"Yes, yes, yes," I cut her off. "You're welcome. Please lady, I'm really busy."

"I just..." she sighed. "I just wanted to thank you, and..." she hesitated now.

"Yes?" I replied. "And what?"

"And, well, I met this man afterward, and he told me some great things about you, and about what you've done for hundreds of other people. How you saved his own life more than once, and then, well, he said that you sort of shied away from it all."

My heart sank.

"All right," I said. "That's enough. You're welcome. Now get the fuck out of my face."

I tried leading her away but she pulled back, as though she actually had something meaningful to say. Goddamn it!

"He asked me to come by and talk to you; see if you had given any thought to what he had said?" she smiled. I stared back at her in full rage now. I was going to snap. "I'm an editor, and I was wondering if you were interested in branching off your business, you know, keep helping those you have, and will help in the future. You could write your life philosophies, and your thoughts about..."

"Here's what I think!" I exploded, and she stepped back a little, slightly on guard. "You tell Grant that if I see him again, I'll blow a goddamn hole the size of my fist right through his fucking head. And if you speak one more word to me about this bullshit, I will do the same to you. Now get the fuck out of here! Out! Get out, now!"

She shuddered, stunned.

"But..."

I reached behind me and whipped out the Glock, shoving the ugly thing right into her pretty little face, causing her eyes to fill with terror. "I want nothing to do with you goddamned freaks!" I snarled into her stoned face. "I want nothing to do with Grant, or with you, or with anyone who places me on some demented pedestal. Got it?"

She nodded quickly. Her breathing a series of quick, sharp gasps.

"Now turn around, and get out. The warning is the same for you as it is for Grant. Don't let me catch you near me again because there will be no exchange of words next time. I will use force."

She nodded again quickly, and was already pulling away from me, but seemed unable to keep her mouth shut.

"Have some compassion for the poor..."

I snapped, "You have 3 seconds before I shoot you. You should probably start running now."

She turned and ran, breaking a heel, but never stopping to pay much attention to it.

"Goddamn, motherfucking, Grant!" I snapped. I was dangerously balancing on the edge of murderous violence. It seemed like I was saving every one of these idiots, setting them free like confident, reformed psychopaths, and all of it was at the cost of my own soul! Well fuck that! And where in the hell was Steve?!

The girl left, but the misguided did not. There was a constant mixture of them storming through the doors with gifts, and thanks, and hugs, and each one of them were met with my savage attempts to shove them back–but to no avail.

A strange mixture of contradicting sounds constantly raped my ears. "Thank you so much!" from the front office was met with, "You are a stupid little pissant with no meaning in life!" from the back. "You saved my life!" contrasted with, "You deserve to die!", "I love you!", "You mean nothing!", "You are our master!", "I should put a fucking bullet in your stupid, rotten, shit filled head!"

Crack!

Like a tsunami, I was being inundated with dangerous ideas. I was being lashed back into the corner with my very own whip. My own gun was being shoved into my face, and through it all I was totally, absolutely, and hopelessly alone.

I told myself, "Well, if people think I'm some kind of god, then fuck em! It's their loss." Of course, I could have embraced it all. I could have reveled in it like some ecstatic televangelist in the back of my Rolls Royce, in the name of God, of course, but there was something so inherently wrong with that on all levels of existence that I could never righteously accept any of it. An idiot with a conscience is no plan for success in a capitalist market. It was hopeless. No matter how much I screamed back, "I'm more messed up than the rest of you! I'm just a man! I have no answers." they just kept on coming. And when I tried to simply ignore people's retarded notions of who I was, to just put my head down and push through with blinders on, I began finding notes taped to the windshield of my vehicle. Hideous little things with scribbled messages like, "You owe it to these people, Mickey! You have saved them already!" and, "We love you, Master. Why won't you heed the requests of those who love and care for you?" and, "Your path is already laid out before you. All you need to do is take the first step."

This is ridiculous! This can't be real!

But there was no mistaking it. It was horribly real. Eventually, I faced no other choice but to resume my role and take on new kidnappings, because the majority of callers began refusing the service unless, "The master would be present." I needed the money. I couldn't deal with Grant's bullshit for much longer, but I knew even more that there was only one way to properly deal with a gangster like The Terror. You took care of him first, delivering every penny, on time, into his hands.

I kidnapped. I beat. I got paid.

Every street I waited on, seeking my prey, I knew he was around, somewhere, lurking in the shadows, staring back at me with desperate eyes. Every black van I saw instantly triggered the urge to pull out the Glock and fill it with lead. I could feel him around me, watching me. I could feel his purpose everywhere I went. The people with the horribly damaged faces walking along the sidewalks, I knew, would soon be snatched up by Grant and told blatant fucking lies. From bank tellers, to restaurant waiters, to bus boys, to door men, and on, the experience of Crypto Fear had scarred them all. Their emotions had been set free and left raw enough for Grant to impose an impression. Every one of them, I knew, would eventually be the destruction of me.

The warehouse was running twenty-four hours a day. Filled to the seams with screams, and blood, and gasps. I was becoming a preternatural beast.

"Here's your goddamn freedom!" I would scream. "Here's your stupid fucking life back!" Crack! "Go home and put a fork through your eye!" Crack! "Feel free to swallow a shotgun!" Crack!

And still, through all of it, no sign of Steve. I was worried that perhaps he had gone too far and possibly lay dead somewhere in the gutters. Yet another victim of the primitive drug culture. *"Here's a donation. Save the children! Try sodomy, not drugs!"*

The thing kept going with all pistons screaming, and the money was as relentless as Grant's attempts to get me to heed to his diluted purposes. So much of it was coming in that I didn't even have the motivation to really do anything with it. I no longer cared about any of it. I wanted out. Fuck money! I wanted to be poor and helpless, not rich and forced into a corner from every angle I turned. I had lost all control. The harsh truth was that this was exactly like every other situation in all of our lives. Nobody really wanted the money at all, what they wanted, was the control. We were all hopeless.

And then, for the second time in a month's time, and without any history of it at all, the doors of my business opened to a highly enthusiastic gangster with money in his eyes and elation on his face.

"Mickey! My boy!" The Terror laughed, looking around and taking it in. Everything had the look of money, of control. "Things are well?"

I was exhausted. Completely beaten in every sense of the word.

"Yes, Mr. Labelle," I said sullenly. "Everything is fine. Money's rolling. All is good."

"Good! Good, Mickey!" he boasted. The big smile never leaving his face. "I was just noticing, maybe you should hire some gorgeous girls to do some of the beating. Get the horny toads in here at three thousand bucks a pop!"

I sighed loudly.
"I'll think about it," I replied.

"Good," he smiled. "You'll have my money for me early next week?"

"Yes, sir."
"All right then, I'll see you later, Mickey. Good job here. Looks good!"

I smiled, nodding him off. The anger in me rising as the realization of what was happening became apparent. Ironically enough, Grant and his rising army of delinquents wasn't necessarily the thing that irritated me the most. What did, was The Terror walking into my place, into my business, my creation, and spewing out random suggestions like, "Maybe you should add other tortures to the experience. Maybe you should have some naked girls running around. Maybe you should include a reading room for friends to come along, and get a sense of what this is all about."

What the fuck? I thought. I imagined doing what I would never dare do in reality–simply snap and scream wildly into his face, "I have enough goddamn pressure, all right! Now fuck off, and I'll pay you when I pay you!"

Of course, none of that would end well. Not with my tongue cut out, or my fingernails beautifully fashioned into some little girl's necklace. I rubbed my temples with intensity. My head was pounding. My head was always pounding lately.

"I used to be a gambling addict."

"I don't give a shit! I could lend you some money for the casino if you'd like. You don't even need to pay me back."

"I used to be unable to stop masturbating."

"Good, you finally lost your virginity! Finally became a man. Get out!"

"I used to need to be choked."

"Ha!... You have no fucking idea. Please, just leave me alone."

I found endless notes on the doors of the warehouse, and inside the warehouse, and inside the vans, everywhere, Grant's little pleas were there, but I pressed on, completely ignorant of them all. I kidnapped. I beat. I got paid. I was a methodical, calculated, and frightened money spewing machine.

It wasn't long before The Terror reappeared one day, talking about adding a drug trade as an extra dimension to the business, or maybe even prostitution.

"Please, Mr. Labelle," I muttered, my face hope-

lessly drooped, my body folded over like a lifeless mannequin–exactly what I had become–a goddamned mannequin.
A pond in someone else's twisted little game. "I just need to
think right now."

He looked at me with lowered eyebrows.
"Jesus, kid," he said. "You look tired."

I scoffed and shook my head.
"You need to get laid or something? Want me to call my
girls?"

"No thanks," I replied, and sighed. I was absolutely
beaten.

"Hey, Mickey," he said, and pushed a hand up
against my shoulder. "Why don't you take a holiday? Take a
break. I'm paid. You're off the hook, and everyone else here
seems to know what they're doing."

I laughed solemnly at the thought of it. A vacation.
Christ!

"No, I'm okay," I replied. "Maybe I'll just sleep for
a few days."

"Right, well, whatever you do, just keep this thing
rolling. Christ, it's making a lot of money!" he smiled and
looked around again. "Did you know these people want you
to lead some kind of new religion or something like that?
What a bunch of fucking retards!" he laughed. "But it could
make some good money. Shit, you could probably write
some books."

"No!" I snapped now. "Thank you, Mr. Labelle, but I
have a lot of work to do. I'll see you later."

"Yes, yes," he said. "Don't let me keep you. Do what
you must."

I smiled feebly and walked away, but I could still
hear him speaking to his body guards, "You know what
would be nice here? A brothel! I'm telling you. Get kidnapped. Get beaten. Get fucked. It's beautiful!"

I shook my head and kept walking, trying to avoid
that stupid conversation. For one of the most successful
gangsters of his age, he could be one stupid motherfucker.

I went upstairs and tried calling Steve–still, no answer. I let my head fall back against the sofa and closed my eyes. Goddamn it I was tired. I was alone. I was... In peaceful darkness for a change.

CHAPTER 35

I was lost in the heavy fog of some alien wilderness. The air was cold, and smelled like the fresh mountain forests from when I was a boy. The only lighting was provided by the moon, reflecting brightly off the fallen leaves and the thick green moss. My breath was labored and on edge, my hands numb. I was turning in circles, around and around, trying to get my bearings, trying to figure out just where in the hell I was. The trees around me stretched a confident two hundred feet to the top. I was looking through the fog, peering to see something, anything, but there was nothing else. I was all alone, lost, and lacking all memories. And then, I saw them! Eyes! Red eyes, like a cartoon demon. Faint at first, but undoubtable once the realization was set that I could see them. They did not blink. They did not sway. A rush of chills ran up and down my spine like I had jammed my hand into an electrical socket, and then, an explosion! Just the sound of it, no flashes, and I was three feet in the air, jabbing hard fists in every direction.

I then realized exactly where I was. I was in the living room. I was home, in the warehouse, on my feet, screaming and flailing fists at nothing. Or was I? I watched as figures rushed toward me with intense speed. I counted 4, or maybe 5 of them before I felt something smash against the side of my face, throwing me backward with incredible pain flashing through my skull. I winced and felt the hard, abrupt thump against the floor.

"No!" I garbled, my mouth suddenly throbbing in pain, my voice assaulting the back of my throat. "What the... What the fuck?"

"Shut him up!" one of them snapped.

"I... I'm trying. I..."

"Move!" the voice said, but I was still fighting back with everything I had. I managed to kick one of the figures in the crotch and vomit suddenly spewed all over the floor. I heard it, more than saw it. It was near pitch black.

"Move, goddamn it!" the same voice snapped again, and I heard stomping footsteps rush toward me. I clenched my jaw hard, contracting every muscle in my body before feeling a warm rush of pain spread through my face and down the back of my neck. Bright flashes exploded in my vision from a shaken brain. Sullen confusion. And then... Nothing. Back to darkness.

***

The eyes stared unflinchingly through the thick fog like smoldering embers from the deepest pit of hell. Threatening. I didn't move. I didn't breathe. I didn't think. No movement came from the eyes. They were forever fixed on their prey. I stared back, trembling. I wanted to run, I wanted to scream, but I didn't dare move a hair. Suddenly, I heard the rustling of leaves. The eyes were stalking my death from behind the cover of the banks, basking in my terror, and before I could even comprehend what was happening, they darted for me, revealing teeth like jagged razor blades. I felt its ugly breath feverishly snapping for my throat.

I felt my body jolt violently, tensing in reaction to everything real, and not. I heard my voice whimper, feeling nothing else but the incredible, skull splitting pain blasting through my head. After an incredible struggle, my eyelids opened, but my vision was horribly hazy, skewed. I could only see dark shapes contrasting a painfully bright background. My head weighed three hundred pounds.

I tried moving my arm to feel my face, trying to understand the true pain of it all, but I couldn't move it. I was stuck, and with no energy to try it again. I managed a small, excruciating cough, and a rush of blood flooded my taste buds. My ribs felt like they were caught in some kind of mechanical clamp. An oppressive hydraulic machine.

"Welcome, Master," the voice was soft and calculated. Concise, and confident. Terrifyingly confident. I forced my eyelids open just long enough to receive a stabbing of light and see a dark shape in front of me.

"Wh... Where am..." I coughed, and another bolt of pain rushed through me.

"Shh," the voice said. "Shh, just relax. Just enjoy the pain for the moment."

I winced and forced my eyelids open again, keeping them open longer and longer each time. Taking the pain, taking the madness, trying to understand what was happening. My vision slowly cleared, but my head continued spinning wildly, like a drunken fool who had passed his limit 15 shots ago. My nostrils were caked with dry dust and mucus. The hot, humid air pressed uncomfortably against my skin, forming a glistening coat of filthy sweat over my entire body.

"Wh... Where am I?" I feebly tried again. "What... Do... You want?" My voice was so weak I wasn't even sure if I had actually spoken, or simply thought about it.

"Shh," the voice came again. "This is the beginning of your experience."

With my vision adjusting, I could see a few dark shapes shifting eerily in front of me, and I knew, without a doubt, that one of them was that psycho son of a bitch, Grant. A single light bulb hung above my head, swaying this way and that, making my head spin with it. I coughed and tasted more blood. I cleared my throat laboriously.

Then a face approached mine. From the shadows, it came in slowly, and calculated, like a curious beast. The photons reflected the features back to me in layers, like an appearing ghost, and even in my condition of utter uselessness, I could feel rabid rage bubbling inside of me.

"How are you feeling?" he whispered, and smiled, as if I would suddenly recover, ready to party.

"Fuck you!" I snarled, absolutely exasperated with him. Blood misting from my lips as I did.

He held his smile. "Well," he said. "I see you're

conscious enough to get the full extent of it now. Are you ready?"

I frowned hard, feeling the creases of my face ply up against the filth and sweat. I squirmed uneasily.

"For... For what?" I said. "Are we hosting a party? I forgot to bring my famous potato salad. Sorry."

He chuckled in amusement and held a wide smile, coupled with a disheartening stare of admiration.

"Oh, yes," he said. "We are having a party. No need for potato salad though, Master. You are here. That is all we need."

I chuckled in disbelief. A snort. The nerve of this son of a bitch! I painfully lifted my head and squinted my eyes, carefully, and methodically moved my corneas over the other fools standing around me. I knew none of them. Three were male, three female, but all of them were holding a disgusting look of idolization. And for the first time, it seemed, I realized the full extent of my situation. I was sitting on a hard steel chair, my hands bound tightly behind it, my feet together. The rope was digging into my ankles and wrists. My pulse felt massive in my rotator cuffs.

Grant smiled again.
"Do you recognize any of them?" he asked.

I chuckled, painfully shaking my head. "No," I laughed. "No. Ha! Ha! Ha!"

Their eyes turned to disappointment. Stone cold. "You've saved all of them," Grant said.

"I don't care, Grant," I muttered. "I don't fucking care!"

"Well," he sighed. "You should. Because of you, these people, me, and hundreds more out there on the streets are truly alive now. And it's all because of you, Master. The only thing we want is for you to appreciate the meaning of that. We want to show you how grateful we are."

I snorted again. My head still swelling with pain. "Why don't you all blow your heads off then?" I smiled. "That would please me just fine, thank you. Now go forth and follow thy word. Ha! Ha!" Blood spewed out of my mouth with every one of my rebellious bellows, but his face was very serious. Almost offended. Dangerous.

"We do not appreciate such comments, Master," he said. "We owe you our lives, you know." He stepped back, and stood in line with the others.

"Tell him," he said to them.

A girl I have never known, would never want to know, stepped forward.

"Master," she said softly. "I used to cut myself. I used to need pain in order to function in the world. I had to smash my hand in drawers. I had to slit my arms with razor blades. I had to..." She paused, and then gasped. A wisp of blond hair fell into her face. "I had to... I had to try and kill myself." Her eyes welled with tears.

I closed my eyes in nonchalance. Who was this person? And why did she think I cared? Why? I didn't care. In fact, if my condition was any better, I would have attacked them by now and taught every one of them a lesson in pain. Yet, on she sobbed against my sighs of frustration, and my quick chuckles of disbelief. Unbelievable! Then, another girl stepped forward. A tiny little Asian girl, mid-twenties, I guessed, with shoulder length black hair and a tank top that hung from protruding collar bones.

"I used to be addicted to sex," she said with a heavy accent. "I used to sleep with anyone. I had to. Anyone from a bar, to the office, to the... To the streets. But you helped me. You showed me a new way. You saved me."

I swallowed hard, suddenly thinking that if I did get access to a gun, I would turn it on myself instead of trying to pop off these idiots. It would be so much less painful.

She stepped back, and was followed by a man stepping forward. A tall, burly, lumberjack looking man, properly attired with an old ball cap and a checkered flannel shirt. He smiled at me shyly.

"Hello," he said softly.

"Oh, hi there," I replied sarcastically, still tasting the blood seeping from somewhere inside of my cheek. I tongued at the pain.

"My name is Henry, and I used to be a junkie," he said. "I used to sleep in the gutters, and steal constantly just to support my habit. I barely ever ate. I barely ever was conscious enough to do much actually," he chuckled nervously, as if in the presence of greatness. I hated myself. "I heard about what you were doing on the streets. I heard about the help you offered to all sorts of folks. But I had no money. I managed to find Grant here, and I told him what I needed. I needed help, sir. Master. I needed big help, and from the goodness of his heart, he lent me the two thousand dollars I needed for your service," he simultaneously smiled and sighed, as though relieved. "I ain't got no junk anymore, sir. I don't even crave it no more. I see life through new eyes because of you, Master. I would be dead, without you."

"Come on, man," I said. This couldn't be real. This wasn't real! "Okay!" I exclaimed. "I get it, all right. I helped you. You're welcome. Now please, just leave me alone! This is fucking crazy! This is–this is crazy, you assholes! LET ME GO!!!"

Useless–they proceeded as though I wasn't even there. Another women stepped forward. Older. Mid-forties. Short, and sporting a wrinkled smile. She reminded me of my own mother with her soft voice. Her eyes were sullen, and her demeanor timid.

"I... Ah," she swallowed with difficulty. "My husband used to beat me–a lot," she smiled uncomfortably. "And the kids. He used to drink, and beat us all to a pulp. For years, I lied. I hid, and I lied some more. I cried in silence. I suffered in lonely pain. When I heard about what you were doing, I figured, what the hell, right? What's another beating? I could take it. I saved up for weeks after this woman I know went through it, and she couldn't stop raving about how real, and how, how helpful it truly was. It's not about the beating. It's about the words. The beating is only to break down your walls," she sniffled. "Two weeks ago, I... Ah... I beat my husband with a baseball bat. I beat him with the same intensity he had beat us for so long with. I broke him. I bled him!" her voice was backed with painful intensity. "And then... Well, then I left. I packed the kids and left him unconscious on the floor, and I left," she smiled. "I am free now. What you did for me, I will never be able to thank you enough for. I... I'm free! You gave me courage, sir. You gave me my life back."

I took a deep breath, trying not to hold eye contact, trying not to sympathize.

A black college kid came next.
"Hey," he said shyly.

I forced a sarcastic smile. The debilitating offensiveness apparent.

"I ah... I used to be into meth, man," he said. "Like that guy. I was... I was messed up real bad. My family, they're rich and all, and you know, it was always easy for me. I wanted to get off, you know? My family did this intervention thing. My girl, well, my girl left me, man, and I really loved her, you know? I tried rehab and all that, but, I just couldn't kick it. I tried so hard, but I guess it was always just too easy for me. I went to your warehouse, and, I haven't touch a line for 6 weeks. You help people, man. You helped me. All of us here. So, thanks a lot."

I snarled my blood covered teeth like a rabid pit bull and snorted some filthy mucus. The last insipid disciple stood in front of me, and I suddenly felt an air of relief wash through me. I didn't think that I could handle much more. I would puke. I would choke, and implode, and hopefully die a crude, filthy death. Even I couldn't help myself now.

This guy was older, like the mid-wife punching bag. He smiled like the others, but I continued to stare back with expressive despair.

"I'm a father of three kids. Nice kids. Good kids. My wife, she left me after she..."

"All right!" I exclaimed, taking the brutal pain that flashed through my head. "I get it! Goddamn it, you demented fucking lunatics! I get it! Enough! Please, just let me go. Please, let me go. This is fucking crazy!"

They all stared back at me in surprise. My little outburst upping the massive tide of pain in my head. The last fool was caught in confusion, turning his head to look at Grant, then back to me.

"Get back!" I yelled, causing excruciating jolts of pain throughout my body.

"All right!" Grant said, pulling the idiot back. "That's enough. I think he understands all of us just fine now. Don't you, Mickey?"

I sat with my eyes closed, trying to concentrate on weening off the reality of it all.

"And then, well, there's me," he said. "But you already know all about me, don't you?"

I offered no response.

"Yes, of course you do."

I lifted my heavy head, completely irritated. "Why are we here, Grant?" I muttered, my voice horribly hoarse.

"You know why, Mickey."

"No!" I exclaimed. "No! I don't! What I know, is that you've assembled a cast of guilt ridden freaks and made them believe in some kind of fabled semantics that don't make any goddamn sense! Now tell me, why are we here, Grant? Why?"

"They make sense," he replied strangely, softly.

"No they don't, goddamn it!" I snapped. "I am not a savior, and I am not a god! What the fuck is your problem? This is entertainment! This is bullshit, extreme entertainment! Like bungee jumping, or skydiving! This is not a fucking religion! Get it through your thick skulls! I hate you! I don't give a shit about you! And if I could, I would destroy each and every one of you! Got that? This is about making money! Nothing else!"

My freak out sent my blood pressure skyrocketing, and I could suddenly see my pulse in my vision. Heavy, pulsating torment. Grant pulled back, sighing loudly, looking at the others still huddled around me like a pack of football goons. The light bulb above me flashed with spastic interruptions of electricity. The air felt hot, and moldy, and was irritating the soft membranes of my nose.

"You had your chance," Grant whispered.

I frowned hard. Confused.

"What?" I replied, still steaming with anger.

"You had your chance," he said louder now. "I gave you the chance. I gave you the option to embrace this. To keep helping the same poor people you have already helped. You are a legend out there. Don't you understand that? Don't you know what your very existence means to hundreds of people? You are a Savior."

"No!" I snapped. "I meant my warning, Grant. I am going to put a fucking bullet right through your head. First chance I get, Grant! Bullet through the goddamn head!"

He quickly retorted, completely unaffected by my threats, "You're not only a flesh and blood, real life Savior, but you are a symbol. A symbol of hope, and of help. A symbol of life, and of freedom. A symbol of something higher than what we are. An attitude. A way of life. A path toward our very own salvation."

I could see his eerie smile through the zoned out light.

"The religions of our world are... Outdated, at best, and you my friend, my Master, have brought us the answer. The answer every conscious being constantly searches for. Why are we here? Why do we exist? What is our purpose? These things," he held his hand out in front of his face like a passionate Italian chef. "Are timeless questions. These things are haunting, and they rob us all of true life. These things are what make us all human, and not Gods. It keeps us in check, below the higher standard. But now, you have presented all of us with a proper path toward finding the correct answers. Regardless of what you think, Mickey, regardless of your personal opinion on the subject, the reality is right here in front of you. In these people. It is everywhere on the streets. In a world that is oppressive, dangerous, and filthy in more ways than we are capable of conceiving, there is so much hope for something like you. So much, and it's right in front of you. Just please, have a look," he pulled back and stared at me as though he was going to cry. "Hope," he repeated.

I sighed, incredibly frustrated. I wanted to rip out of

my own skin.

"Together," he continued, while the other robots behind him nodded in agreement. "With your concepts, and with our willingness to help spread the message, we will make a difference in this world. And you, my dear friend, you will forever be regarded as the founder of a new way of life."

The room fell silent, as if everyone expected a bomb to explode at any moment. I could tell from Grant's eyes, from the shimmering insanity that flashed through them, that he was hoping, probably more than ever in his entire life, that his little speech had finally gotten through to me and stimulated the coveted nerve that would magically send me exclaiming something like, "By God, you're right, Grant! You're absolutely right! Let's change the world! Let's gather the heathens and convert them to our ways. Let's save our children from the hellishly evil, big scary future that inevitably awaits them!" What a bunch of fucking idiots!

All eyes were hopelessly focused on me, and then, it happened.

"Haaa! Haa! Ha! Ha! Ha! Ha!" I filled the empty space with loud, echoing laughter. My diaphragm convulsed maniacally through the pain, through the madness, through the horrified looks. "Ha! Ha! Ha! Ha! Ha! Ha! Ha!"

Grant suddenly hung his head like a scientist failing his one, life defining experiment.

"You!" I exclaimed. "Ha! Ha! You, Grant, are one crazy motherfucker! Ha! Ha! Ha! Ha! You're fucking nuts, man!" I smiled like a stoned teenager.

His shoulders rose high with a deep, sullen sigh. He lifted his head and stared at me with the expression of a beaten, hopeless soul. Anger danced in his eyes like wildfire.

"You're fucking crazy!" I said again.

"Well," he said softly, defeated. "I guess there's only one thing left to do then."

I nodded in gleeful agreement, off my rocker now, smiling madly back into his angry face. My head was thumping with so much pain I actually thought I was getting used to it.

"Let's do it!" I smiled. "Give it to me, Grant! Make me understand!"

He leaned back, shifting his weight into it, and then crashed a lightning fast fist into my face.

Crack!

I felt his knuckles smash against my cheek bone. My jaw vibrated with intense pain.

"You have no purpose in life!" he screamed.

"That's right, Grant!" I yelled. "You tell me! Make me know it!"

"Shut up!"

Crack!

The bridge of my nose shattered into splinters. Blood gushed out like a flood.

"Your life is failed! You are nothing to no one! What is your purpose? What is it?"

Crack!

Chunks of teeth cut into my tongue, jagged fangs still dangled from the sockets.

"To lead you, Grant! To lead you! Make me lead all of you fucking morons!"

Crack!

"Why are you alive? Why are you here? Do you think anyone gives a shit about you?"

Crack!

More jagged flecks of enamel flew into the back of my throat. I suddenly thought about how Grant really wasn't very good at doing this at all. I would have rightfully fired him as an employer.

"You suck!" he screamed. "You're a parasite! You are an infectious scab, and you should put a goddamn bullet into your head!"

Crack!

I saw stars. Bright flashes, and misty blood flying upwards.

"You hit like a girl, Grant."

"No one loves you! No one hates you! No one even knows you're alive!"

Crack!
My eyes rolled back into my head. My neck cracked. My lungs filled with blood.

"Fuck you!" he snapped. "Fuck you, and fuck everything that you love!"

Crack!
I felt the hard thump against the concrete floor. The cold cement felt good while the blood pooled around my head. Grant had officially beaten it all out of me. I struggled for breath, struggled to stay conscious, struggled to stay alive. I felt the swoon coming on fast, gripping every cell of my brain. I was suddenly floating. I was suddenly weightless. I was finally dead.

I could hear Grant's voice moaning in pain from a broken hand. I could hear the shock in the room. I could feel the hope in the air.

Hands suddenly grabbed at my arms and legs, and I was carefully raised into the air. A wasted hunk of flesh. I felt myself be lowered to a fairly soft surface. I heard a door close, and although I couldn't physically pull it off, inside, I smiled. It was my turn to spend some time in the Monkey Den. No hope of salvation now. No hope of escape. No hope, for anything. This had gone much too far already. Much too far. Something had to be done. Something drastic, had to be done! I had to kill Grant.

CHAPTER 36

The Monkey Den. A cold, hard, lonely cell. The room feels closed in the same way your claustrophobic soul does. It's a place where the same bitter loneliness you've always felt, always whined and cried about, seems horribly magnified. The room, the empty, sullen space–I had never taken much time to consider the meaning of it all. It was just a room, a place meant for recovery rather than a place to change your life. More for the experience of forceful confinement, than for spiritual enlightenment. But as my face sucked the sweet, cold moisture from the floor, I realized that the very idea of such a room was probably the true cause of everything that was now lashing back at me. The Monkey Den was the cause of Grant and the rest of his demented disciples. The Monkey Den had been a stupid fucking idea!

When they first drop you in, your body's adrenaline level is so high that you barely feel them placing your wrecked cadaver on the floor. Those around you speak in tongues, and for a moment, you try hard to decipher the gibberish, but to no avail. You gasp, frantically trying to catch your breath. You wince horribly with every hair that moves. You think... You think that at any moment now, you are going to die, so you feebly hold on to some vague fear that maybe the beating was a little too harsh. That maybe, during the wild frenzy, the shock accidentally blew up one of your essential organs, like your liver, or your kidneys. You think that maybe your face will never truly recover from openly showcasing splintered bones. Your body suddenly succumbs to wild convulsions, like bacon in a frying pan, and then, finally, the release. An ugly, nasty nightmare of hallucinations. This lasts for a long while, during which time, all of

your feeble energy is forcefully concentrated on control-
ling the pain, on weening it off somehow, demanding more
dopamine, more endorphins from the brain, anything. You
feel your pulse everywhere, in every joint, and every digit,
and every point of impact. You know that you're a mess. You
know that you may die, and yet, you still feel too weak to
fight back against it.

You tongue your gums, where teeth used to be. You
swallow ungodly amounts of hot blood, and cough it up, and
inhale it. You feel it pooling around your head, drying to a
hard crust over every part of your body. You think that your
nose has been ripped off your face. It's all pain, it's all heat
radiating from your forehead like a dangerous fever, and it's
all struggling. And then, things begin to slow down as your
mind eerily cruises deep into some dark paradigm you never
even knew you carried. The pain recedes into a weird thumping experience and you hear some distant song echoing
through your mind. Cosmic music. Not a real song from the
outside, but an internal hum you're dimly aware of. You lay
there, somewhere in between lucidity and madness, dreams
and reality, with no line clearly separating the two, and you
think that perhaps this is it. The total psychological breakdown that will finally crush you forever. Silence pounds at
your ears, and glimpses of other worlds invade your reality until you no longer know where you are. You no longer
know what has happened. You no longer care.

Your life suddenly becomes a well laid path before
you. Clear. Horrifyingly clear. The kind of exact dissection
of life that makes you squirm uncomfortably. This is the
point where all of those fools out there had figured it out.
This was the source of their beliefs. This was the existential
orgasm. The frantic misfiring of brain waves disguised as
spiritual enlightenment. Suddenly, the problems that pounded against you in real life, they seem minimal. The solutions
seem clear, and you begin to feel slightly stupid for never
having put them into action. You feel free. You feel numb.
You feel comfortable.

You never open your eyes, but you no longer care.

What matters are the lucid dreams lashing out at you from all sorts of hidden crypts in your mind. What matters are all of the simple solutions to your life rushing at you like lightning bolts. What matters, is that you feel nothing. Nothing at all. You are enveloped in a strange cocoon, emersed in peace. The natural drug that eradicates everything around you. You have reached the oasis of your mind, and your soul is caught up in a prolonged orgasm.

Hours pass, but the dreams continue. Reality is something you suddenly cannot conceptualize. You are lost, and you cannot remember anything. Something else takes over, and you suddenly feel as though you're falling freely through the air. Falling, racing, falling, until the mind shuts down, and you are gone. You never were.

CHAPTER 37

I heard the rusty hinges of a door swing open. I heard something thump on the ground, and soon smelled the aroma of hot food coursing through the air. The sound of water being poured. I slightly jerked my head to one side, but never opened my eyes. Only for a second, I thought about the hunger I felt, and then quickly returned to unconsciousness.

I watched bright clouds float peacefully over a mountain range, the sun shinning through them in rays, and I thought about God. I thought about the meaning of God. I thought about peace.

I crept an eyelid open, instantly feeling the extinguishing pain. I feebly moved my body an inch to the left, and then lost it again.

I saw a man standing around the corner of some unknown street, staring at me from the darkness of the night. Eyeing me like a predator. I looked around, feeling my chest tighten. I turned and ran. He was behind me, running faster. I was at top speed, any faster and I would trip and face plant the dark sidewalk beneath my feet, but still he closed in. I heard his voice like a monstrous echo, "You will die!" I felt the wild slash of a knife rip across my upper back. I screamed, and soon realized–I was screaming out loud. My body jolted, the savage pain relentless.

I managed to turn to my side, but kept my eyes closed at all costs. I saw the face of the devil. He told me that I was a joke. He told me that I would forever be condemned to a dark pit of hell where all of those I had hurt would torture me with endless rage. I snapped my eyes open at his laughter. I shuddered at how stupid it all was.

My eyeballs were on fire. I coughed and winced, and then laid still for a moment. I wondered how much time had passed. How long had I been lost in the bowels of my own mind? How long had I slept through ridiculous hallucinations? There was no way of knowing for sure, but what I did know, was that I had survived. I was still alive.

I knew that sooner or later, they would come and get me. They would shove me into a van, and drop me into the gutters somewhere. I knew this, because it was all part of the Crypto Fear experience. My very own stupidity in action. I could feel their hopeful assumptions that they had somehow succeeded in convincing me, but the reality was so much further from the hope.

I considered proclaiming to them that it had worked and briefly acknowledge my new role as savior, only long enough to lower their guard, and then strike back with vicious ferocity. I would claw their idol-like gazes right out of their sockets. I would smash not only their bodies, but their very souls into the depths of nonexistence. Deep inside of me, the rage of a true god was erupting. I had to end it. I had to!

I understood how they felt, and how they could have constructed these notions of me, but the truth of the matter was that the entire experience was a trick of the mind. Hallucinations. I had given them the same rush, the same intense kick that a blotter of acid would have done. The psychological near death experience.

I closed my eyes and I was in the African wilderness. The oppressive heat seared my skin while I aimed a mighty riffle. I stared directly into the face of an elephant swinging its trunk wildly, snorting in anger. I put a bullet into its head.

The door swung open and I heard a voice say, "Get up. It's time to go." It was Grant's voice. Grant's stupid, decrepit voice, assaulting my ear drums like a high pitched wail. Hands grabbed me, lifted me off the ground like a limp rag doll. My head swung back, cracking my back. Horrid, messy pain. I felt them shove my body into their van, and heard the door slam. I felt the transmission shift into gear,

and the acceleration push us back. Total silence now. A snif-
fle. A cough. I simply laid on my back with my head tossing
back and forth, side to side, seizing my neck with cramps.

The momentum stopped and the transmission shifted
again with the engine revving up. Still, not a word spoken. I
felt Grant's body creep up high above mine. I smiled wildly,
showing my smashed teeth.

"I hope you understand, Master," he said, very
seriously. "You have time to think about it, but think hard,
Mickey. We need you to head this for us. We need you. We
love you."

I smiled again and mumbled a weird, "Bah!"
"I'll be back for your decision," he said. "I trust you will
make the correct one."

I said nothing and stared through half glued eyelids.
He sighed loudly.

"All right," he said. "Dump him."
They grabbed me, and I heard the side door slide open. I
felt my body lunge forward and I didn't even put my arms
out to break the fall. I hit the asphalt and moaned as the van
screeched away. I rolled up against a mound of filthy garbage
and closed my eyes. I slept.

$$***$$

I was a mess, but I was feebly able to move around,
at least. The pain was incredible, but my basic motor skills
were functional. I slowly sat up, and leaned against the
mound of garbage bags behind me. I lifted my arm and gingerly inspected my face. Horrible. Ugly. Nasty. I had no idea
of how much time had passed since I had been at the warehouse, or even of where I was. I sat in between two giant
brick buildings lining an alleyway. I dug my hand into my
pocket and found a few clumpy bills, amazed that I hadn't
been robbed while I slept. Too ugly to mug. I painfully irked
my way up to my feet and took a deep breath, desperately
trying not to vomit. I cracked my neck, and began walking
very slowly toward the intersecting street, but when I got

there, I leaned against the building for a moment, trying to catch my breath. Across the street was a drug store. I hurriedly made my way toward it, straight through the horrified pedestrians rushing to me, asking if I was okay, did I need an ambulance? I ignored them and blasted through the doors of the drug store, stumbling down the aisle where an old Korean man was suddenly waving a broom in my face, yelling at me.

"What you want?" he demanded. "What you want? You get out. Get out. You filthy with blood. You filthy."

I held up my hands, a sign of peace, a plea, *just give me a fucking break, man.*

"You go now," he snapped. "I call police."

"You," I replied, exhausted, and weak. "You do whatever you have to do, old man, but I'm not leaving here without a bottle of painkillers in my hand."

He quickly snatched a bottle from the shelf. "Here," he said. "You no pay, you go. You go."

"All right, all right," I said. I snapped off the top of the bottle and let at least 10 pills slide into my mouth. I painfully crushed them with whatever was left of the jagged sockets housing remnants of teeth. I moaned in pain, swallowing with difficulty.

"You go now," his temper was getting dangerously thin. I couldn't handle a single strike from his broom, so I turned and left the store, stumbling back onto the sidewalk, back into the shocked stares of unsuspecting pedestrians quickly covering their mouths with their hands. I shoved the bottle into my pocket and stumbled weakly into the street, trying to wave down a cab.

No luck. The sight of me was causing engines to rev higher, and hurried lane changes. Finally, one cab was in the wrong lane and had no escape. I lurched toward the vehicle, landing directly in front of it as the brakes screeched, and the hood nearly ended it all for me. I could see the immigrant man shaking his head through the glare of the windshield. His lips repeatedly forming no, no, no. I raced for the passenger side and swung the door open just as I heard the locking mechanism kick in. Too late, Mister. I hopped in fast.

"No! No, Senior. No ride, man. No ride."

I dug into my pocket and pulled out two fifties.

"Here," I said. "Just drive. Just get me out of here." The driver sighed loudly, not wanting to go, but still unable to resist the lure of cash. The car began moving and I gave him the address to the warehouse. The ride was incredibly silent, aside from the steady hum of the engine and the manic traffic around us. He didn't dare ask a question. He didn't even look at me. I rested my heavy head against the head rest and closed my eyes. Solace now. At least momentarily.

By the time I arrived at the warehouse, the pills were kicking in, slowly beating back the erratic jolts of pain to a bearable level. I could keep my eyes open. I could feel my legs. I opened the door and whimpered a "Thanks."

The sight of the building made me want to burn it down. I hated myself. Reluctantly, I went inside, and immediately, I could tell that something was wrong. I could feel it in the air. Something had gone very, very wrong.

The place was empty. No employees. No victims. No money. The echoing silence was oddly disheartening, and felt quite alien to me. I hurried up the stairs as quickly as I could, my ribs searing in pain, my lungs crying for air. When I opened the door upstairs, the place bled with a crack house-like ambience. It was so incredibly rancid and vile.

"Jesus Christ!" I said. I wasn't sure of what had happened. It was wild. There were people sleeping everywhere amongst vials of white powder and half empty liquor bottles passively reflecting whatever light still shone from the unbroken bulbs in the ceiling. The walls were littered with strange, multicolored scribbling of mindless proclamations. Things like, "Freedom is death," and "Eat my soul," and "Heroes do not understand," were written everywhere by trembling hands with no real meaning behind them. Twisted.

From somewhere, muffled by a multitude of walls, I could hear music playing in the distance. It heightened my sense of uneasiness with the place. I stepped over the naked bodies of beautiful women, unashamed in their drug

induced comas, and headed toward the back rooms. It had
all the hallmarks of Steve's twisted mind. Had he come back
while I was out getting my very own piece of understanding? There was no doubt in my mind that he'd had a hand in
it, but where was he? Was he still living? Was his mind still
functional? Or had he, as I always expected, finally gone too
far and cracked under the pressure?

I opened the first door in the hallway and the smell
of the room made me gag. A horrid stench that seemed like
a hybrid cross between wet garbage and a busted sewer
line. There were people in there, unaffected by the cloud of
hazardous stench as it probably emanated from their pores. I
wondered who they were. These drug riddled scum. Where
had they come from?

Through the next door, just down the hall, I found
more stinking, foul individuals looking like wasted carica-
tures from some hellish carton. More writing on the walls,
and I suddenly wondered if these people were followers.
Would they be in the future? Were these delinquents also
caught up in Grant's defamed notions? Had they expected
the savior to arrive at some point during the party?

I toyed with the idea of simply loading the Glock
and going to town on the unsuspecting comas, blasting the
vileness straight out of them, but I was desperate to find
Steve and figure out what had happened. Get these parasites
out of the warehouse and try to deal with the consequences
that were coming my way. Grant would not be able to contain himself for very long.

I shut the door and continued my search, my chest
flooding with uneasy fear. I headed directly for the door at
the end of the hallway where the muffled music was blaring
inside. I kicked it open like a raiding police officer, but was
stopped dead in my tracks at the sight of a hellish scene.

There was violent blood splatter on the walls, and
the ceiling. The music was incredibly loud, the smell unbearable, and on the floor, next to the bed, was Steve! Passed out,
and completely naked. His long hair was stuck to his sagging face with a mixture of blood and dried vomit, but that

was not the sight that made my sweat turn cold. Two women lay on top of the flame seared bed, naked, and covered with hundreds of violent stab wounds. Their dead eyes stared out into space with nothing inside of them.

"Shit!" I yelled. "They're dead! Holy shit! They're all dead!" Panic rushed through me like a bad chemical trip. How long had it been? What the fuck had happened?

I rushed out into the hallway and puked on the floor. A horrible scene of decay. My abdomen heaved in painful convulsions. What the hell was I going to do? I ran back into the room and headed directly for Steve, straight through the filth, and the blasting music. I kicked him hard in the side, screaming wildly, "Get up, you fucking lunatic! Get up! Get up! Get up!!!"

He jumped up and began smashing anything he could grab, screaming incomprehensible gibberish as if he was still locked in a nightmare–and that's exactly what he was in–a twisted, mind-fucked nightmare! He was beside himself! I grabbed the blaring stereo and smashed it on the floor next to him, the wild sparks ending the unbearable decibels and snapping him out of his mindless attack.

"You fucking idiot!" I screamed. "What the fuck are you doing? What did you do?"

I could taste blood seeping into my mouth. He seemed stunned for a moment, trying to focus his eyes on the grim reality that now surrounded him. He stared at his blood covered hands, and then up to the bed, before losing it again, but it wasn't in a rage this time, it was now on par with my own panic. The frontal lobes of his brain were flat out refusing the signals being sent to it. He was terrified now, probably realizing that he had done something incredibly cruel, and brutal.

"What happened?" he yelled frantically. "What happened?" I snapped. "You tell me what happened! You killed two girls! You fucking killed them! You...."

"I didn't do it!" he snapped back. "I couldn't have! I love women, man! I love em'! You know that! I was framed!"

"Framed? You degenerate bastard! You fucking killed them, and now they're gonna fry you for this! Shit, they'll probably fry the both of us, you crazy fucking asshole!" I punched him in anger.

"No!" he snarled. "This isn't real! This isn't real!" He was attempting to convince himself that he was only trapped in a bad trip, just a very bad hallucination.

"Oh, it's real, you fucker! What happened?" I screamed in panic.

"I... I don't know, man," he yelled.
I began assaulting him with questions.

"Tell me what happened! How long have you been here for? Who the fuck are all of these people?"

"I don't know! All right! I don't fucking know! I don't fucking know, man!"

He began crying.
"Goddamn it!" I snapped again. "Get a fucking grip and focus!"

He suddenly looked up to me.
"Where were you, man?" he asked as if he hadn't disappeared for 2 weeks without a single trace.

"Where was I?" I screamed. "I was being kidnapped and tortured by a bunch of fucking lunatics, while you were here, for who the hell knows how long, partying like an unhinged junkie and STABBING TWO FUCKING GIRLS TO DEATH!!!"

I punched him in the head as I said it. I was enraged.
"Please, man," he whimpered. "Please! Don't say those things, man. Don't..."

"You degenerate!" I snapped. "I can't help you! You're fucked! You are fucked!"

"No, man!" he cried, rocking his body back and forth on the floor like a schizophrenic. "Please. Get me out of here, man. Please, I need you to save me."

"Save you?" I replied. The thought of it reflected everything back to me in an unsettling rush of rage. "Save you? Fuck you! I can put a bullet in your head! That should save you! Or give Grant a call, he'll show you the way! Call

Polaris, I'm sure she's doing just fucking great far, far away from me. Fuck you, man!"

"Please, man," tears streamed down his face like rivers. "Please. We can frame one of these fuckers. We can put a knife in their hand and drag their ass in here. Cover em' with blood. Please, man. Please, I need your help."

I stopped. He had a point. We could simply drag one of the naked catatonics into the room and frame the bastard for double murder. Why not? There were no reliable witnesses. Everyone in the place was horribly lost in some distant dimension of time, and place. Lost on the existential edge of madness. I thought about it, but just as I was about to agree with him, some very important questions began flooding in.

Here he was, caught with two dead girls in a completely annihilated dwelling. Quite obviously, drugs had been the main contributor to the situation, so no one could possibly be trusted to say no, it wasn't that guy, it was him. But what about the hard facts? These were junkies. Steve was a junkie. The real questions had to be asked. Questions I knew even he could not answer with certainty.

How many times had he left his filthy seed inside of these two wound riddled bodies, and where? There was no denying hard evidence. How many people had seen them in here, or anywhere? How long had it been? What other kind of incriminating evidence was hidden in this repulsive room? Too much to even begin counting.

His eyes flooded with tears and he stared at me like a child. Beady, and terrified, and ravaged by guilt.

"Please, man," he pleaded. "Please, Mickey! You have to help me," he shuddered, and gasped, letting the tears pour out. I could tell that he was still caught in some obscure crystal meth haze. He was fucked.

"Please, please, please..." his body rocked back and forth. I simply stared at him. Wasted. There was no returning from anything anymore.

"I need a line!" he suddenly exclaimed, sounding frantic and out of focus. "I need a... I need a line!" he began thrashing through the broken garbage around him, searching for a vial, searching for the only escape he currently understood.

"Stop it!" I snapped. "Hey!"
He suddenly stopped and stared at me with unsettled eyes. I held his gaze while his hand crossed into my field of vision, it was waving a big stainless steel knife at me. His voice was possessed. His face a mask.

"Are you going to help me, or not?" he asked, very seriously, frightening in its desperation. I sighed, and bit my swollen bottom lip. I wanted the pain. I winced and bit harder. I needed the pain.

"No," I whispered. I was a foul example of a friend, but there was nothing I could do. "I'm sorry, but I can't help you. I love you, man, but it's too late."

He said nothing for a moment, his expression not even changing.

"Fuck that!" he screamed in rage. "Fuck you, you goddamn hypocrite! I fucked up! I'm sorry! But please, please, man. Don't do this to me! We're best friends, goddamn it!"

He was incredibly hurt, as was I, but it had to be done. He tried to get up and attack me with his blade, but he was too off balance and fell back to the ground in a fit of tears. Desperate, heartfelt tears. It was too late.

I said nothing. My head was exploding. I needed to run.

"Take care of yourself, man," was all I could think of saying. I turned and left, and never stopped to look back. When I was finally outside, my body went numb, and I began running. My only destination–was away! Far, far away.

I ran.

CHAPTER 38

I found myself thinking about Polaris. Where had she gone? Where had she hunkered down, far away from the savagery? Madness had been the only sensible thing I could afford her, the only attraction that had bonded us together like a sad sack of carnival freaks. How twisted.

Rain drops smashed painfully into my broken face while I ran. The cold relief immediately gave way to more pain. Eventually, I sat alone on a park bench, the entire place around me empty save for a few homeless men with long beards and dark plastic bags dragging behind them.

I wondered what was I going to do. My life was getting worse by the day. I swallowed hard, wincing in pain. I was done. This was it. I couldn't afford any more madness. Polaris was gone. Steve was finished. My dream had evaporated right before my eyes and the only thing left standing, was me. Petty, little, broken me. I felt unbearably alone. I had no one. No one I wanted, at least. I had money, I had a following, I had an identity, and still, I had nothing. Nothing!

The best thing I could think of doing was to approach The Terror and quite bluntly say, "I'm sorry, but I'm done." Death was the obvious downfall of that situation, but somehow, I felt that what I was already living was far worse than what death could provide. It had to be ended, and if that meant an eternal debt owed to The Terror, then so be it. If it meant death, well, then, what's a man to do? I felt shoved so far down the pits already that I had to look up in order to even see hell.

I sat in the park for hours under the dripping heavens, thinking until my skin reached the sensitivity level of an oozing sore. I was decided. I had to muster up the nerve to call The Terror and announce my intended visit. If I was to run, I felt I should at least have the decency to pull the stunt off face to face. Realistically, there was no way to truly out-run the man. For all I knew, he had satellites floating around in space watching my every move. I found a phone near the edge of the park and dialed the number with a shaking, nervous finger.

I spoke with Mr. Gordon, his voice as straight and serious as always.

"Yes, Mickey. Mr. Labelle is very excited to speak with you. I would advise you to make it here as quickly as possible. His patience is running thin."

"I know," I said, trembling. "I'm on my way now. I have a major emergency to deal with."

"I will advise him. Thank you, Mickey. See you shortly."

My nerves were shot. I had no vehicle, but there wasn't a chance in hell I was going back to the warehouse to pick one up. I hopped on the city bus with my face man-gled and multiple bones broken. I didn't care what people thought. I had a giant goddamn mess on my hands that had to be dealt with swiftly, and quietly.

The bouncers at the front doors didn't recognize me at first and tried to stop me from going anywhere near the building until I began screaming wildly at them, "I'll have The Terror down here and feeding you your own testicles before you even have a chance to protest against it! I owe him money! Now get the fuck out of the way!" Of course, the properly trained employees immediately recognized the obvious. Money was owed, let the poor bastard through at once! I plowed through the classy establishment like a human bulldozer. The rich customers and strippers alike all gasped in horror at the sight of my face, probably expecting to see me come crashing through the ceiling at any moment once I made it to the boss's lavish headquarters. I trampled up the stairs and into the room, never knocking; I was impor-tant now, I felt–I owed a lot of money–I had VIP status in the place.

The Terror was sitting at the bar, speaking with the bartender. The body guards immediately drew their pistols at the crashing doors, and even Mr. Gordon seemed excited by the commotion, but not The Terror. I didn't believe the man was capable of feeling fear, in fact. Why should he? He lived by a very simple set of standards. If someone is not doing what you want them to do, torture them in the most inhumane way you can think of and set the proper tone for the next fool who tries to screw you. Make an example of him. If something moves in an unpredictable way, shoot at it until it stops, and then continue on with business. Nuts and bolts kind of stuff. Nothing was uncontrollable. With enough force, everything eventually moved under the pressure.

The Terror's eyes grew wide at the sight of me. He seemed very serious, and in a very foul mood.

"Hi," I said, almost casually. "I'm here."
He stood up and approached me.

"Mickey," he said sternly. "Where the fuck have you been? I've been trying to get a hold of you."

"I'm sorry," I said quickly. "I ah..."
"And please, enlighten me," his French accent echoed monstrously through the room. "What the fuck happened to your face?"

"Ah... I know. I ah..."
"No," he interrupted. "I mean, have you seen it?"

I was suddenly aware of the full weight of my body, as though I was fighting hard against gravity to keep from being pulled down to the floor. He continued speaking, examining the gashes and the swollen pools of black and blue collected under the skin.

"It looks like the face of this woman I know. A few years ago, she had decided to have a girl's night out, or whatever they call it these days, and failed to return home after a bar hopping stint. It was fairly harmless, it was in Montreal, after all. Unfortunately, this woman is my sister, and her piece of shit boyfriend suddenly believed that he was tough enough to unleash a blind rage on her."

My eyes were shifting wildly, trying to keep focussed on what was happening. I had bigger problems to deal with, but no one pushed Mr. Labelle to move faster. He was the boss, and if you didn't like his pace, well, you could happily eat 15 or 20 lead projectiles to the face.

"Luckily," he continued. "His opinion quickly changed after his hands were accidentally chopped off in a horrible meat cleaver accident, and the big man, quite unfortunately, choked to death before even getting to the ring finger of the first hand." He smiled and looked upward as if remembering a cherished memory.

I frowned and closed my eyes, letting the blood stained saliva painfully slide down my esophagus.

"You fed him his own fingers?" I asked in shock. "I never said such a thing," he said, waving his index finger through the tense air. "All I said was that he choked on a few finger chunks and died before the whole deed could be done."

"Jesus Christ!" I said. My mind was knocked off balance, and suddenly, I had nothing to say. Why was I even here?

"I'm just saying," he shrugged. "You reminded me of it." He smiled, but it was the kind of sarcastic expression you would give a man before you shot him in the head. "Now, where the fuck have you been? The business is suffering, do you know that? It's about to crash, Mickey! There hasn't been a goddamn person in the place for days now. No one. This is unacceptable!"

I suddenly felt a mixture of fear and embarrassment. I was weak with exhaustion.

"Here," he extended his hand. "Have a seat and talk to me. I want to know what's going on. I won't allow anyone to fuck around with my money. I'm trying to save your life here. So tell me, what's the problem?"

I could still taste thick blood at the back of my throat. "I ah... Mr. Labelle... We have a big problem," I stammered.

"A what?" he cocked his head. "A problem?" "Yes... Yes, sir."

"Well what kind of fucking problem, Mickey? And please, tell me what happened to your face."

"Well, that's part of the problem... Sir," I could tell that his patience was running dangerously thin. "You see, there are two problems really."

"Get to it, kid," he warned. "I'm getting sick of this."

"Sorry," I replied. "First off, the warehouse, well, it hasn't been empty, really. My ah, my partner, Steve, he disappeared for a few weeks and I had no idea where he was. He's been having a little bit of a problem with drugs lately."

"I don't give a fuck about your personal life, Mickey. Get to the fucking point, now!"

Without hesitation, I starting ranting. "There's a guy out there on the streets. The one who started these bullshit rumors about me being some kind of savior. Well, he's... He's gone too far. He's got the whole thing organized like some degenerate religion, and they're after me to, I don't know, be their leader. They're losing it. Anyway, I refused, and they kidnapped me. They did this to me. I guess, to try and make me understand or something, but they'll be back soon enough. I don't know what to do. These people are dangerous."

He nodded.

"Ah... Anyway. They kept me in a warehouse for a while and then dumped me, but when I got back to the warehouse, well, my partner, Steve, he was back, but there was a major problem, and I need your help with it. Please, I desperately need your help, or else this whole thing will be over for all of us. It's–it's serious, Andy," I said. "It's really bad."

He looked around the room to the others, slightly confused.

"I... I can't go back there!" I broke down in tears. "What the fuck?" The Terror replied, disgusted, and utterly repulsed by my overwhelming rush of emotions. "All right!" he said quickly. "Everybody out! Out! I need to speak to Mickey alone."

Quickly, those present vacated the room. "All right,"

he said. "Listen to me, Mickey. Tell me what happened. What did you do?" His voice was calculated, and I suspected that he would soon put a bullet into my pumpkin sized head and cut his losses.

"Nothing," I moaned painfully, sobbing like a little girl. "He ah, he stabbed two girls. He killed them. Both of them. Upstairs, in the office. He... He fucking killed them. We're fucked!" I exclaimed. "We're... We're finished, Andy. It's too late."

He licked his lips, frowning pensively.
"He stabbed two girls?" he questioned. "When?"

"I... I don't know," I replied, still sobbing. "But there were lots of people there. They had been partying for days, and they were passed out everywhere; but in the back room, Steve was in there, and on the bed, there were two dead girls!"

"Are you fucking kidding me?" he demanded. "What the hell are we supposed to do about this now? This is bad, Mickey! This is very bad for business!"

"I know," I nodded and tried wiping my tears, but the flesh was far too sensitive. He stood up and walked toward the bar, pouring two whiskies on the rocks. He chugged one and filled it again, bringing me the other.

"Well," he said. "I can't let that place go, it's too profitable. Business there is only going to get better."

I sipped the drink and the alcohol stung every sore molecule, causing an angry sensation all the way down to the pit of my tangled stomach.

"We gotta clean it up," he said. "We have to get rid of everything and reorganize, understand?"

I reluctantly nodded in agreement. As much as I hated the thought, I had no choice in the matter. Steve was my best friend, but he had screwed up on a monumental scale. Either way, no matter what I did, he was done. I gingerly rubbed the scabby, rugged texture of my forehead.

"I'll send a team out there to clean it up. Your friend, Steve, is it? Well, I'm sorry kid, but forget you ever knew him. He, and anyone else present when the team gets there, do you understand?"

"Yes," I nodded sullenly, defeated.

"I'm only telling you this once, Mickey. This is a major fuck up! If you let anything even remotely close to this happen again you'll be chewing on your own asshole!"

I nodded, and an awkward silence came between us, catching us both in dark reflections.

"Jesus Christ," he muttered. "You better hope to Christ that no one got out of there, Mickey. For your own good, you better start praying! Goddamn fucking amateurs!"

"I know," I replied. "I'm sorry."

"How long has it been since you were there?"

"I don't know, maybe four hours."

"Four hours?" he exclaimed. "Next time, you fucking call me immediately. You do not leave! You do not do anything! You call me, and you fucking wait!" He was screaming at me now like a father who had just found out that his son had totaled his car. "You stay there and you wait for me! Don't be fucking stupid!"

"I'm sorry," I said.

He shook his head violently, snatching his phone from his breast pocket, and jabbing at the numbers.

"These goddamn phones!" he yelled.

Whoever answered on the other end was swiftly given directions by the boss.

"*Assemble l'équipe et envoie la a l'édifice de Crypto Fear. Bleach it, vous comprenez? .... Très bien!...* Get it done fast. Clean and fast. Goodbye!"

He slapped the phone shut.

"Well," he said. "That's that. You want another drink?"

"No thanks," I said, my emotions under control again. Somber. Doomish.

"Now," he continued. "Tell me more about this other problem. The less dramatic one. Tell me about the man with the rumors. Is he a threat? Can he cause more damage than you've already done?"

"I... I think so. I think he's a very disturbed man."

"Great," he replied. "Another goddamn moron running

around and stabbing holes in my business. Where do you find these idiots?"

I shook my head in despair. I could sense from the tone of his voice that he was desperately trying to contain himself and not destroy the place like a powerful tornado.

"Who is he?" he asked.

I told him the entire twisted story, "He used to be my boss. I blackmailed him. I punched out an executive and encouraged him to do the same. He did. He then came to me, wanting to be kidnapped, wanting to be beaten. I did. Then he started following me on jobs. He confronted me with his demented notions of who I was. I refused, but he pushed on and gathered many people to follow him. He spread my name everywhere and the business swelled. He stalked me for a while, then kidnapped me, beat me, and tried to make me understand. And now I do. He's a goddamn fool. And here I am now. Beaten and scared, and I don't know how to deal with it.

"He'll be back for me, Mr. Labelle. I don't know when, but it won't be very long. And then what? Will he kill me? Will he, I don't know. All I do know, is that it won't be pretty, and I may have to shoot him."

He smiled strangely. I was confused by his reaction. Why was he smiling? This was no joke! This was serious goddamn it!

"That makes a lot of sense," he said, rubbing his chin.

"What does?" I questioned. "Grant?"

He swallowed the rest of his drink and stared at me intently. What now? What was he thinking?

"You know, Mickey, I am a very well connected man." I nodded yes, of course, I was no fool. At least not in that context. "And there is something brewing out there that has been catching my attention lately, but I could not quite figure it out. But now, it all makes perfect sense."

I stared back with painful eyes. My head was throbbing.

"I've noticed a trend on the streets lately, that is,

how do you say in English... Let's say, disheartening."

Disheartening? I thought. What could possibly be disheartening for this man? He ripped people to horrible shreds on a daily basis, and some *trend* was suddenly disheartening?

"There are people everywhere lately," he continued. "Here, in Los Angeles. In San Francisco, and apparently, all the way up to Seattle, and straight across to the east. In Michigan. In Detroit. In New York. Christ, my associates even have reports coming out of Vancouver, and Edmonton, and Toronto, and even beautiful Montreal city. Everywhere, it seems, there are people walking the streets with swollen faces, like yours, which I know, of course, you did not put there."

"What?" I frowned in pain.

"Yes," he replied. "These people are being kidnapped off the streets and beaten to a pulp, just as you're doing here. Christ, next I'll be hearing it from Japan, and France, and Russia."

"What?!" I felt terror seize my heart. This could not be.

"Mickey," he said sternly. "They all know your name."

My stomach turned to lead. My vision blurred, and I was far too "disheartened" to even tremble.

"Wha... What did you say?" I asked as though I had completely misunderstood the statement, even though deep down I knew I had not.

"They speak of you," he said, and stood up, calmly pacing the room. "They chant your name, Mickey. They kidnap, in your name. Apparently, they have all these websites where they gather and talk about this whole thing and probably jerk off to your picture. I will never understand this new generation of idiot kids, but that is besides the point, isn't it? The point here, is that to these idiots, you are a savior. You are a leader of low lives, Mickey," he said and came very close to my ugly face. Sweat poured from my mangled pores. "You are getting famous, my friend."

I closed my eyes. The room was spinning violently,

my chest tightening, and suddenly, I couldn't breathe, I couldn't concentrate, I was having a panic attack!

"I... Uh.... I...." I mumbled, but the strength of the panic was far too powerful to subdue. This could not be! This was a nightmare! Please, anything but this! Anything!

"I don't think I have to tell you what this means," The Terror said, pulling away from me. I placed my head in between my legs, trying to catch my breath. I was blacking out. I was mumbling, "This is not good. This is wrong. This is wrong!"

But The Terror's face held a malicious smile. "This is good, Mickey," he said valiantly.

"No!" I shrieked. "This is not good! This is no fucking good!"

"You listen to me!" he said, matching my intensity. "This is very good. Your little psycho friend, Grant, is it? Well, he's been very busy spreading the word all over the country. Shit, it's spreading into other countries as we speak, and as we speak, right now, people from all over the place are being kidnapped, and they are being beaten, and they are all reading, and hearing, and talking about Mickey Tyler. The Master. The Savior. The God."

"Fuck!" I screamed. The very idea of it shifted my stomach into a ball of poisonous lead. "I'm gonna kill that motherfucker! That's it! I can't take this anymore!"

"No you will not!" he roared. "You will not do anything to him because he is making you famous. You have the opportunity to become very rich, my friend, and you owe it all to him. Millions of dollars can be siphoned from this. If you do anything to him now, you risk screwing it up, and I will not have that happen. Do you understand me? It won't happen!"

The idea of having legions of geeks chanting my name and talking about my supposed life philosophies was sickening. All of them claiming me as their savior. All of them, supposedly owing their lives to me. I would take it. I would take everyone of their sad, depressive little lives and dispose of them in an industrial sized incinerator.

"Please," I moaned, knowing exactly where this was going. "Please. Don't make me do this. Don't make me head this like some..."

"Quit being such a goddamn pussy!" he snarled. "Were you born this stupid, or did you have to learn it? Don't you understand what's happening here? This is the greatest opportunity of your life. This is the greatest thing that will ever happen to you. Right here, and right now, you have the opportunity to make enough money to take care of yourself for the rest of your life. No success comes without sacrifice, remember that."

I winced emotionally at his words.

"Listen," he continued. "Who really cares about these people? Screw em, you have everyone from respected citizens, to scum bag losers, to salad tossing hipsters hanging off your every word. They are paying for this. They are warranting your presence in order to head this into a real thing, to make it concrete. Who cares about if it's right or wrong? Why do you even care what they think you are? Get your sorry little ass in there and start collecting from it, goddamn it! You started this, Mickey, and at the first sign of success, what do you do? You start running away like a little bitch who just got kicked in the side of the head. Get a grip on it. Get all of that available money, and keep your mouth shut. No one cares about your feelings, Mickey, and no one ever will. You're set up for life. You've won the lottery. Now go and collect your prizes."

I felt a stabbing pain in my liver, my kidneys felt swollen, and my heart was throbbing in erratic jolts. I was crushed.

"You should be grateful for this, because I warned you not to fuck this up, and quite frankly, if it wasn't for your little psychotic friend, Grant, I would never have helped you. Ironic, isn't it? Yes, quite ironic. I've always told you that I like you, but as I've said, there is no room for feelings in business. No one gives a fuck about them because they cause irrational and unnecessary decisions to be made. Become a robot and use your head, ignore your heart, it has nothing profitable to say."

Bad waves of despair washed through me. This could not be! He could not be telling me to go back. Not like this. Not with Grant around.

"Where are your employees now?" he asked.
"I have no idea," I muttered. Thick, sticky phlegm blocked my airways.

"Well," he sighed. "We'll find them. Forget them too. They're too much of a liability now. I will assign new employees for you. They will be faithful, and they will know exactly how to handle this with you."

I pressed my hand against the ragged edges of my face, causing me incredible pain. I wanted the pain again. It was the only way I truly knew that I was still alive, and that this was real. All of this, painfully real.

"What about Grant?" I asked.
"What about him?" he replied simply. "When you see him, you tell him that you now understand his purpose, and that yes, in fact, you are ready to accept your new role as the leader of this obscenely profitable business venture. Don't be stupid, Mickey. I'm warning you."

I gasped at the thought of it, seriously contemplating suicide.

"You should have time to regroup and reorganize by the time you see him again," he said. "Apparently, from what I am told, he, or somebody out there, is stating that you are temporarily gone on some soul searching expedition. Ha! What a bunch of idiots! They're comparing it to Jesus in the desert, forty days of personal challenging, alone, and debating the true course of your life. These fuckers are serious, and you better take them that way when they come back to you."

"What the fuck?" I whimpered. "What the fuck?"
I shook my head, trying not to crack under the unrelenting pressure.

"Jesus," he said. "You really are a mess, aren't you?"
I said nothing and panted.

"Tell you what," he continued. "I'll have my driver

bring you to a hotel. I want you to rest for a few days. I want you to get back into shape, and then get back to work. Forget about all of this and just get back to making some money. You will be a millionaire before the end of the year, Mickey. Smile, and be happy. Money really can buy you happiness, just give it a chance, you will thank me in the long run."

I couldn't feel much of my body anymore. I couldn't feel much of anything anymore. Here I was, broken, and beaten, and completely cornered into becoming a social product. A poster boy for things no one truly understood, but everyone assumed with a crude, primitive herd psychology. The truth didn't matter, only the illusion did. The lure of someone who seemed better, and smarter, and who was shrouded in mystery was more than enough to hold the interest of the general public. I was weak, and scared, and suicidal, but this was to be my life. I should have smiled–all of my dreams had come true.

All of my stupid fucking dreams had come true.

CHAPTER 39

Bleach. The horrid stench of sterile surfaces battered the soft, sensitive membranes of my nose. The smell of death hung in the air. The "special team" had been swift, and obviously knew exactly what they were doing. They had rampaged through the warehouse and made everything disappear. There were no bodies left, no furniture, no sign of any of it. The industrial carpet was gone; ripped out and probably burned somewhere in a black cloud of plastics and chemicals. No evidence. No proof. Everything was wiped down, leaving only the stench behind to mask the truth of what had truly happened.

They told me that Steve had already slit his wrists and lay dead by the time they had arrived. I didn't believe them, but he might as well have. I knew that regardless of the circumstances upon arrival, he had, in one way or another, committed suicide a long time ago. I missed him, but I was having trouble feeling it. I was cold, and absent of any real feelings.

As far as they could tell, no one else had made it out before they had arrived. One other girl was already dead with thick yellowish foam around her lips. No one got out of there. Not willfully, anyway.

I spent 3 days in a hotel room, sleeping, crying, and pleading with the walls for some kind of release. The scabs on my face were black and had glazed over hard, but the swelling was almost completely gone. I could finally feel the bones underneath the thin flesh of my face, a monstrous improvement from the swollen disaster I had been; but when I finally did return to the warehouse, I was met by The Terror towing a cast of goons behind him.

"Mickey," Mr. Labelle said. "Say hello to your new crew. This is Paul," a big bouncer looking man with hair like a carrot stepped forward and shook my hand. "This is Pete, Jason, Dave, and Jack." I nodded hello to the assembled crew, but wanted nothing to do with them. I was bitter, and angry! Injustice!

"Oh, and for the women who like this service of yours, say hello to Holly," a brunette stepped forward and extended her hand.

"Hi," she said happily. "I look forward to working with you, Mr. Tyler."

"Whatever," I answered. I hated these fools. I wanted nothing to do with this!

"Now, now, Mickey," The Terror said. "Be nice to Holly. She's a champion kick boxer. I'll have her make a little girl out of you before I fashion your tongue into a new tie for Mr. Gordon here. Now, let's get to work, shall we? Let's get this money machine a'rollin!"

There were days of hands on training, and before I even understood what was happening, the whole place was buzzing as loudly as ever. Business was good, but I was not. I took to a slew of chemicals in response to my newly reached rock bottom; drinking heavily, and fouling my nostrils with a seemingly endless supply of white powder. Without it, I didn't think that I could deal with any of it. Crypto Fear wasn't even my business anymore, it was The Terror's business. He owned all of it, and I was nothing more than a puppet, nothing except the poster boy used to lure the limp and broken minds through the doors and keep the gears turning at top speed.

Mickey Tyler was back! Or at least the illusion of it was. In reality, I was out of my mind with anxiety. I'd snort a line, drive out, beat the life out of some idiot right there on the sidewalk, shove him into the van and get him into the warehouse, snort another line, and then go to town on his face with my voice horribly unconvinced with the shit spewing out of my mouth. I had lost control.

"Your life is worth less than dog shit!"

Crack!

"Do yourself a favor and jump off a bridge!"

Crack!

"Why did you come here? Huh? You're an aborted soul. You're only worth an overdose!"

Crack!

Things were rolling, but there was no soul in it anymore. The motivating factors that had launched me into this mess in the first place had long ago withered away and died. Everything was now calculated, monotonous, generic, and still, it sold to the mainstream with unwavering loyalty. I simply went through the motions. When I told someone they were worth less than my warm spit, I no longer meant it in that moment. When I felt my knuckles connect against someone's skull through the cocaine induced force field I carried with me at all times, it meant nothing. When I heard any mention of the words master, or savior, or god, another piece of my shattered soul sunk deeper into the pit.

The Terror was acting more like a manager/agent/publicist than the ruthless gangster he was known for. His smiles were big, his excitement bigger, his control, relentless. He walked through the warehouse with the corners of his lips touching his ears while the money piles fattened like swine in a pen.

"Have a look!" he exclaimed like a man who had just won the lottery. "Look at this! Isn't it amazing!"

He turned a laptop toward me; the soft light of the screen caused my body to shudder.

"What the hell is this?" I exclaimed. "A website? You had a website made?" I stared in disgust. Sad realities. There was my face! My eyes looked like they were trapped in deep, intellectual thought, my face reflected the aura of a man who knew things. Deep, important things.

"Your website!" he continued. "Look at this! It's beautiful, kid! These people are insane over you! I love this technology! I fucking love it!"

He was terribly excited, but I failed to meet his level of enthusiasm.

"What's wrong?" he questioned quickly. "You don't like the picture? Don't worry. People love it." And he smiled widely again.

"You can't mass produce this," I protested. "This isn't a fucking fast food joint. This–this is wrong."

"Yes, I can mass produce it, and I am," he quickly replied. "What's wrong with you? I told you, this will make you rich. Christ! I've never seen a man whose depression rises in sync with the money he earns. Are you retarded or something?"

"You have no idea," I whispered, walking away. "Mickey," I heard him in the distance. "Mickey, come on, kid. This is great!"

"I need more cocaine!" I declared. "I need a drink." I was a recluse as often as I could be. While the dedicated employees beat the endless throngs of losers and freaks, I hid. I drank profusely. I snorted wildly. I binged until my eyes crossed and my heart felt as though it would cause a hematoma on the inside of my rib cage; until my mind reeled with gibberish, and my body was so far beyond numb, something very close to peace moved through me. A wonderful blanket of substance abuse.

I feared the day I would see Grant again. His idolizing stares crushed my insides like a press. The Terror's voice echoed through my skull every time I thought about Grant; "These people are serious, you better take them that way!"

Despite the pressure, and the pain, and the incredible paranoia I was causing myself, I simply could not bring myself to do it. I simply could not slip into the role, and play the part, and laugh all the way to the bank because of it. I was nothing like The Terror.

If I went out, I was on high guard. On a job, my eyes relentlessly scanned the surroundings for any sign of the psycho staring back at me from a distance. Oddly enough, he seemed nowhere to be found, and it somehow caused me even more worry. The longer his absence endured, the stronger the anxiety pounded at me and filled my head with ghoulish possibilities. How long before the inevitable came knocking at my door like unwanted preachers? I needed a release, and quick.

Unwillingly, I continued working under The Terror's threats to eat my Adam's apple, and feed me my own intestines. I continued, but as I did, I also began growing increasingly reckless. I had no problems with grabbing a girl off the sidewalk by the hair and dragging her very calmly across the street to the waiting van while she screamed for people to call the police. I had no objections about shoving my gun in someone's face in the middle of a mall, or even firing a few warning shots into the air. I couldn't have cared less. Arrest me. Do me a favor and throw my stupid ass in jail. Beat me savagely and hang me publicly in an example of what happens to those who dare make our society uncomfortable. Fight me back. Kill me. Please, somebody just fucking kill me.

Unfortunately, for myself at least, The Terror's employees were highly trained in these tense situations, and were always just a little too quick in containing the damage and leaving the scene before any consequences reached us. Always too soon. Always too fast.

In the warehouse, the echoing gasps and moans emanating from the cells sounded like claws screeching down a chalkboard. The hard packing sounds, and the breaking bones, they sounded like knives to the heart. The swollen faces leaving in the morning, they looked like reflections of my devastated emotions. I was lost in the same question over, and over, and over again. Why did I do this? Why did I do this?! Why did I DO THIS!!!!!

CHAPTER 40

"Check it out!" The Terror exclaimed, opening a huge cardboard box in front of me and excitedly reaching inside.

"Are you kidding me?" I was stunned, disgusted. "No, Mickey," he snapped. "I am not kidding you. You better smarten up or else I'll slap you in the face with a fucking chainsaw. Now man up, goddamn it!"

I couldn't believe it! In the box were T-shirts, and coffee mugs, and pens, and... And fucking bookmarks! All of them covered with slogans. The shirts said, "Freedom through confinement. Master Mickey, L. A." and across the mugs, "You mean nothing, enjoy it," and, "Beat your problems," engraved into the pens. It was ridiculous! This gangster, this man of the underground, he was whoring me out to the corporate citizen like a pimp. He was making my name common and safe with their sheltered little morals, and their comfortable suburban illusions. He had me hooked, and he would be goddamned before ever letting me go. I was his shinning empire of pure profit.

He began pulling shirts from a second box, these proclaiming to the world; "Crypto Fear saved my life. Crypto Fear is my life. Thank you, Master Mickey."

"Fuck this!" I snapped again, ignoring The Terror's previous warnings. "This isn't a retail store! You can't let people walk out of here with those! Please! Please, Andy, don't put me through this!"

"Too late," he replied nonchalantly, lighting a cigarette and offering me one. I frustratingly accepted. "We've already started selling these," he said, blowing a thick cloud of smoke toward the ceiling. "Pre-ordered through the web-site, we've sold one hundred and forty two already. This is real, Mickey. This is real wealth."

I felt like putting my cigarette out on my arm. I felt like strangling The Terror with the same intensity I used to choke Polaris with; until his lips turned blue, and his eyes swelled, and his body went limp. I would never let go of that death grip. I hated him so much. He was just as bad as Grant was. The two of them had ripped all control from my hands and incarcerated me into a situation I wanted absolutely nothing to do with. One wanted money, the other wanted salvation, but both wanted me. Little, broken me.

I was furious! I sat there with mounting despair, day after day, watching the website counter pass 10,000 hits, then 20,000, then 30,000. I watched people walk out of the warehouse with immense smiles on smashed faces because of a goddamn T-shirt! I wanted to kick them in the throat. I wanted to kill their dogs. I wanted to destroy each and every one of them.

People poured in out of nowhere, already knowing the philosophies and the teachings of Grant, the "success" stories from others. The website was an instant phenomenon. The number of followers expanded like an ugly balloon about to burst. One beaten face after another came to me, thanking me for having saved them from whatever ridiculous existence they had come from. Who were these foul ex-amples of modern existence, these unknown faces? And just what in the hell did they even want, exactly? Did they know? Had they ever stopped to ask themselves, even for a second? They had not. They were following the fad, jumping on the band wagon, blindly following the internet to whatever ridiculous trend was currently popular for the next fifteen minutes. It was pathetic. As always, the reasons were beside the point when everybody else was doing it.

Every time I heard, "Thank you so much for liberat-ing me from my (insert stupidest thing you've ever heard here,) I wanted to kick them in the crotch and gouge out their eyes. Every time I saw a smile, the rage in me bubbled to a level I was no longer sure I could contain. Every time I was forced to personally carry out a kidnapping, I wanted to shoot the goddamn idiot in the face right there on the sidewalk. Make a mess of his confused little brains; reduce him to a big red puddle of mud.

I was making more money than I knew what to do with aside from piling it up high and setting fire to it. None of it made me feel good. None of it mattered. Money might make some people happy, but it can't save your soul. The universe doesn't give a shit about your money.

Every time The Terror raved about some obscure news report on TV or some sprawling article in newspapers from different points of the country, I felt ill. Journalists from New York, and all the way to Seattle, to Vancouver, to Montreal–from North America, to Europe, to South Asia, to Russia, to Australia, all of them were caught up in the hype of it all. I couldn't help but wonder if the entire population of the planet had gone psychotic, or if I had just managed to bring it out of them. Crypto Fear was supposed to be an experience, it was supposed to be entertainment, but what it had become was too ridiculous to even contemplate. I could no longer even fathom the sheer scale of it.

Suddenly, I was famous. Suddenly, I was the greatest man to have lived in the last millennia. Suddenly, I put a gun into my mouth and tried harder than ever to pull the trigger–I couldn't do it. I just could not.

My cocaine habit had quickly spun out of control. Not that I thought so, but The Terror did, and so limited my available amount. Only enough to keep me in line, not enough to, in a single sitting, indulge in enough to kill a small village. I was a baby now. I was an infant, begging his mommy for more food.

Some girl sporting dark gashes on her forehead told me that I helped her get over her fear of germs–I broke down and cried right there on the floor in front of her. The Terror had her quickly escorted from the building and lashed out at me like an embarrassed mother.

"What the fuck is wrong with you? You can't be

weak like that! Be a fucking man and quit being such a pussy! I'm getting really tired of this, Mickey. I'm getting really fucking tired of your shit! You're about to go for a swim all the way to the bottom of the ocean!"

I smiled through my tears.

"Fuck you," I said, like a boy trying it out on his father, and just like a father, his knuckles smashed against my eye socket so violently that I flew backward and never even attempted to block him. I laid there and laughed at him. His rage was so high that he kicked me in the ribs, but still, I did nothing but smile back. I was carried upstairs by the loyal employees while The Terror roared like an angered beast.

"I'll have someone eat your goddamn face off! I'll have your balls on a silver plater, you ungrateful little shit! You're almost finished, Mickey! You're almost fucking there, you piece of shit!"

I let myself be carried through the air, refusing to move a muscle until they lowered me to the floor, shut the door behind them, and left me alone with my nightmare. I thought about Grant, about how strange it was that I had not seen a sign of him for weeks now. Why? Where was he? With any luck, at least I hoped, he had already perished in a horrendous accident. With any luck!

I could still hear The Terror downstairs raving wildly and throwing things against the wall. I heard him slam doors and leave the building, squealing his tires in the parking lot. I spread a long line of white powder and snorted all of it in one swift motion. I felt my face go numb, and at the same time, I felt my stomach turn and seize like gears in a blown engine. I cocked my head and vomited. Then, again. And then–again, splattering all over the bleached floor.

"Jesus," I muttered and I wiped my mouth. "Blood is always good." I stared at the stinking puddle, streaked with bright red blood. It was my soul escaping. Who cares?

"I've gotta get out of here," I moaned to myself. "I have to go somewhere. I'm losing my fucking mind."

I hadn't actually left the warehouse to go anywhere aside from kidnapping spoiled idiots in what seemed like months now. I had made no other human connection aside from my fists landing hard on unknown faces. No conversation except the ridiculous rhetoric being screamed into their faces. I had failed myself on all fronts.

I quickly headed back down the stairs with a sore rib cage and a swollen eyeball. I snuck out without anyone noticing and made a break for my van. I jammed the key into the ignition, waking the engine, and made it scream down the street. It was a jail break, a momentary lapse of surveillance, and for the first time in excruciatingly long months, I felt slightly better. I felt a slight shimmer of freedom. I felt... A little bit of something.

CHAPTER 41

The multicolored lights swirled in erratic flashes. The music came from every angle, loud, and conflicting with all of the other sounds of the carnival. I heard the joyful yelp of someone winning a teddy bear, and the prolonged screams from those on roller coasters. All around me, children laughed and ran excitedly through throngs of normal people, on normal dates, and on normal family outings, eating giant balls of blue and pink cotton candy. Sticky lips stuck to candy apples. Gigantic wheels with circling lights rose high above the crowd into the dark sky. There were clowns making balloon animals, and mimes trapped in invisible boxes, and walking cartoon characters posing for pictures with babies, handing out free lollipops to big eyed children. Roller coasters crisscrossed each other at regular intervals and soared toward the heavens, looping up and around and down. Crypto Fear was once supposed to look something like that. It was supposed to feel like that. Exhilarating. Exciting. Fun. Unfortunately, it seemed that I had managed to tap into something so powerful in the human psyche that there was no escaping it. No hope. It was too far gone, and far too late.

I had made it to the amusement park after driving aimlessly for hours, crisscrossing streets through downtown, until it dawned on me. I hadn't been to a carnival since I was a boy. A fond memory. The lights, the people, the rabid excitement, it was careless, happy, fun.

I walked around observing people of a breed I had long ago lost touch with. Normal people with children running around, walking aimlessly through the excitement, holding hands, kissing, laughing–normal.

I saw no swollen faces, no grotesque looks of impaling idolization, no fanatical beliefs shoving me further into depression. All I saw with silent contentment, were normal, regular, mundane things. It was beautiful.

I shot down a row of metallic ducks and then gave my prize bear to a little girl who was crying to her parents that she wanted one too. The smile on her face was genuine, and her level of excitement was amazing. Had I really felt such a thing once upon a time? Where had it gone?

I bought my own giant mound of cotton candy and picked at it while amiably making my way through the sea of people. Everywhere I looked, happiness was what I saw. I bought a ticket and rode a roller coaster. The powerful G forces rocked my head involuntarily from side to side, and caused, for the first time in a very long time, a genuine, honest smile to stretch across my face. My eye socket throbbed with the forces of nature pushing more blood into the swell, but it still felt righteous! I felt free and alive while rushing through the loopty loops, racing up toward the sky, and then back down toward the pavement, the faces below me nothing but a smear from the high speed of the wild train.

After the ride, I walked for a long time, eating my way through a giant bag of butter covered popcorn. Fantastic! I smiled at the happy faces. I paid the man who handed me a basketball to launch into the distant ring hanging from the back wall and... and...

No!

I wasn't sure, but from the crowd to my left, I swore... I was almost positive... Had I seen Grant's face? I peered intently through the squirming wall of bodies, scanning feverishly, but I couldn't see him anymore. It had only been a shimmer, but it was enough to shake me from my new escape drug; vicarious happiness. Jesus, I really was losing my mind.

"Hey buddy, you gonna shoot or what?"

"Oh... Yeah, sorry."

I had 5 attempts and missed them all.

"Sorry, Chief," the man said.

"Yeah," I replied. "No problem. Thanks."

I was heavily distracted. Was I being watched? Was he here?

I walked, filled with anxiety, searching through throngs of
smiling faces filthy with cotton candy. I turned this way, and
then that, swinging my head wildly, smearing my environment like the roller coaster had. I felt my heart pump faster,
harder. I felt my knee caps tremble, and weaken. I lit a
cigarette and took a deep drag from it. "Calm down," I mur-
mured. "Calm down. It's just your imagination. It's just your
imagination. Just relax."

I made my way across the park balancing on the
edge of a panic, frantically searching for affirmation that he
was near me–somewhere–watching. I was terrified that this
night would be the one I had been fearing for weeks now.
The confrontation. The questions. The fear. Would I accept
my role as savior? Not a chance in hell. Would I heed to The
Terror's demands? Fuck him. But could I continue with this
savage ride, already far past the pits of hell? I could not. I
had to start climbing up. I had to fight back and reclaim my
life. My life, was mine! It was mine, and no one else could
have it. No one!

I couldn't find him. If he was at the carnival, he
would be very difficult to find. There were too many factors
moving in my field of vision. Too much noise and confusion.
I felt fear creep up my spinal column, and before I knew it,
I was feverishly heading back for the van. Run! The instinct
came even without proof. Perhaps I was losing my mind.
Perhaps all the powder was beginning to cause the early
onset of a permanent delirium. High powered psychosis.
Whatever the case, I felt it was important to get away from
the lights and drive away at top speed. Escape the phantom
threats. Run away, far away, and never look back.

I got to the vehicle and hopped in, scanning every
direction around me. Was he there? Was he watching? My
hands were numb, my face drenched in sweat, my eyes watery, and burning. I decided that no one was around. No one
suspicious that I could see, anyhow. I pulled my resealable
plastic bag from the glove compartment and shoved my nose
into it, Tony Montana style. I snorted hard like a gluttonous
pig and fell back against the driver's seat, letting the rush

overtake me.

"Jesus," I muttered. It was powerful stuff, and suddenly, all was calm again. Solace. The incredible illusion of strength masked the reality of how frail my body truly was. I looked around once again. Nothing. Only a mother cradling a baby in her arms, her husband trailing with a sleeping toddler.

"All right," I said, and felt myself gnashing my teeth with cocaine induced tension. "Let's get out of here." I started the van and backed out of the spot, but almost instantly, there was a pair of headlights riding my bumper, causing my body to tense horribly. I scoured the rearview mirror to see what it was. Was it a van? A black van from hell? The horn blew, warning me to either drive or get the hell out of the way. I put the car in gear and began driving, narrowly missing a parked vehicle in front of me, all of my attention focused in the mirrors. I pulled over to the side, hoping the angry vehicle behind me would pass; it did with a revving engine and a muffled, "Fuck you, asshole!" assaulting my window. I sighed with deep relief and drove off, but it wasn't long before I felt like a schizophrenic again. Frantic, and totally unfocussed on the situation in front of my vehicle. Every headlight was suspect. Every van was shuddered at. Every stop light took my breath away. I had to get away. I had to get back to the feeble, enclosed, claustrophobic safety of the warehouse. As sad as it made me, it was all I had left. Fuck my life.

It was a long ride back, and the bag had disappeared quickly into my nasal cavity, but I had made it. My body was incredibly numb, my tongue as thick as a slab of meat, my eyes like black holes. I parked in front of the building and stood by the vehicle for a moment, listening, expecting no traffic anywhere near. I held my breath and listened... There was nothing.

"It's just your imagination, goddamn it! Calm down!"

I ran up the stairs and locked the door behind me. I sat down on the floor, as I no longer had any furniture left, and rolled a fat joint. I had a shot of whisky. I smoked the cannon. I calmed myself down. I had more cocaine.

Suddenly, the realization crept over me. I was losing it. My mind, it was cracking. My spirit, it was broken. Jesus– I was going insane! My mind was finally collapsing under the pressure. How many things in my life had been nothing but rabid hallucinations from a frayed mind? Was that possible? Was that real? Christ, what was I doing? Was I here? Grant... Was he... Was he real?

My God, what was happening? Who was I?

CHAPTER 42

I was standing in a long stream of clear water, abandoned in some long ago forgotten forest. The fog was thick and cool in the night air, caressing my body, and limiting my vision to only a few feet in front of me. The moon was out, bright and beautiful, as only a spatial object can be. The running stream sounded like peace flowing through the darkness. The water cool, but not quite cold, enveloped my ankles while I looked around for a signpost, a clue to my whereabouts, but I could not see anything aside from my direct surroundings. Nothing but the hazy moon up above like an eerie light bulb in a grim dungeon.

I turned in circles, peering through the thick cloak of floating clouds, feeling dizzy, and lost. I suddenly stopped and listened to the silence. A deafening wall of it pressed against my ear drums. A few moments of debate resulted in my decision to walk. To where, I didn't know, but anywhere from my current position felt better. The illusion of progress provided a slight relief. The water splashed with every footstep while I observed the embankment for a path, a break, anything to get out of the water, but the banks were nothing but thick slabs of mud and brush, forbidding a feeble fool to cross.

Splashing through the water, I suddenly heard the rustling of leaves from behind me. Instantly, I stopped with wide eyes and a clenched jaw, my fists as tight as the first time I had beaten Grant.

"Was that real?" I wondered.

I listened like an old man who'd forgotten his earpiece at home, peering through the darkness with the eyes of an eagle. And then it came again, and I didn't even give myself the chance to wait for it. I pounced and lunged through the water, frantic, feverish, panicked.

I hopped up and over the water, then splashed in again, and then back out at top speed. I was blinded, but somehow, I could feel something else near. I was not alone! The feeling was so strong it caused me to stop and listen to my surroundings once again, but this time, I saw it! The fog flowed with the speed of the river, enveloping the shadow before me. It was almost shapeless, ill defined, but it was there. The eyes were its only distinctive factor. They stared at me like Satan himself was standing before me, silent, and waiting. In shock, I ran, but the alien footsteps quickly approached mine, splashing feverishly in the water. Thump! Thump! Thump!

My legs suddenly gave out from under me and a scream ripped through the air like a clap of thunder. The voice of Satan spoke, "Now you die, you god-like fool!"

I tried to scream. I tried to protest, "No! I'm not a god! I'm not a savior!" but it was too late. I felt the mighty slash of a blade rip through my back, exposing my blood-ied ribs and spilling out my essential organs. I felt my heart struggle to keep beating, my lungs filling with water, my soul dying. I was turned over by a powerful hand and I could feel his breath on my face. Hot, putrid filth. Head to head with the beast himself, and still, I could not see his face. Only the eyes. He grabbed me by the shirt and pulled me toward his headless vacuum.

"You!" he snarled. "You are a foul example of humanity. A waste of flesh with no purpose, and no place in the world. Your soul is mine and I will make you pay, you baffled fucking ass! Now DIE!"

I felt him thrust the blade into my chest, paralyzing all organs. I was suffocating on my own filthy blood, sul-lenly realizing that I could no longer fight back. I could no longer move. I could no longer exist.

I laid in the shallow stream, trying to breathe, my vision pulsating with every labored pump of my heart. I focused my hazy vision on the moon above, unaffected by the horrors happening below it. Uncaring for its closest of all neighbors. And as I felt the awareness begin to leak out of my brain, something else took its place, carrying visions and illusions of the mind. I saw Polaris. I saw her blue lips and her bloodshot eyes bulging out from her skull, begging me to clamp down harder. I saw her panting with pleasure. I saw her eyes focussed on mine, and her mouth was moving, but all I could hear was, "You give me nothing. You are empty."

I wanted to speak, but nothing worked. There was nothing allowed to escape.

"You killed my soul."

I was trying to say, "No! Please, no," but her face suddenly dissipated like the fog of the stream, and all I could see was Steve, snorting Crystal Meth, and running around like a lunatic in a Christmas orgy, shoving himself into countless women, lost in lust. But then the background shifted and we were in the warehouse again, still trapped in our ugly, final scene. Steve lay motionless on the floor, apparently unaware of the two dead girls on the bed. The blood was so thick, and so dark. I stared at him in full repulsion, but I still couldn't move, or turn away. Suddenly, Steve sprung back to life, his eyes filled with craziness. His blood covered mouth quivered and said, "I'm so cold man. I'm so fucking cold. Why did you do this to me?" I felt ugly shock, terrible guilt. I felt terror, but still, I could not utter a word. His face was suddenly caught in anger, and he screamed, "Why did you kill me, man? I was your best friend! Why did you fucking kill me? Why? Why?"

I felt myself collapse into darkness, but from there, far away, a shape was floating toward me, zigzagging like a curious insect attracted to a corpse. It circled, up and down and around, and I could hear laughter, but it was the kind that makes you frown in suspicion. The kind that induces a special type of terror in your heart. The shape floated freely, and quite suddenly, it picked up speed and came toward me, astonishingly fast, and stopped only inches away from me. It was Grant's Face! No body. No hands. Just his repulsive, maniacal face, coming in and out of focus like a malfunctioning camera lens. The color of his eyes shifted from brown, to hazel, and then from green, to red, to yellow, to purple. He laughed, and laughed, and uttered creepy whispers, smiling like a monster. His mouth was suddenly flapping wildly, and his voice erupted in echoes.

"Say it!" I heard him say, his face shifting shapes. "Say it!" he screamed. "You are the answer to our lives! You are the final revolution of our evolution! You are the one! The chosen one to save us all from ourselves and each other! The chosen one to show us the way!"

I tried to speak, but there was still nothing. I tried to nod my head, but I was no longer sure I had one. Did I exist? Was I real? The size of his face swelled, then shrunk, and then came back to inches away from me. It was like watching him through a shifting magnifying glass.

"You are the all one, all eternal god of our lives! You are beyond material, beyond moral, beyond physical! You are the one who will break the sullen fools down and save the decaying, depleted, and hurting souls! You are the answer, Master! You are the one! You are the meaning we've all been searching for! Now, say it!"

His menacing eyes crept into my soul, disturbing something valuable in there. Me. His ill fated smiles were like belligerent nightmares. I suddenly felt pressure against my forehead, and although I couldn't see anything, somehow, I knew it was a gun.

He spoke with dangerous conviction, terrifying totality.

"Say it!" he whispered. "Say IT!" he roared, his voice echoing through my soul. "Say that you will save us! Say that you will forever hold us dearly! Do it! Say that you are our God!"

I was speechless, motionless, forever trapped in a hellish dimension of doom. From a distance, I suddenly heard another voice screaming while Grant laughed like an unhinged beast. It came from very far away, and then ripped to the forefront with vehement rage, and I soon realized that it was my voice!

"I'm your God!" my voice roared.

"Ha! Ha! Ha! Ha!" Grant was screaming. "Say it again! Say it!"

"I'm your master! I will save every one of you! I will crush you all!

I had no control over the words or the intensity. It didn't even seem to be escaping from my own mouth. It came from somewhere else in space. Distant. Behind. Like a wave of fury blasting through the fabric of reality.

Suddenly, Grant's face was out of focus again, shrinking, getting far away, light years into nothingness, and then coming to the forefront like a slimy caricature, oozing filth from his every pore. He now had a body, a twisted, mangled form that stretched, and shrunk, and widened into indeterminate shapes. He was wielding a knife, and laughing while his body lurched upward like a diabolical genius. I watched in horror as he raised the blade high above me and brought it crashing down with enough force to split a log in two. I felt a rush of pain.

Grant bent over me, closer, still smiling crazily. He spoke in tongues at first, but then became deafly clear.

"I belong to you now, Master! There is the first sign! My life is now your scar. I am a part of you forever now. Forever. You are my Savior! You promised! Promised! Promised! Promised! Promised!"

The words seemed to echo eternally through space while Grant began swirling around like an angry bee. Shrinking and growing different parts of his body simultaneously, until, there was nothing. I was alone. The pain I felt, it was gone. The horror, it had somehow transmogrified into a sort of sullen comfort. I was alone, and all was dark. I was dark.

***

For a very long time, I didn't move. I came through the darkness and waited for the vague visions in my mind to dissipate. I felt like a ghost trapped in a fog, and when I finally did try to move, I found that my limbs were noodled and useless. I tried to sit up and stretch, but a slashing pain ripped through my chest. Instantly, I looked down at it, and everything came back to me like a painful regurgitation.

"No!" I yelled out loud. "No! It can't be!"
I felt my skin crawl as though millions of little worms squirmed beneath it. There was a slash across my chest, dark red, undoubtably caused by a knife! I couldn't breathe! I remembered Grant's ugly face, his manic smiles, his pressing rhetoric, demanding my purpose in this foul world. It couldn't have been real, it was a hallucination. Too many drugs. Too much, too much!

I shook my head in disbelief and wondered how it could have happened. Could I have done this to myself? Could this have been a bad case of nightmare psychosis; carrying out reactions in response to a bout of sleepwalking terror? That could happen... Couldn't it?

Perhaps it could, but I failed to find a blood covered knife. And what about the other dreams? What about Polaris, and Steve? What about Grant? Had he been in the warehouse? Had he slithered in like some demented snake intent on slashing my chest open? Had it been a dream, or reality?

Painfully, I rushed to the door, but it was still locked! The frame was still intact and lacked all evidence of a forceful entry. I scanned the mostly empty room for clues, anything that would please affirm that I had done this to myself, but there was nothing.

"What the hell?" I paced the room frantically. "What happened? Did it happen? Fucking hell! I'm losing my mind!"

My chest heaved with panicked breath, stretching the fresh scab slashed across it, inducing more panic, more pain, more aimless questions!

"Ah man!" I panted. "What am I gonna do? What the hell am I going to do?"

I was frantic, and frayed, and suddenly, my phone was ringing, and for a moment, it pushed the confusion even further.

"Hello?" I answered forcefully.

"Jesus Christ, kid! Were you still sleeping?" it was The Terror.

"Ah... Yeah... What?"

"You fucking dope fiend!" he snapped. "Take it easy on that shit! It'll bore a hole straight through your brain like a parasite."

I said nothing. What did he want? Why was he calling me?

"Anyway," he continued. "I have some things I want to talk to you about. Get your ass out of bed, I'm coming over right away."

"What time is it?" I asked.

"It's time to get ready, now get to it. I'll be there in 15 minutes."

The line went dead and I was filled with despair. What now? I thought. Grant coming in here and slashing my chest like the Son of Sam wasn't enough? Now The Terror had to come in here and push me around like the playground bully?

I ran to the bathroom and flicked the light switch, closely examining the cut across my chest in the mirror. It was a fairly clean cut stretching across the flesh diagonally from the top of my left pectoral and all the way to the right nipple. Not deep enough to kill, but definitely enough to leave a scar. The echoing words filled my head again, "My life is now a scar! I belong to you, Master!"

I shook my head. It was a macabre obliteration of all that seemed sane and true in my world. Soon, those feelings slowly mixed in with rage as I was once again filled with the overwhelming urge to capture Grant and blow his head off. Make him suffer like he'd made me. A sweet revenge. An eye for an eye, plus interest, and applicable taxes! I wanted my pound of flesh. I wanted my righteous revenge. I wanted my goddamn life back. No hope. No hope. I quickly washed off the blood and got dressed for The Terror's visit. I decided not to tell him about Grant, mostly because I couldn't be sure that it had actually happened. I had no hard facts, but deep down, I knew. I felt it. That psycho had done this to me.

Somehow, I knew he had.

Moments later, The Terror burst through the doors with a big smile, carrying the air of a man who truly felt like he was walking on the top of the world. A man stepping on the heads of the middle class, snatching bills out of the air.

"Mickey!" he smiled and approached me with a stack of legal looking papers clutched in his hand. "Mickey," he said again. "Are you ready to be a star?"

CHAPTER 43

It is the director's responsibility to choreograph the action and make sure that all of the actors are hitting their marks and babbling out the correct lines. When things go wrong, it is the director's responsibility to unleash a flurry of crazy reactions in an attempt to get things back on track again. Many directors, especially the overly egotistical type, do not fend well with actors who prance around the set following their own agendas. This was Los Angeles, after all, and I suddenly found myself wondering about what kind of strained relationship develops when an over confident young director attempts to direct a high ego A-list actor through a scene. The tensions there must be incredible, especially if the actor thinks the director is a moron, as was presently the case with me, while the director screamed in frustration, "Cut! Cut! Cut! Goddamn it! What the fuck are you doing?"

This little showdown was part of what The Terror called "the commercializing plan," which was only an effort to make Crypto Fear a little more socially acceptable. We were filming a commercial to be released on the internet and attract more idiots into my crippled life. At least, that was the intention, if this up and rising director could get his shit together and actually get me to do something he wanted.

The entire thing was blatantly ridiculous, but The Terror had asked me how I would handle holding my own eyeballs in my hands, thus giving me the strong suspicion that I had no other choice in the matter. From which I thought, "Fuck em. If they want anything out of me, I would make them work some serious labor for it."

This most recent outburst from the director was apparently due to the fact that I had somehow lost sight of my victim and "accidentally" threw the camera against the hard concrete wall.

"I'm sorry," I said. "I was so into it, you know?"

"You fucking idiot!" the short, blond streaked director snapped. "Do you know how much these things cost?"

"No," I said calmly. "Is it a lot?"

"Yes it's a lot!" he snapped. "These are twenty thousand dollar cameras!"

"Wow," I replied sarcastically. "You're right. That is a lot. Do you own them?"

"They're rented, all right. Just, please, be careful, okay?"

"Sure," I said, smiling. "I hope you took insurance out on them. Is that how it works? Like a rental car?"

"Just please, let's just do the scene and get this over with. Please?"

"Absolutely!" I exclaimed. "This acting thing is really fun you know. I feel like Brad Pitt, or maybe like, Matt Damon, or someone like that."

He sighed loudly and shook his head, returning to his fancy chair, ready to once again, direct.

"Okay," he said. "Just hit the three combos on his face. That's all we need for this scene. Got it? And remember the angles we taught you. This is only acting, all right?"

"Yes, sir," I smiled and looked at the fool sitting on the chair in front of me. This poor kid, flying into L.A. from the backwoods of Nebraska with big stars in his eyes and a deep yearning for fame in his heart. He stared at me suspiciously, mildly terrified.

"Have you ever been punched in the face?" I asked him.

He shook his head. "Not since I was a kid," he said. "Playground stuff."

"That's unfortunate," I said. "Don't you know it's the only way to cleanse yourself?"

"Well, I am a little bit familiar with your work. You're pretty big out there. I think what you're doing is actually pretty great, and gutsy."

"What I do is bullshit," I replied. "There's nothing great about it. Don't be sucked in like the rest of the idiots."

"Everyone on set!" the director's voice came. "Rolling, okay... Action."

I cocked my arm back and smashed it into the poor fool's face, sending him flying backward and onto the hard concrete floor with a thump. Instantly, the director almost fell off his chair.

"Motherfucking goddamn stupid fuck head! Are you demented? What are you doing?"

"What?" I replied. "He said he wanted it."
"Fuck!" he screamed. "I have to pay insurance on these guys. Come on!"

He ran frantically toward the kid as though a terrible tragedy had just occurred, attempting to tend to his wounds.

"You should get an ice pack or something," I mumbled. "Better yet, just enjoy the pain, it builds character, and you can never have too much of that. You'll thank me later."

"Shut up!" the director screamed. "Get the fuck out of here! Get out! This is bullshit!"

I chuckled and took a vial of white powder from my pocket, dumping a few bumps on the back of my hand.

"Jesus, you people are serious. Don't you know this is just acting?"

"Fuck you!" he screamed again. "Get out!"
I snorted the tiny mounds and did a little feel good dance.

"All right," I replied. "I'll just be... Whatever." I stepped out of the room and instantly felt the despair. Sure, I was being an asshole in there, having a little bit of fun with the squares, but inside, I didn't feel so light. All I could really think about, strangely enough, were the words of Marilyn Manson. "The camera will make you God," and, probably most prominently here, "We're not fantastic motherfuckers, but we play them on TV."

I felt the slash on my chest burn underneath the material of my shirt. The eeriness of it was still lingering thickly in the gallows of my mind.

Moments later, The Terror burst through the door as

angry as a bull, gun in hand, and pressing it hard against my forehead.

"What the fuck is your problem, huh? I ask you to do one thing, one little thing, and you fuck it all up! Don't make me, Mickey!" he snapped. "Get your fucking ass back in there and get it done or I will destroy everything you've ever cared about!"

I stared at him expressionless, like a child getting in trouble.

"You're spreading yourself really thin here, kid. Really fucking thin. Don't make me break you, because I will in ways you've never imagined possible. Now go!"

After a few reassurances from the boss, the camera was once again shoved into my face and the overly dramatic director shouted choreography at me while I pretended to beat the life out of the poor Nebraska kid. I screamed, "Not too violent words," as the director referred to them, into his make up caked face. I wondered how he had felt after I punched him in the face, realizing that it wasn't exactly what he had signed up for. This vile, borderline snuff film that surely would make his mother cry in shame.

The video was supposed to induce all of the idiots of the world to cause a huge buzz over it. The new thing. The new style. Getting your ass kicked into a blob was the new trend. Freedom through pain. Orgasm through torture.

"Tell him he knows nothing about himself!" the young director shouted. "Tell him the path toward truth is through Crypto Fear."

The camera angles would properly accentuate the action, and make-up was added to make him look more bloodied, and bruised. Of course, I wondered why I couldn't just beat the hell out of the guy for real. No need for all of the make up.

"Reality is too boring!" the director said. "Not dramatic enough. Don't worry, it's going to be beautiful!"

Kill me now.

I shot clips of single sentences in different settings, and clothes.

"He needs to look flashy!" The Terror insisted.
"Make him look cool, and mysterious."

So they did.

The result was a furiously wild two minute commercial,
heavy with undertones of subcultured truths, and commer-
cialized rhetoric. The sight of a room, dark and gritty, thick
with unnerving ambiance. An empty chair. A shot of the
Monkey Den. A single swaying light bulb. Then my face
with a few days of beard growth and dark sunglasses on, saying, "Crypto Fear is not for the faint of heart." Then a quick
clip of me blasting the fool from Nebraska in the side of the
face. My face again, music blaring, "You do not understand
yourself." Another punch. "You do not understand your life,
or the ones around you." A splatter of blood. "You do not
know your purpose." Hot sweat pouring from my face, red
lights, the frames changing quickly from unsaturated, to
over-saturated tones. Bloody knuckles. Broken faces. A pulp
understanding.

The Terror was stupefied with it. Proud and bewildered with the final result.

"Perfect!" he exclaimed. "Absolutely fantastic! It's
dark and gritty and nasty, yet still slick and cool. This will
work wonders for us!"

Wonders indeed. I wanted to kill something. Drill
some living thing in the head with a fat lead projectile. I
wanted to watch it squirm and fight and finally wither away.
The slash on my chest was still throbbing with hot pain.

**

When the video hit the internet, it did exactly what
The Terror had wanted it to do. It spread like wild fire. It cat-
apulted the entire thing to a level so common that it was being copycatted all over the world. From the ghettos of distant
Asian countries, to the sun bathed coasts of Australia, Spain
and a slew of South American countries; under the doomish,
gray skies of massive cities all over the planet, Crypto Fear
was there too. Somewhere. Hidden in the shadows, like a

myth cloaked by a heavy fog. Like a legendary bogeyman. Crypto Fear, and right next to it, was the name Mickey Tyler. As always, it seemed that no one could possibly be content with simply letting the band wagon pass by. They seemed possessed with a blind necessity to jump aboard until it collapsed under its own weight and ruined us all, but it did beat risking the ridicule of having been left out. What a shame.

Suddenly, Crypto Fear was on the tongues of millions. Suddenly, Crypto Fear was at the forefront of some kind of social revolution that was so ill advised and misunderstood, the only real perversion of it was an obscene and blatant confusion. I hated Crypto Fear. I hated The Terror, and Grant, and all of the fools who subscribed to it for whatever diluted reasons they saw fit. I hated everything, but most of all, I hated myself for being so goddamn stupid.

The Terror chuckled and seemed to be nothing short of absolutely fascinated with the phenomenon. He spent endless hours crawling through Crypto Fear forums from all angles of the internet, belting out howls of amazement which turned to sheer bewilderment, and then to stunned looks of misunderstanding.

"Listen to this, Mickey!" he exclaimed. "Listen. This guy says, 'Crypto Fear has saved my life. I will forever be a part of it and spread the goodness it has to offer,' and then this other guy just flat out calls him 'A faggot eating Nazi pig who should stick to cutting himself in the dark while hanging from a noose,' Ha! Ha! Ha! Ha! I fucking love the internet! These people truly are the lowest form of existence, aren't they? Don't they have anything better to do with their time than argue with complete strangers from halfway across the world? Ha! Ha! Ridiculously beautiful!"

He was right, but such was the state of our world. In fact, the most direct factor contributing to the stunning success of Crypto Fear was the fact that no one had any real, concrete relationships with each other anymore. We were all digital, expendable, and caring about nothing more than our 15 measly minutes of fame with no returns, no impact whatsoever.

The forum pages stretched on endlessly, and The Terror was truly captivated with the digital fights. He gawked at the sheer number of different opinions people could have on the exact same subject.

"I'll tell you, kid," he said. "This is the most fun I've had in years. Christ, people are stupid. All over the planet, in all countries of the world, rampant stupidity. It's fucking hilarious!"

Dixiegirl234 posted: Crypto Fear is just another excuse people use to cop out and not deal with their real problems.

Mypenisishardxxx posted: Shut up dixiegirl! Crypto Fear is the new answer to our sad existence. You should try it one day. You might be surprised what you find out about yourself and those around you. Don't judge a book without having read it first.

Lonelysadtrapped21 posted: Fucking faggots!

Bowtome posted: Yet another bullshit religion to confuse the masses even further. When will people stop believing in superstitions and just be human?

Andmo1052 posted: Fuck religions! You people are missing the point! Crypto Fear is for entertainment. What the hell are you retards talking about? Religion? What a bunch of morons?

Hannafreshdaisy posted: In Korea, Crypto Fear saved my brother from drug overdose, and even suicide. It saves lives.

Lonelysadtrapped21 posted: Did he try to kill himself because of his small penis or because you're his sister?

Hannafreshdaisy posted: You American's are so stupid! You always have to be so violent and rude. This is sensitivity to me and my family.

Lonelysadtrapped21 posted: Yeah, real "sensitivity" subject for me too.

Hannafreshdaisy posted: My grandmother will put a hex on you!

Lonelysadtrapped21 posted: Really? Cause she didn't mention anything in my bed last night.

Hazycornea posted: Come on people, there's no need for such profanity. This is supposed to be a forum to discuss Crypto Fear, where everyone can freely express there own opinions, not to settle personal quarrels. Send each other emails if you want to fight. Please, can we get back on topic here?

Lonelysadtrapped21 posted: Fuck off!

Awesomeorgasm posted: I love Mickey Tyler!!!

Huntedandtamed posted: Me too! Mickey Tyler rocks my world!

Momotyver posted: Who is Mickey Tyler, anyway?

Awesomeorgasm posted: Who cares? He created Crypto Fear. He's my personal Jesus! I want your children, Mickey!

Pothead423_x13 posted: Whore!

Lesliedancingbaby posted: I hate Asians too!

Hotbodyboy posted: Fuck Americans! And Canadians too for that matter! Fuck all North Americans! They may have started Crypto Fear but they do not understand the true meaning of it all... As always!

Pothead423_x13 posted: We have all the best porn though! We understand that!

Swedman_les143 posted: I love Crypto Fear from Sweden.

Happybunnyf=girl posted: Crypto love from Spain!

Pussymonster posted: Crypto Fear = Real Life. No questions! There are your answers! Believe in it and it will believe in you, wankers! Britain loves Crypto Fear!

CHAPTER 44

Paranoia. Sheer and disjointed, blunt and urgent. When your mind falls into such a trench, everything else loses meaning. Your body reacts with unpredictable aches and every muscle seems to tense tighter than a tourniquet.

I was out of touch. The faces that sat in front of me, I didn't know them. The eyes staring at me with dedicated awe, they meant nothing. They felt like mustard gas filling my lungs with bubbling death. When noses collapsed like a soda cans under the wrath of my fists, or when cheekbones cracked and the lacerations gushed with bright red blood, I didn't even feel ill about it. I would simply take a deep breath and wonder how much longer it could go on for. How much longer before the stares of adulation disappeared and the throngs of idiots left me alone? How much longer before the masters pulling at my puppet strings finally cut me loose and left me behind like a rotten piece of meat? How long? How long?

It seemed like I was perpetually trapped in the disillusioned psychosis of a man locked up for far too long in solitary confinement. Nothing but four walls only inches from my face. No door. No key. No hope.

I feared the fact that I could not tell with absolute certainty that Grant had actually slashed my chest, becoming a "part" of me, as he had said in the dream. I had not seen him. I had seen no other sign of him, but a paranoid intuition somehow told me that I was correct in my assumption. The fear was taking over every molecule of my body, causing me to suffer through long nights hyped up on too much powder, allowing my mind to reel with irrational nightmares. I would stare out into the darkness for hours, listening, holding my breath, trembling. Sleeping seemed like an impossible natural process, insurmountable, even though I often found myself snapping out of hellish nightmares at odd times of the day. I needed to get a grip. I needed to get a hold of reality.

On other nights, those dark, starless evenings I spent being a good employee with a gun pressed against the back of my head for that extra nudge of motivation, I channeled my fear into rage. I kidnapped and beat people so viciously through my concentrated hate that The Terror had assigned me my very own referee. He was charged with standing in the room with me while I savagely beat the God stare right off of the morons who had paid good money for it. He was charged with stopping me from gouging out their eyes and putting my fist straight through the thick bone of their skulls. He was responsible for keeping me in check, and making sure I killed no one on purpose, which, oddly enough, had become my sole purpose in life. Eradicate the scum. Destroy the monsters. Kill the soul.

Despite this, the money still poured in like impossible waterfalls, and The Terror was nothing but smiles about it. Big, boastful smiles. He carried the face of a child getting his first puppy. Amazement.

"Come on, Mickey!" he pleaded with joy. "Take it. It's your money! All of this is because of you. Take it. You deserve it."

I stared at the swollen stack of bills he shoved into my face and I truly, honestly, had no interest in it. No use for it. What would I do with it, after all? Buy a house? Buy a car? Buy myself some nifty new slacks and a tie? All of it was worthless! All of it.

I sighed and stared at him with minimal expression. "Just make sure I have my drugs, all right? That's all I want. No money. No fame. Just drugs. Thanks."

"Mickey," he smiled. "Come on, kid. This is your doing. Reap the benefits of your hard work. This is working beyond our dreams."

"I know," I said over my shoulder as I walked away. "That's the problem. Just get me my goddamn drugs."

When I saw a fresh face sit in front of me, I let my fists explode, and when I heard a moan of pain, I just wanted to strike harder, but when I saw eyes of envy, of adulation... I wanted to cry. My chest and throat would fill with tightness, but no emotions were ever allowed to escape. There were no tears. There were no gasps or chaotic convulsions of my diaphragm in a fit of sorrow. There was just nothing.

***

"Are you going to heal me, Master?"
"Shut up! You're a fucking cockroach! There is no hope for you. You cannot be saved."
"Are you sure about that, Master?"
"I told you to shut your fucking mouth. Shut up, or I'll save you with half of your skull blown off."
"This is a dream come true, you know?"
"Eat shit."
"I've been needing your saving my entire life. I've led an empty, broken life."
"You should hang yourself then. Why are you here?"
"Because you perform miracles, sir. You save the broken, and give them hope. You help them find the meaning of their lives."
I said nothing and shook my head.
"Would you like to know my name, Master?"
"No! Just shut up!"
"My name is Henry. Henry King. I've led my whole life bar hoping, drinking, sleeping with strangers... Alone..."
My temper was flaring.
"Well Henry, I hope you die by the end of tonight."
"I have three kids. Two girls, and a boy. They all hate my guts. Even changed their names on me."
"Yeah, well, I'd hate you too. Jesus Christ, look at you."
"I had a family. I had a life, with a home, and kids, and a wife, and a little dog running around. I had toys thrown everywhere around the house. I had it all. I had..."

I watched his eyes swell with tears, and I lost my mind. In a flash, I was an inch from his ugly, sweaty face, roaring like a lion securing his territory.

"You son of a bitch! Fuck you! I don't care! All right! I don't give a shit! I hope your fucking house burns down! I hope your kids are trapped inside! I hope your stupid fucking dog becomes a hood ornament! This is a game, you fool! This is not real! This is make believe! Got it! Got it, you fucking demented shit head cocksucker!"

Before I knew it, I punched the side of his face so hard he went crashing to the concrete floor, his body stiffening into a rigamortis type of shock. Instantly, I jumped on top of him, bludgeoning his head with fists like bolts of lightning. Crack, crack, crack, crack.

"Fuck you!" I screamed. "I hate you! I fucking hate you!"

Crack! Crack! Crack!

"Crying to me about your pathetic little life!"

Crack!

"What do you know about loss? What do you know about losing everything? Huh?"

Crack! Crack! Crack! His face was a bloodied mess and he wasn't even conscious anymore, but I never stopped raging under the dim light of the single incandescent light bulb hanging above us.

"What do you know about meaning? We are all nothing! We are nothing! You stupid fucking parasite cocksucker!"

I felt giant paws hurl the mass of my body backward into the wall. I could see the referee's lips flapping wildly, but nothing was getting through to me. Muffled screams. Angry faces. I was lost in rage, confusion.

The referee snatched me up again, still screaming nonsense, but his face was tinged with a tiny bit of fear at the sight of the bloodied fool on the ground, frightened with the fact that he might have already let the boss down. He threw me out of the room as though I weighed nothing.

When my heart began to calm a little, I noticed that

Mr. Gordon was standing only a few feet away from me, calm and calculated as always. Serious.

I stared at him in disgust.

"What?" I asked angrily.

"Mr. Labelle wants to see you, Mickey."

"Where is he?" I asked.

"I'll bring you there," he said, and then sighed. "Jesus, look at you. You're a mess, kid. You look like shit."

"Really?" I sounded surprised. "I've been working on it all day."

He shook his head solemnly.

"Come on, kid. Let's go."

I followed him into a Cadillac, and off we were. I felt nothing aside from regret that I hadn't managed to kill the whiny little turd in the warehouse. I stared out of the passenger side window in absolute silence, shifting my weight every so often. Mr. Gordon could sense my overall discomfort, but he offered nothing in way of comfort, which I appreciated. I wanted none of it. He pulled a fresh cigarette from its package and offered it to me. I stared for a moment, and then accepted.

"Thanks for the...."

Smash!!!

I felt shards of glass fly into my face, into my mouth and nose, and for a second, one long, eternally stretched out second, I had the distinct sensation of being completely weightless. The momentum twisted my body with incredible force until I felt a final blow; the sound of metal vs. asphalt was like thunder.

Sheer confusion. A dizzying shock overwhelmed me, and I was suddenly aware of the enormous heat engulfing my face.

"What the.... What the hell?" I mumbled, and realized that I was hanging upside down from my seat belt. With terror filling my heart, I started screaming.

"Help! Someone help!"

I felt like I couldn't move my head, but from the corner of my eye, I could see very distinct flashes of yellowish light against the darkness outside.

"I'm on fire, goddamn it! Somebody fucking help me!!!"

I could smell the threat throughout the vehicle and I tried to squirm out of it, frantically jabbing for the belt buckle, but I couldn't reach it! I was trapped like a horse cornered by a wall of fire. Pure panic!

"Help Me!!!"

Finally, I heard voices outside the vehicle. Salvation was coming, at last! The voices echoed against the crushed tin of the car's panels, coming closer, faster, to save me from my heated metal tomb. A leather glove reached in, clutching a knife, and in one swift motion, I was cut from the belt and crashed head first into the demolished ceiling. Instantly, countless hands reached in through the non-existent windows to pull me from certain death and back toward safety, toward life, toward....

"No!" I screamed, and suddenly resisted being dragged from the fiery hunk of steel. "No! No!"

I knew what this was. I knew what was happening even through the melee of confusion and terror. I knew, the instant I saw black ski masks on the head of five or six men, that I was fucked!

I screamed, but the scene was much too chaotic to offer any kind of salvation from bystanders. Salvation it seemed, was a comfortable myth.

"Get him in the van!" one of them yelled. "Now! Now! Let's go!"

I was hurled in through the side door and the van speed off at its maximum acceleration.

I felt vomit burning at the back of my throat. I knew of only one thing for sure. However this would end, it wouldn't be pretty for anyone.

CHAPTER 45

"Are you hurt, Master?" his voice was soft, and calculated.

I moaned, my body felt as stiff as a corpse.
"You know, Grant," I replied. "I feel fantastic! Just fucking amazing! I mean, getting t-boned by a speeding car, it's gotta be better than sex, right?"

"It was a necessary evil, Master," he replied, and his face radiated with humility for a moment.

"Really?" I said. "Necessary, huh? And what about all of this? This beautiful suite you've so elegantly prepared for me. Thanks a lot, Grant, you really are a great guy, you fucking prick."

His eyes twinkled eerily.
The "suite" I was referring to, was really more of a prison cell. I was locked behind a thick steel door, surrounded by concrete walls, bruised and bleeding from the accident. There wasn't a single photon of natural light to be found, and the stench of stale, moldy air was trapped deep inside my nasal cavity. There was a ragged, lumpy cot in the far corner for me to sleep on, and a single light bulb shedding its depressing yellow glow from not too far above my head. Elegant.

"First, I must apologize for requiring that a man of your stature be confined in such a room, but it is actually for your own protection."

"My protection? I can take care of myself, Grant! Goddamn it! You're a fucking lunatic!"

"Somebody had to do something!" he screamed in rage, and I was taken back by his drastic reaction.

I shook my head. "What are you talking about,

Grant? What is this all about, huh? Can't we just work something out here?"

"You," he said calmly, and stared deeply into my eyes.

"What?"

"It's all about you, Master. All of this, and it's about to get even better from here on out."

I was suddenly aware of the scab across my chest. It was pulsating, sickening.

"Grant," I began, but he quickly interrupted.

"I am a part of you!" The shock of it made me shudder, sending a cold chill down my spine. "I am, we all are, a part of you now, Master, and something had to be done to keep it that way."

I was astonished! Could it be?

"Did you cut me, Grant?"

"The first sacrifice," he beamed. "The first sign of your acceptance to lead us all toward a better existence for generations to come. In your name we will prosper. In your name we will conquer."

Vivid flashes came back to me. His manic face, stretching, and pulling, and twisting in all directions, mumbling nonsense before slashing a knife through me. I wanted to puke.

"You're fucking nuts!" I exploded, the pain in my head surging. "You're fucking crazy, man!"

"I had to save you!" he said.

I frowned in disbelief. "You're completely insane! Save me? Save me from what? Nothing out there is more dangerous than you are, Grant! You've completely lost your mind and you need some fucking help!"

"Don't patronize me!" he stood from his chair and paced the humid room with his hand up to his mouth. "I had to... To save you from that fool. That idiot who's trying to undermine everything this stands for. The one who's trying to destroy everything we've worked for."

"Who?" I asked. "The Terror?"

"That fucking fool running around in your warehouse! That

is your place of healing, and he is bastardizing the entire concept into some filthy thing. Into some meaningless money machine, just like the rest of them. This is too important to fail. Too important! This is real! This is life! This is setting free all of those people who do not know what is wrong with them. It is something to belong to. To live for, and to believe in. I will not let anyone undermine any part of it. I had to protect you, Master. I had to protect the entire organization."

I swallowed and my throat felt like it was lined with needles. Every time I saw this man, he was topping his previous high scores for complete insanity. He was a dangerous thing to be associated with.

"Grant, listen," I said, not really sure of what to say. "A fucking commercial!" he interrupted, completely repulsed. "A commercial for Crypto Fear? What does he think this is, a sitcom? That this is just some kind of big joke? Some big parade of clowns? He is a stupid man!"

"Grant, please, I can talk to him. I can, you know, try to..."

"It's too late for any of that!" he snapped. "It's too late now. You are here. You are safe, and you are wanted, and right now is the time to stake our claim and make it official. Right now, is the moment Crypto Fear becomes real, and all of the world's broken and weak and struggling will once again be able to feel hope. True hope, and true faith in the fact that someone out there does care. You... Care."

I snorted.
"Grant!" I said sternly. "This is crazy, all right? I... I don't care about this! Okay? I don't want any of this! I don't fucking want it!"

"Yes you do, you said so yourself! You accepted your role! You welcomed my scar, my sign to you, and now, you will accept the scars of all of those in need. It's too late, Master! This is your life now! This is your destiny, whether you accept it now or later, this is what you were meant to do. This is why you were born."

"Goddamn it, Grant!" I screamed in frustration. "Let me go! Let me out, now! This is bullshit! This is bullshit!"

All he did was smile. "Rest well, Master. There is a celebration in a few days."

"A what? What are you talking about? What the fuck are you doing to me?"

"It's time for you to prove to everyone that you are serious. It is time for you to accept the scars of all those who believe in you and carry their lives on your flesh. Carry their troubles with you like the divine soul that you are. It is time for you to meet your followers."

I was speechless. What was he talking about? "Wait! Wait!" I was desperate. "What do you mean? What are you saying? Accepting their scars?"

"It will be a beautiful affirmation of your love for us all. You will be tied to a post, naked, and one by one, the followers will approach and offer you a single strike of a bull whip. A testament of their love for you, their belief. It's not to hurt you, but to love you. It is to symbolize that you are with us at all times, and we with you. The ultimate symbol of love and dedication for all of the believers. The ultimate sacrifice."

"Grant," I pleaded. "Please don't do this. Please... Don't do this! This is insane! This is–this is fucking insane, you goddamn lunatic! I'll fucking kill you, you bastard! You're a fucking vulture! You're picking at my bones and I'm gonna eat you from the inside out! Don't fuck with me, Grant! Don't do it!"

He smiled.
"Too late. After the ceremony, you will address your followers from across the world with a live broadcast over the internet. They are waiting with baited breath, Master. You must deliver. We must save this before that other fool destroys it for us. It is too late to turn back now, get some rest, preparations for the ceremony begin tomorrow."

He turned and a man on the outside unlocked the door to let him out.

"Good night, Master."
"Grant!" I screamed in panic. "Grant!!!"

He neither turned nor replied. I was his prized pos-

session now. I was his ape to be flaunted and exploited by the
world like some mythical legend. I was the reluctant leader
of psychos, the beaten master of fools, and I was absolutely
furious about it. When this was over, at the first opportunity
to present itself, without hesitation, I would kill Grant.

CHAPTER 46

I festered. I sat, and I fermented like a swollen bag of hooch. I was a decaying fruit decomposing into a grotesque, desperate alcohol. I waited through hot sweat covering my body like a cocoon, and through agonizing nightmares, and high octane anxiety that caused my body to tremble and stiffen. The forced separation from my beloved powdered crutch was unbearable. I sat and waited in my filth riddled cell with the light bulb smashed on the ground, and the hollow bars of the cot broken in many places. In the stagnant air, unbearably thick and heavy, I waited with my foot in severe pain from relentlessly kicking at the door like a beast caged against its mighty will. I smashed and screamed and ripped my clothes off in desperate fits against the humid heat. I broke down, I threatened, and yet, still they came. They came and they cleaned, and they tended to my needs. They changed the light bulbs, and replaced the cots, and even brought me lighter clothes to wear, but all I wanted was out of the cell. It would take death to stop me after that.

A young woman with pale skin would come and deliver food for me day after day, never uttering a word. Her eyes were filled with a deep fear that forbade her to speak a word to the almighty Savior. For fear of judgement, fear of punishment, fear of... Whatever in the hell psycho Grant had told her to be afraid of. Ridiculous! But there was something else about her that was hitting me like a brick to the face. I couldn't place her at first, but I knew her. Somehow, I had known her, and when I finally did make the connection, I couldn't help but spew my guts out. It was Alice! Alice! The girl I used to work with, the one whose boyfriend had chased me wildly through city streets after I ruined his life forever.

Alice! Goddamn it! What's wrong with you? Please, please, help me!

I was bewildered, shaking, and desperate to make a connection with her. Desperate to get a friend in my corner. Anything, please! I spoke to her incessantly, but she seemed possessed, unable and unwilling to communicate, but it didn't stop me from trying every opportunity I had.

"If you let me out, I will make you my wife," I would say, trying to hollow out her delusions and tweak them over to my side of the table, but to no avail. "I will make you my queen! I will make love to you, and we will be the rulers of this circus!"

Nothing. Always nothing. But it couldn't end there, I had to try the entire spectrum, never give up! I shifted my focus.

"If you don't let me out, I will personally make sure that you suffer like a filthy sow, regardless of your dedication! Do you hear me? I will make you suffer, you whore!" Still, no words. "I am your Master, goddamn it! Now, I demand that you let me out of here! Let me out! Now!!!"

Unwaveringly ineffective.

I had no idea how many days had passed, no idea of what was happening beyond the heavy steel door. I could sometimes hear muffled voices of people going about some type of important business, but in reality, I knew nothing. All I could do, was fear the worst.

I wondered about Mr. Gordon. Had he survived the accident? And where was the backlash from it all? Was The Terror losing his mind? Was he planning some sort of violent rebuttal? Would he crush Grant with his vengeance? I could only hope. It was unbelievable. Only a few days ago, I wanted to abandon the sick monster, I wanted to run and hide and never see a sign of him again, and now, I was begging for him to save me. I wanted him to be my savior, my salvation. I wanted him to break me of this lunatic's grip, and set *ME* free.

I thought about Steve and his feverish tailspin of self-destruction. I missed him so, so much. And Polaris, too.

I missed her. I worried about her. Was she living a different life? I couldn't deny to anyone that I had loved the girl–no–I still loved her. I loved her despite all of the madness and the deranged fetishes. Son of bitch! Like everything else in my life, she was gone forever. Nothing but a memory. Nothing but a yearning that festered like an emotional sore.

Outside, on the other side of the door, I could feel the tension rising in the air, even from the confines of my tiny cell. I could hear the excitement in their footsteps, their muffled voices a little more chipper. The time was quickly approaching. Madness was already at my door.

***

"Are you ready, Master?"
His face was drenched with sweat and his anxiety was highly evident.

"Grant," I said softly. "Please. Just let me go. I..."
"Absolute nonsense!" his voice shrilled as he paced the room staring at the floor. "Nonsense! This is the greatest moment of not only your life, but the lives of all of those who are attending. Even those who will not, those you will address after the ceremony, those people are desperately awaiting your words. They are waiting for your face, and your acceptance of them... And you want to leave? Oh no, sir, I don't think so."

I stared at the floor, defeated.
"Listen, Master," he said. "You are the king here, and I am your servant. I will heed to your every demand, but I also have a responsibility to the rest of the following, and if they demand their savior, then I have no other option but to ignore your requests and deliver you to them."

"Screw you, Grant," I screamed. "I will never be your savior! I will never lead you fools anywhere! Do you understand that? I hope all of you die. You can torture me all you want, put me through any type of emotional carnage you can dream up, but I will not give in, Grant! Never!"

He smiled crookedly.

"I am truly disappointed, Master. I just wish you could see the fantastic opportunity that has been presented to you. I wish you would accept your destiny with open arms, and develop what you have. But, if you will forever refuse, then I suppose the culture has no other option."

I frowned.

"Wait, what?" I asked. "What are you saying? That you'll let me go? You'll set me free?"

He smiled eerily.

"Yes, Master," he replied. "Your freedom is imminent now. You will do the ceremony tonight. Afterward, you will address your followers with a speech, and then, well, I suppose you will not be needed anymore."

Suspicion caused my eyes to twitch. My heart sank for a moment.

"What do you mean, I won't be needed anymore?" I demanded. "What are you saying?"

"Shh," he smiled. "It's okay, Master. Everything will be fine. I don't want you to worry. What I want, is for you to prepare for the greatest moment of your life. The classic affirmation of who and what you are. What you mean to the world. This is our greatest moment in history. Today, you become a god."

"Grant!" I sounded desperate.

"Shut up!" he snapped. "They are coming. Things are in place and they cannot be undone. You will attend. You will take their scars. You will take their lives. And you will address them like a god. You will, single handedly, give hope to thousands of people tonight. Regardless of your beliefs, Master, this is something that will change all of their lives, and it is something to be proud of. It doesn't matter what you think!"

I gave up trying to reason. All of it was useless, and falling on the ears of a lunatic with only one thing in mind. Egotistical salvation.

"It's getting close now. I will have them prepare you for the ceremony."

I wrung my hands tightly together. The pressure in

my chest was so great I was hoping it would crack open and offer me some type of relief.

"Where is all of this going, Grant?" I asked. "What's after this? A god tour? Are you going to prance me around like a rock star? Like some mythical creature that all should adorn?"

His face was very serious. Calculated and calm. "Don't worry about the future, Master, it's out of your hands."

"How the fuck do you expect me to lead anyone if I don't even have the freedom to lead my own life?" I yelled in anger. "Why don't you take it, Grant? Why don't you become the savior and lead these brainless sheep around your little dream world. Shit, most of them don't even know what I look like! Go ahead, Grant, it's my gift to you! You take it and run with it! You become the face of Crypto Fear. You become the Master that all will envy."

He chuckled, and his eyes flashed wildly about the room.

"As I've said, Master, don't worry about the future. It is out of your hands."

I felt rage explode inside of me so intensely that before I even knew what was happening, I had my hands around his neck and I was screaming furiously into his face.

"You destroyed my life, you son of a bitch! I'm gonna kill you! I'm gonna fucking kill you!"

I clenched harder, a skill I had luckily already mastered in the past. His face turned bright red while he gasped for air. Bubbling spit collected in the corners of his mouth while his eyes rolled aimlessly.

"You fucking prick! Look at me!" I demanded. "I want you to watch me kill you! Watch me!"

His body twitched and convulsed like a crushed spider, and still, I clamped down harder, the rage in me magnified when I did.

"Watch your master destroy you! Watch your savior annihilate you, you fucking lunatic!"

It takes longer to actually kill someone by strangulation than we are led to believe in the movies. The body has lots of richly stored oxygen in its blood as reserves. It will instinctively fight and twitch and try to flee as the reserves slowly run out and the heart begins to fail. I was close to it now. The bastard was mine.

I then felt a sharp pain in the side of my head, and my vision went blurry. I heard muffled voices, screaming and frantic, and then felt a blow to the ribs. I soon realized that I was on the floor, and somehow, Grant was already up to his feet and kicking me in the rib cage with absolute ferocity.

When it was all over, I couldn't catch my breath, and neither could Grant. There were 3 or 4 other bodies standing over me in the cell. Big men, dedicated fools, staring at me in despair.

I saw Grant wipe crusting saliva from his cheeks. His face was still bright red, but there was no mistaking his psychotic determination.

"Get him ready!" he snapped at the others. "The ceremony starts in two hours."

CHAPTER 47

The zombified orderlies ripped off my clothes and shoved me into a tiled shower. There were two men standing by the stall with tazer guns, just in case. My head was pounding with terrific flashes of pain while I washed the incredible filth from my body. Grant was standing by in anticipation with my "special attire" for the big event. A massive lump of velvety dark blue material with golden seams. A glorified bath robe.

"Here," Grant said very seriously, and wiped a sleeve full of sweat off his extended forehead. "Put this on him. Is everything ready?"

"Yes, sir," one of the women responded. "He is ready to go."

"Excellent!" he exclaimed. "Perfect! Perfect. Everything is almost ready. Everyone is almost here. Five more minutes and we will begin."

He approached me and stared deep into my eyes. "Tonight, you become a god," he said. "But even gods must be restrained at times."

"Your sore throat is only the beginning," I replied. "I'm not finished with you, Grant."

"If you mess this up in any way," he snarled. "There will be serious repercussions! This is not about you, it is about them. They need you as their hero. Do not disappoint them, Master, or another, more terrible sacrifice will not be out of the question. Understand?"

I leaned in close and grinned, showing my teeth, "It's not gonna happen, Grant!"

"DON'T!" he shrieked and slapped me hard in the face. "Don't! This is too important!"

He sighed loudly. The madness in his eyes potent with concentrated dedication.

"Get him ready. Five minutes. I'll be back," Grant said, and went to check on the horrid scene somewhere else in the building.

I felt weak, drained, and tired. They threw the thick cloak over me, stringing my arms through the sleeves, and adjusted the front of it for maximum comfort.

"Anyone got a smoke?" I asked, but none replied. I took a deep breath and tried to control the trembling. It felt like a massive ball of fire was sloshing around in my chest. When Grant returned, his eyes were wide like glossy marbles of bad craziness.

"Okay, here you go," he said without looking at me, handing pistols to everyone around me. My heart sank.

"You need guns?" I asked.

"Nothing, will stop this. Nothing!" he replied very seriously, sending a cold chill rushing down my spine. "Not even you! Now let's go."

They led me down a long hallway, dim with twitching fluorescent light bulbs and old, gritty walls. I was suddenly filled with the sensation of a man being led down skid row toward the electric chair, toward the final scene, and for the first time really, I felt a strong, deep worry that perhaps I would not make it through this insanity. That maybe, just maybe, I would die on this night, in this unknown building, at the hands of unknown faces, and at the mercy of fanatical propaganda designed solely for the biggest fools to have ever walked the earth. Delivering their savior to the land of phantoms. Making him beyond human.

I clenched my jaw tightly and held iron fists at the end of my arms. My legs were a consistent mess of rubber bands. When they opened the doors at the end of the long, stale hallway, my heart walloped at the scene.

There were hundreds of them! Hundreds and hundreds of faces sat impatiently, their heads swooping about the room in frantic anticipation for the one who had come to deliver them from themselves. Instantly, the muttering ceased and all the faces turned, all eyes were focussed on me.

The place was set up like a concert hall, or a church gathering. Cheap steel chairs sat in row after row of perfectly spaced patterns, all facing the front of the hall where a long stage stretched out before them. Spot lights blazed down on it like artificial suns, illuminating the microphone stands. Security guards stood everywhere, sporting heavy weapons. At the middle of the stage was a single wooden post, thick in diameter; the thing I already knew I was going to be tied to and whipped by everyone of these misguided delinquents.

The lighting over the crowd was dim, and haunting. Their faces were like ghoulish phantoms peering from the darkness, staring at me in bewilderment. The heat of the place was outright offensive. All those sweating, swollen viruses sitting in their chairs with baited breath and explosive excitement for the arrival of the big boss was disheartening, sickening. The walls were covered with propaganda posters, fouled with the foolish words these people refused to let go of. Pillar torches, six feet tall, stood on the edge of every third or fourth row, framing the way to the stage. The tension in the air was so thick, so repulsive, that I thought I would lose consciousness before even making it to the stage.

"Go," Grant whispered from behind me, and then, something happened that made me nearly vomit all over the place. It was applause. Only one clap at first, that led to others quickly joining in, exactly like the sheep that they were, until the entire building resonated with an explosion of cheerful applause. Their beaten, tired, spiteful hero was here.

They led me toward the stage like a celebrated boxing champion, the heavy hood covering my head. The applause intensified as though I was the first extraterrestrial to visit the earth. As if, goddamn it, as if a god had descended to earth and was about to give his first speech to the poor little insignificant earthlings. They bit their lips and stared with glossy eyeballs. They clapped relentlessly, and the only thing I could think of was how any of this could have happened. How?

I stumbled like a drunkard, but the orderlies instantly latched on, each grabbing an arm, forcibly leading me to the stage, up the stairs, and into the savage heat of the spotlights. They stood and clapped for a long time while I fought off the express urge to collapse and drop dead. A welcomed thought, but if I didn't die, then Grant would surely see to it afterward–with god-like severity!

Finally, Grant approached the microphone and let his deranged voice blast through the speakers.

"Thank you. Thank you. Please, sit down. We are about to begin."

The applause slowly tapered off and bodies began sitting on their stiff chairs. My body trembled, but sweat was pouring out of me. I was drenched underneath my cloak. Naked and soaking wet.

"First," Grant resumed. "I would like to thank you all for coming tonight to witness the official inauguration of our new god."

Another quick applause erupted, and then silenced. "His name, his human name, is Mickey Tyler. He is the original one. The creator of Crypto Fear. The one who has, and will continue to change each and every one of your lives for the rest of time. He is the founder of the greatest organization on the planet, and he is also the author of the words that have so drastically altered your lives."

Another quick eruption of claps.
"He is here tonight to welcome you all to his fantastic world of free existence. Here to attest to your love and to accept you all as dedicated and saved followers. Here to carry your lives with him forever. Wherever he goes, whatever he does, you will all be with him, and vice versa."

This time, there was no applause, there were only disgusting smiles and crazy eyes peering at me like rabid raccoons.

"Our Master, our Savior, is here tonight to accept the responsibility of leading us all toward a better life. A better path. A better existence. Toward freedom! True freedom, the kind none of us have ever known!"

The crowd resembled a buzzing bee hive. High tensions, and high hopes.

"On the front of his chest," he continued, while the orderlies pulled the cloak open, revealing my naked flesh for all to see. "He has a scar. A deep cut that symbolizes his acceptance of my personal servitude. My personal sacrifice to him. My life is forever etched into him. He will carry me with him no matter what happens, and tonight, each one of you has the opportunity to do the same. To give up your lives to him and prove your dedication to all of this. To mark your life as a physical manifestation. To give up, and follow him into freedom."

The crowd stood and applauded again, the tension in me proving too much to handle.

"Please," he held up his hand. "You all must know, that once this is complete, it is forever. Your dedication to our Master, and to Crypto Fear will forever be sustained. There is no turning back after tonight."

Eerie, cryptic silence.

"Now, are you all ready to prove your love and dedication to Master Mickey Tyler?"

"Wooo!" there was another loud explosion of applause.

"Are you ready to give up and follow the teachings of Crypto Fear?"

Again, more manic responses.

"All right then. Let's begin."

Grant turned and I could see the savageness in his eyes. He carried the stance of a man who had put everything on the line and finally succeeded. I wanted to tell him what a sham it all was. Success was bullshit, have a look around. He came very close to my face, but said nothing, his eyes blazed with madness. Sweat poured off of my body and the scar on my chest was searing with pain.

"All right, Master," he said with a demonic smile. "It is time."

The orderlies pulled the cloak off of my body and I stood completely nude against the sea of faithful eyes watching me. The sight of their faces felt like gun scopes, ready to blow my head off at any moment. They turned and walked me toward the wooden post, the horrid, repulsive place where I was to be whipped like some ancient heretic who had basked in blasphemy. My legs gave out from under me, and my head swirled in mad confusion. I felt so weak. So beaten. So terrified. There was a crushing pressure on my chest. This couldn't be happening. This couldn't be real.

Grant returned to the microphone.
"Behold, your Master. The new god of our lives!"

The crowd erupted in wild cheers, standing and flailing their arms through the air. My head felt like a lead weight. My legs non-existent. They forced me to hug the post with my back to the crowd like some kind of tree hugging activist. A heavy doom settled on my shoulders. All hopes were officially extinguished. An orderly came around and faced me with handcuffs in hand.

"Thank you for this, Master," he whispered.
"Burn in hell, asshole!" I snarled back. "I'm not done with you either, you prick."

He seemed jarred for a moment, but then returned to his duty, snapping one loop around my left wrist. The sound of it smashing my soul.

"Please, no," I pleaded. "You fucking bastard! I'll kill you!"

He tried grabbing my other arm but I fought against him, and suddenly, something ripped through the air like an explosion, and all attention was diverted away from me and toward the side door of the room. People were dangerously excited and scurried about like vermin at the sound of a mighty voice.

"Where the fuck is Mickey?" the scream came, and instantly, I knew who it was. "Get these faggots in order!" he yelled.

It was The Terror! Bursting through the doors like my very own knight in shining armor, and with an army of gangsters ready to exact revenge on those who stole his money machine. His very words echoed through my head,

"No one fucks with my money!"

Everyone was up in arms in a chaotic melee; running and hiding and screaming. I heard Grant's voice roar like an angry lion, "You will not destroy this anymore, you stupid man!"

I turned and saw that The Terror was quickly approaching the stage with homicide flashing through his eyes, absolutely vicious. I felt freedom dancing at the back of my throat. It was my turn to be salvaged. My turn to feel hope. True, deep hope that I would forever cherish. A slew of monsters followed behind him, but Grant was staring back like a threatened demon holding his ground.

"You will not stop this!" Grant shrieked, and just as my orgasmic freedom was climaxing, gunshots erupted, and all hell broke loose. I kept my eyes on The Terror, his gun in hand, almost at the stage, and then, I saw a flash of blood splatter across his thugs' faces behind him, stunning them for a moment while they searched for the source of it.

I saw Grant with his gun in hand, still smoking, and right then, I knew it was all over. My salvation was gone. My hope annihilated. The back of The Terror's skull blew open like a bomb had exploded inside of it. He hit the floor hard with only the sides of his skull left intact.

"No!" I screamed. "Goddamn you, Grant! You fucking psycho!"

He began shooting wildly into the crowd of gangsters, refusing to lose the fight. The gangsters shot back at him. One bullet narrowly missed him, then me, and then hit the orderly with the cuffs right in the face. His blood splattered all over my naked body and he fell like a dead weight to the ground.

Immediately, I grabbed his gun and ran, picking up my cloak on the way. Bullets were hitting everything, the screams were deafening, and suddenly, fire was ripping through the place. I ran behind the heavy curtain at the back of the stage and looked behind me. I could see the rage burning in Grant's face when he turned and saw me. I ran. I reached a door and smashed through it with more force than a bulldozer.

Outside, it was night time. I had no idea where I was, but I ran, the gun tightly gripped in my hand. I heard the door smash open behind me and I knew it was Grant coming after his prized possession. The muffled explosions of gunfire inside the building echoed loudly through the streets. I turned right and ran down a sidewalk through a string of prostitutes asking me if I wanted a date.

"Fuck off!" I snarled.

I ran and ran, knowing that Grant was close, until I saw an underground parkade and followed the paved ramp underground, hoping to lose Grant. Desperately, hoping to lose him. I ran past row after row of vehicles. The place was empty of people, but filled with silent cars of all kinds. My harsh breath banged against the walls. It was dark. It was stingy, and eerie, and gritty with exhaust and grime. I finally hunkered down next to a van and achingly tried to catch my breath while listening intently for any sounds of trouble. For a moment, it was deafeningly silent, and all I could hear was the booming of my pulse in my ears.

"Shit!" I whispered. "He fucking killed The Terror!" I was absolutely astonished. "Shot him right in the head! Ah man, what do I do? What do I do?"

I was desperate, bubbling with intense fear, and then I heard it.

It came slow and distant, almost calculated and unworried–footsteps. The echoing steps bounced off the vehicles as though ten people were walking down the ramp all at once. I held my breath and closed my eyes, trying desperately to get a grip.

"You know, Mickey, the bastard got what he deserved," his voice sounded like it had in my dream the night he'd slashed my chest. Creepy, dark, and sick. "He was using you for money. Money! Doesn't this mean anything to you?"

I said nothing and stayed where I was, but he was approaching. Any sudden movement would surely be heard.

"You betrayed me, Mickey," he accused now. "From the beginning, you have fought against this. You have led me on. You have saved me, and now, you have tried to destroy me. The damage you have caused tonight can never be forgiven. It can never be repaired. It can never be forgotten."

I was concentrating on my breath. Keeping it slow and steady.

"And by never forgetting it, well, I suppose this thing can still keep going, but only in a different fashion. I know you did not like the way it was going, Mickey, but unfortunately, you have forced my hand without knowing that it had been the better of the two options available to you. I now have no choice. There is only one option left in order to save Crypto Fear."

I tried to block him out and concentrate, but the echoing voice came from all angles.

"You must become a Martyr," he said, and my heart skipped again. "That's right, Mickey! You must die for Crypto Fear. You will be of more use to it dead than alive anyhow. You fight too much being alive. Of course, the world will be saddened to learn that you were killed in the middle of a gunfight during your ceremony, but because of it, your name will be set in history, and you will be a god forever. You sacrificed for them. You saved them. And now, you will die for them."

He must have heard a sound because I heard his feet spin quickly and he cocked his gun in a direction that was far from where I was. He then relaxed, and continued walking. Slow, steady, careful steps.

"After your death, I will turn your name into a household item, as common as a toaster, or a dildo. As common as the internet. I will etch your name deep in the minds of all who are lost, of all who are in pain, and you will be their symbol of hope. Their personal hope. The one who gave his life for them. The one who was accepting the lives of his followers onto his body, but tragically died in the melee of a mindless attack. A tragic tale. Everyone loves tragic tales."

I gripped the gun tightly, noticing that it was not unlike the Glock I was used to. I could see him now, in the blurred distance through tinted car windows. I could see his hands gesturing through the air while he spoke. Trying to reason with me. Trying to convince me. Trying to kill me.

"Goddamn it, Mickey!" his patience was wearing thin. "Come out, now! Now! There is no other way! You will not escape this! You cannot run from your own creation! You created this! You made this what it has become! Now fess up to it! You have a responsibility to the people! The people love you! They adore you! They believe in you!"

Nothing but silence.

"Show yourself! Show yourself to me! Show me a sign that you are brave and powerful, and that all of my work has not been wasted! Show me your strength! Show me your power! Show yourse..."

He hit the filthy concrete in surprise when I fired a bullet his way. It was hard to aim for him due to the placement of the vehicles, but it was enough to scare the life out of him. Almost instantly, he fired two shots back in my general direction. Exploding glass flew everywhere in the parkade, and my eardrums were nearly blown out from the sound waves. I quickly ran away from him and hunkered down behind a pick-up truck, keeping a close eye on my hunter, and trying to line up my sights.

"Goddamn you, Mickey!" he screamed in rage. "Goddamn you, you fool!"

I shot again, but missed. I shot one more, and sent him diving for cover and shooting back at nothing.

"I love you, Mickey! We love you! You are the Savior!"

"Fuck you, Grant!" I screamed back and shot again in his direction. A tire exploded, countless windows shattered, debris flew everywhere. We shot at each other in quick interchanges and screamed nonsense. A bullet narrowly missed me and I was forced to run again for a different cover.

"You were supposed to deliver salvation to us! You were supposed to save us!"

He shot again, but hit nothing but thick vehicles.

"I am your Master, Grant! And now, I will destroy you!" I yelled and was met with heavy gunfire. I shot a quick succession of bullets in retaliation, but hit just as much of nothing as he did. I could hear the blistering frustration building in his voice. The devastation. The sense of betrayal. He was screaming furiously, his mind cracking like a desert floor.

"Stop fighting this!" he screamed. "This is for you! This is all for you! There are greater things than life, or death! You will have immortality!"

I said nothing. He was scanning the scene frantically like a hungry velociraptor. Listening, watching, sensing the air around him.

"Immortality!" he screamed, and I could hear his tears now. His savage breakdown. His incredible sadness. "Argh!" he screamed and shot wildly. I shot back and quickly realized that I was out of ammunition. I had nothing left.

"Fuck!" I snarled. "Fuck! Fuck! Fuck!" I ran my hand through my hair, drenched with hot, matted sweat. I took a deep, courageous breath and started running, staying low to the ground. But this time, I wasn't running away from him, I was running around him, and then, toward him. I could not leave him like this, he would never stop. I had to end this, somehow.

"We fucking love you! Huh huh huh huh!" he was crying now like an unhinged drama queen. "I love you!"

I stalked him like a leopard and heard him reload the clip of his gun. I crawled in between cars, getting very close. Sweat was making my hands slippery, and burning my eyes, blurring my vision.

"Show me your salvation!" he screamed. "Show me your..."

I pounced and knocked him to the filthy ground, sending his gun flying through the air and clunking on the ground.

"No!" he shrilled. "No! You have to die! You have to die!"

We struggled with each other's masses and flying

limbs. He pushed my face away from him, trying to grab for the pistol, but I would have none of it. I landed my fist squarely into his face so powerfully I thought I had hit the concrete on the other side of his skull. Immediately, his arms fell to the ground in pure star gazing shock. His knee came up and smashed into my crotch, a jolt of brute pain ceased my stomach and paralyzed me, but I refused to give up. Not now. Not while I had the psycho in my grip. Not while I had nothing left to lose. Not while I was finally winning. He slashed at my face and arms wildly, but I managed to punch him again, and then again, but he was relentless.

"You're supposed to save us!" he garbled. "You're suppose to be life!"

I punched him once more, trying to break his jaw, and before I even knew how I did it, I snatched the pistol from the ground and hit him in the face with the butt. I grabbed him by the cuff of his shirt and brought his face inches away from mine. His eye sockets were smashed. His teeth were crushed. His lungs were choking on hot death. Blood spat from his nostrils and ears and mouth. I felt like a volcano of rage. I felt a massive eruption of hate. I felt death!

"Here's your goddamn salvation!" I roared, lost in the rage. "Now you're fucking safe, you worthless piece of shit!" I stabbed the barrel of the gun directly into the bridge of his nose and a massive explosion sent blood and dirt flying into my eyes and mouth. I felt the heat of it. I felt the power of it. I felt savaged.

His body instantly went limp. A lifeless carcass, free of mindless psychosis, lying in a pool of its own filth. The blood collected into a puddle that grew bigger and bigger with every second.

"Argh!" I moaned. "Argh huh huh huh huh!" The tears were unstoppable. A monstrous release of emotions rushed through me. "Fuck you! Huh huh huh huh!" I cried and banged on his empty, silent chest with my fist. "Fuck you!"

I fell off of his dead weight and sat on the ground, staring at him for a long time. The tears eventually receded, but the taste of fresh blood swirled heavily in my mouth.

This man. This lonely, batshit crazy man. A lunatic for which there were no reasonable words. He had succeeded in single handedly ruining my life. Everything I had loved, everything I had, and wanted to have, all of it, evaporated into nothingness. My success had become my horrid, haunting nightmare. It had ruined me and extinguished my soul. This man, this fanatic of crazed ideas, he had deceived us all. I stared at his motionless hunk of flesh, as dead as the broken glass that surrounded us, and I knew that it was finally over. His dream, my dream, The Terror's dream, all of it, shattered in a single night. I had finally reached my salvation. Finally! There was only one thing left to do.

CHAPTER 48

The green light came on and flashed into the depths of my eyes. My face, beaten and seemingly aged, beamed with a determination I had not felt in a very long time. I had slashes and lacerations everywhere. Beneath my skin, everything hurt, but I had never felt so good in my entire life.

The screen flashed a count down, 3... 2... 1... On air. I stared at my own image up on the screen for a moment, gathering my inner courage, channeling my frustrations, and then began to speak.

"Welcome to all of those who are in attendance. First, I would like to thank you all for your dedication and hope for Crypto Fear. I understand that for the majority of you, perhaps all of you, the organization has seemingly altered your lives for the better. The things you have heard, the experiences it has brought to you all have succeeded in changing your lives and your habits, and seemingly freed you from your emotional prisons."

The bottom of the screen flashed with outside posts. **Ladybug32** posted: Welcome, Master. Glad to finally see your face.

Bradley_gu1 posted: Thank you, Master. You have saved many lives and we are all grateful to finally hear your words from your own mouth.

Maxigirly posted: He's hot. Like Jesus.
Happyhap posted: You saved me, Master. I am forever in your debt.

I tried ignoring these.
"I am happy that my ideas and success have been able to influence you, and perhaps even offer you the sense that there is more to life, or perhaps a better path through which

life's hardships and tribulations are better handled. I am truly happy that I could be a part of each and every one of your lives. I am grateful for your love and dedication to me, and to Crypto Fear, and I hope that you will all continue doing whatever it is that has altered your lives so drastically–but there is something you must all understand."

Laughingclowngrl posted: I masturbate to you.

Annieflex posted: Master, without you, I would have committed suicide a very long time ago. You breathe new life. You help and save. You are my strength forever.

Harryfly posted: I teach your concepts to the troubled children I work with. Their improvements are remarkable. Thank you on behalf of all of them, Master.

Marylandhobo posted: You got me laid!!!

Ihatepeople posted: I can't cut myself anymore. Thank you. I feel like the weight of the world has been lifted from my shoulders. Cliché, I know, but it's the only true analogy. Thank you, Master.

"Ah... Despite what you have all been led to believe, despite the radical changes you have made, you must all realize that you have made them all on your own. That in reality, I truly had nothing to do with it. I regret to inform you all of this in such a crude fashion, but you have all been lied to."

Frankyfivetwo posted: Master, you are God! The God of all Gods

Hankypanky posted: I love you. You are forever in my heart.

Anybodywilldo posted: Wait, what's going on? What is he saying?

Weirdflash posted: Is this some kind of joke? I thought this was supposed to be Mickey Tyler. The Master. The Savior.

"I can see that many of you are concerned, but please, just... Hear me out. I am Mickey Tyler. I am the original creator of Crypto Fear. I am responsible for the experiences you've had and many of the words that you've heard, but what none of you know, is that you have all been fooled.

I am sure you all know who Grant is. You have probably, at least most of you, heard about who I was through him. But Grant is a sham. There is no easier way to say it. He is a liar, and he has lied to all of you. He has somehow managed to spin a mighty web of lies that has fooled more than saved. He is a lunatic. He is a fanatic. He is lost and scared and searches only for adoration instead of the true salvation of your souls. What you have done to yourselves, you have all done by yourselves. You are all strong. You are all capable. You... You are all believing under false pretenses. You do not need me in any way."

Davidian2 posted: Is he serious? What's going on?
Slayergirl posted: Are you rejecting us, Master? I'm confused.

Henryrenedad posted: This is bullshit! Grant is the most dedicated of us all! He is the ultimate servant. Where is the respect?

Lesbopornqueen posted: I'm so horny right now!
"No!" I continued. "You people are not understanding me. I am not your master! I am not a god, or a savior, or... Or anything else you may believe me to be. I am a man. A human, flesh and blood, man. I am broken and beaten and tired just like the rest of you. Please, please understand that Crypto Fear is not a religion! It is not some gathering place or some ridiculous set of rules to live your lives by. It was born out of frustration with my own life and it somehow morphed into... Into something it was never meant to be. Do you understand that? Do you get it? Like all other religions, some people have taken something very bleak, and very primitive, and have spun a grand story filled with shameful propaganda. Crypto Fear was created with the sole purpose of getting rich, in which it succeeded, but now, it has gone much too far."

Lesliebaby posted: Master, you are the sun of my life. I love you!

Asiansideways posted: You got me off of my junk addiction.

Amitiverypot posted: I used to razor blade my

wrists.

Helenpopodo posted: So what? I used to put a noose around my neck and dare myself for hours to jump off the chair.

Favoriteplayerboobs posted: Master. Please? What are you telling us?

"Listen to me!" I demanded. "You are all being fools. You have been scammed! Understand? You've been lied to. You've been cheated and your souls have been raped. You have all taken a simple notion and blown it into an unrecognizable bastardization. You have all taken a regular man, a simple, lost and broken man, and you have made him seem divine. You have made him seem better than everyone else and have filled your heads with obscene notions of life and prophesy and propaganda. None of it is real. None of it is concrete or even close to being seeded in reality. I am not God. I am not your Savior. The very idea of a savior is completely obscene and incredibly egotistical of you all, and I do not even want to be compared to it. Get it? This is an illusion that you have fallen for, and I am sorry that you have, but I have nothing left to offer you. I have no salvation. I have no answers. I have nothing for you."

The posts seemed to stop for a moment. Were they paying attention? Were they listening to what I was saying? The screen began flashing again.

Beethovenrocks posted: Master? What is happening? Why are you rejecting us like this? What can we do to please you?

Heavenandearth posted: How can we better serve you, Master? How can we please you? What can we do to garner your love?

"No, goddamn it!" I snapped. My patience was wearing thin. "There is nothing you people can do! Nothing! I want nothing from you except for all of you to leave me alone. I do not judge you. I do not watch you. I do not CARE... I don't... I don't care! Got it? I know you people love me and want to please me, but goddamn it, I don't want any of it. You must understand, right here, and right now, that I do not care about any of you. I do not love you. I do not ever want to meet any of you. I don't want to be friends, and I don't want you to serve me. What I want, is to be left alone.

"This Crypto Fear thing, it's over. Do you understand? It is over! Done! Finished! I have nothing to do with it anymore and neither do you. Go back to your lives. Go back to whatever it is that you do, and leave me alone. There will be no more kidnappings. There will be no more beatings of any kind. It's done. It's fucking done. Now please, this broadcast is over. If you prosper from here on out, I wish you all the best of luck. If you stay the same, then that's fine too. But if you decide to do something drastic over this, like killing or hurting yourselves or others, please understand that I will not care either way. You will not get my attention, because I don't care about you. No one cares about you. It's just you, alone in this big scary world. You need to deal with it. You, and you alone are responsible for what and who you are. No one else. Stop being weak, and scared, and ignorant, and take control of your own lives. This is not a difficult concept. It is called reality. Stop believing in me. Stop speaking my words. And please, please, just forget I ever existed. I will never remember any of you, and I hope you will all return the favor."

I sighed and bit my bottom lip.
"So, that's that," I said. "Thank you all for subscribing tonight. I wish you all a good night and the best of luck... Goodbye forever."

I hit the button and my face disappeared from the screen. The posts were silent for a long time, but I continued staring, waiting to see what the reaction would be. Had they listened? Had they understood? Would they move on?

Nothing. Nothing. Nothing. And then...
Andymalice posted: Fellow followers. Please do not feel defeated. We have somehow upset our Master. There is no need for a man of his divinity to explain such matters to us. Keep your faith in him and his words alive, and one day, we will all be rewarded.

THE END.